Outstanding praise for Lisa Jackson!

"No one tells a story like Lisa Jackson. She's
headed straight for the top!"
—Debbie Macomber

"Lisa Jackson takes my breath away."
—Linda Lael Miller

Outstanding praise for Mary Burton!

"Burton delivers action-packed tension . . . the number of
red-herring suspects and the backstory on the victims
make this a compelling romantic thriller."
—*Publishers Weekly* on *The Seventh Victim*

Outstanding praise for Mary Carter!

"A marvelous combination of wit and heart and a reflection of the way a couple can endure one another's faults
for the sake of love and devotion."
—*RT Book Reviews* on *The Things I Do for You*

Outstanding praise for Cathy Lamb!

"*Julia's Chocolates* is wise, tender, and very funny. In
Julia Bennett, Cathy Lamb has created a deeply wonderful
character, brave and true. I loved this beguiling novel
about love, friendship and the enchantment of really good
chocolate."
—Luanne Rice, *New York Times* bestselling author,
on *Julia's Chocolates*

Books by Mary Burton

I'M WATCHING YOU
DEAD RINGER
DYING SCREAM
SENSELESS
MERCILESS
BEFORE SHE DIES
THE SEVENTH VICTIM
NO ESCAPE
YOU'RE NOT SAFE
COVER YOUR EYES
BE AFRAID
I'LL NEVER LET
YOU GO
VULNERABLE

Books by Mary Carter

SHE'LL TAKE IT
ACCIDENTALLY
ENGAGED
SUNNYSIDE BLUES
MY SISTER'S VOICE
THE PUB ACROSS THE
POND
THE THINGS I DO FOR
YOU

THREE MONTHS IN
FLORENCE
MEET ME IN
BARCELONA
LONDON FROM MY
WINDOWS
HOME WITH MY
SISTERS

Books by Cathy Lamb

JULIA'S CHOCOLATES
THE LAST TIME I
WAS ME
HENRY'S SISTERS
SUCH A PRETTY FACE
THE FIRST DAY OF THE
REST OF MY LIFE
A DIFFERENT KIND
OF NORMAL
IF YOU COULD SEE
WHAT I SEE
WHAT I REMEMBER
MOST
MY VERY BEST FRIEND
THE LANGUAGE OF
SISTERS

Published by Kensington Publishing Corporation

OUR FIRST
Christmas

LISA JACKSON
MARY BURTON
MARY CARTER
CATHY LAMB

ZEBRA BOOKS
KENSINGTON PUBLISHING CORP.
http://www.kensingtonbooks.com

ZEBRA BOOKS are published by

Kensington Publishing Corp.
119 West 40th Street
New York, NY 10018

All Kensington titles, imprints, and distributed lines are available at special quantity discounts for bulk purchases for sales promotion, premiums, fundraising, educational, or institutional use.

Special book excerpts or customized printings can also be created to fit specific needs. For details, write or phone the office of the Kensington Sales Manager: Attn.: Sales Department. Kensington Publishing Corp., 119 West 40th Street, New York, NY 10018. Phone: 1-800-221-2647.

Zebra and the Z logo Reg. U.S. Pat. & TM Off.

First Kensington Books Trade Paperback Printing: October 2014
First Zebra Books Mass-Market Paperback Printing: October 2016
ISBN-13: 978-1-4201-2504-7
ISBN-10: 1-4201-2504-4

eISBN-13: 978-1-4201-4328-7
eISBN-10: 1-4201-4328-X

10 9 8 7 6 5 4 3 2 1

Printed in the United States of America

CONTENTS

A RANGER
FOR CHRISTMAS

MARY BURTON

Chapter 1

Austin, Texas
Friday, December 19, 7 P.M.

You're a hard woman to find. Professor Marisa Thompson stared at the text. **You're a hard woman to find.** Was this a joke? No one was looking for her. She'd barely been back in Austin forty-eight hours. But as she reasoned this was a mistake, silent warnings whispered.

As she considered responding to the number with the Texas area code, a knock at her office door had her sliding her phone back into her back pocket.

"Professor Thompson, bet you don't know what the other professors are calling you?"

Marisa raised her gaze to the junior professor's smiling face. Kyle Stone wore a Santa hat cocked sideways over shoulder-length sandy blond hair and his nose glowed red, a sign he'd had too much tequila punch at the history department's holiday party. She tugged off her glasses and tossed them on a pile of manuscripts she'd marked up in red ink. She reached for a cold cup of coffee, stood, and moved to a small microwave in the corner of her office.

Christmas music drifted through the hallways of Garrison Hall. "I don't bet. But it's Scrooge, no doubt."

Laughter rumbled in his chest and he strolled into her office. "How'd you know?"

"I have a reputation."

"Their teasing is good-natured."

"No, it isn't."

He pouted, clearly making fun of her sour mood. "Why didn't you make an appearance at the party?"

"Just didn't." She put the mug in the microwave and punched in one minute. Behind the lectern or cutting through the jungles to a Mayan ruin, Professor Marisa Thompson was at home. Ancient languages buried by time, neglect, or malice were easier to grasp than a holiday packaged in disappointment and wrapped in bows of false promises. The Christmas season was a time to be endured, not celebrated.

"More sour than usual."

"I miss the jungle."

You are a hard woman to find. The text tugged at her concentration before she brushed it away.

She'd returned two days ago from a six-month sabbatical spent in the jungle west of the Yucatan in Mexico, hunting for evidence of the Mayans who'd lived in the region one thousand years before the Spanish had arrived. Two weeks before she was to leave, she stumbled upon a hole in a large limestone mound. The hole had been carved out centuries ago by grave robbers and offered a glimpse into a tomb. She'd been able to squirm inside the hole and with a light had found a cavern covered with ancient writings. It had been the single most important find of Mayan language in decades. She'd wanted to keep digging and work until the entire site had been mapped and catalogued. But her time and money had run out thirteen days later and she'd been forced to leave her ruins behind, until she could find sponsors to pay for her return.

"Everyone was asking about you. This is your first Christmas back in Austin in several years."

The seasonal travel had been deliberate. Life was easier when she vanished during the holidays. However, this year a lack of funding and the university's schedule dictated a return to campus to teach graduate classes in the spring semester. And so here she now sat in her small office, trying to immerse herself in her ancient languages and hide from the holidays and festive coworkers. Of course, she could go home to her Hyde Park home in central Austin, but that would mean facing too many unpacked boxes delivered this morning from the storage company. The boxes had valued papers and books and memories—items that belonged to her mother, items she'd not been able to look at in the seven years since her mother's death.

"Bradley and Jennifer were there. He's been talking nonstop about your trip to Mexico and your find."

She allowed a twinge of disappointment with the mention of the ex-boyfriend. "That so?"

Kyle lowered his voice a notch, speaking in a conspirator's whisper. "He's itching to work with you on your find."

Six months ago Bradley had dubbed her adventure a fool's errand. "He wasn't the one sifting through rubble and rock in one hundred degree heat."

"He's never loved field work." Kyle picked up a limestone rock from Marisa's bookshelf. "Hard to chase the financing when you're in the boonies."

Marisa studied the rock in Kyle's hand. Found at her latest dig, it reminded her that she belonged in the jungle, not here. "I suppose." The microwave dinged; she removed her coffee and sipped. The coffee tasted bitter.

"Aren't you supposed to pick up toys for your brothers?"

She glanced at the clock on her desk. "Damn."

Thanks to her trips to Mexico, she had avoided family gatherings, but this year had no credible excuse exonerating her from her father and stepmother's big holiday party. She wasn't close to her dad and his second wife, but they had two sons, Travis and Tyler, seven-year-old twins. As much as she dreaded the holidays, she had a begrudging affection for her half brothers, whom she'd not seen in over six months.

Kyle glanced at his black explorer's watch. "If you hurry you can make it."

The shopkeeper had called and warned her that today would be the last day he'd be open before Christmas. He was closing early this year to go on a holiday vacation. If she didn't pick up the toys today, she'd not get them until after New Year's.

Marisa grabbed her leather jacket and slid it over a black T-shirt embellished with a glyph symbolizing life. Pulling her long dark hair out from under her jacket, she reached for her satchel purse. Silver and beaded bracelets rattled on her wrists as she shut off her desk lamp. "I can't believe I forgot. I swore to myself I'd not mess this up." She might not love the holidays now, but when she'd been seven, the holiday spirit had zapped through her body like electricity, just as it did her brothers now.

"Why didn't you order online like a normal person?"

"Because my stepmother said the boys wanted these specialty trucks from this particular store. She had the shopkeeper set them aside for me." She shrugged. "It would be nice if I bought a nice gift for the boys. I haven't shared Christmas with them in years."

"I didn't think you were motivated by guilt."

If she hadn't liked her brothers, she wouldn't have taken the bait. "Easier to get the trucks, put in an appearance at their Christmas party, and be done with it all." She scooped up her papers, dropped them in the bottom desk drawer, and digging her keys from her purse, fastened the lock. "I'll see you after the holidays."

"Tell me you aren't doubling back here to the office and working on Christmas Day."

"Okay, I won't tell you."

"Give yourself a break."

"I love my work." *And it's all I really have.*

"You are hopeless." He kissed her on the cheek. "Merry Christmas."

"Back at you."

Christmas music chased after her as she hurried along the hallway and out the front door. Cold winds had her drawing in a breath as she tugged up her collar and ducked her head. With her mind squarely on reaching the toy store in time, she didn't see the large man until he was feet from her.

"Dr. Thompson, you are a hard woman to find."

The familiar deep baritone voice echoing the text message had her turning to face a man with broad shoulders. He wore a Stetson, white shirt, red tie, a heavy dark jacket, and silver-tipped boots that peeked out from crisp khakis. The Pecos star, clipped to his belt buckle, confirmed he belonged to an elite group of lawmen, the Texas Rangers. Only one hundred and forty-four men and women wore the Rangers' star.

For a moment, she struggled to reconcile the man before her to memories she'd done her best to forget.

They had met six weeks ago on the Day of the Dead celebration that had beat with a fever pitch in Merida, Mexico, the centuries-old city that was the heart of the Yucatan. Music reverberated around the small university café built in the European style of the Conquistadors and coated with the white limestone of the Mayans. She'd been savoring a spicy hot chocolate and watching parading revelers, dressed in brightly colored Indian garb and carrying large gold crucifixes in honor of their Catholic faith.

The Day of the Dead festival was a remembrance of dead ancestors, and when she was in Mexico she always made a point to attend. A toast to her late mother had been on her lips when he'd crossed her path.

He'd worn a simple white shirt, jeans, and that Stetson. If not for the hat, certainly his commanding attitude gave him away as American. He sat at a table beside hers and ordered a beer in fluent Spanish spiced with a subtle Texas drawl.

Texans might squabble and carry on while inside their borders, but once they stepped over the state line, they shared a kinship. She'd been feeling festive that day, perhaps lonely, and so she'd done what she'd rarely done. She'd struck up a conversation with the man, Lucas, which had led to drinks, dinner, and later his room.

The next morning she'd awoken, satiated and chagrined over their encounter. Sleeping with strangers had never been her style, and she'd felt awkward. While he'd slept, she'd slipped away and returned to her jungle, certain the past would stay dead and buried.

Now as Marisa watched Lucas walk up the stairs with slow, purposeful steps, her heart dropped into her belly. What were the chances of them ever seeing each other again?

"Lucas Cooper."

The sound of his name sharpened gray eyes. "Good memory."

"Some say too good." She glanced at her watch. Forty minutes until the store closed. Grateful for the excuse, she said a little too quickly and candidly, "I'm sorry to run off, but I have to pick up a gift for my brothers or I'll be blackballed from my family. Have a good evening."

As she descended the steps, he followed. "I came to see you."

She fished her keys from her purse, energy flooding her veins. "Why?"

"Not for the reasons you might think." He kept pace with her easily.

Heat now burning her cheeks, Marisa let the comment drift past, hoping it would carry away the night they'd shared. She tipped her head forward, letting the curtain of black hair obscure his vision of her face.

"I hear your thing is ancient languages." His tone remained steady, though she sensed a vague insult simmering below the surface.

Her *thing?* She'd dedicated the last decade of study to the subject. Like her mother before her, she'd established herself in international circles as the premier linguist in the Mayan language, whose origins could be traced back over two thousand years. "Yeah, you could say that."

"I hear you're mighty good." His face softened, but avoided a smile.

"So I've been told." She burrowed chilled fingers into the pockets of her jacket.

"I'd like to run an idea by you."

"What? Why?"

"I'm on a case." Ah, so Merida hadn't mattered much after all.

Pride piqued, her voice was more clipped. "Maybe you could call my assistant, Kyle, and make an appointment. Like I said, I must get these presents picked up. I'll have plenty of time after the holidays." Truth was, she had plenty of time, but his blatant dismissal of that night had her digging in mental heels. Stubbornness, she'd been told, was her greatest asset and her worst fault.

"Now would be better than later." Steel coated the words barely softened by a slight smile.

She glanced up, conscious of the difference between her diminutive height and his six-foot-five frame. To appear a bit more intimidating, she tilted her chin and raised a brow as if staring at a tardy student. "I don't imagine you as a student of ancient languages."

Amusement danced in his gray eyes at her attempt to claim command of a situation he'd owned before he'd uttered the first word. "You'd be surprised what interests me, ma'am."

"Are you trying to be clever?"

"Wouldn't know how to be clever if I tried."

False modesty didn't ring true. "What do you want?"

"Got a research question for you."

"Regarding?" He wasn't the relaxed man with the easy smile she'd met in Mexico. This man was harder, tougher, the kind of man who didn't seek out anyone without an express purpose.

He glanced from side to side and dropped his voice a notch so that only she could hear. "I'm not here to interfere in your personal life. I'm working on a drug case. It's the same case that took me to Merida. A drug dealer has developed a code that's been used to communicate information about an upcoming shipment, and no one can break it."

She drew cool air deep into her lungs. "And you want me to break the code?"

"I'd have asked you in Mexico if you'd let me get to know you better. I figured we'd talk more at breakfast."

Color warmed her cheeks. "Breakfast."

"You vanished into the jungle until a few days ago. I never forgot you, and it's taken me this long to track you. Like I said, you are a hard woman to find."

Chapter 2

Lucas had hunted down Marisa. He'd tracked her to Mexico and now here. She wasn't sure if she was upset or pleased. "I see."

"No one has figured the code out so far. It's made up of dots and dashes and pictures. We think perhaps Mayan or Aztec, but no one can read it."

"There are glyphs?"

"Say again?"

She unzipped the folds of her jacket to show him her T-shirt. "Like this?"

His gaze dropped, lingered. "I suppose so."

She zipped up her jacket. "Why didn't you talk to the folks here at the university? I'm not the only one who could have figured this out."

His gaze met hers. "We had Rangers interview the professors here. None could help us out."

Despite the situation's awkwardness and the ticking toy clock, her interest flickered. "Do you have it with you?"

"I have all the pieces and parts back at Ranger head-quarters."

"Is this time sensitive? Can I look at it tomorrow?"

"We don't have much time, now. Days maybe. Now would be best."

The front door to the building opened, and a woman's laugh drew their attention to a couple—her ex-boyfriend and his new girlfriend, a tall blonde dressed in a silk dress and fur jacket. Awesome. Marisa had Ranger-from-the-Past and Bradley and Jennifer to contend with at once. Awesome. And thirty-eight minutes until the toy store closed.

"Marisa," Bradley called from the top of the stairs.

She watched as Bradley's girlfriend whispered in his ear, and he nodded. Her frown suggested she clearly did not want to meet Marisa any more than Marisa wanted to meet her. The power duo descended the stairs, both all smiles.

When they approached, Marisa straightened her spine just a fraction and tried not to focus on her lack of makeup or her faded jeans. How many times had her dad told her to lose the homeless look and dress like a professional? "Bradley."

"We missed you at the party. Mrs. Lorraine was looking for you. She had lots of ideas for the spring semester pro-grams."

Mrs. Lorraine was a sixth-generation Texan and a large donor. The last time she and Marisa had talked, she'd wanted Marisa to include more Texas history in her cur-riculum. When Marisa tried to explain she taught Mayan history, Mrs. Lorraine had said she didn't really care about any history other than Texas history. "Right."

Bradley's mouth twitched. "There's a lot of buzz about your work. Had some alumni at the party who wanted to meet you. Your kind of find could mean lots of donations."

"I don't have concrete information yet." Aware of

Ranger Cooper's gray gaze assessing every move, she itched to be gone.

"Who's your friend?" Bradley asked.

Marisa swallowed. "Bradley and . . . Jennifer, I'd like you to meet Texas Ranger Lucas Cooper."

Lucas took Bradley's hand in his, and she savored a moment's satisfaction when Lucas squeezed the professor's hand a bit too hard. "Didn't catch the last name."

"Rogers." Bradley pulled back his hand. He had enough pride at least not to grimace or shake the cramp from his hand. "Marisa, Jennifer and I were hoping you could join us for drinks. She was just telling me how fascinated she is with your work on ancient languages."

Jennifer smiled and nodded. "We'd love to have you."

As obtuse as Marisa could be about reading body language, she realized Jennifer's flat smile and distracted gaze telegraphed total disinterest. "I can't."

"Give me one reason why you won't join us, Marisa." Irritation had crept into Bradley's voice. So far her work had kept her job safe in the department, but she didn't have tenure yet and he'd been hinting about budget cuts. She might be sitting on the breakthrough of the century or nothing. "You can't hide from Christmas for the rest of your life."

"Not the rest of my life," she said. "Just six more days."

"She was like that when we dated," Bradley said to Lucas. "Hated the holidays. Always a sore point with us."

Embarrassment mingled with anger. She was not going to have a blow-by-blow of her failed relationship in front of a man she'd slept with and abandoned. "No one's interested in our history. Now, if you all will excuse me."

Bradley's smile vanished, and he looked as if to block her path. Lucas shifted his stance just a little closer to Marisa as if making a claim. "She's got a real tight schedule. Just time for me this evening."

Bradley didn't hide his shock. "You have a date?"

Marisa enjoyed his shock too much to correct him. "We do."

When they'd dated, she'd never said no when he'd asked for her help, whether it was interpreting some of his work or covering his classes. However, her patience had been stripped away. "Girls have fun once in a while."

Bradley frowned. "You owe the department an appearance with the alumni party. I'm tired of covering for you."

"Then don't."

Bradley's BlackBerry buzzed, distracting him from his comeback.

Lucas took the opening and moved a fraction closer to Marisa. "We really have to get going. Have a nice evening."

"You aren't coming?"

"No," Marisa said, grateful Lucas had the sense not to answer for her.

Bradley glanced at Lucas, who stood tall, an immoveable wall of muscle and determination. Frowning, Bradley cut his losses, took Jennifer by the elbow, and said his good-byes.

As the duo left, gratitude jostled Marisa past embarrassment. "Thank you."

Lucas's gaze lingered on Bradley, much like a wolf stalked prey. "You aren't comfortable around the guy."

"It's not that. I just don't have the reserves to deal with him tonight." She glanced at her watch. Twenty-nine minutes. She'd never make it to the store in time. "And like I said, toys for my brothers. The shopkeeper is closing up tonight and won't reopen until after the holidays."

"What's the address?"

"It's on North Highway. I'm not going to make it."

"I know the place. I can get you there."

"You?"

"Yeah, but you are going to owe me. Toys first. Code second."

Not a question. A done deal.

"Sure, why not." The puzzle was a reason to avoid her empty home and the boxes crammed with memories. "But this is just about the code."

A staggering power radiated behind those gray eyes. "Sure."

Stubbornness had her wrestling for the control that remained out of reach. "As soon as I get those toy trucks."

"Best if I drive. And I'm parked right out front. We'll get there faster. Wait right here."

"Sure." The chill cut through her jacket as she moved toward the SUV. Lucas opened her door, and she slid inside. As he crossed in front of the truck, he pulled his phone from his jacket and spoke quickly before ending the call. He tossed his hat in the backseat and slid behind the wheel. He smelled of fresh air and the faintest hint of soap, scents that had clung to her skin as she'd driven back to the jungle alone.

He put the car in gear and flipped on the lights. "Hold on."

When he gunned the engine, she grabbed hold of the door. He wove in and out of the streets as if he'd lived in the area all his life. Soon they were headed north.

On any given day she loved the silence, but now it weighed heavy and awkward.

Lucas broke it with, "How did your dig go in Mexico?"

"You've been asking around about me?"

"For months. No one in Mexico could quite figure out where you were in the jungle."

"That's the idea. Keep the dig location a secret." She folded her arms. "You never mentioned you were looking for me in Merida."

"I was looking for Dr. M. E. Thompson. Not a woman wearing a white dress in a café."

Her cheeks warmed. "Did you know who I was in the café?"

"No. Like I said, you didn't look like a professor of ancient languages. And you never mentioned your work at dinner."

"Too many people think the Mayan ruins are stocked with gold. I didn't need any unnecessary trouble." She glared at him.

"You thought I was trouble?"

No. Not then. "You never know who's listening." She tilted her chin up. "And what does a professor of ancient languages look like?"

He tossed her a look. "That was a compliment."

She'd heard enough about the stereotypes to know what he must have imagined when he'd gone looking for her. "When did you put the pieces together?"

"After you left."

"Not much of a detective."

He tightened his grip on the wheel. "I found you, didn't I?"

She dropped her head back against the seat. Could this Christmas season get any worse?

She didn't know what to say, so she kept silent. Lights from cars and buildings whisked past.

"Word is, you have a major find on your hands," he said.

No one wanted the blow-by-blow of her findings. Too many times, she witnessed eyes glazing over after she launched into a detailed description. "Bits and pieces. I'm hoping to string it into something worthwhile."

Ahead, she spotted the lights of the toy store sign, and soon he'd parked in front. Inside, she saw the clerk waiting, two bags on the counter.

"I'll be right back," she said.

"I'll be waiting."

Disregarding the meaning humming under his words, she

dashed into the store. Bells jingled over her head as she hurried through the door. She glanced at the clock, fishing her wallet out of her purse. One minute past closing time. "You waited for me."

The older man, eyes heavy with fatigue, shook his head. "Ranger said to wait."

"A Ranger called you?" She pulled out her credit card and handed it to him.

He swiped it. "Said not to close and to wait." He looked past her to the dark SUV. "He sounded insistent, so I figured it was best to wait."

She pocketed her card and the receipt. Normally, she'd have argued. Taking any kind of favor led to dependency and that led to heartache. But tonight she was too grateful to complain. "Thanks."

"Merry Christmas."

"Same to you."

She wrestled the heavy bags from the counter and moved to the front door. Lucas got out of the SUV and opened the door for her. Without asking, he took the bags from her and placed them in the backseat.

"Thanks."

"Glad to help."

She slid back into her seat, and he settled behind the wheel and drove. "So tell me about this code."

"Not much I can tell you. Experts can't crack it. They thought if they could create a key, they could translate the symbols. But no one can figure out the key."

Silver bracelets jangled on her wrist as she ran her fingers through her hair. "Well, ancient languages are what I do best."

"Exactly what I've heard."

"Show me what you have and I'll take my best shot."

"Great."

They arrived at Ranger headquarters minutes later and Marisa followed Lucas past security. He led her to his locked office, flipped on the lights, and moved to a small conference table where a stack of papers rested. "These are the coded messages we have. Feel free to have a look. If you don't mind, I'm going to order pizza. Haven't eaten much today."

Her stomach grumbled. "I'll go halves with you on the pizza. I'm starving."

His powerful gaze reflected a mixture of humor and deadly intent. "You crack that code, and I will buy you all the pizza you can eat."

"Deal."

Her mind shifting from him to the papers, she quickly found herself pulled into the documents and the swirl of symbols. To the untrained eye it was chaos. To her, it was heaven.

Lucas met the pizza delivery guy at the front desk, and when he returned to his office he found Marisa exactly where he'd left her, frowning over the ciphers, oblivious to him and the world around her.

A fellow Ranger, Brody Winchester, had a smart wife, Dr. Jo Granger, who'd put Lucas on to Dr. M. E. Thompson a couple of months ago when the first coded messages had appeared. Lucas considered Jo one hell of a smart woman, and when she'd commented that Dr. Thompson was another level of smart, he'd known she was in the big leagues.

After learning Dr. Thompson was in Mexico on a dig, he'd gone to Merida, Mexico, to ask around the university. He had learned she was a bookish, odd woman who lived for her dead languages. A dull sort, one professor had said, but the best in her field. She was expected in town to replenish supplies, but no one knew exactly when she'd appear.

When he'd arrived at that sidewalk café, he'd been looking for good grub, a cold beer, and a chance to recharge after forty-seven hours of nonstop work while he waited for Dr. M. E. Thompson.

When he'd spotted the woman in the white dress, rational thought vanished, and when she'd smiled at him and teased him about the Texas seeping through his Spanish, he'd been lost. The ensuing conversation, dinner, drinks, and sex had momentarily banished thoughts of work. That night had been all about the woman in the white dress. And then she'd vanished.

He'd asked around and discovered the woman in the white dress was Dr. Thompson. He'd called himself every form of dumbass before deciding that finding her would be easy. However, he'd not counted on the jungle or that it would swallow her trail so completely.

Hours ago, when he'd received word she'd returned to Austin from her jungle dig, he'd dropped what he was doing and come straight to the university. There was a code still to be cracked and if he were honest, one night with Marisa had not been quite enough.

How many times since had he dreamed about her in that white dress? Hell, even now he thought her glasses accentuated rather than hid bright green expressive eyes and a high slash of cheekbones. And the frown grooved in her forehead added to her allure.

"Pizza," he said.

She glanced up from the pages, her eyes a bit vacant and lost. He could almost hear the gears in her brain shifting and grinding as she refocused on the world outside her scroll. "Great. I'm starving."

As she cleared away her papers and stacked them neatly, he set the pizza box on the table along with a bag stuffed with napkins and drinks. "I wasn't sure if you liked soda. There's water in the cooler if that's what you prefer."

"Soda's great." She rolled up her sleeves and placed napkins in front of him and herself. He flipped open the box and the scents of pepperoni, mushroom, and onion drifted around them. She took a piece of pizza and laid it on her napkin. "I haven't had pizza in ages."

He sat and rolled up his sleeves, exposing forearms dusted with dark hair. "It's a mainstay for me."

She took a bite and glanced toward the papers to her right. "It's an ancient language. I'm fairly sure it's Mayan. It might take me a couple of days, but I can figure it out."

"A couple of days?" No hiding his surprise.

"Shouldn't be that hard."

He laughed. "Don't tell the forensics team."

"They shouldn't feel bad. Unless you study this all the time, you wouldn't have a clue."

"I'll be sure to pass it on." Already, he pictured the team's frustration when he told them Marisa had dubbed the task easy. They'd endured many sleepless nights trying to figure out what the dealers were communicating to each other.

"So what exactly am I looking for?"

"There is word of a major shipment arriving from Mexico into the area. It's a new supplier trying to make a name for himself, and we want to stop him before he gets established."

"When's it expected?"

"We've heard around Christmas Day but don't know exactly where or when."

"Time is running out." She plucked the cheese off the pizza and ate it. "I'll work fast."

"Thanks." He sipped his soda, unable to rein in his curiosity. "So you dated that Bradley?" She looked up at him as he paused, pizza inches from his mouth.

She picked a piece of pepperoni off her pizza and then set it aside. "Ours was a fairly classic tale. We dated. We broke up."

"Been reading body language for a long time, ma'am. More to that story than meets the eye."

"You read body language?"

"As well, if not better, than you read those dead languages."

She shrugged. "People are a mystery to me. Must be why I like my dead languages. They may take years to figure out, but there's always a pattern, clues to lead you to the message. That's not so true when it comes to people."

"Meaning you didn't read Bradley well?"

She straightened. "That doesn't really matter."

"Then there's no harm answering the question."

She nibbled an edge of pepperoni. "I thought he was the one. When I received a grant to travel and study, he asked me not to take the trip though I'd been dreaming of going for years. I refused to give it up. He was angry and annoyed. A week before I left, Kyle told me Bradley was dating Jennifer."

"Ouch."

"Long story made short, I broke it off."

A slight wavering in her voice and wrinkling in her forehead betrayed her feelings. Bradley had hurt her badly. Lucas did not fully understand why this mattered to him, but it did. "He's a chickenshit."

A flicker of amusement fired in her eyes. "Not an exact translation of what I said but the connotation is a match."

"Why's he hanging around?"

"He wants access to my research material. I think he's realized that I might soon eclipse him in reputation."

"He'll live."

She plucked a pepperoni from the pizza. "My thoughts exactly."

Curiosity nudged him to ask, "Big plans for the holidays?"

"My mother passed away seven years ago, so other than an appearance at my father and stepmother's house tomorrow, where I deliver my presents to my brothers, no." She plucked off another pepperoni.

"You don't like Christmas."

"I didn't say that."

"Ninety-three percent of communication is nonverbal. Your nonverbal cues scream humbug."

She laughed. "I'm not quite a Scrooge. I just don't love all the fuss and the work for one day. Far too much work for so little return."

"Little return?"

"It's not super fun for me." She lifted her pizza. "So what about you? I'm sensing you like Christmas."

He nodded, no hint of hesitation in his voice. "My folks always made a big deal of the day. They're gone now, so my sister carries on the tradition. We always do up a big dinner, and she makes a point to work around my crazy schedule. One year we didn't eat the turkey and trimmings until January 1. But it didn't matter. Felt like Christmas."

"That's nice."

"So why do you hate Christmas, Dr. Scrooge?"

She laid down her pizza, suddenly not hungry. "My father left my mother on Christmas Eve." She sighed. "He didn't mean for it to happen that way. But they'd fought and he blurted out he was leaving. He moved out that night."

"I'm sorry."

"It is what it is. He's done his best to make it up to me over the years. He and his wife go all-out for the holidays."

She'd been left twice, and now she did the leaving. "Sorry to hear that."

He realized she'd not eaten much. He'd expected talk of Christmas would have been positive neutral territory, but instead it robbed her of her appetite.

"Don't be. We all have to deal. That's life." She sighed. "Could I take copies of this code home? I've got a few days off, and I'll have better luck with all my books to reference."

"Sure. But do me a favor and keep the work a secret. No sense letting anyone know about this."

"Sure."

He picked up a manila envelope from his desk and handed it to her. "Copies for you."

A delicate brow arched. "You were that sure I'd come and help you."

"I'm mighty persistent."

"You haven't met stubborn until now."

A smile curved the edges of his lips. "You keep telling yourself that."

Chapter 3

Marisa was far too wired to sleep after Lucas Cooper dropped her off. The toys balanced in her hands, she pushed open the front door to her tiny Hyde Park home with her foot. The house had been built in the twenties and her mother had bought it shortly after her parents' divorce. What little time her mother spared from her work went to Marisa and so the house remained ignored. Marisa knew she'd soon have to sell the place, fix it up, or risk having it disintegrate around her.

Renovation, she'd discovered during her sole meeting with an architect last fall, took time and creativity and she had little in reserve after she pushed aside her work at the end of the day.

And so her home remained a dark and dingy space. She'd sold most of her furniture before leaving for Mexico. Yesterday, she'd bought a clearance lawn chaise at the hardware store as well as a patio table and chair that would serve as a stopgap for dining, work, and general tasks until she figured out what to do with the house.

She dropped the toy bags and glanced at the boxes stacked in her living room. As luck would have it, the box on top was marked CHRISTMAS. The thick block lettering had been her mother's, and Marisa guessed after the divorce she'd boxed up what few decorations she chose to keep and put them away forever. Marisa had glanced in the box but closed it immediately. She just didn't have the courage to see what about the dreaded holiday had been so important to her mother.

Kicking off her shoes, Marisa moved into the kitchen, where she snagged a carton of takeout rice from the fridge that she'd not finished last night. She popped it in the microwave and set a pot of coffee to brew.

She'd barely eaten with Lucas Cooper. She was too stunned and off-kilter to really think. She'd never been nervous when she'd met Bradley. When he'd first approached her, he'd not come bearing sweet words, flowers, or chocolates. No, he'd known her too well for that. He'd brought her a word puzzle. Granted, she'd solved the puzzle in under thirty seconds, but the gift had shown her that he'd been paying attention to her thirst to unravel mysteries. His schoolboy-ish attempt had charmed her. Later she would figure out his charms had hidden motives.

Lucas Cooper had come bearing a far more interesting puzzle and a history of their shared night that still made her blush. As she sat at the kitchen table and thumbed through the copies of his documents, she thought back to the person she'd been the night they met. Unguarded and happy, she'd been in her element, still buzzed from a consultation with experts in the local university's ancient studies department.

She'd thought she'd almost moved on from Lucas, and then he'd appeared and unsteadied her with a glance and a puzzle that couldn't be solved in under a minute.

Despite his controlled manners tonight, his flinty warrior's gaze suggested a very dangerous man. Born into a different time, the tall, broad-shouldered Ranger could easily have worn a warrior's mantle, wielded a battle-ax, and sported a shield bearing the likeness of a fierce spirit god.

The image coupled with this very intriguing puzzle flooded restless energy into her veins. She rose and moved to a drawer to dig out a rubber band and tie back her hair, which suddenly now annoyed her with its weight.

She changed out of her jeans into sweats and an oversized T-shirt. She moved back into the kitchen, pulled out her steaming bowl of rice, and sat in the chair in front of this new mystery.

Major drug shipment, Lucas had said. This was no whim on his part but a mission. As she scooped a ladleful of rice, she bent over the first page and studied the symbols. Their origins were clearly rooted in the Mayan culture, though some symbols reminded her of the Aztec.

Whoever had strung the symbols into words was clever. To the untrained eye, the Mayan and Aztec symbols were similar and few understood the differences. Much like the United States Army had used the Navajo code talkers during World War II, this cryptographer had drawn upon history to create a modern message. And it made perfect sense. Why invent a new code when a look to the past gave you the perfect solution?

As she studied the glyphs and the dots and dashes, her heart beat a little faster. Yes, this demanding puzzle was quite intriguing.

As she allowed the symbols to swirl in her mind, she knew she would decipher this code. It might take a day or two, but she would crack it.

The shrill tone of her phone had her raising her head and glancing around for her cell, which was always a little lost or misplaced. She found the cell on the fourth ring and by the time she said hello she sounded breathless and a bit annoyed.

"Marisa?"

Her father's voice sounded relaxed and happy. Not the clipped, perpetually angry man who'd shared the house with her mother. No, this man was a man right with the world thanks to her stepmother, who had given him the life, and the sons, he'd always craved.

"Dad."

"Just checking to make sure you're still coming tomorrow. Susan's been cooking for days. You know how she loves Christmas."

Susan, her stepmother, was eighteen years younger than her father. Blond and lovely, she never stepped outside without donning makeup and designer clothes. To her credit, she was not a bad woman. She'd not been behind her parents' divorce and had, in fact, not come into her father's life until four or five years after the final decree. She went out of her way to make Marisa feel welcome whenever she visited. Marisa, out of politeness, had done her best to play her part as the dutiful daughter. But no matter how many presents Susan bought or how many smiles and thank-yous they exchanged, she never felt comfortable in their home. She was the outsider and no time of year made her more attuned to her outlier status than Christmas.

"I know she loves the day." She pictured the three Christmas trees that Susan put up, the thousands of white lights that now adorned their front lawn, and the row of pictures featuring her brothers sitting with Santa Claus lined up along the mantel.

"She's gone all-out for you this year. Put a lot of thought into your gift. You're going to be pleased."

Marisa felt ungrateful and small when she thought about the bottle of perfume she'd hastily purchased online for Susan. Expensive and nice didn't trump the lack of thought or love that had gone into the gift. She'd checked the Christmas Gift box, so to speak. "I can't wait."

A silence crackled through the line. "How's work going?"

"Great. I'm steeped in ancient cultures."

"What about the modern culture? All work and no play . . ."

He let the words trail. "I love my work. Hard to say no to it." Her work never disappointed, lied, or left. "The work is so thrilling."

In the background she heard the boys' polite chatter. Her father had set up a special desk for the boys so they could work alongside their dad. The voices grew louder and a door opened. "Well, we look forward to seeing you."

"Me, too. Can't wait."

She hung up, sadness fisting a knot in her chest. Pity she couldn't bond with people as well as she connected with her dead languages.

Marisa had lost track of time when her phone chimed with a text. She rubbed her eyes and stretched her tight shoulders as she glanced at the clock on her phone. It was just after 2 A.M. The time had slipped away from her again. She picked up her coffee and sipped. Ice-cold. Grimacing, she moved to the sink and poured out the stale coffee before setting another cup to brew. As the machine gurgled and spit, she picked up her phone.

Sacrifices will be made.

What sacrifices?

Rubbing her tired eyes, she studied the words and phone number. The caller was Unknown. Not Lucas. Who would send her such a text? She had a friend, Doris, who drank too much on occasion and would send Marisa texts. But those were all jokes about the men she met in bars.

The reference to sacrifices made no sense and did not fit the profile of anyone she knew.

Sacrifices will be made.

Assuming the text had arrived in error, she moved to the coffee machine and picked up her cup. With a splash of milk, the fresh coffee tasted good and revived many of her lagging senses. Foolish to drink the brew so late at night, but she knew herself well enough to know she'd work until dawn and then, with no school tomorrow, fall into bed to sleep the day away.

Her phone buzzed again.

She picked it up and read: **Sacrifices will be made.**

More annoyed than worried, she imagined a drunk in a bar texting a girlfriend or someone's ex too hammered to make sure the call was sent to the right person.

As she set the phone aside and settled back in her chair to review the notes she'd written, there was a loud bang on her front door. She jumped, sloshing her coffee. Hissing as the brew scorched her hand, she rose and backed away from the door until she bumped into her kitchen counter.

The pounding grew louder, and when the handle of her front door rattled as if someone was trying to tear the door-knob out of its setting, she realized the text was no mistake or joke.

Her phone buzzed a third time and she glanced at the word, **Sacrifice.**

Someone was sending her a message. A warning. A threat. She looked toward the scattered, coffee-stained pages on her table and at the door. The rattling and pounding stopped, and a shadowed figure passed in front of her thick sheer-covered front window.

Her hands trembled as she drew in a breath and catalogued the names of the people she could call. The cops made sense, of course, but that would put her in the position of explaining the documents, and Lucas had asked her to keep the work she was doing for him a secret.

There was Bradley, but she imagined him nestled next to Jennifer, waking to take the call. He would come, but there'd be some price, no doubt, to her pride. Her father would lecture and demand she stay at his house for the holidays.

The door handle rattled again, not with the urgency of a madman but of someone trying to calculate its strength. Whoever was out there was stalking, searching for a chance to strike.

She scrolled through her list of contacts and settled on one. Embarrassment fluttered for just a brief moment and then she dialed.

Chapter 4

Lucas parked in front of the Hyde Park house within a half hour of receiving Marisa's call. Lights in all the rooms burned bright and set the house apart on the darkened, quiet street. Out of his SUV, he put on his hat. Hand on his gun, he surveyed the porch that stretched across the front of the house, the tall windows, and the brick façade. It was a fine house, no doubt expensive, but it was in need of work.

He saw no signs of a threat, but still kept his hand on his gun as he moved to the front steps and knocked. He could easily imagine Marisa meaning to tend to the house just as she'd meant to buy those presents before it was almost too late. Cracked brick and peeling shutters weren't enough to pull her from work.

Footsteps inside the house ran to the front door and hesitated. "Marisa, it's Lucas Cooper."

The rattle of chains scraped against locks and the door opened. Light from the interior shined behind Marisa, casting a glow on the long black hair hanging loose around her shoulders. Her skin was pale in the light, and the spark of annoyance had vanished, making her look a bit fragile. "You had some trouble."

She pushed open the screened door, which squeaked and groaned. "I'm feeling just a little foolish right about now. It's been quiet since I called you. Not a rattle or a text."

He stepped inside the foyer, removing his hat as he surveyed the living room. As worn and neglected as the exterior, it was furnished with just a few brand-new outdoor chairs and a table that looked more suited for a picnic. One chair still had the red clearance tag dangling from an arm. He guessed she'd sold her furniture before her Mexico trip, likely still angry over Bradley's affair, and believing she'd not return to her life in Austin.

What she couldn't bring herself to sell had gone into storage. What Marisa valued enough to keep, fit in a half-dozen dusty boxes. One box marked CHRISTMAS had a loose top flap as if she'd pried it open and stopped. He doubted if she'd ever get around to putting up the decorations.

He closed the door behind him and eased his hand away from the gun. "I'm glad you did call. Can't be too careful."

"I'm not the nervous sort. Not at all." She scrolled through her phone and showed him the messages. "I've camped in the jungle and dealt with unsavory characters and wild animals. But these texts . . . they were creepy. And then someone came to the door and rattled it as if they wanted to get inside. I kind of freaked." An apology hummed under the words.

"Like I said, glad you called. There a backyard?"

"Yes. Not big, but it's through those double French doors."

He strode across the small home, his boots thudding steadily against the rough pine floor. In the backyard, there was a nicely built deck in need of refinishing and no furniture. No potted plants. "Looks clear."

She hovered fifteen feet from the door. "I ran around the house checking all the doors and windows to make sure they were locked. I also checked under the bed and in the closets."

He frowned. "I'd rather you'd have waited for me to do that."

She grimaced. "I felt a little foolish after I talked to you. I don't panic."

"No trouble. No trouble at all."

She hugged her arms around her. "Can I get you a coffee at least?"

"Sure. That would be nice."

He followed her into the kitchen and noticed the scattered papers he'd given her earlier this evening. Red marks covered each page. He tried to read her comments but found her writing just as elusive as the ancient language. "Looks like you were working."

She pulled a UT cup from the cabinet. "It pulled me right in. I lost total track of time."

"Come up with anything?"

"I think your encoder pulled symbols from two ancient languages. Mayan and Aztec. Very clever to mix the symbols. Both languages have been dead for thousands of years, and only a half-dozen people in the world can read it."

He studied the spark in her eyes. "But you can."

"I can." No bravado. Just stating a fact. "I will break it in the next few days."

He thought about the hours and hours experts had spent on the letters. "I can't believe it."

She shrugged. "I have a very defined skill set. Most days those skills are as useless as a relic. But in this case, it's the perfect skill."

The coffee gurgled and she moved to open a refrigerator. "Do you have any idea who might have wanted to harass you?"

"No. At least I don't think so."

"What's that mean?"

"I dated a guy a couple of years ago and we went out a

couple of times. This was before Bradley. I ended it by the third date. We had nothing in common. He didn't take it well."

When had her pattern of leaving men begun? "What did he do?"

"Sent me a few annoying texts and e-mails after I ended it. It was getting really tiring. Finally, he stopped bothering me. I quickly put him out of my mind."

He reached for a notebook he always kept tucked in his coat pocket. "What was his name?"

"Reed North. But do you really think it could be him? It's been almost two years and I've not heard a word from him in eleven months. Odd he'd just forget about me and suddenly pop back up."

"You never know what's happening in his life. He could have been traveling out of the country, in jail, or dating someone else. We don't always know why stalkers reactivate."

"Stalker. Sounds dramatic."

"They're a real danger." He glanced at the papers. "And the texts could be connected to those. Mayans did their share of sacrifices."

She shook her head. "'Sacrifices must be made.' Sounds too generic."

He wasn't so sure, but didn't want to spook her any more tonight. "Good coffee."

"I can only cook a few dishes, but I cook them well."

"Part of that defined skill set."

"Yeah."

Remembering something else she did real well, he rubbed his index finger over the mug's handle. "I've called DPS and they're going to step up patrols in the area."

"Thanks." She skimmed her palms over her jeans. "You don't have to stay."

He took hold of the mug and sipped his coffee. "I can stay."

She met his gaze. Her cheeks brightened with color, and the look in her eyes reminded him of Merida.

Clearing her throat, she pressed her palm to the base of her neck as if calming a racing heart. "I'm fine. And I've kept you long enough."

He glanced at the papers while hiding a smile, wondering if she remembered the warm, musky air of his Mexican hotel room and the way she'd sucked in a breath when he'd trailed his hand over her flat belly. "You going to sleep?"

She rose. "I'll sleep some. Got to get my act together and get myself to my dad's house later tonight."

He stood up, in no rush to leave. "You wrapped those trucks?"

"Not yet."

"Life does get in the way," he said.

She swallowed as if realizing he wasn't talking about Christmas now. "Thanks for coming. I'll call you tomorrow with an update."

He heard the stress weaving through the words. "Call me tomorrow."

"Will do."

Ignoring the cool night air that seeped through the thin jacket, the figure stood in the shadows, waiting and watching Marisa's house. There'd been a rush of excitement when the rattling door had made Marisa shriek and pace in front of the sheered windows. That moment had been better than any Christmas present.

When the Ranger had shown, he'd moved with quick precision, closing the gap between his SUV and her front door in quick, purposeful strides. She'd let him in immediately, and when she'd looked up into his face, her relief had been palpable.

Clenching chilled fingers, the figure stepped back farther into the shadows. Frustration ate at him, and for a moment, thoughts swirled as anger boiled.

Finally, several deep breaths calmed a racing heart. This job was going to be far tougher than first imagined. The next move would have to be more aggressive. Marisa needed to be stopped. She needed to be taught a lesson. Needed to be brought down a peg.

This battle might be lost, but the war was far from over.

Chapter 5

Lucas sat at his desk, coffee in hand and phone cradled under his chin. He'd arrived home about 5 A.M. and had fallen into bed, hoping for a few hours of sleep. But thoughts of Marisa raced through his head. She had spunk and fire. And if she was right about breaking that code, well, it would be one hell of a break in the case.

But he'd not dreamed about the code. He'd dreamed about sliding his hand up under a white lace dress and along sun-kissed legs. He'd dreamed of stroking her and watching her climax.

A knock on his door had him sitting straighter and raising his gaze to Ranger Brody Winchester. He'd known Winchester from their days working the border area. "So did you find Dr. Thompson?"

Lucas sat back in his chair. "I did. And she thinks she's close to cracking the code."

Winchester shook his head as if he'd just heard a tall tale. "Is that so?"

"Smart as a whip."

"Jo said she was the best in her field."

"She had some trouble at her home last night. A couple of odd texts, and someone tried to break into her house."

Brody folded his arms over his chest, his good humor vanishing. "Think this has to do with the code?"

"I do. She doesn't. Suggested it could be a guy she dated a couple of years ago."

"But you don't think so."

"Trouble really started after I passed off the documents to her. That's just too much of a coincidence for my taste. I've stepped up police patrols in her neighborhood, and she has promised to call today with her findings. She has a family party tonight and can't put it aside."

"Does she have theories about the meaning behind the coded messages?"

"Says she'll know once she's cracked the key." He drew in a breath. "We're close."

"Damn." Brody shook his head. "If we can read these messages we'll be able to break this drug smuggling ring before it gets a foothold. We'll put this new dealer out of business for good."

Lucas drew in a breath, trying to break the stranglehold of tension banding his chest. "Lot riding on the good doctor."

"Keep me posted."

"Will do."

After Brody left, Lucas traced the number that had sent the texts to Marisa. Took less than a few minutes to discover the phone was a burner. Untraceable. Whoever was trying to get to Marisa wasn't a complete novice, though he doubted the person was aligned with the cartels. If the cartels saw her as a threat, she'd be dead. A car explosion. A stray bullet. They didn't waste time with cryptic messages. They acted. So why the need to rattle her cage?

He thought about the man she'd dated a couple of years

ago. A background check was already in the works. One way or another, he'd get to the bottom of this mess.

The wrapped presents piled haphazardly in the backseat of Marisa's car wouldn't win any beauty contests. She'd gone back to the office early and meant to stop work by midday to wrap the gifts. But just as she'd pushed away from her desk, she'd had a major breakthrough. Much like finding the key piece of a puzzle that joined large but separate sections, she'd found the component that had broken the text. She hastily translated meaningless symbols into words and sentences. Before long, she'd had two messages completely translated.

She'd been ready to dial Lucas's number when she'd glanced at the clock and realized it was past five. As much as work called, the pull of family jerked at her. She'd quickly locked her papers in her desk drawer and scurried home.

After a quick shower, and hair still damp, she'd put on minimal makeup and shimmied into her go-to simple black dress. The gifts for her father and stepmother had been easy enough to wrap—nice square boxes. But the trucks, well, she'd been forced to wind wrapping paper around them and slap tape on each crease and corner. The red and green Santa paper was at least festive.

Hair drying, Marisa gripped the steering wheel of her sedan as she took the exit off I-35 into the Texas Hill Country. The closer she drove to her father's country house, the tighter her stomach became. Her mind tripped back to the night her father had argued with her mother and declared he could no longer live with a woman who only cared about her work.

Her mother had been a history professor and her father a professor of psychology. They'd met at the University of

California Berkeley, but it had been her mother's career that had brought them to Texas. Her father had eventually landed a job at the university, but he'd felt as if he wallowed in his wife's shadow. She was a rising star in Mayan archaeology. By the time Marisa had turned seven, her father's resentment and anger no longer simmered but boiled.

Too much wine on Christmas Eve had fueled the last and final argument. He'd been annoyed because her mother had half-decorated the tree and had failed to make the tamales that had become a holiday tradition since their move to Texas. She'd been working as always, lost in her dusty papers, when he'd confronted her. She'd not understood his outburst and quickly had become annoyed because it had taken her away from her work.

He'd moved out and it would be almost a month before Marisa saw him again. When he came to see her the first time, it had been a chilly January day. He'd driven her to his new apartment, a barren and sterile place. He'd made a room for her, and though he'd decorated it with pinks and yellows, it wasn't her room. He'd pulled out a brightly wrapped gift and told her he was sorry her Christmas present was late. Marisa could still remember peeling back the neatly wrapped paper and finding a carbon copy of the doll she kept at home. "You can keep her here," he'd said.

She'd stared at the doll, marveling and hating its perfection at the same time. Her real doll had smudges on her arms and *her* doll's dress was stained and dirtied from so much holding. That doll she loved. This doll was as strange and scary as the apartment.

She never spent Christmas Eve or Christmas Day with her dad, a point her mother had demanded at the custody hearing. It was always the week before or the week after.

She glanced at the clock on the dash. If she hustled she would cover forty-five minutes worth of road in thirty.

Twenty-three years had passed since that sad Christmas, and still she and her father never saw each other on Christmas

Day. After she turned eighteen, her mother always found a reason to travel with Marisa over Christmas. She'd never put up another tree again, and though she gave Marisa a gift, she always claimed it had nothing to do with Christmas. Though her mother had died seven years ago, Marisa had found her dislike of the holiday lingered.

Shifting in her seat, she tried to embrace the positive. She really tried. But the more she thought about the coming gathering and the explosion of reds and greens waiting for her, the more somber she grew.

Shoving out a breath, she shifted her thoughts from the holidays to Lucas's puzzle, the one she'd cracked. She took pride in the accomplishment, remembering Lucas's stunned face when she'd told him she'd nearly broken his secret messages.

She fished her cell phone out of her purse on the passenger seat. Excitement stirred with an energy she'd not felt in a long time. Reminding herself it had to do with the code and not Lucas, she punched in his number. As she readied to hit SEND, she noticed the headlights in her rearview mirror. She glanced at her speedometer and realized she was driving a little slow and assumed the driver behind her was impatient. She sped up and focused on her driving. The headlights faded into the distance.

She hit SEND and after one ring his crisp, deep voice echoed in her ear. "Lucas Cooper."

"It's Marisa. Marisa Thompson."

"I know who Marisa is," he said, his voice heavy with an unnamed emotion.

She swallowed, pushing aside the feelings she'd had in Merida when they'd been together. Frightening, how alive one person could make another feel. She cleared her throat. "I cracked the code."

"Really?" The surprised pleasure in his deep voice warmed her heart.

The headlights returned, bright and annoying. "I created the key barely an hour ago."

"Marisa, that's great."

"I'll be back in town early in the morning, and I'll come by your office to review what I've discovered."

"Excellent."

The headlights grew closer, and she checked her speed. She was driving exactly five miles over the speed limit. She glared into the mirror as if willing the driver to back off. The other driver drew closer and closer.

"Marisa?"

Lucas's deep voice cut through her worries. "Sorry. Look, I don't want to sound paranoid, but there's someone right behind me on my bumper. I'm on Route 290 headed to Fredericksburg."

"How close is the car?" His voice had dropped and a low menace hummed under the words.

"Five or ten feet."

"I'm calling the sheriff's office and having them send a car in your direction."

As much as she didn't want to sound the alarm bells again, now was not the time to wonder if she'd made a mistake. The car edged closer and in a split second it bumped her back bumper. "He just hit me."

"What?" She imagined him standing and reaching for his gun as he headed for the door.

"He bumped my bumper."

"Speed up."

"I'm tossing the phone in my lap."

"Keep me on the line."

She gripped the wheel with both hands, the instruments of her dash lit up by the glare of the other car's headlights. Despite her increased speed, the car caught up to her again. This time it hit her harder. Her car swerved left before she made a hard correction to the right to keep the tires on the road. If there had been another car approaching in the other lane . . .

Heart hammering, she refused to consider what might have happened. She pushed on the accelerator. Again, more inches separated her from the other car and, again, the gap closed as the stranger matched her speed.

This time the car cut left and quickly came up on her driver's side. She glanced over, but shadows obscured the other driver's face. Before she could think to speed up or slow down, the car jerked into her lane, and this time when she swerved, she couldn't correct in time. Her car ran off the road, banging over a ditch and plunging along a rocky ravine toward the dry bed of a creek. She screamed.

Chapter 6

Marisa's screams echoing in his memory, Lucas raced from his office to his SUV. He had the sheriff's office on the radio before he left the Ranger parking lot and shot out orders for Marisa's phone to be tracked and officers in the area to respond.

He'd never driven so fast. His mind detailed all the worst-case scenarios as he bounded down I-35 toward the Hill Country exit.

"Marisa! Marisa!" He'd shouted her name into the phone after she'd screamed, but the line went dead. Though the call had been terminated, the phone still pinged a signal from the cell tower.

The roads out in this part of Texas were flat for the most part, but there were ravines and deep gulches that could easily swallow up a car.

Damn.

He'd thought about when he'd seen her emerge from the history department last night. He'd told himself he'd keep his emotions in check and that personal and professional would stay separate. But the instant he'd called her name and she'd faced him, he only thought about peeling off her clothes and making love. He'd gone searching for her in Merida so she could help him with the cipher, but he'd found the lady in white and she'd snagged him hook, line, and sinker.

This time he would not lose her.

When he saw the flashing police lights ahead, his stomach lurched. He'd barely put the car in PARK when he got out of the vehicle and raced toward the rescue crews. As he approached, the rescue squad hoisted a stretcher up from the gulch. He studied the steep grade to the ravine, his stomach sinking as he looked at Marisa's mangled car. Steeling himself, he raced to the stretcher, where he found Marisa.

Her pale skin was ashen and there was a large gash on the side of her head. The EMTs had bandaged it with a swath of fabric that covered her right eye. She was unconscious.

Lucas jogged alongside the EMTs as they carried her to the open bay of their rescue squad. "How is she?"

An EMT at the head of her stretcher held up an IV bag. "She sustained head trauma and is unconscious. She's responding to stimuli, but she's not rousing. We'll know more when we get her to the hospital."

He reached out and took Marisa's small, pale hand in his, marveling how delicate and limp her fingers felt in his. Gone were the energy and the fire.

"Marisa." Her name sounded like a strained plea.

She did not move. Did not squeeze his hand.

Lucas glanced at the EMTs. "Where are you taking her?"

The paramedic named the Austin hospital. "Her family needs to be contacted."

"I'll take care of that."

The paramedics loaded her in the back of the ambulance

and slammed the double doors shut. Lights flashing, they drove away.

Feeling helpless and of no use, he pulled his phone from his breast pocket. She'd mentioned her father, but he didn't know the man's name. Who would know? Bradley, no doubt, but Lucas would call him as a last resort. In the end he called Brody Winchester.

Winchester answered on the first ring. "Yeah."

"It's Lucas. I need to talk to Jo. I'm trying to locate Marisa's father. She's been in a car accident."

"How is she?"

Lucas supplied what little details he had and waited as Brody brought the phone to his wife.

"Lucas?" Jo Granger's voice was filled with concern.

He explained the situation and soon had the name and number of Marisa's father. The call had been tense and direct, and he'd tried to keep as much distance as he could from his emotions as he chronicled the facts, including where she was being taken.

When he hung up the phone, he glanced toward the bend in the road where he'd last seen the ambulance. As much as he wanted to follow, he was of more use to Marisa investigating the accident. Just the idea of finding the man who did this calmed his mind with renewed purpose and allowed him to box whatever feelings he had for Marisa.

He grabbed his flashlight from his vehicle and made his way to the accident site. The county sheriff's deputy was taking pictures, but the forensic team had yet to arrive.

The deputy lowered his camera. "We usually don't get a Texas Ranger at accident scenes. This case special?"

Lucas hesitated as he studied the mangled vehicle. "Yeah. This one's special." Unwilling to elaborate, he circled the car, a panther pacing. "What do you have?"

The officer glanced at his notebook. "Best I can figure, she was driving on the main road and was sideswiped. It was a blue car, judging by the paint on the wreckage. She skidded off the road and went over into the ravine. Seat belt and air bag saved her."

He fisted his fingers, and it took a moment before he could unfurl them. He moved closer to the car and spotted the brightly wrapped presents. Peeking from the torn edges of the paper was the wheel of the toy Range Rover Marisa had bought last night. Though the toy had been through an accident, he guessed the mangled wrapping job had more to do with Marisa's distraction with his code yesterday.

The work.

She didn't believe her late-night visitor was connected to her work with him, but he wasn't so sure. His reputation for busting cartels was indeed well known, and he knew in his gut she'd been attacked because of her association with him.

His work was dangerous, and he understood the burden it placed on a wife and children, so he'd stayed clear of any lasting relationships. *"You come and go as you please. You're like a cat."* How often had his sister said that? He'd been fine with that decision until he'd seen the petite woman dressed in white, sipping chocolate in the café six weeks ago.

From his coat pocket, he retrieved one of his business cards. "When you finish with the scene, send me those gifts in the backseat. They belong to the driver's younger brothers."

"Yeah, sure. Might not be before Christmas."

"Just get them to me."

"Sure."

"What else can you tell me about the accident?"

"I found a chunk of tire on the road. Seeing as this car never made it that far, the rubber could have belonged to the second driver."

"What kind of tire?"

"That will take me time to figure. I'll check the database. I should have information for you in a day or two."

"The sooner the better."

The deputy accepted the order with a weary shrug. He'd likely gotten the short end of the stick and was pulling holiday duty. "Right."

"Any witnesses?"

"No. Out here it's so desolate. If she hadn't been on her cell with you, she could have languished in that creek bed for a long time. And with temps getting so cold over the next few days, no telling if she'd have been found alive."

Lucas shoved aside a dark image. "If the second driver damaged his tire, he's going to have to stop sooner or later."

"Stands to reason. And I can tell you, judging by the tire marks, the second driver was headed west."

Odd. If it had been the cartel, bad tire or no, her attacker would have doubled back to make sure the job was done . . . that Marisa was dead.

"Assuming he kept heading west, where could he stop along the way?"

"If it were me, I wouldn't stop until I crossed the border or found a place to stash my car."

"Say this guy isn't as savvy. Where would he stop?"

"There's a gas station up ahead about ten miles. He'd be getting closer to Fredericksburg and there would be plenty of places to stop."

Plenty of places meant more people to notice a banged-up car and disabled tire. "Thanks. Keep me posted on what you find."

"Will do."

With a weight bearing on his shoulders, he moved up the embankment to his car. He removed his hat and slid behind the wheel. Reason dictated that he not call the hospital and check on Marisa. *Let the docs do their job. You focus on the mission.*

Firing up the engine, he allowed the heater to warm his skin, far more chilled than he realized. As he sat in the silence, his skin tightened with worry. Any other time he'd have listened to reason.

But not tonight. Not with Marisa.

He dialed the number of the hospital, and when he identified himself he was routed to the right person. He asked about Marisa.

"No news yet," the nurse said. "She's pretty banged up and still unconscious. They're running scans and X-rays now."

"How long before you know?"

"Morning at the earliest."

He gave his contact information and placed his phone back in its belt holster. Fifteen minutes later he pulled into a gas station, now dark and quiet. It was past midnight, and it made sense that a garage owner out here wouldn't be expecting much business.

The headlights of his SUV shining on the station, he searched for signs that a driver would have come through this way. By the pumps he saw a chunk of tire. With the beams of his lights still shining, he got out of his car and studied the section of tire. This close, he could also see a depression in the dirt as if the driver was working on a rim. Moving ten paces away, he found more tire tracks, but these marks weren't those of a damaged tire. Had the driver stopped here long enough to change his tire before moving on?

In the dark, it was impossible to tell, and he spotted the small red light mounted on the top edge of the garage. A camera. He scribbled the name of the gas station and called Information. It took minutes before he heard a gruff and tired, "What?"

"This Skip Donovan?"

"Yeah."

"This is Texas Ranger Lucas Cooper. I'm working a hit-and-run accident case, and I believe the second driver might have stopped at your station about an hour ago."

"I've been closed since six. Holidays. I'm on vacation in Mexico. Just landed about an hour ago."

Lucas tapped an impatient index finger on the phone. "What about your surveillance cameras? Do they work?"

"Yeah, they work. And I can give you the tapes when I get back in three days."

"Is there a way to access them before then?"

After a beat of silence and a sigh, "I can call my brother-in-law. His name is Rafe Jeffers. We both own the station. He's in Austin visiting his girlfriend for a few days. I'll have to track him down. Might take me a few hours."

"Do that. I need to see those tapes sooner rather than later."

"Sure. And Merry Christmas."

"Right. Thanks."

Lucas stared up at the surveillance camera. "I'm going to find you, you son of a bitch."

Chapter 7

Sunday, December 21, 6:45 A.M.

Lucas arrived at the hospital just before dawn. He'd contacted Rafe Jeffers, and the man had promised to get the tape as soon as he sobered up or found himself a designated driver.

As he strode across the lot, his cell rang. He glanced at the number and, recognizing his sister's name, hesitated an instant before he hit the ANSWER button. "Hey, Sherry, what are you doing up this early?"

"I could ask you the same, but I know you probably can't tell me." Her voice was light, friendly with the excitement of the holidays.

"Just following a lead on a hit and run. About to talk to the driver of the car."

"They hurt?"

"Will know in a few minutes."

"I'm sorry. No one should have to spend the holidays in the hospital." She sighed. "Are you going to make it up here for dinner tomorrow? I know you said you were working this week, but I thought I could practice a few recipes out on you. Bill's working so we won't have the official holiday celebration until next week."

He glanced up at the hospital and imagined Marisa in her bed. "I'd like to, Sherry, but I can't promise."

"At least say you'll try."

"I'll give my all. I'd hate to miss your world-famous pork tamales."

"Well, I wouldn't say they're world-famous, but they've won their fair share of blue ribbons."

Sherry had graduated from culinary school and worked as a chef before she'd married and quit her job to stay home with her boys, now six, eight, and ten. She was working on a cookbook but joked she was lucky to scratch out five hours a week of work time.

"I'll do my best."

"That's all I can ask." Since their folks died, Sherry had done her best to create occasions that included him. Birthdays, Fourth of July, Thanksgiving, and Christmas were all showstopper events. Family was important to her. It was important to him, as well.

He rang off and headed into the hospital. Removing his hat, he entered through the hospital's double doors, immediately greeted by the buzz of machines, the hum of conversations, and the controlled chaos of an emergency room. He found the nurses' station, identified himself, and learned that Marisa had been moved to a room. She was conscious but still very confused.

Hat in hand, he moved along the hallway, steeling himself as he pushed open the door. He'd hoped to find her alone but instead discovered a couple at her bedside. The man was tall and gray-haired and had Marisa's eyes. The woman was in her early forties, blond with flawless make-up, clothes that sparkled a little, and big jewelry. Dad and stepmom.

Lucas's gaze barreled past them to Marisa, who lay in her bed. She was awake, but her skin was as pale as the sheets, and she sported a dark bruise on her left cheek. She looked small and fragile. Her gaze didn't burn with the sharp curiosity he'd grown to like, but had a vacant dull look instead. Her eyes drifted closed.

The man moved in front of Lucas. "I'm Daniel Thompson. And you are?"

"Texas Ranger Lucas Cooper."

"Marisa said she was working on a project for the Rangers when we spoke last night. She said the project was why she was running late." Anger rumbled under the man's words like thunder before a storm.

The blonde moved to stand beside her husband. She placed a gentle hand on his arm. "Marisa loves her work. Puzzles excite her, Daniel."

Daniel's jaw clenched. "Until now, dead languages have held her interest. I don't like her traipsing around in the jungle looking for ruins, but at least that's territory she understands. She takes your job and the next day she ends up in the hospital."

Guilt banded his chest. "I'm investigating the accident."

"It was no accident. Marisa was mumbling about being run off the road before her MRI. Who would run her off the road?"

Lucas would not allow this guilt to muddle his thoughts. Later, he'd second-guess and worry. For now, he had to remain on point. "I will find who did this to her, make no mistake about that."

Daniel shook his head. "I can't believe we're here."

Lucas hesitated, staring at Marisa as if willing her to see him. She blinked, studied him, but there was no recognition. "How's she?"

"She's got a bad concussion. Her thoughts are rattled and confused."

"She'll get better." Not a question but a statement.

"That's the hope." Daniel drew in a steadying breath. "I'm going to have to ask you to leave. It's too much stress on Marisa to have people here."

Lucas kept his gaze on Marisa, wanting to hold her hand and tell her it would be all right. But Daniel was right. His job was to track the man who did this. He didn't belong here.

An hour later, Lucas removed his hat as he passed through the arches of Garrison Hall on the campus of the University of Texas. The ninety-year-old building, in the shade of the Texas Tower, housed the history department as well as Marisa's second-floor office. No doubt, if Marisa were at his side, she'd explain to him all the architectural nuances and give him a history lesson behind the names etched in the building's stone façade. But Marisa wasn't here. She was in a hospital.

Pushing his anger back, he approached a campus policeman, who stood just a little straighter. "Dr. Thompson's office."

"You here about the break-in?"

He received the call a half hour ago. Marisa Thompson's office had been ransacked. "Yes."

He took the stairs to the second floor and quickly noticed the collection of officers hovering outside a small side office. His stride was purposeful and direct as he approached the head of campus police.

The man easily recognized the garb of a Texas Ranger, and his eyes sparked with some pride as if glad to be involved in a case that caught a Ranger's attention.

"I'm Officer Stewart," the man said. "I wasn't expecting a Texas Ranger."

"Ranger Lucas Cooper. Can you tell me what happened?"

"Received a call from the officer on duty. He saw a flashlight in the room. We know Professor Thompson works late hours, but, well, she doesn't work by flashlight. He came up to investigate and found the place as you see it."

Lucas looked past the officer to the small ten-by-ten office. A few feet from a tall window stood a desk far too large for the office. It was made of bulky oak, and the heavy carvings on the legs and sides reminded him of another generation. The floor was littered with scattered papers and upended and open books as if someone had taken a hand and swiped it across the desk. A handblown glass lamp lay on the floor, its base shattered. Shelves on the walls, crammed full of books, had been pulled out randomly and also lay on the floor. "Do you know what was taken?"

"Hard to say with these professors. They have so many papers and projects. I couldn't tell you what was valuable or not. I've called Professor Bradley Rogers. He's on his way. He's more familiar with Dr. Thompson's work."

He studied the mess again, thinking that this was the work of an amateur. If it had been a seasoned drug dealer, the office would have been swept clean and likely set on fire. They'd not have risked leaving behind evidence and would have destroyed the place as insurance.

Donning gloves, he moved behind the desk and sat in her chair. He tried to imagine her sitting here and wondering how she could stand such a confined, overcrowded space.

"What the devil?"

He turned to find Bradley standing in the doorway. His

neat hair, brushed off an angled face, accented dark blue eyes. What the hell had Marisa seen in this man?

"Dr. Thompson's office was vandalized," the officer said.

Bradley studied the room, shaking his head. "Was anything taken?"

"You would know better than any of us," Lucas said.

Bradley didn't take his eyes off the confusion, as if Lucas hadn't spoken. "She kept her recent work in the bottom right drawer of her desk."

Lucas glanced at the drawer that was wide open and empty. "This drawer?"

Bradley came around the desk. "Yes."

"What was she working on?"

"It's hard to explain to a layman."

"Try me."

"She was able to snap pictures of the interior walls of a temple. Inscribed on the walls are messages that predate the Mayans by one thousand years. If she's correct, her find is huge and will make her a rock star in our world."

He found no traces of the work she'd been doing for him. The neatly annotated pages from the other night were gone. He touched his fingers to the wood damaged, clearly, by some metal device used to pry open the lock. "She didn't keep important work in a more secure location?"

"Her photos are stored on a secure server, but the notes she'd been taking since the discovery were in that drawer. I told her so many times to get a real safe. Finally, she ordered one. It will be here in a matter of days. She believed the locks on the desk, her office door, and the building would be enough."

"It wasn't."

"No."

Lucas studied the desk. "Did she use a laptop?"

"She did."

"It isn't here."

Bradley frowned as his gaze roamed the mess. "No."

"I need a list of people who have access to this building."

"Will take me an hour or so, but I'll get right on it."

"Thanks."

He spotted an overturned picture and righted it. The image was of a much younger Marisa and a woman who clearly was her mother. They appeared to be in a jungle setting and her mother was holding up a stone carving.

As if reading his thoughts, Bradley offered, "Her mother. Dr. Ellie Thompson. She was a professor of archaeology. Marisa inherited her brains and love of history. I never met her. But she was well-known in her field and, from what I've heard, liked by her students."

"Look around the desk. What's missing?"

Bradley frowned as he surveyed the scattered papers splashed with coffee from an overturned coffee cup, random sticky notes filled with Marisa's scrawled handwriting, and an upended pencil mug and her calendar. "If not for the books scattered on the floor, I'd say it looked like it normally does. Chaos. But she's only been back a couple of days and hasn't had time to really mess it up. I'm always telling her she should organize, but she's never listened. Said she has a system."

The need to defend Marisa rose up sharp. "She did just have a major career breakthrough."

Bradley's chin lifted a fraction. "Well, she had yet to prove her theories."

"So what does a discovery like that do for a person like her?"

"She's on tenure track but, of course, none of that is a guarantee. But such a find would have assured her spot on the faculty as a tenured professor."

"That's a big deal."

"It is. She'd have been awarded more grant money. Would have been able to travel back to Mexico to investigate further. It would have been quite the coup for the university."

Lucas studied the man closely, not so sold on his generous acceptance of Marisa's find. "That must rub other professors a little. I mean, she's young. No one likes the new kid on the block taking the lead."

"We aren't like that here. We are supportive of each other's work. A win for one is a win for all."

Lucas didn't believe Bradley. Earlier, sparks of glee in his gaze as he'd scanned the room told Lucas that Bradley was enjoying this.

Bradley made an effort to smile. "What was Marisa doing for you?"

"Helping me with a case."

"Funny that this happens right after she agrees to help you."

Lucas's anger rose up as sharp as a saber. He didn't like being questioned by this man, especially when his words struck at the core of his own guilt. He resisted the very primal urge to punch him. "Who had access to her office?"

Bradley glanced back at the undamaged door frame. "A key was used."

"Who had access?"

"Me. The department chair. And I'm sure maintenance has a master key."

"What kind of car do you drive?"

"Why does that matter?"

"Just asking."

"SUV."

"What color?"

"Black."

"Where is it?"

"Parked out front." He frowned. "What does my car have to do with a break-in?"

"Marisa was run off the road earlier tonight."

"What?" His face paled.

Lucas supplied the barest details, studying the man's expression closely. "Her family is with her now."

Bradley's eyes narrowed. "I would never hurt her." He rubbed the back of his neck with his hand. "I was with my girlfriend at a Christmas party until midnight."

"That so?"

He leaned in a fraction, dropping his voice a notch. "There was a time when I loved her."

Lucas didn't comment.

"Look, I see the censure in your eyes. She makes it impossible to love her. I wanted to get closer, but work is her sole priority. The rest of the world matters when she has a spare minute or two."

"That why you strayed?"

"Yeah. I was tired of being second fiddle. I wanted to be number one in the life of my girlfriend."

Lucas rose from the desk. "Thanks for your time."

"If I can help, let me know."

"Get me a list of witnesses who can verify your alibi."

His lips flattened into a thin line. "Am I being accused?"

"Just get me the list."

The afternoon light shone into Marisa's room, making her head hurt all the more. The discomfort really kicked in an hour ago when she'd stopped taking the painkillers. She'd grown tired of muddled thoughts and had decided the pain was a fair trade for a clear mind.

Her father and stepmother had left around lunchtime but had promised to return tonight. They were talking about keeping her in the hospital a few more days, but she already questioned that decision. She wanted out of here.

She sat up and winced as her head pounded. For a moment, she teetered back toward the pillow before catching herself. She could not lie here. She had a sense of urgency as if important information had been locked in her brain.

Instead of falling back to her pillows, she stayed upright and blinked until her gaze focused. She breathed deeply until her head steadied. She studied her hospital room, noting a bright bouquet of flowers. She couldn't make out the card but suspected her stepmother had ordered them. Susan had perfect taste. If her mother had been alive, she'd have gathered wildflowers from the side of the road or drawn Marisa a picture of glyphs that communicated some kind of get-well message. Her heart ached as she thought about her mother.

Her gaze was drawn to a chair in the corner where two brightly wrapped, if not mangled presents sat. Gaze narrowing, she studied the presents. She'd wrapped them. For her brothers. But how did they get here?

A knock on the door had her turning slowly to see Kyle carrying a big handful of flowers.

"You're alive," he said.

"Seems so."

Kyle grinned and came into the room. He held up the flowers. "I got you these."

"They're lovely."

"So how're you doing?"

She sat taller, wincing as her bruised muscles screamed. "Feeling foolish."

Kyle put the flowers in a water bucket and sat on the edge of the bed. "Don't feel foolish. You could have really been hurt."

"What happened? The accident and the hours before it are all a blur. I'm trying to remember, but no memories are shaking loose."

"I talked to your dad, who talked to the docs. You've a

nasty concussion so a little memory loss isn't unusual. It might take a few days or weeks for all the details to come back."

"My pieces of memory feel like a dream."

"What do you remember?"

"I remember those presents. Trying to wrap them and saying a couple of bad words when the toy wheels kept poking through the paper. Did Dad bring them?"

"I don't think so. They weren't here this morning when I stopped by and saw your dad. They must have come this afternoon."

"Odd that they'd make it to my room."

"Worry about getting better. What do you remember about the accident?"

She raised her fingertips to the bruise on her face. A slight touch made her wince. "After putting the presents in the car, my memory goes blank. What day is it?"

"Monday."

"What happened to Sunday?"

"You slept through it."

As tempted as she was to lie back and close her eyes, she didn't. Instead, she swung her legs over the side of the bed. "Kyle, I have to get out of here."

"You really shouldn't be going anywhere."

"You just said all I really need is rest."

"You should be resting in a hospital."

She pulled back the top blanket. "I can rest anywhere."

Kyle rose, clearly surprised. "Why are you so determined to leave?"

"There's something I have to do."

"What? You have no work until mid-January, and you said last week in an e-mail that you planned to kick back over the holidays."

She stared at the mangled presents. As she studied the packages closer and saw the tiny wheel sticking out, she remembered Lucas. He'd driven her to the toy store on time so that she could get . . . so that she could get two trucks for her brothers.

"Did the nurses make any comments about a Texas Ranger visiting me?" When Kyle didn't answer right away, Marisa cocked her head. "Spill."

"Yeah, as a matter of fact. He came by a few hours ago and he checked in on your status. He's been by every few hours since you arrived."

"I was doing a job for Lucas."

Kyle's lips flattened as if he'd bitten a sour apple. "Translating some document."

She'd known Kyle for six years and could read his many moods easily. "What aren't you saying?"

"Your office was ransacked after your accident. All the papers locked in your desk drawer were taken."

"Papers?"

"The ones you were translating for the Ranger."

"All my papers are gone?"

"Yes."

She pressed her fingertips to her temple. Memories came in and out of focus, and no matter how much she tried to corral one, she couldn't. "My work for the Rangers was important."

"I'm sure that it was."

"There was a time limit. He wanted me to hurry."

"How about you not worry about the Ranger and worry about getting better? I was thinking you could come and stay with me for a few days. I know the holidays aren't your favorite."

"Yeah, maybe."

"It's either me or your dad's place."

The drama of Christmas had faded to a distant second. What worried her now was retrieving the memories that would not focus. Lucas had said her work was really important. He'd said lives were at stake. They were running out of time.

"Kyle, I want you to spring me from the hospital."

That statement startled a laugh. "You can't just leave."

"Of course I can. I'm an adult. I stay as long as I want and I want to go."

"Where are you going?"

She didn't have the energy to explain or to argue with Kyle. "I need to get dressed and get out of here."

Chapter 8

Monday, December 22, 3:45 P.M.

Lucas sat at his desk staring at the map of Texas and doing his best to cage his roaming thoughts. He kept thinking about Marisa. She was going to be okay, but that didn't stop his worries that this accident stemmed from her translation work. She'd unlocked the key about the next shipment. He had ideas and theories about when and where the drugs would land, but he had no concrete clues. Texas was too big to strike out blindly. He needed Marisa's key.

But she now lay in a hospital bed, bruised and battered. Time was running out. Soon the drugs would pass into Texas and he'd be helpless to stop them.

He sat back in his chair and pinched the bridge of his nose, trying to chase away the image of her on that stretcher being loaded into an ambulance. She needed to be safe. Needed time to heal. As he ticked through each logical point, he couldn't deny he wanted to be at the hospital. He could not explain this pull he had to Marisa, but it was as strong as a cattleman's well-seasoned lariat.

His phone buzzed, and he snapped up the device and offered a far too gruff, "Cooper."

"Ranger Cooper." The cool, smooth voice belonged to a staff secretary who was rarely rattled by the big personalities of the Rangers.

"Fran." He dialed back his frustration.

"You've a visitor."

"Not now."

"I told her that and she insists on seeing you. Her name is Dr. Marisa Thompson."

Cooper's stomach dropped. "I'll be right out."

Grabbing his jacket from the back of his chair, he slid it on as he made his way to reception. He found Marisa standing by the desk. She looked pale and small, but the rock-hard determination had returned to her gaze. He released the breath he'd been holding for what seemed like thirty-six hours.

"Dr. Thompson."

She glanced up at him. "Ranger Cooper."

"Why aren't you in the hospital?"

The man standing next to her sighed as if he'd grown tired of hearing that question. "She should be in bed, but she's not listening. We were driving close by when she announced I had to bring her here."

Marisa waved away Kyle's concern. "I'm fine. But I want to talk to you."

"In my office."

Kyle frowned. "I'll wait out here."

"I'll see she gets home," Lucas said. She was his, and he'd take care of her.

Kyle's eyes narrowed. "I don't mind waiting."

"Kyle, it's fine," Marisa said. "I'm feeling a lot better already just being away from the hospital."

Kyle studied her face. "If you feel the least bit bad, go home."

"I promise."

Kyle shook his head. "You won't."

Marisa smiled. "I'll be fine."

When Kyle left, Lucas escorted Marisa back to his office. He had the urge to settle his hand on her lower back as a steadying guide but decided it was best to keep contact to a minimum.

In his office, he directed her to a chair and after closing his door, sat on the edge of his desk and faced her. "I'm amazed you're here."

"I don't like hospitals. I spent a good bit of time in them when Mom was having her chemo." She settled back in her chair with a soft sigh. "I hear my office was ransacked."

"It was. I inspected it myself, and whatever notes you might have been keeping on my case are gone. Also your laptop was taken."

"Damn." A resigned shrug. "I'm a fanatic about backups so at least I have my data on my professional work. Computers can be replaced. Work cannot be so easily duplicated."

"The docs tell me your memory is fuzzy."

"It is. I sustained a concussion. The pieces are drifting just out of reach. I understand that's common with concussions, but it's frustrating."

"What do you remember?"

"Not much. The last memory I have is wrapping presents. I think I was close to figuring out your puzzle."

"You called me while you were in the car. You said you'd cracked the code."

"I don't remember the call or the code." An irritated sigh escaped her lips. "I hate not remembering."

She was here. With him. That was what really mattered. "You will. Give it time."

"I don't want to give it time. You said yourself this was time-sensitive information."

"The accident is not your fault. You have to be patient."

She leaned forward. "I'm not a super-patient person. I had more than a few professors tell me to ease up and not push so hard. I've never figured out how to stop and smell the roses."

A smile tugged at the edge of his lips, softening the tension banding his body. "I've been accused of the same."

Green eyes, glittering a mixture of determination and hope, lifted to his. "I want to go back to the accident site."

"Why?"

"That was the last place where I had all my memories. I think I might be able to jog my memory if I can travel the road again."

"That doesn't make much sense."

"Re-creating steps can be highly effective. It's helped me find countless sets of lost keys, shoes, and sunglasses."

"We aren't talking about shoes. Memories are a little different."

"I don't think so." She closed her eyes and pressed her fingertips to her temple. "The memories are so close. They're literally hovering below the surface of my mind and I feel as if I can reach out and pluck them up." She arched a brow. "I'm going. I'm here to ask you to come with me, but either way, I'm going."

"I can't imagine your father would be happy about this."

"I'm an adult." Her annoyance crackled like lightning. "I make my own decisions. Are you going to take me to the site or do I go it alone?"

He leaned toward her a fraction, his tone hard and clipped. "You can't be driving now."

"I'll take a cab."

"No." The response shot from him like a bullet. Of all the people she could have turned to, Marisa had come to him. "No cabs." She opened her mouth to argue as he reached for his phone. "I will." He called his secretary, told her he was leaving for the day, maybe two. "Let's go."

She sat straighter. "I need to swing by my apartment and grab a bag?"

"Sure. Let's go."

This time as he guided her out of the office, he did put his hand on the small of her back. It felt good to touch her, and he remembered the softness of her skin when he'd stroked his palm over her flat belly that night in Mexico.

"Did you drop the presents off in my hospital room?" she asked.

It pleased him she'd noticed. "A shame to have them land in evidence over the holidays after seeing all the trouble you went to in order to get them."

"Thanks."

"I'd have been pretty excited to get a truck like that when I was seven."

"It's the bells and whistles. It's been my observation that males like loud and noisy toys."

He pushed the elevator button. "We do like our toys."

She looked at him with genuine curiosity. "Why is that?"

He chuckled. "I suppose we don't quite grow up."

Marisa nodded as if she agreed.

Outside, the air was cool enough to send Marisa burrowing deeper into her coat. He opened the passenger side door of his car, and she climbed into the seat. As he crossed to his side of the car, he saw her relax as if she'd arrived home. She likely wasn't aware of the move, but he was. She felt safe with him. Knowing that nearly coaxed a smile.

The drive to her house took less than fifteen minutes, and she packed an overnight bag within minutes.

"Why haven't you unpacked?" he asked, fingering the flap of an open box.

A sly grin tipped the edges of her mouth. "It makes no sense for me to really unpack. I don't plan on being here long."

He stilled. "Where are you headed?"

"Not sure. I don't really need a house because I travel so much."

"I had the impression you were going to be in town for a while."

"For the next few months at least. But I can barely take care of myself, let alone a house."

They were on the road almost immediately.

"Aren't you going to stop and get a bag?"

"My sister lives in the area, and I can always swing by her house if need be." He wove through Austin traffic, wanting to be headed south before rush hour. He flipped on the radio, which played a Christmas song. She stared out her window, unmindful of the jingle. They'd been on the road twenty minutes when he noticed she put her hand to her temple.

"You getting a headache?"

"The doctor said I might." She smiled. "I'm fine. I'd rather keep going."

Caught up in the rush of seeing her, he'd not really thought about how a car ride would make her feel. He considered the remaining hour of traveling and weighed turning back. He chose the next option.

"Where are you going?"

"To my sister's house."

A frown furrowed. "Why?"

"You aren't feeling well."

"I feel fine. A little headache is not a big deal."

"It's a big deal when you've had a head injury. By the way, did you eat?"

"I ate breakfast at the hospital."

"What, a fruit cup or pudding?"

"Fruit cup."

"Not enough." He slowed and took a right onto a small road not marked with a street sign.

"Where are we going?"

"To my sister's house."

He and Sherry had inherited the family ranch. Though he'd received the lion's share of the land, their parents had deeded her the house. That suited him fine. He was far from being ready to settle down, and she and her husband had just found out they were expecting. His brother-in-law worked in the high-tech industry and Sherry stayed home with the boys.

Marisa shifted in her seat. "I don't want to interfere with their holidays."

"Sherry loves guests. She invited me to dinner tonight."

"She invited you. Not me."

"The more the merrier for her."

"Don't the holidays overwhelm her?"

He sensed if he stopped the car, she'd bolt. "It'll be fine."

"I don't like this."

"Don't be a baby."

She glared at him. "I'm not."

"You're whining."

"Am not!"

Smiling, he realized her headache couldn't be so bad if she was willing to argue. He turned down the gravel drive and wound into the Hill Country until they rounded a corner.

An explosion of colorful lights lining the drive greeted them. Lights dangled from the trees and wound around shrubs and a collection of wagon wheels. More lights outlined the front porch as well as the steep roofline of the house.

Marisa shook her head. "I think my stepmother has some serious competition."

"No one can out-Christmas Sherry. No one."

Chapter 9

Monday, December 22, 6 P.M.

Marisa blinked as she stared at the lights. Whereas her stepmother chose white lights, this home was decorated in bursts of bright color. Each twinkling light winked an invitation, beckoning her inside. Despite her headache, her spirit lightened.

She got out of the car, and with Lucas at her side, climbed the three steps to the front porch. Lucas rang the bell and seconds later the thunder of feet echoed in the house. The door snapped open to three boys, all with dark hair and gray eyes much like their uncle's. The boys—the youngest looked to be about six, the oldest three or four years older—were wearing cowboy hats and vests.

Their faces split into grins when they saw Lucas and they dove into his arms. He gave them a bear hug and lifted all of them up off the floor. They laughed and kicked and tried to wrestle free, but Lucas held tight until he set all three on the floor.

She couldn't imagine her brothers jumping and yelling like this. They were more subdued. That was one of the reasons she'd taken her stepmother's suggestion and bought the trucks.

"That's Billy," Lucas said, pointing to the boy on the right. "The other wranglers are Nate and Zeke. Where's your mom?"

"In the kitchen." They turned, each yelling *"Mom"* as they scrambled around a corner.

The house smelled of cookies and bread and cinnamon, and drew Marisa in like a welcoming embrace. The large, open room had a vaulted ceiling made of roughly hewn beams. The furniture was large, overstuffed, and looked as if it had been well used. She imagined the boys plopping on the sofa, eating a snack while they watched television or diving into a pillow fight with the cushions. The walls were filled with family photos. Most featured the boys, but she saw a few that featured a young Lucas. She resisted the urge to study each more closely.

Lucas pulled off his hat and tossed it on a table. "Sherry!"

"Lucas!" A woman appeared. Tall, she wore an apron over well-worn jeans and a T-shirt. Her raven hair was pulled up in a loose topknot. Wisps framed an oval face. Faint crow's-feet feathered out from her eyes, a sign she smiled often.

She hugged Lucas. "Boy, I didn't think we were going to see you this year."

"I wasn't sure myself." He pulled away and angled his body toward Marisa. "I'd like you to meet Marisa Thompson. She's helping me with a case."

Sherry wiped a floured hand on her apron and extended it. "Well, I'm pleased to meet you. Lucas told me he was on the trail of an expert to help him."

"It's great to meet you." Sherry's soft welcoming energy melted some of Marisa's nerves.

"You must have been the gal in the car accident."

Marisa touched her bruised cheek with her fingertips. "I was. But I'm on the mend."

Sherry studied the dark bruise on Marisa's cheek. "Well, give me your coat and let's get you both into the kitchen. Looks to me like you could use some real TLC."

"That cookies I smell in the kitchen?" Lucas asked.

"It is, but I'm going to serve you two up some stew first. I made a big pot, hoping you could make it, Lucas."

"Bill working late?"

"He is so he can have the holidays off. I'm keeping dinner simple tonight. Hope that's all right."

"Smells great," Lucas said.

Marisa's stomach rumbled. Lucas had been right. The fruit cup had not cut it.

The kitchen was a large open room. To the left was a huge island, complete with a stove and sink. Beyond the island stood a double refrigerator covered with pictures and art projects. The granite counter behind Sherry was covered with cooling racks filled with cookies. A loaf of bread cooled on the counter.

To the right stood a long rustic table flanked by two long benches and capped by two chairs at the ends.

"Sit," Sherry ordered. "I'll grab you two a couple of bowls. You do eat meat, don't you, Marisa?"

"Yeah, sure."

"Never know these days. I can always whip up a grilled cheese sandwich."

"No, stew is perfect."

Lucas pulled out the chair at the end of the table and she sat, not relaxed enough to ease back. No one had cooked for her since her mother had died, and those meals had been haphazard at best. Her mother, like her, preferred to work rather than cook. Lucas shrugged off his jacket, the muscles in his wide shoulders flexing under his shirt as he hung it on the back of the chair next to her. He unfastened his cuffs and rolled up his sleeves, revealing muscled forearms.

Sherry quickly appeared with a tray that held two heaping

bowls of stew, silverware, and glasses of lemonade. She set the tray on the table and served a bowl to Marisa and Lucas. "Go ahead and eat. I'm going to grab a coffee. Marisa, I know Lucas will take a cup, what about you?"

"That would be great."

Marisa took a bite of stew and marveled at the rich tastes of beef, potatoes, and rosemary. For several minutes, she and Lucas sat in silence. With each bite she could feel her headache ease.

A loud crash boomed in the other room as the boys yelled. Sherry, shaking her head, said she'd be right back before disappearing into the other room. Seconds later silence returned.

"Those three rattle like thunder when they get going," Lucas said.

"It's nice. They add life to a house."

"Chaos is more like it," he said, grinning.

Sherry returned, shaking her head. "Marisa, tell me about your work."

"I work at the university. Ancient studies. I just returned from Mexico a few days ago after a six-month dig."

"Mexico," Sherry said. "Lucas was just in Mexico."

Marisa could feel her face warm, but if Sherry noticed she didn't say anything.

"Find anything interesting in Mexico?" Sherry asked.

Marisa cleared her throat. "A portion of a stone tablet covered in glyphs. It tells the story of a Mayan ruler, I think."

"Think?"

"The language shares similarities with the Mayan language that has been deciphered for the most part. But there are other glyphs that don't fit."

"Your boss says it could be a huge find," Lucas said.

She arched a brow. "My boss? Bradley? So far, he's dismissing the find. He thinks I'm overestimating it."

"What do you think?"

She carefully scooped more stew. "I think it's going to be huge."

Lucas chuckled.

"What's so funny?"

"I'd like to see his face when you get his job. He's not going to like it."

She grinned. "I don't want his job. Too much paperwork."

"So are you two going to spend the night?" Sherry set coffee mugs in front of Marisa and Lucas.

"Is that all right?" Lucas asked.

"Of course it is. I'll put you in the boys' room and Marisa in the spare room."

Marisa scooted to the edge of her seat, her unease returning. "You don't have to host us tonight."

Sherry, sipping her coffee, waved away Marisa. "Too late to go anywhere. And you look like you could use a good night's sleep." When Marisa considered a protest, Sherry said, as if the matter were settled, "So tell me about this work you're doing for Lucas."

Marisa hesitated, not sure what she could or couldn't say about the work.

"It's a code," Lucas said. "We've had a team on the case for months with no luck, and she cracked it in a day."

"I don't remember what I did," Marisa said. Symbols skirted on the edges of her mind. She had the sense again that time was running out, but she couldn't grasp facts to articulate.

"It will come in time," Sherry said. "A good night's sleep and a country breakfast and you will be good to go."

"I hope it's that easy."

"Do you have any information on the second car?" Sherry asked.

Lucas set his coffee cup down. "We did get surveillance of a driver stopping and changing a tire. He's in the shadows and it's hard to make him out much. Our computer tech guy will be back from holiday in a couple of days and can enhance the image."

"Marisa, did you see him?" Sherry asked.

"No. I was just a little freaked out." More memories swirled in her mind, rolling in and out like the lapping waters of the Gulf. For a moment, one memory skittered nearly close enough to grab. No words or thoughts. But a sound.

"Are you getting another headache?" Lucas was staring at her hard.

"I thought I was remembering. No words but a sound. Like a ringtone on a phone. I have this odd feeling that whoever ran me off the road approached my car, but stopped when his phone rang."

Lucas set his spoon down. "What was the sound?"

"A song. It was classical. Mozart, I think."

"Did you see his face?"

"No. I don't think I could open my eyes. But I heard the crunch of brush under boots and the song." She shook her head. "That's all I have. Why can't I remember more?"

"Don't push it."

"Lucas is right, hon," Sherry said. "You'll remember and Lucas will find the guy who did this. No one gets away from Lucas Cooper."

Color warmed Marisa's cheeks as she lifted the cup to her lips.

No one gets away from Lucas Cooper.

Chapter 10

Lucas had insisted Marisa go to sleep. He'd declared her pale and exhausted, and when Sherry had agreed, she'd gone to the spare room. By the time she'd changed into a gown and slipped under the covers, sleep had taken her swiftly.

But even the deepest sleeps can be penetrated. Most nights when she awoke it was with worry over work. Tonight, it had been to the scrape of metal, car against car, and the sound of her own beating heart hammering in her brain. Damp palms gripping the steering wheel, she'd dreamed of a car swerving into her as fear ripped screams from her lungs and her car careened over the embankment. So helpless.

Marisa woke with a jerk, hands covering her face as a cry escaped her lips. Her breathing labored as if a weight rested on her chest.

She'd had plenty of bad dreams as a kid after her parents had divorced. All left her weeping in the middle of the night, alone because her mother, lost in her own grief, had turned to sleeping pills and rarely heard Marisa's cries.

She glanced around the unfamiliar room, trying to anchor herself in the present just as she'd done as a child. Catalogue. Analyze. She searched for her belongings, but when she didn't see her battered backpack, muddied hiking boots, or her clothes strewn in careless piles on the floor, panic flared. Sweat dampening her brow, she reminded herself to breathe. Breathe. In and out. Finally, sleep's haze evaporated like the morning mist, and she could analyze the room's puzzle pieces—a cherry dresser and mirror, pastel curtains, a rocking chair, and a handmade quilt warming the bed. Sherry's house.

A light clicked on in the hallway and after a soft knock on her door, it opened. The light illuminated a man's large, broad-shouldered frame. "Marisa?"

She recognized Lucas's deep voice and sat taller, ashamed that she'd cried out in her sleep. "Sorry, did I wake you?"

His shirt open over worn jeans, he hovered in the doorway as if he approached uncharted territory. "I was awake. Not much of a sleeper."

She pushed the hair back from her eyes, realizing the sound of his voice had slowed her runaway pulse. "I'm sorry."

He leaned against the doorjamb, in no rush to leave. "Don't be sorry. You've had one heck of a week."

"It's one for the record books." A ghost of a smile tugged the edges of her lips as she rose up out of bed. She needed to stand on her own two feet and prove to Lucas and herself that she was just fine. Her gown brushed her ankles and billowed around her small frame. "Did anyone else hear me?"

"No. Just me. I'm bunked with the boys and those three rascals sleep like the dead."

"That I envy. I've not slept through the night in years."

His head tilted a fraction, as if she'd piqued his curiosity. "Why's that?"

"Who's to say?" Of course, she knew. It was the constant feeling that if she didn't keep working and pushing, that she'd somehow be left behind. The feeling had stalked her since the night her father had moved out of the house. Reinforced when her mother died. Sleep was an unaffordable luxury.

A shake of his head told her he didn't believe the evasion, but he was too polite to call her out on it. "I can brew us a pot of coffee."

"What time is it?"

"Just after four."

As much as a cup of coffee tempted, if she drank it now, hope of any sleep would vanish. And she needed to rest and give her body time to mend. "Thanks, but I better not. Still a little early, even for me."

She'd refused him but remained rooted in the same spot, not willing to return to her bed alone or act on a rising temptation to move closer to him.

He pushed away from the doorjamb, but instead of taking a step back, he moved toward her two steps. One single step would have put him within an arm's reach of her. He flexed and unflexed the fingers of his right hand before he stilled them, as if recognizing the nervous gesture. "There's no rush tomorrow. We can leave whenever you're ready."

"I'll be ready early. I'm not much good at sitting around. And I want to remember the accident and the key to the code."

"You will. Just takes a bit of time."

"You sound sure."

"I am."

"Are you always this confident?"

"For the most part." A twinkle in his eyes softened the arrogance of his tone.

"Good to know."

"What did you dream about?"

A frown furrowed her brow. "I remember hearing the scrape of metal and feeling a hard jolt when the other driver hit me."

A scowl darkened his face.

She thought for a moment. Until now, she could not say it. "I tried to speed up to get out of his way, but he gave chase. When he pulled beside me, he swerved into me."

The twinkle vanished, replaced by a dangerous fire. "We'll find him."

"Like a needle in a haystack."

"Finding people is what I do." No doubt lingered under the words. "I found you. Twice."

She edged a little closer, afraid if she didn't take the next step that he would leave. He'd met her more than halfway, but the rest was up to her. Dark gray eyes studied the way she moistened her lips, the drape of a stray lock of hair, and her pulse beating in her neck.

She wanted to kiss him. Wanted to taste his lips again. Feel his hands on her body again. Her gaze lowered to her hands and the shorn nails that had been digging in dirt just a week ago.

A jolt of electricity drew her closer. With Lucas, the kissing wouldn't be polite. It would be primal, hot, and as dangerous as a rattler, as it had been in Mexico.

She wanted to taste dangerous again, knowing that it couldn't last and that one day, life would pull them apart and in separate directions.

Moistening her lips, she looked into his darkening gaze. Inches separated them, but still he didn't move. He wanted her to come to him. Really living was exciting and terrifying.

She took another half step and could feel the heat of his body. Inches to go. She stared up at granite features made all the sharper by the light cutting in from the hallway. He looked at her as if no other person in the world existed.

Could a kiss be any riskier than what she'd survived? The answer came easily. With Lucas, loving would indeed be a hazard.

She laid a hand on his chest and felt the drumming of his heart. He might look as still as a mountain, but underneath, his energy stirred like a volcano.

He put a hand on her shoulder, using his thumb to trace the bone alongside it. Her nerves danced and her senses sharpened. "I never forgot how smooth your skin felt."

She thought of the calluses marring her palms. "You remember?"

"Every detail."

"When you woke up in Merida, I was gone."

Gray eyes darkened with a mixture of anger and passion. "Roses have thorns. That's what makes them interesting."

He raised his hand to her cheek and grazed his knuckle along her cheekbone. "You're interesting. Intoxicating. Frustrating. I like the challenge."

He leaned forward and kissed her gently on the lips. The touch reminded her of butterflies skittering across her skin. Again, he kept the pace slow, as if he wanted her to set the tempo.

She wrapped her hands around his neck and, rising on tiptoes, pressed into the kiss. His arms immediately banded around her narrow waist, and he lifted her off the ground as he deepened the kiss.

The moment swept over her like a tropical storm and she found herself longing for the touch of his hands on her body. In the house, footsteps creaked on the second floor. His hand, moving from her shoulder to her breast, stilled. He pulled back and allowed a sigh of frustration. "This is not how I pictured our reunion."

She moistened her lips, trying to push back the wave of desire that had come with the force of a twister. "You imagined?"

He cupped her face with his hand, coaxing her to open her eyes and look at him. "More times than I could count."

Heat warmed her cheeks. "Oh."

Another creak echoed in the house, reminding them both where they stood. His hands glided over her arms. "We'll wait until we have a proper bed and more privacy than my sister's house can give." His voice deepened with a promise he sounded determined to keep.

Disappointment circled around and howled that promises were meant to be broken. With an effort, she released her grip. "I don't know what to say."

His head cocked a fraction. "Mind, this is no rejection. It's an admittance the timing is bad, and we will return to this. That's a promise."

A nervous laugh bubbled in her throat. "I'm supposed to sleep now?"

He glanced back at her, a lightness humming under the remaining passion. "I did try to offer you coffee."

With his scent still lingering on her, she crawled back into bed, quite sure she would never sleep again.

Chapter 11

Tuesday, December 23, 10 A.M.

When Marisa awoke, the bright sun streamed in her window. She glanced at the clock and realized it was late.

She tossed back the covers, shocked and amazed that she'd slept so long. With the rumble of the boys laughing and talking and the television humming in the other room, she got out of bed, showered, and dressed. Purse and overnight bag in hand, she emerged from her room to the smell of coffee and cinnamon. The scents coaxed her to the kitchen, where she found Lucas talking to Sherry.

Sherry greeted her with a cheery good morning. Lucas's nod was casual, but his gaze devoured her as he raised his coffee cup to his lips.

Color warmed her cheeks as she thought about the kiss they'd shared last night. "I can't believe I slept this late."

Sherry waved away her concern as she plucked a Santa mug from the stand and filled it with coffee. "You needed it."

Lucas's eyes twinkled as if he'd remembered decrying her inability to sleep.

"So you two are off to the accident site today?" Sherry asked.

"We are." Marisa shifted her attention to Sherry. "I'm anxious to get to the site now that I'm rested."

Sherry pushed scones in her direction. "Eat up. It's going to be a big day."

Marisa's phone rang. She dug it out of her purse and glanced at the number. "That's my father. I better take it."

"Sure," Lucas said.

She offered a brisk hello and moved into the living room, away from Lucas and his sister. She couldn't predict what her father would say and didn't want to risk them overhearing.

"Dad."

"Marisa, where the hell are you?"

She rarely heard her father swear and knew he was upset. "I'm at a friend's house."

"What does that mean? According to Kyle you're with that Ranger and you're helping him again."

She lifted her chin, annoyed that he spoke to her as if she were twelve. "Dad, I know what I'm doing."

"Do you? You've just been in an accident. You're lucky to be alive, and now you're running around with that Ranger."

"I'm not running around. I'm trying to remember what happened to me."

"You need to come home and let Susan and me take care of you."

Home. His house, purchased after the divorce, had never felt like home. When she'd stayed the night she'd been an anxious guest, hesitant to use too many towels or stay more than a night.

"Dad, I'll call you when I have more information. But for now, I have to go."

"We're not done with this conversation."

"Yes, we are. I'll talk to you soon." She hung up and immediately put her phone on silent. Sooner or later she'd have to deal with the outside world, but for now, she needed to shut it out.

Lucas watched Marisa hover by the front window, her face tucked forward and her hair draping her face like a thick curtain.

"I like her," Sherry said.

Lucas let the comment stand and didn't respond.

"So do you," she prodded.

He sipped his coffee.

"And the fact that you aren't talking is proof enough for me that you *really* like her."

"That so?"

"Yeah."

"And how do you know?"

"In all your days, Lucas, I've never known you to bring a woman home over the holidays. You've had your share of dates at barbecues, but the holidays have always been kind of sacred for you. You met her in Mexico, didn't you?"

"Yes."

"Something happened?"

"False start. Nothing that can't be overcome."

She shook her head. "Why bring her here?"

"I could see she needed a break before we headed to the accident site."

"I'm a good hour out of your way. Makes no sense to detour to my place when you could have gotten a good hotel room in Fredericksburg."

"Seemed to me, she'd be more comfortable here."

"I don't mean to give you a hard time. She's more than welcome. And like I said, I like her."

He set his cup down. "But . . ."

"I just worry for you. You like her. A lot. Whether you admit it or not. And I'd hate to see you get hurt."

A smile tugged the edges of his lips. "You're looking out for me?"

"Yeah, that's what family does. We look out for one another. I don't want you to get your heart broken."

He and Marisa were from different worlds. Chemistry in a bedroom didn't mean any kind of commitment. But he knew they were right for each other.

"Right now she needs you. She's hurt and she's scared. But when she gets back on her feet, she'll go scrambling back to her world, and you're going to go back to yours. Like oil and vinegar, they mix when shaken, but after a while they separate and return to where they came from. Sooner or later you're going to get called away. And she's going to end up back on one of her jungle digs."

"Why don't you stop thinking? Let's see how it plays out."

"I'm all for letting it play out. Just keep your guard up, big brother."

Marisa and Lucas were both quiet in the car. For a long time, she stared out over the dusty land dotted with scrubby trees that reminded her of an old man's scruffy beard. Texas wasn't a lush or easy land, but it had a beauty that she'd always found hard to resist.

She thought about that night she was driving to her father's house. The sun had set, and she'd been disappointed that her first trip out of the city in over a year had been blanketed in darkness. She'd yearned to see the rolling countryside and the bright sunshine and, for the first time in a long time, she'd realized she needed to push away from her buried ruins and dusty documents and step into life. But, of course, she'd been late because she'd been working. Always working.

Marisa again questioned her choices when she'd stood in Sherry's house last night. The home was full of life. It was a happy place. Connected.

Feeling Lucas's gaze slide from the road to her face, she heard herself saying, "Your sister has a lovely home."

The sound of her voice eased some of the tension in his body, as if he'd worried she'd slipped away from him for good. "She does. She has a knack for making anyone feel part of the family."

Her mother had never had stews simmering on the stove or cookies in the oven. "No one can out-Christmas Sherry."

He smiled. "I told you."

She thought of her mother's paltry collection of lights and decorations that still remained in the box. She wanted to love Christmas and wanted to embrace the holiday. But each time the season approached, she drew deeper within herself, counting the days to the New Year and the end of the holiday reverie. What kind of person didn't like Christmas?

She closed her eyes and pushed aside questions she could not answer. Her focus shifted to what she could fix. Her memory. The accident and the documents.

As she allowed the tension to seep away like water from a cracked urn, she cleared her mind and collected the broken pieces of the night of the accident. But as much as she stared at the pieces and searched for the missing ones, she could not create a coherent image.

"You're trying to remember?"

"Yes. But no matter how often I assemble or reassemble the pieces, I can't create a recognizable picture."

The seat leather creaked as he settled back in his seat. "Were you playing music on the radio?"

She opened her eyes and studied his profile. His was not a classically beautiful face. Too many flaws to approach beauty. But there was an energy, a strength that made him far more appealing than the most perfect statue of a Mayan god. And when he smiled . . . well, her knees went just a little weak. "What does that have to do with remembering?"

"It's just a simple question. Music?" When she continued to stare at him, he said, "Close your eyes. Music."

She closed her eyes and let her mind drift past the broken pieces that refused assembly. In the distance she heard the faint sound of a strumming guitar mingled with the deep melody of a man's voice. A smile tipped the edges of her lips. She'd been listening to country-western music. Despite all her connections to the ancient civilizations, she loved country music. "Willie Nelson."

"Willie Nelson."

Laughter rose up in her. "Crazy."

"I never figured you for a fan."

"I'm not all dusty documents and dead languages."

"I know you aren't."

A vibration under his words hinted at Merida. Color warmed her cheeks. She wanted to open her eyes and see his expression but didn't dare.

After a heavy hesitation, Lucas asked, "Was the sky clear or cloudy?"

Welcoming the question, she allowed her mind to drift, and as she did, thousands of lights twinkled in her mind. She'd been so rushed to get to her father's, she'd not really noticed the night sky full of stars that winked and sparkled like polished gems. It had been a lovely night, but she'd not really seen any of it. She'd barely heard a favorite song on the radio. How much of her life was she missing because of work? "Stars. Lots of stars. And the road was empty. I remember wishing I were making the drive during the day because it's one of my favorite drives."

"When did you notice the headlights?"

Ah, there was one of the pieces she could not connect to the others. Instead of being afraid, she felt safe cocooned in the car with Lucas. Memories couldn't frighten her here. "I don't think I noticed until shortly after I dialed you. I'm good at getting lost in thought."

"I've noticed." A smile softened the coming words. "You called me as the headlights appeared."

"He could have been following me for a while, but I didn't notice him."

"When did you notice him?"

"I was near the bend in the road near the creek bed. I remember glancing up from the radio dial and looking in the mirror. I saw the lights, distant at first, and wasn't surprised when they grew closer. I drive slowly when I'm distracted, which is why I assumed the other car was closing ground."

"The lights were bright."

"Very bright. He had on his high beams. I had to adjust my mirror because they were too bright. And when I took my hand off the wheel, he bumped me." A cold chill rushed through her veins.

The memory of scraping metal grated against her mind. The sound grew louder, filling her ears and startling her heart into a gallop.

"You said you had to toss the phone aside."

"I needed both hands on the wheel." Fear constricted her throat. "I was so afraid."

"What happened next?" His voice deepened, soothing her as if she were a wild horse.

She squeezed her eyes shut. "I don't remember."

He held back his next question, giving her time to slow her heart and get control. "The music was still playing."

"Yes. Did you hear it?"

"All I heard was your voice."

"What do you remember?"

"The excitement in your voice and your promise to see me the next day with a full translation. And then the sound of a crash, and you screaming." His grip on the wheel tightened until his knuckles were white.

He'd never once frightened her. Not even when she'd seen him sitting alone in the café in Mexico. But in this moment, she knew she'd glimpsed a formidable warrior.

Chapter 12

Tuesday, December 23, 2 P.M.

They arrived at the accident site a half hour later and Marisa felt tension building in her as they drew closer and closer. Silence wrapped around her like a shroud.

As they approached a bend in the road, she saw the skid marks that cut sharply to the left. Those had been her skid marks.

Lucas slowed the car before pulling off the side of the road onto the dirt shoulder. Marisa moistened her lips. "I used to love this stretch of road. Even at night. Now I'm not sure I can ever drive this again."

His wrist rested easily on the steering wheel. "I never figured you could be scared off easily."

The unspoken challenge nipped at her. "I'm not scared. But I had a near-death experience right here."

"Not the road or land's fault. This is all about a driver who wanted to hurt you."

"You're being far too logical."

"Logic has a way of cutting through the fear."

She looked at him and a half laugh startled from her. "I bet you're never afraid."

"Only crazy people don't feel fear from time to time. Fear keeps us alive and our senses sharp."

She unhooked her seat belt. "So I suppose you want me to get out."

Wide shoulders shrugged under his jacket. "If you want to."

The fear whispered in her ear. Told her to stay and run from the memories that were sure to bring heartache. "Fine. I'm getting out."

"I didn't ask."

"You didn't have to." She opened the door, burrowed deeper in her coat as the cold air bit and snapped. Her shoes crunched along the dirt as she followed the skid marks marring the road. Like Dorothy on the Yellow Brick Road, she walked toe-to-toe, following the black rubber tire marks, hoping they'd lead her to the missing pieces in her life. As she grew closer to the edge of the road, tension tightened around her chest. Memories of the metal tearing and bending accelerated her heartbeat past the safe speed and straight to dangerous.

Lucas hovered close, not speaking but a silent sentinel there to chase away the darkness.

She moved to the ravine where the imprint of her tires remained gouged in the dirt. A trail of flattened brush burrowed down the hillside to the spot at the bottom of the ravine where she'd crashed. The air bag had deployed, smashing her face and jerking her against the seat.

Marisa closed her eyes, remembering that she'd felt suffocated by the bursting bag that had saved her life and left her face bruised. She'd clung to consciousness as she'd heard Lucas's voice still echoing from the cell phone that had been tossed about the car in the fall.

"I'll find you," he'd said. *"Hold on."*

She'd clung to bruised and injured thoughts that wanted to scurry into the darkness. Her body ached from the battering. And then there'd been . . .

"A flashlight. At the top of the hill."

"Who was it?"

"It was the other driver, I think. I don't know if he'd checked to see if I was okay or if he was coming to finish the job. I closed my eyes and didn't move. I barely took a breath." She raised fingertips to her breastbone. "My heart beat so loudly I thought he'd hear."

"Did he come down the hill?"

"Partway. I barely lifted my lids, and I could see the light. But he stopped. His phone rang. An odd ringtone."

"Can you place it?"

Eyes closed, she chased the memory that darted back into the shadows.

"Don't worry about it. What happened next?"

"The light lingered on the car for a long time, and I was sure he'd come the rest of the way and kill me. But he didn't. Finally, he turned and left."

"Just like that?"

"I heard the rattle of his car as he drove off."

"He had a busted tire. He stopped at a gas station a few miles from here."

"Do you think it was an accident? I mean, why not finish the job?"

"Maybe he didn't want to kill you. Or maybe he was sloppy. My guess is sloppy. Assumed the accident had done its job."

A cold shiver shuddered through her as she studied the isolated land. "The accident didn't get me but this land would have. Doubtful anyone would have found me for days, and with the cold temperatures, who's to say if I would have made it."

"Your father would have gone looking for you."

"He was having a huge party. Tons of guests. I knew I'd barely see him, and I could have easily been missed until morning at the earliest. I have a reputation for being late."

Lucas worked his jaw, as if chewing on a retort. "You were found, and that's all that counts."

"The papers were stolen from my office along with my memory."

"You'll remember."

"But when? You said time was critical."

"Don't worry about time. This is not your fault."

"It feels like my fault. If I'd left on time, none of this would have happened."

"You can't say that."

"It would have at least been daylight, and I'd have seen who was trailing me."

"Let it go."

She touched the broken branch of a scrub, knowing she'd snapped it when she'd slammed past.

"Let's get out of here."

"Where do we go?" She felt so weary now. Home for her was a plain, cold house littered with dozens of unpacked boxes. She couldn't return to her office, not now when she felt so vulnerable. It had been her safe haven, and it had been violated.

"There's a motel nearby. It's clean and doesn't get much traffic this time of year. We can hold up there for the night, and tomorrow I can take you wherever you want to go."

The night's reprieve lifted her spirits. She liked being with Lucas, and though she doubted they had a future beyond the case, now was good enough. "Sounds good."

When she climbed into the SUV, his scent, a blend of fresh air and soap, wrapped around her as he turned on the heat. She held her hands up to the vents, letting the warmth spread through her chilled fingers. She didn't know the area well, only venturing out here when she made the annual drive to her father's Christmas party. With unspoken emotions hounding her each year, she'd vowed to find the joy in this trip but it always eluded her.

For a while, they drove as the sun slowly dipped and vanished into the horizon, leaving a wake of reds and yellows that slowly faded to blackness. "I'm starving," she said.

His face would have been lost to the shadows if not for the light from the console. "I know a barbecue place. If we hurry, we might be able to grab some takeout before they close for the evening."

"Why would they close so early?"

"Holidays."

"Right. I keep forgetting." A half smile teased her lips. "There are people who love the holidays."

He tossed her a curious glance. "You must have liked the holidays at some point?"

"Sure. I loved them before my parents' divorce."

"Favorite memory?"

She carried in her heart a box of dusty memories and from time to time opened the lid to peer inside. Most times, it was too painful to view, so she kept the lid closed. But today was about remembering, and if conjuring a forgotten Christmas moment helped her remember the rest, she'd do it. "I was six. And my dad bought me a new bike. It was blue with streamers and training wheels. It was awesome. My parents weren't ones to splurge at the holidays. They believed it was a time for family and not huge presents. They kept telling me it was too expensive. And I accepted that I'd get the customary gift-wrapped socks and shirts. But when I came downstairs and saw the bike under the tree, I squealed. Both my parents looked pleased with themselves."

A smile softened his face but he remained silent.

"Mom explained that Dad had put the bike together in his office and stowed it at the neighbor's until Christmas

Eve after I went to bed. It was a cold day, but I didn't care. I rode for hours." Two years later, her parents were divorced. "After the divorce, Christmas was not fun. Mom insisted on having me for the holiday, but she also refused to cook that day so we ended up at the Chinese restaurant eating our Christmas dinner."

When her mother had gotten sick, Marisa had brought a small tree into her hospital room. Her mother had thanked her, but when Marisa had returned the next day the tree was gone, her mother making the excuse that she'd given it to the nurses to enjoy at the front desk.

"Don't know if we can scrounge Chinese out here."

"That's fine. I love Chinese food any other time of year but now. Barbecue will work."

He called in an order, and twenty minutes later he pulled into the parking lot of a dive that had a BBQ sign glowing red neon in the front window. Her stomach grumbling, she climbed out of the car and met him by her door before they walked inside. The interior was dimly lit, but a strand of chili-pepper Christmas lights wrapped around the empty hostess station. There were at least two dozen tables and most were filled. A haven for the misplaced at Christmas.

A blond woman wearing a BBQ T-shirt and a Santa hat moved to the stand and collected two menus. "I've a table in the back."

"I called ahead for takeout. The name is Cooper. Pork tamales."

"Oh right. I think that order just came up." She moved back toward the kitchen, weaving through the tables. She vanished behind swinging metal doors. Seconds later, she appeared with two large brown bags. She read the ticket and the price and Lucas gave her his credit card.

Marisa knew enough about a real Texas Christmas to know that pork tamales were a staple. "We ate pork tamales in Merida."

"I know." He smiled. "They make the best."

Her skin warmed at he stared an extra beat. In the SUV, the smells of tomatoes and vinegar quickly filled the interior. "How'd you find a place like that?"

"Rangers are on the road a lot. Most of us learned the best places to eat when we were rookies with DPS."

It occurred to her how little she knew about his work. She'd shared a night with him, glimpsed a personal life she imagined he'd shown to few, but she knew little about his career. "How long have you been a Ranger?"

"About ten years. Before that, eight years with the Department of Public Service and before that a football scholarship to Texas Tech."

She could imagine him on the football field shoving his way through the throng of players, football tucked under his arm. His was a warrior's heart.

"I will tell you that history was my worst subject."

"Really?"

"I didn't mind Texas history, but all the goings-on in Europe, well, I just didn't see how it mattered."

"Of course it mattered. We think we're living life for the first time, but countless others have walked our paths before. We can learn from them. Those who do not study history are doomed to repeat it."

"You use that line in class much?"

She nodded. "Sure. I want to bring the past alive for my students. I want them to know that the dead have lessons to teach. I mean, really, do you think our generation has a lock on dreaming big, greed, or broken hearts?"

"Suppose not."

"We don't."

"So tell me about this discovery of yours. This big find in Mexico."

"It's fascinating." Just thinking about the work brought a smile to her face. "I've found evidence of a lost civilization."

"One hell of a win career-wise."

Pride warmed her voice. "It's exciting."

"Why were you in Merida in November?"

"I needed a few days off, and I like the Day of the Dead celebration. Mom loved it, and it was a time to drink a toast to her."

"How did Bradley feel about the discovery?"

"Supportive, I suppose. The day I returned from Mexico, he wanted to work with me, but given our history, I refused. He tried to pull rank, but I went to the dean. He told Bradley to back off."

"He couldn't have been happy about that?"

"No, he wasn't. That's why I was surprised to see him smiling and friendly the other night."

"Why the change of attitude?"

"I don't know."

"He the type of guy who would run you off the road because he was jealous of your work?"

"Bradley?" That shocked a laugh. "No. He's not the brave of heart. He's a talker, not a doer, a lesson I learned the hard way."

"What would happen to his career if you could prove your theories?"

"He wouldn't be the star any longer."

"He'll just sit back and watch you climb the ladder of success."

"I suppose."

"When did you two break up?"

She frowned, digging again for another unpleasant memory. "A few weeks before I left for Mexico. He said I was leaving him like I've left all the men I've dated."

A heavy silence settled and he asked, "Why'd you leave me?"

She shifted. "That wasn't right. I'm sorry."

"Why did you leave?"

"I got spooked. I liked you, and it scared me. I have a long history of people I like leaving."

He was silent for a moment. "If this find of yours is as big as you think, it's motivation for murder."

She shook her head, unwilling to believe that someone who had once held her in his arms would savagely run her off the road. "I can't accept that."

"You should consider it. Be thinking about all the conversations he's had with you since that breakup."

"More clues from a murky past."

He pulled up in front of a blinking motel sign. She cocked her head, suggesting that this might be a joke. "Don't let the exterior fool you. The place is clean, and the sheets are fresh."

"A hot shower would hit the spot. My muscles ache as if I ran a hundred miles."

"That's from the accident. You got knocked around pretty good."

She straightened her shoulders. "I'll be ready to put this memory behind me." Though this memory wouldn't go in the same box with the other memories. She needed a new box for memories associated with Lucas. Not only weren't they all bad, but most were real nice.

Chapter 13

When Lucas returned to the car, he had one key. "They're booked. They've just got one room, but it has two beds."

"That's fine."

"You sure?"

Laughter rumbled in her chest. "As you well know, I'm no blushing virgin."

Her words triggered a memory of him pushing into her, watching her eyes close as she called out his name. He cleared his throat. "Good."

The flinty grate of his voice sparked something within her. "I'll likely eat and pass out within the hour."

"Sleep's good for you."

So is love and human contact. The words echoed as he drove to room number six.

As the headlights shone on the door, she smiled. "In ancient cultures, six is a lucky number."

"That so?"

"Means prosperity."

He grabbed the bags of barbecue, realizing she found

the positive in most everything except Christmas. "Here's to prosperity."

She burrowed into the folds of her coat as he opened the door and switched on the light. The rustic double beds were made with plain light quilts that appeared to be made by hand. A television, not the flat screen kind but the old box kind, dominated the dresser hewn from poplar. Carpets were tan and the curtains a dramatic print that reminded her of another era. "Shower's in the back if you want to clean up."

"That would be great." She shrugged off her jacket and dropped it on the first bed. Her jeans fit her well, hugging her hips and narrow waist. She tugged off cowboy boots and headed, sock-footed, into the bathroom. "I promise not to take all the hot water."

"No worries." He might not like a cold shower, but it might be exactly what he'd end up with tonight.

He unpacked the food on a small round table just to the left of the door, setting out and opening the containers. By the time he'd shrugged off his own jacket and tossed it next to hers, the bathroom door opened and, from a fog of steam, she appeared.

She'd finger-combed her long hair and redressed in her jeans as well as a fresh white T-shirt embossed with the word ARCHAEOLOGY. Her skin was dewy and pink. "Smells delicious."

He pulled out a chair for her and when she'd taken her seat, he sat. He watched as she smoothed out a napkin in her lap. "I've never seen so much food."

"They always load me up. They know I can put away the grub."

"You travel a lot for your job?"

"On the go a good bit of time. Though now that I'm in Austin, the pace might slow." He unwrapped a tamale. "Promotion."

She reached for a soda. "Big promotion?"

"Of sorts. My work with the cartels, well, it was noticed."

She sipped her soda, clearly savoring the cool liquid on her throat. "I'm not sure what you did with the cartels."

"In a nutshell, I closed down a major trafficking ring." It had taken him five years. Lives of key informants had been lost, and he'd distanced himself from his family to protect them.

"That was why you were in Mexico looking for me."

"There is a new drug supplier and some believe he's associated with the cartels. Word was, you could read the coded message."

"You came all that way to find me."

"It was important the code be broken." His level tone gave no hint of what had been a dangerous, difficult operation.

"And these messages discuss the new drug shipment."

"Exactly."

"What if the drugs get through?"

"They'll bring trouble and violence." The words carried the weight of worry and frustration.

A frown furrowed her brow. "I will remember what I figured out about the code. I will."

His gaze held no hint of judgment. "Don't sweat it. You'll remember."

A casual shrug didn't soften her frustration. "How do you know?"

"I've confidence in you."

After they'd eaten, he'd watched her rise and stretch. He imagined running his hand along the curve of her back. Her skin would be soft, supple, and he supposed she tasted sweet. "I better take my shower."

"Sure."

He vanished into the bathroom, knowing the shower would be cold indeed.

*   *   *

While Lucas showered, Marisa cleaned up their empty paper dishes, replaced the lids, and placed the leftovers in a small fridge.

When Lucas emerged ten minutes later from the bathroom, Marisa glanced up automatically. He was dressed in his jeans, and though he'd buttoned his shirt partway, some part of his lean chest was exposed to her view.

A heat, strong and demanding, shot through her body just as it had that first night in Merida. She'd tried to shove aside the sensation and blame it on . . . well, she wasn't sure what she could blame it on. In Merida, she'd blamed it on loneliness and frustration over the dig, but now as fresh desire pumped through her veins, she searched for another logical reason why she reacted so strongly to him.

He'd protected her. Looked out for her. And desire was a natural reaction to feeling safeguarded.

"You're staring," he said.

She glanced up into amused eyes and realized her mouth was open. She snapped it closed. "I don't think that I was staring."

"You were staring."

"I was just thinking . . ." What could she possibly say that would dig her out of this mess?

"Thinking what?"

She closed her eyes for a moment, and before she thought about consequences, she said, "I was thinking about Merida and I was trying to figure a reason why I was as affected by you then as I'm now."

"How do I make you feel?" He took a couple of steps toward her and she could see the faint mist from the shower still clinging to his skin.

"Maybe because it's been a long time."

"That's the reason?" An arched brow called out her lie.

"That's the logical explanation."

"And you believe it?"

She shook her head and instead of answering his question, answered the one troubling her. "Lots of men have offered to be with me, but I've never felt the same about them as I do you."

He took another step closer. "And how's that?"

"I can't quite explain it." Her voice had grown as rough as sandpaper, and she found her thoughts skittering around her head like a mouse searching for cheese.

He captured a damp tendril of her hair and twirled it between his calloused fingers. "You have the prettiest hair. You were wearing it down the night I met you in Merida."

"I was thinking I needed a change. I'd been in the jungle for months and I'd not had a decent shower."

"I liked it." He traced her jawline with his finger and again the sparks shot off in her head like it was the Fourth of July.

Impatience nipped at her heels as she longed for a deep, wet kiss. He was letting her set the pace just as he had the other night. And again, he was waiting for her to make the first move.

Emboldened by her desire, she caught his hand in hers and pulled him through the remaining inches separating them. When his chest bumped against her breasts, her nipples hardened. Too drugged with desire to care about tomorrow, she rose up on tiptoes and kissed him.

He stood still for a moment as if asking *Are you sure?* She answered him by wrapping her arms around his neck and deepening the kiss.

Without hesitation, he hauled her against him. His muscles snapped with the intensity of a man reaching for a lifeline as he kissed her and cupped her breast in his hand. Her pulse beat with the zeal of a madwoman. She arched as a moan rumbled in her chest.

"Last chance." His voice, ragged with desire, was barely audible.

"I know what I want."

He backed her up to the bed and lowered her to the mattress, sagging under their weight. Reaching for her shirt, he yanked it up until her breasts lay bare to him. He suckled a nipple and she arched, saying his name as if it were a curse.

His smile was wicked. "You like?"

"Yes."

He pulled her shirt over her head and straddled her. She smoothed her hands over his muscular thighs. They'd been in this moment before. They'd been swept away with desire that had quickly cooled and they'd parted.

No . . . they'd not parted. She'd run away. She'd fled because the intensity of what she'd felt for him had been too frightening to bear. For days she'd thought about him, wondered what he was doing, if he thought about her. But each time he'd invaded her thoughts, she'd pushed him away.

And here she was again, inviting this delicious desire and feeling. As much as she wanted to promise herself she'd act differently tomorrow, she didn't. All she could promise was now.

Lucas raised his head and studied her face. "I can hear your mind working."

She smoothed a hand over his broad back. "It does that sometimes. Time to turn it off."

He cupped her face in his hands for a moment, staring deep into her eyes as if willing the fear away. He kissed her as if he didn't want to think about tomorrow, either.

She reached for the snap of his jeans and unfastened them. The loosened waistband allowed her to slip her hands over his bare skin, and he hissed in a breath as if she'd seared him with fire.

He rose up on his knees, staring at her as he quickly ripped off his shirt and reached for the snap on her jeans. Soon they were both naked, and he entered her. The sensations overtook them both and their bodies, damp with sweat, climaxed.

Lucas collapsed against Marisa. He rolled on his side and pulled her close, nestling her bottom against him. He held on as if somehow he'd find a way to keep her from running again in the morning.

Chapter 14

The next morning, Lucas woke and rolled on his side, expecting to feel Marisa's warm body. His eyes were barely open, and he wanted her. They'd made love twice last night, and he still craved more.

His hand slid across the sheet and hit a cold, empty patch. Immediately, his eyes opened and when he didn't see her, he bolted up. He glanced around the dark, empty room, curtains still drawn, and found no sign of her. He tossed back the covers and reached for his pants, which were puddled on the floor.

As he ran through all the possible scenarios, he glanced toward the bathroom and saw the light on. "Marisa, you okay?"

Silence lingered a beat before the door opened to a bleary-eyed Marisa, who held a stack of papers. "I didn't want to wake you."

"You didn't." Relief washed over him. He resisted the urge to cross and hold her close.

"I remembered the code." She held up the papers. "I

woke up a couple of hours ago, and the pieces fell into place. I found paper and pencil and had to write."

The smile in her eyes eased his tension more. "What do you remember?"

She explained the basics of the code, which was based on the Mayan language. "There's a drug shipment coming in today."

"What?"

She shuffled the papers and frowned as she read. "My handwriting is awful. It's a code unto itself." She studied the page. "Today. Definitely. Twelve noon." She read off the address. "This is where they'll be housing the shipment."

"You're sure?"

She raised a brow. "I know languages. And I'm right."

Lucas kissed her on the lips. When she raised her hand to his cheek, he savored her touch. He'd not lost her again.

She finally broke away. "Don't you have to call someone?"

"Right." He reached for his cell and dialed headquarters.

The next thirty minutes was a scramble to dress, grab coffee, and get on the road back to Austin. Lucas dropped her off at her Hyde Park home an hour later. Instead of racing back to his car, he hesitated. "I don't like leaving you here."

"I'll be fine. And it's time I went through some boxes."

Boxes that held memories she'd been running from for years. The outside world had barreled back into their lives. Would it tear them apart? "See you soon."

"Be careful." She smiled and reached for the door handle.

He captured her arm. "I'll be back soon."

"I know."

He took her hand in his. "I was thinking we could take a vacation."

She arched a brow. "Really?"

He brushed a strand of hair from her eyes. "Somewhere fun. An island. Just the two of us."

"Okay."

"Don't go anywhere."

She laughed before sobering. "I won't if you promise to be careful."

"Copy that." He kissed her again and watched her vanish into her home. When he heard her click the dead bolt in place, he drove off, his gaze in the rearview mirror as he wondered if he'd ever see her again.

"Marisa." Her father's voice cut through the phone line. "Where are you?"

"Home. I'm home." She sat in front of the one box she'd sworn she'd never open again. It was the box marked CHRISTMAS. She pulled out strands of old lights, colorful glass balls, and had just reached several handmade ornaments when the phone rang.

A sigh shuddered through the line. "I've been worried sick about you."

She glanced at the box of Christmas ornaments. "I'm fine."

"This is the Ranger's fault."

"It's not."

"Ancient languages are not cutting edge. They were the center of your mother's life, other than you. We agreed on little, but we both loved you."

Emotion clogged her throat, and for a moment she didn't speak. She dug into the Christmas box and retrieved a handmade star ornament. Recollections flooded of the day she and her mother and father had made it together. "Remember the year you, Mom, and I decorated a cedar tree along the highway? I was about six."

"I remember. You and I spent most of the morning making a paper chain to go on our tree. And your mother made the star."

She held up the star, amazed he'd remembered. Light caught the bits of glitter still clinging to the cardboard. "I remember thinking that chain was a thousand feet long after we'd made all those loops, but in the end it barely wrapped twice around the cedar tree."

"Your mom loved Christmas when you were little."

She cut through time, trying to remember the years before the divorce. "I have few happy memories of Christmas."

"There was a time when she loved the holiday." A heavy silence settled. "I never meant to end the marriage on Christmas Eve. I lost my temper. I didn't think beyond my own misery to you or your mother. I've always blamed myself for ruining Christmas for you and your mom."

She cradled the phone close, tears stinging in the back of her eyes. Her father may have been selfish, but her mother had also chosen to hang on to the anger and let bitterness rob her of happiness. That bitterness had spilled into Marisa's life and she'd allowed it to remain.

She could never gain back the years she'd lost with her mother and father, but she could find a way to embrace the future. "Thanks for saying that."

He cleared his throat. "Come over for dinner. We'd love to have you."

"Thank you, I'd like that. I've a few chores to do here and I'm waiting to hear back from Lucas. I broke his code."

"Did you?"

"Yeah. This is a big break for him."

"Your mom and I always said you were the smartest of all three of us."

Her front door bell rang. "Dad, someone is at the door. I have to go. It's probably Lucas."

"Please be careful. Look before you open the door." She glanced out her front window and saw Bradley standing on the front porch. She groaned. "It's Bradley."

"Good. You're safe."

"Safe?"

"I called him. I thought you two were long overdue for a conversation."

Marisa shoved her fingers through her hair as she watched him standing, hands in pockets, on the front step. "What do we have to talk about?"

"Just talk to him, honey."

She shoved out a breath. "Sure. I'll talk to him."

"We'll see you soon?"

"Yes." She hung up and moved to the door, snapping it open.

Bradley had the good sense to look embarrassed. "You're back?"

"I am."

"Can we talk?"

"Sure." She allowed Bradley past her threshold into the living room. When she closed the door, she turned and faced him. "What's this about?"

"I made a mistake. A terrible mistake. I was hoping we could talk and maybe find our way back to each other."

For a moment she almost laughed, thinking it was April Fools' Day and not Christmas Eve. "You meant every word you said."

"I didn't. I was selfish and hasty."

Her father must have had some talk with him. The emotion behind her father's words had touched her heart, but Bradley's words left her cold. "Is that all?"

"Your office was trashed. You were run off the road. You shouldn't be alone."

"I'm fine. I can take care of myself."

He rattled loose change in his pocket. "This danger you're in has to do with that Ranger!"

"It does not."

"How can you say that? All your work was taken. Your office was ransacked."

"I don't believe the two are connected."

"That's insane. Your office was broken into just after your accident while you were lying in the hospital."

"Lucas said the place was trashed, but it reminded him of an amateur. If it had been the cartels, they'd have burned the place to the ground."

He fisted his hands. "Why burn an entire building? They were after your work."

"To hide evidence."

His gaze narrowed. "What evidence?"

She studied him, noting the tension around his eyes. "Why're you upset?"

He jabbed stiff fingers through his thick hair. "Anyone would be upset. God knows who breached the history building."

"Lucas said there were no signs of forced entry." She shook her head as she watched him. He showed no sign of surprise. "You took my work."

"Don't be ridiculous."

She'd made the statement off the cuff, not sure what reaction she'd receive. But now, as she watched his face redden a shade and his lips flatten, she confirmed her hypothesis. "You've been jealous of my work for months. I tried to ignore it, but you're angry I made the find and you didn't."

"That's not true."

"It's true." She advanced a step. "Did you run me off the road, as well?"

"Don't be stupid! I didn't run you off the road. And I have witnesses who saw me in town at the time of the accident."

So he'd considered the need for witnesses. "But that didn't stop you from taking advantage of my hospital stay, did it? You broke in after my accident and hoped the Rangers would connect the break-in and car accident."

His gaze hardened. "I should have burned your office to the ground."

To hear the admission, despite her accusations, struck her like a slap.

"I should have burned all your papers and destroyed your work."

"Why?"

"I wanted to teach you a lesson."

"Lesson?"

"I'd hoped you'd see the Ranger was trouble and that you'd return to being your old self. You've been different since Mexico. And I know you two met there behind my back. One of the other professors saw you dancing with him in the café."

"Behind your back? My old self?" Anger simmered.

"You used to be easygoing."

Her eyes narrowed. "You mean a pushover."

"You were a nicer person before Mexico."

"Before you dumped me."

"You were selfish. All you cared about was work. You never looked at me."

"I can't believe this." She reached for the door and opened it, allowing a chill to race over her. "Get out of my house."

"We need to talk."

"We're finished."

"Marisa, I did it for your own good."

"Go away, Bradley."

He reached out his hand as if to grab her arm, but she flinched and backed up toward the open door. The sound of footsteps on her front porch had them both turning to face a stunned Kyle. He carried a bag of groceries and a bottle of wine.

Relieved, she attempted a smile. "Kyle."

His steady gaze settled on Bradley. "You all right, Marisa?"

"Bradley was just leaving."

Bradley glared at the two of them, and though he wanted to say more, he brushed past them and stormed down the steps toward his car.

Kyle raised an amused eyebrow. "So what's the deal with Bradley?"

"He just admitted to trashing my office."

Kyle stepped over the threshold and set the groceries on the lone table. "Why?"

"To teach me a lesson." She closed the door.

"So he has all the papers?"

"I suppose. I don't care. My work is backed up, and I remembered the code."

Kyle rubbed his chilled hands together. "How much?"

"The entire collection of messages." She checked her watch, imagining the Rangers storming the storage shed now. "Lucas and his men are on the way."

"You always did have an amazing memory. What was the key to the code?"

"The Mayan and Aztec languages. It's a mixture of glyphs and numbers. Simple, really."

"Simple for you. Not for most. I doubt there's one other person on the planet who could have broken it."

"You could have cracked it."

"Maybe." The phone in Kyle's bag rang.

The ringtone had a familiar melody that captured Marisa's attention. She watched as he grinned and fished the phone from his pocket. By the third ring, she recognized the tune. It was the song she'd heard while she'd been trapped in her car. A unique sound that she'd never heard before.

Marisa watched as Kyle glanced at the number, paled, and pushed the phone back into his pocket purse.

"Who was that?"

Kyle's lips flattened into a thin line. "No one."

"You don't look well." She thought about the code she'd broken. Kyle could have written it.

"I'm fine."

Kyle raised gray eyes that narrowed a fraction, like an outlaw sizing up the sheriff. His hand slid behind his back, and he removed a gun.

Chapter 15

Wednesday, December 24, 11 A.M.

Marisa took a step back. "You were at the accident."

Kyle nodded. "You heard the phone that night, didn't you? They were calling to see if I'd done the job."

Her stomach turned and threatened to upend. "You were sent to kill me."

He glanced from side to side, as if to make sure no one was watching. He swallowed, and his gaze grew heavy with sadness. "Not kill you. Scare you. Buy some time."

"Why?"

"Because the shipment had to get through. Once it was delivered, I would be off the hook."

Kyle's familiar face didn't jive with the words of a stranger. "Why?"

"I owe them."

"We've been friends for years." This betrayal struck directly into her heart.

"I knew you were alive in that car. I planned to send help in the next day or two. Like you said, we were friends."

She pressed trembling fingertips to her forehead. "Who do you owe money to?"

Sweat dampened his brow, and his face had paled. "Bad men who bought out my gambling debts with the promise that I do them a favor."

"Gambling. I thought you'd quit."

"I thought I had, too. And then, well, the itch returned while you were in Mexico."

"Why didn't you come to me? I would have tried to help."

A bitter smile curved the edges of his lips. "You've bailed me out enough. And I couldn't come to you again and see the look of disappointment on your face."

The realization chased a chill through her body that left her cold and numb. "So you did this one favor."

"Make a simple code. That's all I thought I was doing."

"They'll never want one favor."

The scorn in her voice hardened his expression. "I could have told them the Rangers had come to see you, but I didn't. I thought if I could buy some time, this would all be over soon."

Tears filled her eyes. "I can't believe this."

"I like you so much," he said, his voice a hoarse whisper. "I respect you. But I had to do this. You don't know what they do to people who say no."

Overwhelmed with sadness for a friendship she'd never had, she asked, "So what now?"

He squared his shoulders. "Get in my car. We need to go for a drive."

"Where?"

"You'll see." Kyle jabbed the gun. "Move. Now. If I don't get this right today, I'll be sent home to my parents in pieces."

"So I'm supposed to just walk to my death?"

"Don't be dramatic. Just walk."

"No."

"I'll give them the name of your father and stepmother and your brothers."

Blood drained from her face as she thought about what they'd do to her family. "You're a monster."

"No. I'm not a monster. I'm just a guy trying to get by."

The Rangers raided the warehouse just after twelve noon and found huge stores of drugs as well as two dozen men moving and packing boxes for shipment. There'd been gunfire, blood had been shed, but in the end, the drug dealers were no match for the Rangers.

Lucas, as commander, had held back, letting the local SWAT team handle the actual takedown. A deep satisfaction burned inside him as he watched the collection of drug runners led to squad cars. When the building had been secured and declared free of explosives and traps, he'd gone in and inspected the stash. Millions and millions of dollars in neatly bound bundles lined the floor.

Brody Winchester approached, carrying a cell phone. "You might be interested in this."

"What?"

"This is a phone from one of the guys we arrested. Someone called in just before we raided the place. He left a message warning of the raid."

"Who would know?"

Winchester grinned. "It's got me curious, as well." He held up the phone. "Do you recognize the number?"

Lucas glanced at it. "No."

"Does the name Kyle Stone mean anything?"

"Marisa Thompson's assistant's name is Kyle."

All traces of humor vanished. "Kyle's made a lot of calls to this group."

"Shit."

Lucas reached for his phone and dialed Marisa's number. She didn't answer. "I don't like this. I left her at home hours ago."

Kyle's gun trained on Marisa, she drove through the Hyde Park neighborhood, past several homes with children playing in the front yards. He dialed a number and when there was no answer, cursed. "So what's next, Kyle? What happens? Do I just disappear, and you keep working at the university?"

"No one is answering my calls. That's bad. It tells me that the Rangers did a lot of damage."

She laughed as she gripped the wheel and turned the corner that led out of the neighborhood. "You really believe your drug dealing friends will forgive this?"

"I can make another code if I have to. And with you gone, there will be no one to break it."

"Bradley might be able to."

Kyle shook his head and almost looked amused. "He's nowhere near the scholar you are. Without you his work has suffered."

Up ahead, she spotted a Christmas tree lot on the side of the road. This close to Christmas it looked almost deserted because most anyone wanting a tree by now would have gotten it. Before she stopped to think, she slammed her foot on the accelerator and the car zoomed forward. Kyle couldn't react fast enough as she twisted the wheel hard and drove straight for the trees. They plowed through several rows before slamming into the side of a small concrete building. At the moment of impact, the airbags deployed. She braced, remembering the feel of the impact.

Kyle grunted when his airbag hit him in the face.

Stunned, Marisa felt for her door handle, and unclicking her belt, rolled out of the car as her bruised body groaned and screamed from old and new injuries. She stumbled several steps, nearly tripped and fell, but caught herself and kept going.

"Marisa!" Kyle screamed her name as if it had been ripped from his chest. She didn't look back. Kept running.

In the corner of her eye, she spotted the flash of lights. The squeal of sirens pierced her fear, but she didn't dare stop, not knowing who else had arrived. She ran along the side alley of a Mexican restaurant. A dog barked. Her heart felt as if it would explode out of her chest. And as she rounded a corner, she stumbled to a stop when she saw the dead end. She had nowhere to go. Trapped.

She turned, fingers fisted, ready to run toward Kyle. When he appeared at the lip of the alley, he bore a red welt on the side of his face. Rage darkened his bloodshot eyes.

Kyle leveled the gun. "Bitch."

Screaming, she ran toward him. She would die trying to stop him.

And then, a shot fired. Adrenaline kept her moving forward, and she didn't stop until she saw Kyle fall to the ground. He dropped his gun and gripped his thigh, which had been torn and mangled by a bullet.

Sweat dripping from her brow, she looked around until she spotted him. Lucas. He'd held his gun outstretched, trained on Kyle, ready to fire again.

She stopped, her heart pulsing, her hands now trembling.

Lucas kept his gaze and gun on Kyle, who lay on the ground screaming. He kicked the gun away and cuffed Kyle seconds before more cops and Rangers arrived. When the Ranger had control of Kyle, Lucas lowered his weapon and holstered it.

Tears welled in her eyes. She wanted to touch Lucas and hold him. When his gaze locked on her, he crossed to her in three quick strides and wrapped her neatly in his arms. "I thought I'd lost you."

She gripped handfuls of his shirt. "I'm too mean to die." His shirt felt smooth against her cheek. "I love you."

He pulled her back and studied her face. "Did you hear what you just said?"

She nodded. "I meant it. I love you, Lucas. I loved you in Mexico. And I think that's what scared me."

"I love you. Marry me. Now."

She rose on tiptoes and kissed him. Excitement hummed through her body. "It's Christmas Eve."

"I can find someone."

"I'd like my dad and stepmother to be there. And Sherry and the boys."

"That can be arranged."

She laughed. "If you can make it happen, cowboy, I'm there. I'm ready for new Christmas memories."

Epilogue

One Year Later
Christmas Eve, 7:00 P.M.

Lucas Cooper's booted feet clipped hard against the tiled floor of Garrison Hall. Two teaching assistants spotted him, but their smiles died instantly when they saw his dark expression.

Not bothering to remove his hat, he moved past them and a collection of colored lights decorating the entrance and climbed the steps to the second floor two at a time. His entire focus rested on one thing: finding Marisa. Memories of arriving home and finding it dark and empty still haunted him and set his heart to racing anew. When he'd called out her name and she'd not answered, he'd called her cell. The instant her phone had gone to voice mail, he'd thought the worst as he'd raced toward her campus office. He'd already decided if he didn't find her here, he'd put out an all-points bulletin.

At the second floor landing, he spotted the light in her office. Relief doused the dread. "Damn it," he muttered.

He found her at her desk hunched over a collection of

photographs that she'd taken during the spring dig at her Mayan ruin. They'd taken a belated two-week honeymoon in Mexico, one week on the beach and the second week exploring her ruins. She'd taken thousands of pictures.

As he moved toward her ready to scold he saw her hand slide to her very pregnant belly. She winced and the color in her cheeks faded from rosy to ashen white.

"Get your coat, Marisa. The doctor says you aren't supposed to be here."

She looked up, took several deep, even breaths, and nodded. "I know. I hadn't planned to come in to work today. I'd planned to rest, but I had a breakthrough while I was napping today."

He crossed to her desk in three quick strides and closed her laptop. "We're leaving now. Doc says no more work until the baby is born."

Her lips flattened into a thin line radiating a mixture of frustration and pain. "I'm nearly done."

"Don't care, darlin'." He took her gently by the elbows and helped her to her feet. She leaned into him heavily, a sign she was exhausted. His tone softened. "You can take the laptop home and work. But you need to be in bed. Baby's due any day."

She smiled and smoothed her hand over her belly. "That's what the doctor said last week."

"Coopers are always on time," he teased. "This baby has inherited his late timing from you."

"I'm on time. For the most part." She snatched up her satchel and tucked her laptop inside it as he wrapped her coat around her shoulders.

He took her bag and slung it on his shoulder. "Car's out front."

She tossed him a withering glare. "I'm not an invalid. Women have been having babies for millions of years."

"Don't care. This is the one and only as far as I'm concerned. Let's go."

He guided her slowly out of her office and down the hallway to the main doors. She wasn't talking or complaining, both signs that she'd overdone it. She loved her work, and he was proud as hell of the passion she had for it. But enough was enough. Time to rest.

He opened the car door, and she lumbered into the seat. He was reaching for the seat belt when she winced again and this time closed her eyes as she breathed quickly.

His heart skipped a beat. "Damn it, Marisa, how long has this been going on?"

When the spasm passed, she released a relieved sigh. "A few hours. I was hoping to get my notes finished before we went to Dad's for Christmas dinner."

He muttered an oath. "We're not going to dinner. We're going to the hospital."

She looked up at him and instead of arguing nodded. "Their Christmas presents and yours are in my car. I haven't wrapped any of them."

"Don't worry about it. I'll send someone for your car and the presents later."

She smiled at him. "Okay."

If he wasn't so damn worried about her and the baby, he'd have made a joke about her agreeing so easily. But jokes were the last thing on his mind.

Behind the wheel he gunned the engine, cut through evening traffic, and had them at the hospital emergency room entrance in fifteen minutes. She gripped her belly as he came around to her side of the car. He could feel his own heart constricting as he stared at his wife, whom he loved more than anything in this world.

He spotted an orderly and ordered a wheelchair. The man hustled inside and returned moments later. Lucas helped Marisa from the car into the chair.

The next five hours became a blur of doctors, nurses, and more and more contractions. It was close to midnight when they wheeled Marisa into the delivery room. At her side Lucas did his best to look unworried as he reminded her to breathe and not push.

Not long after arriving in the delivery room, the action sped into overdrive. The doctor arrived and on her fifth push Marisa delivered their son. Jacob Alexander Cooper, eight pounds, one ounce, arrived in the world wailing and carrying on like a bronco rider.

When the nurse laid Jacob in Lucas's arms, he figured he'd never seen such a beautiful sight. He knelt close to Marisa so she could see the baby. Smiling, she studied the baby up close, taking inventory. "He's perfect," she said.

He kissed her. "You did a real fine job, Mrs. Cooper."

She glanced at the clock and then smiled at him. "He's officially a Christmas baby," she said.

"And the best damn present I ever will get."

A SOUTHERN CHRISTMAS

MARY CARTER

I'd like to thank my editor, John Scognamiglio, and all the staff at Kensington who work so hard on every manuscript; my agent, Evan Marshall; and all the wonderful people I met in Wilmington, North Carolina. I would especially like to thank Sara Strassle for allowing me to tour her beautiful home and "use it" for the Christmas gala.

To Elijah and Amelia, who keep the spirit of Christmas alive.

Chapter 1

Danielle Bright and Nathaniel Hathaway walked hand in hand down the boardwalk. It was a picture-perfect Christmas Eve. There was a tiny nip in the air, and the skies were littered with stars. Boats along the river were decked out in Christmas lights and displays, floating their holiday cheer up and down the Cape Fear River. The horse and carriage was coming in for the night; the telltale *clip-clop* rang out even before the white beauty came into view. The driver treated the pair to a wink and a wave, and Dani and Nate smiled and waved back. The horse, a Percheron, was one of five rescued draft horses that they rotated in and out of short shifts. They were well-treated and friendly, like most folks about town.

The air had the smell of cookies just out of the oven. Dani could imagine racks of them cooling on counters up and down Front Street, awaiting icing and Santa. Dani smiled at the thought of all the children hyped up even before licking the bowl. She glanced at the skies as if trying to spot flying reindeer. The huge tourist paddleboat, the *Henrietta,* was just pulling in from its moonlight cruise.

The ship honked its horn, as if winking at the young couple on the shore.

Nate's hands were clammy, which wasn't like him. She hoped he wasn't coming down with something. They were having Christmas dinner at his grandmother's house, and Danielle couldn't imagine missing the exquisite feast. She absolutely loved going to Ruth Hathaway's gorgeous historic home on Christmas. Oh, she loved spending the mornings with her parents and sister, of course, but there was no denying the special pull she had toward Ruth's festivities.

Ruth Hathaway had a passion for the holidays that could not be beat. Her home always boasted the best decorations inside and out, the food and drink were a culinary dream, and not a single detail was ever overlooked, right down to chestnuts literally roasting over a roaring fire. And this year, Dani's entire family was invited. Just thinking how special it would be infused Dani with the Christmas spirit. Beside her, Nate cleared his throat.

She would have to encourage him to take some vitamin C before bed, and if he woke up with the sniffles, he was just going to have to power through it. Just ahead towered the town Christmas tree. Dani and Nate were just a few feet from it when the scent of pine reached her nose. Dani stopped, dropped Nate's hand, and gasped. "It's live," she said.

Nate grinned. "You got your wish this year," he said. Normally, it was an artificial tree, something that really got to Dani. But this year. What a surprise. What a beauty she was.

"Did you know?" Dani asked Nate.

Nate nodded. "It's a regal blue spruce specially cut from the mountains in Asheville."

"It's unbelievable. They did it. They finally did it." The multicolored lights glittered like precious gems in the night. Just as they passed the tree, Nate stopped, swung her around, took her hands in his, and gazed into her eyes. There was a twinkle in his eye. Nate got down on one knee. The clues finally gelled. He was going to propose.

Before she could even think, her body reacted. She yanked him back up. He was off balance, and startled. She took a moment to look into his eyes. Normally a greenish-blue, next to the tree tonight they were the color of emeralds. A perfect contrast to his dark hair. He was such a handsome young man, and they had been happily going steady for three years. But she was only twenty-four. And they hadn't had the talk yet, not really, about the future. To Danielle, it seemed a sure thing, but far off. At least three years. Even five. She wasn't ready to settle down and have kids. And as much as she loved Wilmington, North Carolina, their little "Hollywood of the East," she wanted to see other places before they started a life together. More specifically, she wanted to see New York. No, that wasn't the exact truth. She didn't just want to see New York. She wanted to be a part of New York; she wanted to *live* in New York. And Nate had stated numerous times that there was nowhere he'd rather be but right here. It was sweet, but it was also maddening. She had resolved to talk to him about it in the New Year.

"Nate," she said. He smiled and squeezed her hands, and only then could she see how nervous he was. And how well dressed. Why hadn't she noticed before that he was wearing his blue blazer? There were a few other people roaming about, but mostly they had the boardwalk to themselves. An older couple stopped to take a picture of the tree. Music was playing nearby. Danielle couldn't tell where exactly it was coming from, but suddenly she realized what it was. Her favorite Christmas song, "It's Beginning to Look a Lot Like Christmas," sung by the one and only Bing Crosby. Nate had planned that, too. He reached into his pocket. He was so nervous he wasn't picking up on her attempts to stop him.

"Wait," Dani said. The couple who had stopped to take

the picture were openly staring in anticipation. Smiling. Holding the camera up, just waiting to get a snapshot of his face when she said, "Yes. I will. I will marry you." Dani leaned down. "Pretend you're tying your shoe," she said.

"What?" Dani pointed to his shoe. He stared at it, then stared at her, and raised an eyebrow.

The words were out of her mouth before she could censor them, soften them. She clasped her hands as if she was the one proposing. She dropped to one knee, too, so that they were nose-to-nose. Anyone who saw them would probably think they were putting on some sort of strange nativity performance. Dani could have used the guidance of a wise man tonight, preferably all three. Or even a shining star to guide her. But all she had was herself. And the burning feeling in her gut that if he asked her now, there would never, ever be a later. "Please don't ask me," she said. "Please, not here. Not now."

Nate's eyes bore into hers for a few seconds, before he glanced behind her. At first, she was annoyed. He couldn't be that upset if he was so easily distracted, if he didn't even want to hear why she was stopping the proposal. *Delaying the proposal.* Of course she would marry Nate. Just later than sooner. They had all the time in the world. She turned around to see what had captured his attention. What a fright!

The boardwalk behind them was now teeming with people ready to celebrate. So many of them. Piling off the *Henrietta*'s moonlight cruise. All their friends and family, come to witness this romantic moment. Nate had timed everything perfectly. Passing the tree, stopping to gawk. The boat pulling in. The captain playing her favorite Christmas song. So that by the time she said yes, they would turn around to a thunderous cheer, and the popping of champagne. The horse and carriage was indeed waiting to take one more spin that night, this time just for the luckiest couple in the world.

Slowly, it dawned on her. "You had the tree flown in," she said.

"Just for you," he replied.

Oh yes. Nate Hathaway had seen to every tiny detail. Every detail, but one. He had never counted on Danielle Bright saying anything other than a resounding "Yes."

Chapter 2

"Just what is a Southern Christmas?" Adel asked the question and everyone at the conference table looked as if they were pondering it, except Dani, who slid a few inches down into her chair, hoping it wouldn't happen, but inevitably Adel's eyes landed on her and remained. Soon, the entire room was looking at her. Could she really be the only employee here from the South? "Well?" Adel said in a tone that suggested she did not have time for Dani to slip all the way under the table and crawl to the exit on her hands and knees.

"There are three things you need to know about a Southern Christmas," Dani said. Lately she'd noticed that Adel responded to lists of three. She nodded at Dani to continue and took her seat. "One," Dani said, holding up her index finger and stalling for time. "There will be food. Two—"

"We all have food," Adel answered. She sounded suspicious now.

"Do you have cheesy biscuits, and grits, and country ham?"

"No, we do not," Adel said, feverishly tapping on her

iPad. She was back on board now. "Wait. You have that for breakfast? On Christmas morning?"

"Well—my family would often have that breakfast as the main meal on Christmas Day."

"Oh my God."

"But that's just us. Others go all-out. Southern meals at Christmastime, are you kidding me? Beef tenderloin with homemade mustard dip, sweet potato biscuits, glazed ham and sage-crusted pork with pear chutney, standing rib roasts with red wine mushroom, and turkey with figgy port wine sauce—"

"Figgy port wine sauce," Adel echoed.

"—Montgomery punch, cheese dreams—"

"Cheese dreams," Adel repeated as if she was in a dream.

"Mini corn cakes with smoked salmon and dill crème fraiche, cheesy grits soufflé, pecan bourbon balls—"

"Stop or I'm going to wet my pants!" Adel looked as if Dani had been to an exotic new land. "Two?" she asked, grasping her pen like a torch she was about to pass.

Two was easy. Two was one of the things Dani missed the most about Christmas in the South. "Two, there will always be a gala." Instantly, she was in Ruth's gorgeous home. Violinists playing Christmas carols along with the pianist. The table elaborately set with the finest china, and ribbons falling from the chandelier, and skyscraper candles resting in mini-wreaths, and always a show-stopper centerpiece. Dani's favorite was the year Ruth had a gorgeous white swan pulling a red sleigh.

And, oh, the smells. Ham, and turkey, and corn bread stuffing, and so many delicate little appetizers that Dani often fasted for days before the dinner just so she could taste as many as possible. Christmas cocktails and champagne on ice. Mountains of delectable desserts, but Dani's favorite was always Ruth's red velvet white chocolate cheese cake. There should be a book made in its honor. *The one cheesecake to try before you die*. And the people were adorned just as beautifully as the food and decorations. Women in beautiful gowns and glittering jewels, and men in tuxes. A roaring fire, and every inch of space tastefully decorated for the holidays. She'd been dancing with Nate at Christmas galas since she was sixteen. He'd been so nervous that first time, his hands so clammy. She'd wanted him to kiss her so bad. It didn't happen until the second year, and that was only because Dani cornered him on the upper deck with mistletoe. Not that he resisted—

"A gala," Adel repeated. "I love it." Heads nodded up and down the table. They loved it, too. All but one.

"A gala?" Sawyer said. He drew the word out in his Texan drawl like he was a ten-year-old, and she was in pigtails, and they were at recess.

"Yes, Sawyer, a gala," Dani said. "It's a formal affair. Nothing you'd ever be invited to." Danielle knew she was taking the bait, but she couldn't help it. She'd been taking his sarcasm for six months now. Recently she'd stopped ignoring it and started firing back. His grin, however, made her think twice. He was loving the verbal Ping-Pong.

"Frankly, my dear, I don't give a damn," Sawyer said.

"You can read," Dani said. "What a surprise."

"There was a book?" Sawyer said. "I was quoting the movie." He winked. Dani scowled. He winked again and Dani bit her lip before he noticed her involuntary smile. Too late. He sat back and grinned as if they'd just shared a dirty secret.

"Southern women would just eat you up, cowboy," Adel said to Sawyer, treating him to a wink of her own. Dani clenched her fists under the table. They probably would. How irritating. Adel turned back to Dani. "Has your family ever hosted a gala?"

"Oh God, no," Dani said. Adel raised an eyebrow. "We lived by the beach. We were comfortable, but not one of Wilmington's elite."

"Ahhh," Adel said, nodding as if she suspected it all along.

"So it sounds like you weren't invited to this gala, either," Sawyer said.

"Of course I was," Dani said. "I was Nate Hathaway's girlfriend." Sawyer raised his eyebrow. Oh, she shouldn't let him get to her, she just shouldn't, but he did, and she couldn't help but take the bait. He drove her insane! Why did everybody else think his cowboy act was so cute? Couldn't they see how arrogant he was? "Nate's from one of the most prominent families in town." The moment the words were out of her mouth she regretted it. It made him sound stuffy and boring. Nate might have been from a prominent family, but he was just as down to earth as she was. God, she missed him. What did she have to do to get him to speak to her again?

Move back. He is never going to forgive me if I stay here.

"And yet here you are," Sawyer said with a slow smile.

"What?" Dani said. Could he read her mind?

"Slumming it with us," Sawyer said. He pinned her with his eyes. Dani stared back, openmouthed. She had half a mind to throw something at him. Perhaps water in the face. And smack him. She would really love to smack him across the face. How did he do that? Zero in on her as if there was no one else in the room? Pin her with his eyes. He was trying to seduce her in plain sight, and she was letting him get his hooks into her. The nerve to be so brazen in front of everyone. It made her feel a little flushed, and then angry.

"It's settled, then," Adel said. "You'll do a feature on a typical Southern Christmas—"

"No!" Oh no. Did she say that out loud? But she couldn't show her face back home. Not until she worked out her plan to get Nate to forgive her. Two years and he still hadn't spoken to her since that horrific Christmas Eve. Dani back-pedaled. "I really don't think we qualify as a typical Southern Christmas. I mean, we're more of a little beach town, you know? Wilmywood? The Hollywood of the East?" She was treated to stares all around. Apparently they didn't keep up with the shows that were filmed in Wilmington. "*Under the Dome*? *Sleepy Hollow*? *Revolution*? *Iron Man 3*?"

"You watch a lot of TV," Sawyer said. "See? We do have something in common."

Dani went to respond, but instead of words, a growl escaped her lips. An actual growl. She was mortified. The others laughed as if she was trying to be funny. If they only knew that something about Sawyer turned on all her primal instincts to defend and attack.

"Easy, tiger," Sawyer said. He knew, she thought. He knew exactly the effect he was having on her.

"Maybe you could throw in a picture of a celebrity," Adel said. "Or the film crew. But mostly I just want a Southern Christmas theme. I like where Sawyer was going. Give us *Gone with the Wind,* the Christmas edition."

What? "You know that was Atlanta, right?" If they only knew. She'd already burned down the town by burning Nate. Still, Dani hoped she didn't sound too sarcastic. Two years on staff, and Dani was still treated as if she were an intern. Adel ran her magazine the opposite of a ship's captain. She was onboard until things started to sink, and then she was the first to jump. Adel loved this idea now, but if Dani didn't write it to her liking, she would make sure that Dani was the one treading water without a lifeboat. Was this why she had come to New York? To be teased by transplanted cowboys and treated like she had no creative ideas of her own? Had she made the biggest mistake of her life turning down Nate and running off to New York? She had to get Adel off this Southern idea and then pitch something she really wanted to write. Christmas in the City—New York—where she was invisible but not hated. "I don't really think of Wilmington as Southern, Southern—we're kind of Northern, Southern. You know what I mean?" *What are you doing, Dani? She wants to give you a Christmas feature. You're going to shoot yourself in the foot. No wonder she still treats you like an intern.* "Why don't I cover Christmas here in the city?" Dani said. "Maybe something a little more substantial?" She treaded lightly.

Adel frowned. "Like what?"

"Like—an exposé on the men behind the store Santas?"

"Why?" Adel asked.

"Because we let children sit on their laps! Who are these men? Alcoholics, drug addicts—perverts? I mean, wouldn't you like to know how many Santas are on crack?" Adel looked around the table. It was impressive how still the others kept their faces, waiting to see what she thought before they reacted. At least Adel wasn't screaming no. Dani pressed on. "I could do all five boroughs."

"Lucky boroughs," Sawyer said. For once Dani ignored him.

Unfortunately, so did Adel. She was completely focused on Dani. "Do you even read this magazine?"

"Of course." *Full of fluff. And more fluff. And recipes for fluff. And now she wanted holiday fluff.* "I just thought we might like to branch out a little."

"You want to go dark, is that it? Why don't we just cover Christmas suicides?"

"I could do that."

Adel pounded her fist on the table. "I was joking! Are all Southerners this gloomy around Christmas?"

"I'm not gloomy. I just think—"

"Don't! Let me do the thinking. Maybe there's something here. We could expose the South as Confederate Grinches. How does that sound?"

"Horrible. It sounds horrible," Dani said. And true. Kind of true.

"I can see Dani's point," Sawyer said. Heads snapped

his way. "Christmas can be stressful. We could give our readers an ultimate sense of relief by acknowledging that," he said.

Adel smiled at Sawyer. If he had suggested Santas on crack, Adel would probably be sitting in his lap by now. She turned on Dani again. "*Midnight in the Garden of Good and Evil*. Is your town anything like that?" Adel was really excited now. If you gave her a mirror and mistletoe, she'd be kissing herself.

"No. Nothing like that."

"Oh. Is there anyone here from Georgia, or Alabama, or anywhere *really* Southern, not fake Southern where Dani is from?" Adel asked. Heads shook all around the table.

"Okay, so Dani obviously doesn't want a feature for Christmas," Adel said. "Does anyone else want a feature?"

The other writers' hands shot into the air.

"Wait," Dani said. "I do want a feature."

"On what? A 'Not-so Southern Christmas'?" Adel said. "Yawn."

"I'd like to do something on 'The War on Christmas,'" Beth Green said. Beth was always trying to outdo Dani. They both longed to be taken seriously as writers. And here was Beth suggesting something Dani would like to do herself.

"As long as Christmas wins the war," Adel said. "Then I like it."

"No," Dani said. "I said I'll do it."

"And I said you've bored me already," Adel said. "Beth, you and Sawyer need to get as many Christmas-haters photographed as possible. Maybe start with Dani here—our Southern Scrooge. Then hit the streets. If you see anyone kicking a reindeer—shoot it—"

Dani shot out of her chair. "You're right. I am a Southern Scrooge. But I didn't used to be. I used to love Christmas."

"And I care, why?" Adel asked.

"Because I think it would make a great story."

"Not feeling it," Adel said.

"Two years ago my fiancé, Nate Hathaway, proposed to me on Christmas Eve." All eyes were on her again. Especially Sawyer. But she couldn't think about that now. "He had involved the entire town. Flew a real Christmas tree in from across the state. Had a flash mob waiting to congratulate us. Hired out the horse and carriage for the night. And I said no. Because I wanted to move here to be a famous writer. Nate hasn't spoken to me in two years. And all I want for Christmas is Nate. I want to go to Wilmington and win him back. I'll write about it every step of the way, and Sawyer can come with me and shoot anyone he wants."

"I'm starting to feel like an assassin," Sawyer quipped.

"If he takes me back, it will be a Christmas miracle. If he doesn't—you'll get your Southern Christmas."

"Hmmm," Adel said.

"Nate Hathaway," Dani said. "He's like royalty in Wilmington. A true prince."

"You turned down the town prince?" Sawyer said. "They must want your head on a platter." He put his hand over his heart.

"Along with the Christmas goose!" Dani said. "Southerners eat goose, too. And my goose is cooked!" She didn't know why she was going on like that except Adel seemed to come to life whenever Dani put herself down.

"Somebody Google Nate Hathaway," Adel said.

"Already did," Beth piped up. "He's hot."

"You found something on Nate?" Dani said.

"Is he an artist?" Beth asked.

"Yes! He's incredible. He makes sculptures from driftwood and shells, and glass. Although he underestimates his talents. I've always encouraged him to think bigger—"

"Looks like he took that advice."

"What?" Dani said.

Beth turned her e-tablet around. It was a photograph of Nate, beaming ear-to-ear. Next to him stood a statuesque woman with long dark hair. She was smiling, too. Between them was a giant sculpture. Dani could tell right away it was Nate's. Only better. In fact it was the best thing he'd ever done.

"Who's that woman?" Dani said.

"An art curator," Beth said.

"Thank God," Dani said.

"From London," Beth said. "Her name is Anya."

So? Dani wanted to shout. So?

"They're engaged," Beth said.

"What?" Dani lunged across the table and grabbed the tablet out of Beth's hands. She brought the picture in closer. Sure enough, it was in the engagement section. "No," she said. "No."

Beth read aloud over her shoulder. "Nate Hathaway and Anya Pennington announced their engagement—"

"No," Dani said again. "No." She pushed the iPad away.

"Americans versus the British in the South once again," Adel said. "It's beginning to look like a very Southern Christmas after all." She rubbed her hands together. "The feature is yours. And see if you can get me an alligator in a Santa hat." The excitement was back in her eyes. "I want the two of you on the next flight out."

One by one, everyone filed out of the room. Except for Dani, who sat and stared at the table. And Sawyer, who hovered by the door.

"Look on the Bright side," Sawyer said.

"What bright side?" Dani said.

"I'm just thinking of bylines," Sawyer said. "Using your last name." He motioned in the air as if he was skywriting. "Look on the Bright side," he repeated.

"Careful," Dani said.

"Of what?"

"I've got a Santa hat and Wilmington really does have alligators."

Chapter 3

The Wilmington airport was tiny, and even though Adel pulled off the impossible and found them a nonstop flight, just under two hours, it was a relief to finally deplane. Dani waited with each step for Sawyer to make some kind of crack about what happened. She could not believe she did that. Two hours! Was it too much to ask that she stay awake for two hours? The stress of returning home had been eating at her. She hadn't slept since Adel announced she was sending them to Wilmington. Keeping it a surprise from everyone, including her parents, had also overexcited her. So that was why it happened—Dani had been totally sleep-deprived. Still. Of all people. Even after they were in the rental car headed downtown, he still hadn't mentioned it. He was looking out the window and whistling. Whistling of all things.

"Look," Dani said. "I must have been really exhausted."

"Must have been," Sawyer said. God, he sounded smug. She'd never heard anyone sound so smug.

"Lucky it was you, I guess."

"Lucky, lucky, me," he said.

"Because I'm sure I would have fallen asleep on absolutely anyone."

"You're like that, are you?"

"No, I'm not like that. It just happened." She'd woken up with her head on his shoulder! Why did he have to sit in the middle? And she didn't want to admit this, never, ever, again, but she had drooled on him, too. She had literally drooled on Sawyer. He was just waiting to nail her with it. He had probably tweeted it around the world by now. Although, truth be told, she'd never seen him with a smartphone. She didn't even know if he had one. She kind of liked that about him. But that was all she liked. Yes, there was some kind of animal sex appeal about him. The bad boy, she supposed. The cowboy from Texas. He wore ripped jeans and T-shirts and always sported stubble and his brown hair was always tousled as if he had just gotten out of bed. He smelled good, though, a strong clean scent that defied Dani's view of him, made her imagine him sitting in a bubble bath. Chest just out of the water, arms open with a hand resting on either side of the tub. That lazy grin on his stupid face as he arched his eyebrow for her to join him. As if! I'll never take a bubble bath with you, she wanted to shout. Never! Even with all those muscles. Obviously he lifted weights. Or wrangled cattle. She hadn't seen any tattoos on him, either. He was sure to have one. On his hip bone?

They were passing the Black River swamp where the bald cypress stood bare—stripped of life by the infusion of salt water. The dead trees, now hollow inside, had become home to a lot of wildlife, and despite the destruction, their remains were eerily beautiful. They always reminded Dani that life was short.

"I believe you drooled on me," Sawyer said.

Sometimes, not short enough.

"Ghost trees," Dani said as if he hadn't spoken. When she'd woken up, dragged her head from his shoulder, he'd been looking at her. For a minute, as they held eye contact, she felt a pulse in her throat. False intimacy, that's all. She had to stop replaying that moment.

"Absolutely beautiful," Sawyer said. He was looking at her. She wasn't going to buy in to that phony baloney, either.

"I agree," she said. "They are." They fell silent and Dani took it all in. Her home. She missed Wilmington. They were on Third Street now and all her favorite buildings were coming into view. Thalian Hall, the courthouse, and farther down the street the First Presbyterian Church and Saint James Episcopal Church—it looked very much like a town in New England. She wasn't at all surprised that the new television series *Sleepy Hollow* was filmed here. And there was the Burgwin-Wright House on the corner of Third and Market Streets, they were going to have to make sure to go to "A Stroll Through Christmas Past." The tour would be perfect for the feature. Maybe she and Nate could be married on the grounds of the beautiful house, now a museum. Then again, that's where the gallows used to be. Maybe they'd just get married on the beach instead.

But first she'd have to get him to start speaking to her again, and second she'd have to deal with Anya. What kind of name was Anya? It was probably pronounced like *Awnya*. Like she was too good for plain old Ann or Anya. Seriously. *Yawn-ya*. Who did this woman think she was?

Before she could overthink it, she took a right on Market Street. She should have turned left instead, heading for her parents' home near Oakdale Cemetery, just outside of the historic downtown. But Dani wanted to go downtown first. And later, Wrightsville Beach. Oh, how she missed the beach. Coney Island and Jones Beach just didn't cut it. Mostly because Nate wasn't there to walk on the beach with her. Why had she ever given him up? "I just want to walk the boardwalk along the river," Dani said. "Then I can take you to your hotel."

"Cute town," Sawyer said. It really was. The Port City.

Quaint shops, and restaurants, and bars, all leading down to the river. A town steeped in history, and some architecture going back to the 1700s. Dani found a parking spot once they passed Front Street, near where the horse and carriage were awaiting their next tour.

"A horse and carriage parked in front of an ice cream shop," Sawyer said. "Don't tell me—everyone here leaves their doors unlocked, too."

"I wish," Dani said. "Oh, it's quaint all right. But Wilmington has a dark side. Gang violence, thefts, shootings."

"Are the Santas on crack?"

"Funny."

"I guess it's not exactly Mayberry then."

"No—but Mount Airy, where *The Andy Griffith Show* was filmed, is very close."

"Seriously? I was kidding."

"Totally serious." Dani found street parking, another blessing of the winter. She turned off the car but didn't make a move. She stared out at the dock and the Cape Fear River. The *Henrietta* was in its home spot. Across the way she could make out the battleship from World War II, the USS *North Carolina*. It was now a floating museum. Sawyer would probably like to tour that. Not that he was on vacation or anything. Guys liked big battleships, didn't they?

"Are we just going to sit in the car?" Sawyer asked.

"Just give me a minute."

"Sure. I'm going to get out my camera and snap a few while the sun is out."

"It's only ten A.M. The sun is going to be out for a while."

"You must have needed a longer nap," he said. "You're grouchy," he added off her look.

"I'm coming," Dani said. "Wait one sec." She opened the glove compartment and removed a baseball cap and large sunglasses.

"007," Sawyer said. "I like it."

"I just don't want to talk to anyone right now," Dani said. Actually, she didn't want to find out whether or not they were still talking to her. She wanted to see her parents first and scope out the situation. Fiancé! How could he be engaged to someone else? A British girl no less? Didn't they deal with that invasion a long time ago? Dani got out of the car and joined Sawyer on the boardwalk. He was snapping pictures of boats on the river. He turned to take her picture. She threw her hand in front of her face.

"I'm not a subject," she said.

"I thought we were documenting your attempts to win back the heart of Nate Hathaway," he said, loudly and dramatically.

"Shhh," she said. He turned and took a picture of the Christmas tree instead. The artificial Christmas tree. Tears came to Dani's eyes. Nate went to such trouble for that proposal. She should have said yes. Then talked to him about moving to New York together. She should have done anything other than what she did.

"Is this where you broke his heart?" Sawyer asked.

"This is where I'm going to break your jaw if you don't stop talking," Dani said.

"You're a pistol, Danielle Bright," Sawyer said. "A six-shooter, I reckon'."

"That cowboy stuff doesn't work on me," Dani said.

"That's too bad, ma'am. Because that feisty wench stuff does wonders for me." Then, he ducked and ran before she could push him off the dock and into Cape Fear.

Dani and Sawyer stood on Water Street in front of a little shop across from the boardwalk. It used to be an arts and crafts shop for children. It still was, in part. But the sign had changed. It now read:

* * *

Create with Nate

"He took my advice," Dani said. "I told him to open his own gallery and teach classes." It was a good sign—pun intended. He might not be speaking to her, but she was still getting through to him. That's the way it worked with soul mates.

"Isn't his fiancée an art curator? Maybe he took her advice." Sawyer snapped a picture of the sign.

"I said it long before he met her," Dani said. Sawyer started for the door. Dani yanked him back.

"What?" he said.

"I can't just walk in there."

"Isn't that why we're here?"

"We literally just got here. Are you in some kind of rush?"

"As a matter of fact, I wouldn't mind being home by Christmas."

"Why?"

"If you must know, I made the acquaintance of a certain Russian nanny who, it just so happens, is free for Christmas and I'd like to get home in time to come down her chimney."

"Oh my God. You are disgusting!"

"What? No. No. I didn't mean it like that." Sawyer actually blushed. Danielle believed him, but she wanted to tease him anyway.

"I'm sure you did."

"I'm sure I did not. Wow, Bright. You have a very dirty mind."

"I'm sleep deprived!"

"Well, by all means, do us all a favor and take a nap."

"And you need to check into your hotel."

"Oh, I'm not going to stay in a hotel."

"What do you mean, you're not going to stay in a hotel?"

"Relax, Bright. I don't plan on taking over your parents' couch. I just don't do hotels."

"Then where are you going to sleep?"

"Worried about me, are you?"

"Not in the least."

"Good."

"But seriously, where are you going to sleep?"

"I saw a nightly rental sign on one of the sailboats," Sawyer said. "That might be fun."

"Suit yourself. If it were me I'd book the best suite at the Hilton. One of the few perks of working for the magazine."

"You didn't book yourself a suite at the Hilton."

"Because Adel knows full well my parents are here," Dani said.

"A sailboat has way more character than the Hilton."

"Especially if it rains and the boat leaks," Dani said.

"No big deal. If it leaks I'll just get a bucket."

"What if it leaks in the middle of the night? You're not in Kansas anymore, cowboy. Nothing is open twenty-four hours around here except a Burger King and the grocery store."

"Why wouldn't the grocery store have a bucket?"

"You'd have to drive to the grocery store. Unless your little boat comes with a car, you're going to be up the creek without a paddle."

"At least I'll have a sail."

"I could never sleep on a boat."

"Yet you have no problem sleeping on my shoulder on a plane."

"Let's get something straight. I was sleep deprived. And I never, ever want to hear you mention that again."

"Do you always get so worked up about things?"

"Yes," she said. "I do."

"Even more of a reason to go in," Sawyer said, gesturing to the entrance of Nate's shop. "Rip off the Band-Aid before that little head of yours works yourself into a tizzy."

"I can't go in like this. Look at me."

Sawyer looked her up and down. His gaze seemed to linger on her body a little too long. Then he leaned forward and snatched off her baseball cap and sunglasses.

"Hey!" she said. He pulled the band from her hair and arranged it so that it cascaded down her shoulders. Then he leaned in and unbuttoned the top two buttons of her blouse. "Hey!" She swatted his hand away.

"He's engaged, Dani. You're going to have to do more than bat your eyes."

"Fine," she said.

"I'd say," he said, his eyes traveling from her face to her cleavage.

"Stop it," she said.

"Stop what?" he said. The smile increased.

"I'm not going in. You can if you want to." Sawyer slid his camera around to his back, came up behind Danielle, and scooped her into his arms. He lifted her effortlessly. "Hey," she said. "What are you doing?"

"We're going in," he said. He headed for the door, "Open it," he said.

"No," Danielle said. Sawyer continued to the door, forcing Dani's knees to push against it. "Stop," she said.

"Just open it."

"Let me down or I'll scream." Dani flailed her legs. Sawyer held her tighter. He was probably a boss in bed. Some women really liked that. Dani wasn't even going to think about the fact that she might be one of them. Sawyer suddenly flipped around so that his back was facing the door, and with Dani still in his arms, he pushed it open. Soon, their presence was announced by the bell above the door jingling.

"Ho, ho, ho," Sawyer said.

"Put me down," Dani said in a loud whisper.

"Can we help you?" It was a female voice. With a British accent. Sawyer let go of Dani and she dropped to the floor. His hand shot out to touch the woman.

"I'm Sawyer," he said with the tip of an imaginary hat. Anya looked even better than she had in the picture. She had beautiful porcelain skin, black hair, and China blue eyes. She was dressed as if she was in a gallery in London. High heels and a beautiful cream suit. Her buttons weren't undone like some kind of floozy. That was the last time Dani would listen to Sawyer. She wanted to reach down and button hers up but she didn't want to be obvious. This European stunner was in love with Nate? Her small-town beach bum of a boyfriend? Dani wanted to cry on the spot. She thought Nate liked blondes. Like her. What was he doing? Did he really want to listen to that obnoxious accent the rest of his life? Would their children run around sounding like offspring from *Downton Abbey*? *Mummy, can we please have a spot of tea?*

The shop was filled with artwork and worktables. Dani knew immediately which pieces were Nate's. Like the four-foot Christmas tree made entirely out of starfish. It was adorned with little crystals and topped off with white lights. Absolutely gorgeous. She reached out, stopping just short of touching it. The price tag screamed out at her. $1300. Dani gasped. She told him every year he needed to put a worthy price on his work. He normally gave them away. Although she would have suggested something way more affordable. This was Wilmington, not London. This was *her* doing. It had to be. The tree was gorgeous, though. She should show her support and buy it. She should get the magazine to buy it. He also had several wreaths made out of driftwood. She knew what the cover photo for the magazine should be. Dani and Nate, lying naked on the floor with nothing but wreaths covering their nether regions. The starfish trees could encircle them. They would each be quoted on the right.

NATE: *I never stopped loving her. She stopped me from making the biggest mistake of my life.*

DANI: *He's all I want for Christmas.*

"Why are you staring at bits of wood?" Sawyer said in her ear. He had a knack for making everything sound dirty.

"It's Nate's," she said. Dani knew Nate's work like she knew her own heart. *He's mine,* she thought as she looked at Anya. *He's mine.* "Get a picture of the starfish tree," Dani told Sawyer. He lifted his camera.

Anya stepped forward and slapped her hand over the lens. "No photos," she said. Sawyer turned the camera and snapped a picture of Anya instead.

"We're with a New York magazine," Dani said. *"The Softer Side."*

"I've never heard of it," Anya said.

"Have you heard of New York City?" Dani asked without a trace of sarcasm.

Sawyer belted out a laugh. "We're a start-up, but we do have quite a following," Sawyer said. "In New York and beyond. We'll be in Barnes and Noble for Christmas this year. We're doing a feature called 'A Southern Christmas.' But if Nate doesn't want his work promoted on such a scale—"

"We should really ask him directly," Dani said. "Although I'm sure he appreciates his sales clerk being so protective."

"I'm his partner," Anya said.

"His partner?" Dani said. "In what sense?"

"In the sense that I own half of this store and I am engaged to be married to him."

Sawyer was staring at the starfish tree. "I imagine that would start to smell after three days," he said with a loud laugh. Dani glared at him.

"They've been glazed," Anya said. "To smell like pine."

"Pardon me, ma'am," Sawyer said, dialing up his Texas accent. "I'm just a bumbling cowboy."

"Seriously?" Dani whispered. Sawyer reached back and pinched her on the butt. She was going to wallop him the minute they were alone.

"Nate isn't here right now. Where are you staying? I can leave a message with your hotel after I've spoken with him about this. I'm sure we can arrange something."

"I'm sure," Dani said. "We'll be in touch."

"Don't wait too long," Anya said. "Otherwise you'll have to fly to London."

"London?" Dani said. "You're going to London?" *Don't say on your honeymoon, don't say on your honeymoon.*

"Of course," Anya said. "Nate Hathaway is highly in demand as an artist. This sleepy little town isn't meant for someone like him. We're moving to London right after we get married."

"Congratulations," Sawyer said.

Judas. Nate was moving to London? Dani wanted to scream. How did she get him to do that? He must be going out of his mind. Forget that, his grandmother must be going out of her mind. Who did this woman think she was? Nate loved this sleepy little town. And it wasn't that sleepy. It just took a lot of naps. She had to remain calm until she could formulate a plan of action. "When are you getting married?" Dani said. She could barely choke out the words. "In a year or so?"

Anya's eyes lit up and she clasped her hands under her chin. "Christmas Eve," she said. "We're getting married on Christmas Eve."

Chapter 4

"Did you hear that? Did you hear that?" Dani was practically screaming. She and Sawyer had just rounded the corner onto Market Street.

"I'm sorry, Dani, I really am," Sawyer said.

"Sorry! I'm not. I'm thrilled."

"Did you hit your head on the door when I was carrying you in?" Sawyer said.

"Did you not hear what she said?" Dani exclaimed.

"Did *you* not hear what she said?" Sawyer replied.

"They're getting married on Christmas Eve," they said together.

Sawyer threw his arms open. "What am I missing, woman?" he said.

"First of all, don't call me 'woman'. Second of all—he's still heartbroken. He scheduled the wedding for Christmas Eve because he's trying to replace the worst night of his life."

"With what he hopes will be the best night of his life," Sawyer said. "With someone else."

"It just goes to show his state of mind," Dani said. "He's not in love with her. He just wants to stop hurting."

"How do you figure that?"

"Why else would he get married on Christmas Eve, the same exact date he proposed to me, unless he was desperately trying to replace me?"

"Why is it you think 'desperately trying to replace you' is something that works in your favor?"

"Because where I come from, marrying out of desperation doesn't scream true love. You saw that woman. Do you really think she wants to be someone's emotional Band-Aid?"

"I think you're taking great liberties with your interpretation," Sawyer said.

"That's because you don't know Nate."

Without discussing it, Sawyer headed into the ice cream shop and Dani followed. The smell of waffle cones baking enveloped them.

"Ice cream is on me," Sawyer said.

"I'm too excited to eat," Dani said.

"It's not eating, it's indulging. You don't have to be hungry to indulge."

"In that case I'll have a triple scoop—coffee, peanut butter, and chocolate, from bottom to top, in a waffle cone, please."

Sawyer stopped and studied her. "You've given this a tremendous amount of thought," he said.

She laughed. "I've been here before," she said.

"You're high maintenance," he said.

"I am not."

"I'm just getting one scoop of chocolate-chip mint in a cup."

"Can you not smell their waffle cones? You're insane," she said. Soon they were standing outside with her high maintenance order and his boring scoop, just as the horse and carriage came in from a tour. They ate their ice cream in silence. Sawyer finished his first and tossed his empty cup in the nearest bin. Dani realized it was going to take her much longer to finish hers, and ice cream was starting to drip down the side. She was trying to figure out how she was going to finish it when Sawyer snatched it from her and took a gigantic bite.

"Hey."

"You're right," he said, diving into it again. "These waffle cones are divine." He tried to hand her back the last few bites. She glared and tossed it into the trash bin behind her. "What's the matter? Afraid I have cooties?" Sawyer stepped so close to her he could have kissed her.

"No," she said. "I know you have cooties."

Sawyer laughed. A few feet away, the horse whinnied. Sawyer turned to it and winked at the horse as if they had been in cahoots. "Is the tour any good?" Sawyer asked.

"Actually it is. Especially at night, at Christmas." Two years ago she should have been on it with Nate. With a diamond ring on her finger. Getting married on Christmas Eve! That was ten days from now. Could she stop a wedding in ten days? Sawyer was right, it was a disaster.

"Do you think it would be wrong to kidnap Nate?" Dani said. "Just until he's in love with me again?"

"I think a night in jail would be a great addition to the feature," Sawyer said. "You might get lucky and get thrown in with a couple of Santas on crack."

"Very funny."

"Just tell him how you feel," Sawyer said. "And this time I'm not talking about Santa."

"What do you mean?" Dani said.

Sawyer stepped uncomfortably close again. He gently placed his hand on the side of her face. "I love you," he said. "Like it or not, and let me tell you, I don't like it— I've loved you from the moment I laid eyes on you, and I don't think I could stop even if I wanted to." Dani could feel the ice cream in her stomach freezing up all over again. Sawyer held eye contact, then smiled and stepped back. "If he's still in love with you, that's all it will take."

Dani prayed to God that Sawyer couldn't see that he'd thrown her off balance. For a heart-stopping second she actually thought *he* was telling *her* that he loved her. It was a good thing that she absolutely hated him, because otherwise that would have been cruel of him.

"Except I wouldn't end my sentence with a preposition," Dani said.

"What?"

"Even if I wanted to. You ended your declaration of love with a preposition."

"It's all about the romance, Ms. Webster. No girl would give a damn if a man said that to them."

"It's not how I would do it at all."

"Oh yeah? How would you do it?"

"Never mind."

"Oh, I mind. Show me."

Dani walked up to Sawyer, and not to be outdone, she put both hands on his face. She gently rubbed her thumbs along his jawline. They were so still she could hear his heart beating. "You're mine," she whispered. "The odds might be against us, and I might be high maintenance, and you might be the most frustrating man I've ever met, but I'm telling you right here, right now. You're mine." Then, she stood on her tiptoes, slid her hands around his neck, and kissed him like he was going off to war. Then, just as she felt his hands start to wrap around her waist, she pulled back and pushed him off. "That's how it's done, cowboy."

"Well played, woman. Throw in a kiss like that and you can end your sentences with a hundred prepositions."

Dani couldn't help but smile. "Don't call me 'woman'."

"Dude. Should I call you dude?"

"My name is Dani."

"Your name is Danielle. Or Bright. I'll just call you Bright."

They had begun to walk again and were standing near

the artificial tree. Dani could hardly bring herself to look at it. "Nate hasn't accepted one phone call from me since that awful night."

"Doesn't that tell you something?"

"Yes! That he's sensitive."

"Or he's moved on," Sawyer said.

"We grew up together. We went steady for three years." Sawyer was laughing, then coughing, trying to cover it up. "What's so funny?"

"Went steady," Sawyer said. "Never heard anyone of our generation use that term."

"You are unbelievably juvenile."

"Oh, I'm sorry. Ma'am. Did he give you his class ring and letter jacket?"

"We were in love!"

"If you say so."

"He was my first."

Sawyer stopped laughing. He put up his hands as if surrendering. "I'm sure, for you, that's hard to get over."

"Not just for me."

"Okay."

"Why? Who was your first?"

"I'm not having this conversation."

"Too late. Who was your first?"

"You really want to know?"

"Yes, I really want to know."

"Mrs. Bentley from across the street." A large grin spread across Sawyer's face and he raised his eyebrows. "Man, she had stamina."

"Disgusting."

"How dare you. It was a beautiful, albeit secret love affair."

"You were what? Fifteen?"

"I was sixteen, thank you very much."

"Disgusting."

"She made the best corn bread I've ever had."

"Is that a euphemism?"

"No. She put jalapeños in it. It was sweet and set my mouth on fire at the same time." He smiled again and arched his eyebrows. For a horrifying second, Dani imagined him kissing his way down her stomach.

"Are you ever serious?"

"Sometimes. And believe me. If I was, you'd know it." He held her gaze, as if trying to tell her something, plant some kind of future seed. Dani headed for the car, not caring whether Sawyer was following or not.

"Why exactly did you say 'no'?" Sawyer asked. He had a very loud voice. Dani turned around.

"What?"

"You turned down Nate's proposal. Why?"

Dani threw her arms open. "Because. I was too young. I wanted to go to New York, try and be a writer."

"And now?"

"Now what?"

"You're only two years older, and you are in New York, and you are a writer."

"And your point is?"

"Do you really want to give all that up and come back here and marry Nate?"

"Why else would I be here?"

"I don't know. Maybe you heard Beth Green jump on your feature, and the competitive shark in you wasn't going to let her have it."

"First of all, there is no shark in me, competitive or otherwise. Second of all—I love Nate. I want him back."

"If you say so."

"Don't say it like that."

"Like what?"

"Like I don't love Nate. Like I don't want him back."

"Fine. I will keep my opinion to myself." Sawyer vocalized the warning ditty from *Jaws*.

"Fine!" She unlocked the car door. Sawyer stayed on the sidewalk. "What opinion?"

"Never mind."

"I want to know."

Sawyer looked away, then back at Dani. "I think if you had truly been in love with Nate, you would have said yes. I think when we're in love, we can't help ourselves. I think you said no because deep down you knew he wasn't the guy for you."

Dani looked out in the distance. She wasn't going to show him how irritated she was with him anymore. Of course that wasn't why she said no to Nate. She'd always known he was the right guy for her, hadn't she? "Hogwash. Hogwash, hogwash, hogwash."

"Well. I guess I can't very well argue with hogwash, hogwash, hogwash."

Sawyer was even more maddening than she'd ever imagined. "Off I go. Figuratively, and literally. Time to go see the folks."

"Hopefully you can squeeze in a nap," Sawyer said with a wink.

"And hopefully you won't sink on your sailboat," Dani said with extra enthusiasm.

"I think I might just have a drink first." God, that sounded good. Not that she wanted to have a drink with Sawyer. But after meeting Anya, finding out that Nate was getting married on Christmas Eve and then moving to London—she certainly wouldn't mind a cocktail or two. Maybe her parents would have eggnog. "What's good around here?"

"It's a college town, so there are bars all over the place—but I think you might like the Duck and Dive." Dani gave him the short walking directions to the bar and then got in her car. It felt weird to leave him here. And then it felt weird that it felt weird.

"I'll call you in a few hours," Dani said. "Mom will probably want to have you over for dinner."

Sawyer tipped an imaginary hat at her and smiled. "Bright," he said.

Chapter 5

Dani pulled up to her parents' house. She half-expected to see them sitting out on the screened-in porch, but the rocking chairs were still. There was a new Lexus in the driveway. Either Santa was early and way generous this year, or they had company. Dani still had her key from the last visit, and she loved the idea of just walking in and surprising them. She opened the door and stepped inside. Voices and laughter filtered in from the kitchen. She had just stepped into the living room when something flew at her. She saw only moving limbs, and long dark hair, and before she knew it powerful hands were squeezing her shoulders and someone was straddling her, and screaming, and punching her with bony fists.

"Intruder, intruder, intruder," the thing on top of her screamed. It had a British accent.

Dani grabbed her wrists and tried to push her away. "I live here!" Dani screamed back.

"Victoria, stop!" a male voice cried out. Soon arms wrapped around Victoria from behind and pulled her kicking and screaming off Dani.

Then a face appeared from behind the writhing girl. A

handsome face. A kind face. A face she hadn't seen in two years. A face she had really, really missed. Dani's eyes immediately welled with tears. "Nate?"

"Dani?" He looked just as shocked as she was.

"Nate?" He was here, in her house. It was her Christmas miracle. The girl stopped wriggling.

"Who is she?" Victoria screeched. Now that she had stopped flailing, Dani could see it was a very pretty teen-aged girl.

"This is Danielle. She lives here. Or at least she used to," Nate said.

"Oh," Victoria said. "How do you do?" Nate let the girl down. She stood over Dani with her hand outstretched. The little beast now wanted to shake hands?

"Give her a minute," Nate said. He gently pushed Victoria out of the way. Soon an older couple entered the room.

"What on earth is all the fuss?" the woman said.

"I thought she was an intruder," Victoria said. "I tackled her."

"Well done," the man said.

"Seriously?" Dani said. Nate held his hand out, and Dani took it. When she was on her feet, she swayed a little. Nate's arm encircled her waist and remained there until she was steady. Then he yanked his arm away as if it had caught fire. That was a good sign, wasn't it? It was him. Her Nate. It took everything in her power not to turn around in his arms and kiss him.

He introduced her to Anya's parents, Margaret and Richard Pennington. Then he crossed his arms and turned to her. "What are you doing here?"

"I came to surprise my parents," she said.

"Oh," Nate said. "They're in California with your sister."

"What?" They didn't tell her they were spending Christmas with Pauline. Then again she'd missed several calls from her mother. She hadn't answered them because she was lousy at keeping secrets, and she didn't want to give her visit away.

"I still don't understand what *you're* doing here," Dani said.

Nate actually turned red. "The Penningtons are renting your parents' house for a few weeks."

"Why?"

"Hotels are slammed."

"In Wilmington? In the winter?"

"There's a big action flick filming for Christmas and the tourism board capitalized on it by offering all these great rates. It's been like the summertime around here lately."

"I was just downtown," Dani said. "It didn't seem crowded."

"Screen Gems is doing a lot of tours during the day. Plus people are going to Airlee Gardens and the beaches. You'll see the cars return in the evening." EUE Screen Gems was one of the largest filming lots east of California. Over 340 films, television series, and commercials had been shot on the fifty-acre lot. It attracted a lot of tourists. And Airlee Gardens held stunning light displays every Christmas. Those two destinations alone were enough to keep most tourists happy. Dani couldn't believe she was just standing here having a normal conversation with Nate about tourists.

"Are you his ex-girlfriend?" Victoria said. "The one who—"

"Victoria, why don't we go into the kitchen and have a nice cup of tea," Mrs. Pennington said.

"I hate tea," Victoria said.

"Come along anyway," Mrs. Pennington said. They were so polite. Dani hated them.

"I'm sorry," Nate said.

A sudden rush of anger and pain enveloped Dani. "You should be," she said. "You haven't spoken to me in two years." Nate glanced toward the kitchen. Dani couldn't help but notice that he was always worried about what other people thought. No wonder he liked Anya. She probably never spoke too loud or impulsively, or even raised her voice. Victoria, on the other hand, broke the mold. Except for giving her a lump on the back of her head, Danielle kind of liked the girl.

Nate threw his arms open. "I had to move forward," he said. "I wasn't ready to deal with the past."

"I know I hurt you, Nate. But I didn't reject you—"

"Oh, you didn't?"

"No. I was just delaying the proposal. Delaying it."

"It doesn't matter, Dani. It all worked out for the best. I actually have some news—"

"Oh, I know all about your news, Nate. And thank you very much for letting me find out through an iPad."

"What?"

"You should have told me before I read about it on-line."

"It was online?"

"Everything is online!"

"I thought your parents would have told you," he said.

Another reason she should have answered her mother's calls. "I can't believe your grandmother is letting you marry a Brit," Dani said. She knew how it sounded, but it was true. Whereas some Southerners were still bitter about the Civil War, or the War of Northern Aggression as they still referred to it in the South, Ruth Hathaway was equally triumphant about the Revolutionary War. To her, it was as if the British had invaded just yesterday. She was not shy about her feelings about those "across the pond." She delved into Revolutionary victories at every occasion.

"She's coming around to the idea," Nate said. Dani tried to hold in a laugh but ended up snorting. "Please, don't."

"You wouldn't move to New York for me—"

"I wasn't ready for such a big change."

"But now you're moving to London."

"Dani."

"Funny. Because you said you were a homebody."

"I meant it at the time."

"So I just wasn't the right girl, then, was I?"

"I really don't want to do this here."

"You don't want to do it at all or you would have faced up to me like a man and picked up the phone and called me."

"Believe it or not, it's because of you that I'm willing to expand my horizons."

"Is that so?"

"Yes. I regretted saying no. I should have at least considered New York."

"Are you serious?"

"Of course."

"Then why didn't you answer my calls, or e-mails, or letters? I tried everything, Nate. Everything. Why didn't you get on a plane and come?"

"Because I spent months planning that proposal, Dani. You don't know the half of it. The entire town pitied me, looked after me as if I was wounded in war. I couldn't just go running back to you after all they did for me—"

Worried about what other people think. Again. Dani knew well enough not to say it. She was already hot under the collar, and getting into things she hadn't meant to get into. And Anya's parents and sister were listening from the kitchen. Tea, her ass; she didn't even hear the kettle. Sawyer's advice tackled her. *Just tell him you love him.*

Dani stepped up, and before she ruined it by thinking it through, she put her hands on the side of his face. "You're mine," she said. She didn't get to finish the rest of it. Nate took her hands off his face and stepped back. He was furious with her.

"I'm getting married on Christmas Eve," he said. He glanced toward the kitchen.

"And I'm the Ghost of Christmas Past. And I'm standing in front of you. And I'm telling you I love you. I'm telling you you're making a mistake. And I'm telling you it's not too late for you and me." Dani hadn't meant to say any of this, let alone sound so desperate, but somewhere inside this man was the Nate she used to know, and more than anything, she just wanted to get a glimpse of him.

"Tea for everyone!" Mrs. Pennington sang as she burst through the door with two cups in her hands. Her mother's best china. Her mother never let anyone touch it. These Brits were ruining everything.

"Wonderful!" Nate said. He practically lunged for the cups.

The door opened. "Toodaloo!" It was Anya. In that moment, Dani could envision Nate's life without her. Instead, this woman would walk in the door every night yelling, "Toodaloo!" They would drink tea, and cuddle, and smooch by the fireplace, and probably eat crumpets. What the heck was a crumpet? And this season they were going to do it in her house with her mother's finest china. Anya swept into the room. She stopped short when she saw Dani. "You," she said. "How did you? I know I said you'd better act fast, but this is a bit far—"

"You've met?" Nate asked.

"Of course. She's here for you," Anya said. "I guess she couldn't wait to see you."

"And you're all right with this?" Nate said. Dani knew she should say something, but her tongue was made of lead.

"I think it's a fabulous idea," Anya said. "She promised me it's going to be a spectacular spread."

Nate choked on his tea. Luckily, Dani had turned hers down. She still couldn't bring herself to touch the china.

"Nate's ex-girlfriend is going to spread what?" Victoria shouted.

"Nate's what?" Anya said. She frowned, looked at Dani again. "You said you were from a magazine," she said.

"I am," Dani said. *The Softer Side.* She turned to Nate. "We're doing a feature on A Southern Christmas and I want to get you and your sculptures into the feature," Dani said.

"That's Nate's ex," Victoria said. "And I tackled her."

"You're Nate's ex?" Anya said. "The one who—"

"Would you like some tea, Anya, love?" Mrs. Pennington said.

We overthrew your tea once before, we can do it again! Dani wanted to shout. "I'd better go," Dani said. Before she scalded them all.

"Why didn't you tell me who you were?" Anya said. She was following right behind Dani.

"I wanted to see Nate first," Dani said. "I'm sure you understand." She'd learned that from Adel. Whenever Adel had to tell someone something that they didn't want to hear, she always added, "I'm sure you understand."

"Where's your handsome sidekick?" Anya asked.

"Who?" Nate said.

"She's traveling with a gentleman friend," Anya said.

"He's just the photographer," Dani said. A little flush of guilt invaded her cheeks. This wasn't Sawyer's fault. She didn't mean to be so dismissive.

"You two must come to the wedding," Anya said. "Mustn't they, Nathaniel?" She turned to Dani, beaming. "It's going to be at his grandmother's house on Christmas Eve."

Dani felt as if she'd been slammed by a pack of reindeer. She could not possibly have heard that right. His grandmother's house? Ruth's home? Dani wanted to cry. She loved Ruth's home. It was *her* favorite house. How could he? She wanted to beat someone. She wondered where Sawyer was.

"I doubt Dani wants to—"

Anya suddenly grabbed Dani's hands. "This is the best thing that could have happened," she said.

"It is?" Dani and Nate said.

"Yes! Time to heal. And because of you, Nate was single again when I came to town. It was meant to be. You're our Christmas angel."

"Please, don't say that," Dani said. "I came here—"

"For the article, right. But you really came to see Nate, didn't you?" Anya said.

"Yes," Dani said.

"To tell him you wish him well. And to see for yourself. No matter how painful it was for the two of you, it was meant to be. Nate has me now. And you must be thrilled that his artwork is being recognized on an international scale now."

"I've always believed in Nate's talent," Dani said.

"Of course you have. I'm sure if you had the connections I do, he would have been a star already."

"Anya," Nate said. "Let's not—"

"He's so down to earth," Anya said. "I love that about him." Anya strode over and stroked his cheek. Nate didn't take her hand away. "Will we see you at the gala? Or as we're calling it—our wedding?"

"I wouldn't miss it," Dani said. *Because it's not going to happen.* "But remember, I want to feature Nate in my article. So of course I was hoping to see a lot of him before that."

"Of course," Anya said. "I think you should."

"I don't think I have the time," Nate said.

"Why? Your grandmother and I have the gala and the wedding all in hand. The exposure will be wonderful, darling."

Darling. Gag, gag, gag, gag, gag.

"Wonderful," Nate said. He looked as if he was going to be ill.

"Take as many pictures of my man as you need to," Anya said. Then, Anya gave Dani a look. It was the equivalent of a school-yard taunt. *Take a picture. It lasts longer.*

"The magazine would love it if I got a picture of a true Southern bride," Dani said. Then she stopped and placed her hand over her mouth as if she couldn't believe that had slipped out. "Sorry," she said. "You're not exactly a Southern bride, are you?"

"I'm sure your little magazine won't care," Anya said. "It's not like anyone has ever even heard of it."

"Anya," Nate said.

"It must be a letdown. You reject the best man on the face of the earth just to make something of yourself in New York—"

"I didn't reject, I just *delayed*—"

"Anya—Dani—"

"And instead Nate stays here and launches his artistic career beyond your imagination while you—what? Write articles for a magazine people use to line their birdcages?"

"Anya, *please*," Nate said.

"It only takes one little article to launch a magazine to the top," Danielle said. "Say a picture of an alligator in a Santa hat, or—hey, here's an idea—a British girl trying to steal a Southern gentleman."

Anya snorted. "As if anyone is actually thinking such a thing. Nobody is stuck hundreds of years in the past!"

"I'm sorry. Have you not met Ruth Hathaway?" Finally, Anya's face let in a bit of emotion. Dani had struck the nail on the head. Ruth Hathaway was as miserable about this upcoming marriage as she was. Every year she still hung lanterns on her porch on the anniversary of Paul Revere's ride. *One if by land, two if by sea.* Dani touched Anya's arm. "Don't you worry about a thing. Ruth loves me. I'll put in a good word for you."

"Would you?" Anya said. "Would you really?"

"Dani," Nate said.

"I mean it," Dani said. "I really want to help."

"I do want Ruth to like me," Anya said.

"She'll grow to love you," Nate said.

"You say that, but I know her blessing would mean so much to you."

"Leave it to me," Dani said. "I'm at your service."

"I'm sorry I said that thing about birds shatting on your magazine." *And I'm sorry if I want to dump all of your par-*

ents' tea into the Cape Fear River. "I really would appreciate it if you'd help me win over Nanna Hathaway," Anya
said.

Nanna Hathaway. Who did she think she was? Dani had
never even called her Nanna. Dani swallowed her anger,
tilted her head, and smiled. "What are Christmas angels
for?"

Chapter 6

Dani called her parents the minute she pulled out of the drive. Her father answered right away. Soon she was on speakerphone. Dani stopped short of telling them that the Penningtons were using the good china. She didn't want her mother to have an attack.

"You should have told us you were coming," her mother said. "We would have stayed."

"I'm sorry. It was spur of the moment, and I thought it would be nice to surprise you," Dani said.

"Hop on a flight now," Pauline said. "It's not healthy for you to be there."

"I'm on assignment," Dani said. Page one: Break up the wedding.

"Darling, it's been two years," her mother said. "I think it's good that you're going to get some closure." She didn't want closure. She wanted Nate back. But she wasn't going to start a fight. Her parents were the ones who had to deal with attitude from the locals after Dani turned down Nate's proposal. She couldn't very well tell them that it had all been a giant mistake. Surely they would be happy for her when she and Nate were officially back together. "What kind of assignment?" her mother asked as if she had just heard the statement. Dani filled them in. "I don't like it," her mother said. "If we left town for Nate's wedding, you certainly shouldn't be there." So that's why they'd left.

"Your mother's right," her father said. "Why don't you cover 'A California Christmas' instead?"

"It wasn't my idea in the first place," Dani said.

"So what was it like seeing Nate again?" Pauline asked.

Like coming home. And finding out the British had invaded all over again. "It went fine," Dani said. "Look—I'd better go find a hotel." Dani didn't want to talk about Nate anymore. Especially when they sounded as if they didn't want her near him. They said their good-byes, but before Dani could hang up there was a *click* and Pauline was on the line.

"You're off speaker," she said. "I'm going into the kitchen."

"I really have to go."

"Don't do it."

"Don't do what?"

"Danielle, you can't fool me. I can hear it in your voice."

"I love him, Paulie. I've never stopped."

"Nonsense. Breaking up with Nate was the best decision you've ever made."

"How can you say that?"

"Because you made something of yourself! You're a staff writer for a magazine in New York City."

"It's not all it's cracked up to be."

"It's a heck of a lot better than what you were before."

"And what was that?"

"Nathaniel Hathaway's shadow."

"I was not." Was she?

"Dani, I don't want to argue. But you were, hon. I was so proud of you when you turned him down. Your entire life would have been wrapped up in a boring little bow."

"But he's changed. He's moving to London."

"He's moving to London for her. He wouldn't even move to New York for you." It wasn't anything Dani hadn't said herself. She'd just thrown that little fact in Nate's face. But it hurt to hear someone else say it. Instinctually she wanted to argue, defend herself and Nate. Sometimes the truth was just cruel.

Sawyer was at the bar, with no less than three women laughing around him. Dani had to drag a stool over, and when one of the women still wouldn't move, Dani had to put her hand on her shoulder. "We're on the clock," she said. "And I need to sit here."

The girl turned a perfect pout on Sawyer. He smiled. "Sorry, darlin'. But I'm sure I'll see you again real soon." The woman laughed, glared at Dani, and then slunk down the bar with the other two women in her wake.

"They're so friendly in the South," Dani said sarcastically as she sat. She raised her hand, and when the young, hipster bartender came over, she ordered a Dark and Stormy. It was dark rum with ginger beer, and a slice of lime. And it packed a punch.

"Why are you back so soon?" Sawyer said.

"Because the British have invaded my parents' house," Dani said. Sawyer raised his eyebrow. Dani filled him in. She skipped the part about begging Nate to take her back and Nate shooting her down cold.

"Nate, your Nate, was in your parents' house."

"Yes."

"I did not see that coming."

"Did you get the sailboat?"

"As a matter of fact, I did. Got lucky, too. Apparently it was already rented to a couple, but the woman was getting seasick."

"Yes, that is some luck. How big is it?"

Sawyer frowned. "Why? Does size matter?" He was so deadpan she had to laugh.

"Because I'm out a place to stay. And yes, it matters."

Sawyer raised a single eyebrow. "I've no problem in that department, ma'am. But you can always try me on for size if you fancy." The drink was making him more tolerable. And funny. She actually laughed again. He grinned in response. "I just assumed you'd be getting a suite at the Hilton."

"Nate said all the hotels were booked. That's why the Penningtons are in my parents' house."

"That's a shame."

"Come on. Is there room for me on the stupid boat or not?"

"Tell you what. Let's see if you can go the next thirty minutes without insulting me, sarcastically or otherwise. Also, no mention of Nate, or Brits. If you can do that, I'll let you stay on the boat."

"Seriously?"

"Seriously."

For a second she was stung. She thought he liked their verbal sparring. But, whatever. She had been kind of cranky. She wondered how small the boat was. Would she be sleeping close to Sawyer? Maybe it wasn't such a good idea. Not that she didn't trust him. She did, actually. His ego was too big to expect anything less than a woman begging him for it. Dani was grateful when the bartender set her drink in front of her. She immediately ordered a second. Sawyer raised his eyebrow again. She'd never noticed before how expressive he was. "He's slow," she whispered. "By the time he makes it, I'll be finished."

Sawyer laughed, and soon Dani felt a rush of warmth, and noticed how soft the lighting was in the bar, and Christmas carols were playing, and more than once women had glanced their way just to check out Sawyer. Dani could see how, if you didn't know him, you'd think he was a catch. And since she didn't want to spend the night in her car, Dani not only didn't argue with him, but by the end of her second drink, she was even flirting a little. "You have a great laugh," Sawyer said.

"Thank you." She felt a sudden rush of embarrassment, as if it wasn't professional to have a nice laugh. Dani was thinking about ordering a third drink, then worried Sawyer would judge her for it, when he beat her to it and ordered a round for them both. Then, they locked eyes. And somehow, Dani forgot to look away. And there it was, undeniable. They had sexual tension. Was he propositioning her? Daring her to let go and sleep with him? It was unbelievably tempting. Her parents weren't here, Nate had shot her down without even a "I'll think about it," she was feeling rather floaty after two drinks, and Sawyer looked damned good in this lighting.

No. Of course not. Of course she couldn't sleep with him. She couldn't, right? "Penny for your thoughts," Sawyer said.

"I was thinking about how I was never going to sleep with you," Dani said. Sawyer choked on his beer. It was worth it just for that. Dani threw her head back and laughed.

"You're messing with me," Sawyer said. "That's not nice."

"You asked, I answered," Dani said.

"You were seriously thinking about sleeping with me?"

"How I *wasn't* going to sleep with you."

"Which meant the first thought had to be about sleeping with me." Sawyer grinned. "You're worried about being on the boat with me. Because you want to sleep with me."

"I was just thinking that you might be thinking about sleeping with me and then I was thinking how it was never going to happen."

"Where there's a will, there's a way," Sawyer said.

"I don't have a will!"

"Never said you did."

"But you just said—"

"I've been thinking about sleeping with you since the first time I laid eyes on you," Sawyer said.

This time it was Dani who almost choked on her drink. She tried to remember the first time he'd laid eyes on her. She'd been late to work that day. Some dirty old man had grabbed her ass on the subway. Then she spilled coffee on her blouse. And the receptionist had handed her messages that were illegible, but she was a young model and Adel was never going to fire her. So the model just stared at her, slightly openmouthed, when Dani tried scolding her about the messages. And then Adel came barging into her office with Sawyer.

"We want you to do a piece on love on the subway," Adel said. Adel never said "story" or "article." Everything was "a piece."

"Perfect," Dani said. "Because some perv grabbed my ass just this morning."

"You can't write about perverts! I'm talking about people falling in love on the subway."

"Have you ever ridden the subway?" Dani blurted out. Adel glowered. And then somebody laughed. A male, with a nice, deep laugh. Dani's head snapped up and that's when she saw him. Sawyer. Hanging in the doorway just behind Adel. He gave her a slow smile. Dani felt her insides lock up, and she couldn't look away.

"Fine," Adel said, in a huff. "I'll give it to someone else."

"We'll do it," Sawyer said. He must have been trying to make up for getting her in trouble. In the end, they didn't find any couples who actually fell in love on the subway, but there were at least twenty women who fantasized about it, and that had been good enough. It actually turned out to be a pretty good article if Dani did say so herself. It certainly didn't hurt to have Sawyer with her. Women opened up to him like lotus flowers. Maybe she should cut him some slack. Maybe if she were showered with so much attention, she'd be obnoxious, too. And maybe, just maybe, he could pull off his magic with Anya. Lure her away, just briefly, from Nate.

"I have an evil plan," Dani said.

"I think the whiskey has an evil plan," Sawyer said. "Are we still talking about hitting the sack?"

"Told you. Not going to happen, Drake." It was the first time she'd used his last name. She kind of liked it.

"What, then? Are you going to steal everyone's Christmas presents from under their trees?" Sawyer asked in a Grinch-like voice, rubbing his hands together.

"Just one," Dani said. "But you're actually the one who is going to do the stealing."

Chapter 7

After three very strong drinks, a walk was in order. Dani always loved looking at the beautiful homes all around the historic district. In her opinion, the best ones were on South Front, and then Third Street. They began on South Front, the street closest to downtown and the river. The houses were mostly from the early 1900s. Victorian and Georgian-style architecture reigned supreme. Front Street had enough land that many of the houses were set up on the hill, away from the sidewalks. Most had rocking chair front porches and upper decks. Some had iron-wrought fences. Many had turrets and were painted in ocean colors: blue-gray, and sea blue, and light aqua. Christmas decorations were classy, and subtle. Hanging wreaths, and lights, and one with a horse and carriage outlined in lights on the lawn. Many of the houses were so large they were being used as bed and breakfasts. Sawyer's camera was constantly clicking.

"I can see why you like it here, Bright," he said. "It's beautiful. Almost frozen in time."

"Why, Sawyer Drake. You sounded somewhat poetic there."

"And you sound surprised."

"You're saying you're a poet?"

"And you didn't even know it."

"Har har."

"Why don't you stand in front of the lion's head over there."

"Me? I'm not supposed to be in the pictures."

"Just do it."

"Now who's grouchy." Dani went and stood in front of a pair of lions' heads flanking an entrance.

"Would it be too much to ask you to look into the camera, and think of something that makes you happy?" Dani stared at the camera. She thought about Nate. "I said *happy*." She thought about her parents, and sister, all the way in California. Sawyer put the camera down. "Are you crying?"

"No." Dani wiped away the tears.

"You leave me no choice," Sawyer said. He crossed his eyes and stuck out his tongue. Dani laughed. He snapped the picture. "From now on—two Dark and Stormy drinks are your limit, Bright."

"Do you have enough for now?"

"Why? Do you want to go back to the sailboat and resist the urge to jump into bed with me?"

"I was thinking I'd like to go to the Italian market and get a latte."

"That'll do," Sawyer said. To Dani's surprise he took her arm and began to walk with her back toward downtown.

"Ice cream, whiskey, and now caffeine," Dani commented.

"The three wise men," Sawyer said. Despite herself, Dani laughed again. Against her better judgment, she had to admit. Sawyer Drake had charm in spades.

The little coffeehouse was right next door to an Italian market. The market had wine, and pastas, and olive oils, and Italian dishes and delicacies. The coffeehouse was homey, with a sofa in the back and tables and chairs by the window. Local photography hung on the walls, and pretty, young college girls worked the register. Dani had always loved sitting right by the window and writing. Her favorite table was just being evacuated, and Dani practically jumped on top of it in order to save it. Sawyer snapped a picture.

"Stop taking my picture," Dani said.

"You're body-surfing a table," Sawyer said. "Impossible not to snap that action." Dani tried to gracefully get off the table, and then began pushing all the used cups to the side. Sawyer shook his head and picked them up. "What can I get you, ma'am?"

"You're buying?" she asked.

"Adel's buying," he said. "I have a company credit card."

"She gave you a company credit card?" Adel never gave Dani a company credit card and she'd been there two years!

"Are you going to get in a huff, or are you going to give me your order?"

"Can't I do both? I'm an excellent multitasker."

"One regular latte coming up."

"No, no, no. I'll have a Pecan Pie Latte with whipped cream and caramel," Dani said.

"Of course you will," Sawyer said. "Do you want that in a waffle cone?"

"Har, har."

"Right back with your high-maintenance order," he said with a wink. Dani sat back, smiling despite herself, and watched as the college girls lit up at the sight of him. Good God. It was like a superpower. So why was she so immune to it? Was it at all possible that the reason she was always so irritated by him was that she wanted to swoon just as much as everyone else, but the very thought so irked her that she pushed him away instead?

Sawyer was right, next time two drinks would be her limit. Nate never irritated her the way Sawyer did. Oh, Nate irritated her plenty, but not in a way that made her squirm. Nate exasperated her. Especially how stubborn he was about staying in Wilmington the rest of his life. And now look at him. London of all places. She just couldn't picture it. He'd told her it was partly because of her that he was going. Because he regretted losing her to New York. So now he was going to London because he was afraid of losing Anya. Fear wasn't a good reason to get married and move across the pond. She was doing him a favor by trying to break up this wedding.

Sawyer was just returning with their drinks—more whipped cream than Dani had ever been given—when a petite woman with white hair styled in a bob walked in. Dani immediately leapt to her feet, sloshing her latte on her top. Sawyer was instantly dabbing a napkin on her chest. His fingers accidentally grazed her breast, sending a tingle all the way down to Dani's toes. She grabbed the napkin from him and stepped back.

"Sorry," he said. He seemed just as stunned.

"Mrs. Hathaway," Dani called. The woman stopped. For several minutes she stood in the middle of the coffee-house, her back to Dani. Finally, she slowly turned around.

"Danielle," Ruth Hathaway said. Dani couldn't read anything in her tone.

"Merry Christmas," Dani said. She stepped forward, then looked down at her blouse. Ruth had only hugged her once, anyway, the morning of that horrific Christmas Eve. And that was only because she thought Dani was about to become her grand-daughter-in-law. Ruth Hathaway's gaze fell on Sawyer.

"He's a colleague," Dani said. "A photographer." Sawyer smiled at Ruth Hathaway and stuck out his hand.

"Ma'am," he said. Ruth Hathaway glanced at his hand, and then pulled hers in protectively against her stomach.

"It's the cold season," she said. "I don't shake hands during the cold season."

"My apologies. I don't blame you at all." Sawyer grinned. Ruth pursed her lips. Was she always such a snob? Danielle wondered. Probably. Dani had just never seen her through that lens.

"Are you here to apologize to Nathaniel?" Ruth asked Danielle.

"Mrs. Hathaway—"

"Oh, call me Ruth."

Call her Ruth? That was odd. "Ruth. I've been apologizing to Nate for the past two years. I've written. I've called. He's never responded to a single attempt."

"He's always been sensitive. And what a fuss he went to that evening. It was an absolutely mortifying experience for him."

"I know. I can't tell you how sorry I am."

Ruth put her hand up, then brushed a stray hair off her cheek and placed her hands back against her stomach. "That's the past, Danielle. I'm quite sure you've heard of his plans for the future?"

"Yes." Here it came. Ruth was going to forbid Dani from coming anywhere near Nate until he was married.

"And I assume you're as displeased as I am?"

Danielle's head snapped up. Ruth stared at her intently. "Yes," Dani said. "Yes, I am."

"And if you had the chance, a little Christmas miracle—tell me, Danielle. You wouldn't dare hurt my Nathaniel again, would you?"

"No. No, I wouldn't. Of course not. But he—"

"And would you drop all this New York nonsense and settle down here with Nate, where you both belong?"

"Yes. Yes, I would."

"Very well, then. What are we going to do to run off these British imperialists?"

* * *

"What are we going to do to run off these British imperialists?" Sawyer said. It was in perfect imitation of Ruth Hathaway. They were sitting in the lower cabin of the sailboat. It was large enough for two small sofas facing each other and a small kitchen. Danielle had to laugh when Sawyer did his imitation, he even had the facial expression—pursed lips, drawn cheekbones, raised eyebrow—down to a tee.

"You have to cut her some slack," Dani said after she'd finished laughing. "Her family has deep roots here. To her the American Revolution was yesterday."

"So I assume their family kept slaves, as well?"

"Ouch."

"It's an honest question."

"She doesn't speak of it, but there are plantations in her family, so of course they did."

"Grim."

"Indeed. Wilmington is part of the South when it comes to that. But the town does its best to own up to their history. The Bellamy Mansion, and the Latimer House, and Burgwin-Wright House, all talk about slavery on their tours, as well as give tours of the slave quarters."

"Can't wait."

"I think it's important to remember."

"Of course. It's also important to recognize every time we are prejudiced against someone, no matter who, we are backsliding into the mentality of our horrific past."

"I agree a hundred—wait a minute. Are you talking about Anya?"

"Do you think it's fair that Ruth Hathaway is judging the poor girl just because she's British?"

Danielle just looked at him. "I'm sure there's a lot more wrong with her than that."

"Oh, you are, are you? Based on what? The fact that

she's helped his career? Encouraged him to move outside his comfort zone?"

"Encouraged him? He's moving to London out of fear."

"You don't know that."

"He told me! He told me it was because of me that he was moving. He said he regretted not moving to New York City to be with me and he doesn't want to make the same mistake with her."

"I see."

"What do you see?"

"What's next on our list of things to shoot?"

Danielle didn't know why Sawyer suddenly put the brakes on their conversation about Nate, but she didn't understand men in general and she wasn't going to belabor it. "We can go to Airlee Gardens tonight."

"Great. I'm going to take a nap. Wake me when it's dark." The sailboat had two bedrooms: one to the right of the living room, and the other on the opposite side past the kitchen and the bathroom.

Danielle stood as Sawyer made a move to the smaller bedroom. "Wait. What did I say?"

"Nothing. I need a nap. And if you don't mind, I didn't exactly come here to discuss Nate Hathaway ad nauseam."

"Our assignment is to see if I can get him back."

"Our assignment is 'A Southern Christmas'."

"You think I should be nicer to Anya, is that it?"

Sawyer didn't answer. He disappeared into the bedroom and slid the door shut. Danielle was too wound up to sleep. She went up to the deck with her cell phone. The water was calm, and in the distance lights twinkled on the Cape Fear Memorial Bridge. The USS *North Carolina* was stark against the afternoon sky. Danielle took a deep breath and called Nate. His voice mail kicked on. Was he screening?

"Nate. Hi, it's Danielle. I was wondering if you and

Anya would like to meet me at Airlee Gardens this evening. We have to do a shoot for the magazine and so I can get us in free. I thought it might be nice to get to know Anya. I think featuring not only your artwork in the magazine but your wedding, as well, would be great for our feature. I ran into your grandmother today and she was thrilled with the idea—" His phone cut her off. There, she'd done it. Invited him. And lied to him about his grandmother.

Sawyer was right about one thing. Dani hated Anya just because she loved and was marrying Nate. She had no idea whether or not Anya was a good person. Maybe if she had met her without knowing who she was, she would have assumed she was a good person until proven otherwise. But why did Sawyer have to be so judgmental himself? Wasn't all fair in love and war? Wasn't Dani at war? So in a way, she was doing a feature on The War on Christmas anyway. Except hers was personal. Didn't this woman realize that Nate had suggested they marry on Christmas Eve because he was terrified of another woman rejecting him on the same date? Didn't that tell her something about Nate's state of mind? And if Dani and Nate were meant to be together, wasn't she actually doing Anya a big favor even if she didn't see it that way? And why, if she was so in love with Nate, was Dani picturing Sawyer Drake all by himself in that little bed, behind a door that would be so easy to slide open?

Chapter 8

Danielle had grown up a bit of a local history buff. She kept an extensive diary with research of local places. Airlee Gardens had been no exception. On the drive there, she filled Sawyer in on the origins of the public gardens. It was, as were most of her favorite historical stories, a love story at heart.

Because Wilmington wouldn't have Airlee Gardens if it weren't for Sarah Green and Pembroke Jones falling in love. The year was 1884. Pembroke was the son of a captain, and Sarah grew up on a vineyard north of Fayetteville. Prior to the wedding, Sarah purchased the fifty-two-acre Seaside Park Improvement Company for $5,000. Later, she would acquire the adjoining land, bringing it up to 155 acres. Pembroke named it Airlee in honor of family in Scotland, and Sarah called it Airlee-on-the-Sound. On the site they built a mansion boasting hardwood floors, arched ceilings, and a myriad of windows. They also enjoyed a covered tennis court, a ballroom, a banquet hall, and thirty-eight guest apartments. The gardens surrounded the house. Sarah had visions for the gardens that couldn't be satisfied by just anyone. She hired a German kaiser's gardener, Rudolph Topel, to bring life to the garden of her dreams.

"Rudolph," Sawyer interrupted. "That's very Christmas-y."

"Funny," Danielle said. "But truth be known, Sarah and Pembroke loved to entertain. They were a bit like the Gatsbys, holding one extravaganza after another, flaunting their Southern hospitality. Once their guests arrived on a special train of trolley cars. Chefs came from the North, entire orchestras were hired to entertain, and get this—party favors were gold watches for the men, and diamond jewelry for the women." Danielle sighed.

"You so want to go back in time and be at one of those parties, don't you?" Sawyer said.

"Oh God. I so do," Dani said. "You have no idea. They once built a spiral staircase on the grounds leading up to picnic platforms erected in the oak trees. Once up there the guests would find the tables adorned in white linen tablecloths and real silverware."

"Fancy," Sawyer said. They had pulled into the grounds now, waved on by kids wielding glowing orange sticks.

"It was even rumored that on some of the hunts—they dressed squirrels up in little red jackets. Squirrels!"

"I would definitely post that on my Facebook page."

"And the holidays? They would burn barrels of tar just for the glow, and line the drive with Japanese lanterns. If I close my eyes I can hear laughter and singing, and watch as carriages come and go with the guests. It's rumored that they were the original 'Joneses' behind the saying 'Keeping up with the Joneses'."

"You are full of fun facts this evening, Bright," Sawyer said. "Are we getting out of the car?"

"Not until I finish my story. Your photographs will be richer if you know the history of the grounds."

"Yes, ma'am."

"While partying is one thing, Sarah's real love was for the gardens. One day, while walking through the woods, she discovered a clump of azaleas. She had the gardeners transplant them near the house. The main garden consisted of magnolias, azaleas, camellias, and wisteria. They also planted 500 live oaks, 1,200 longleaf pines, 5,000 camellias, and a quarter million azaleas."

"That is a boatload of azaleas," Sawyer said.

"The land is surrounded by Bradley Creek, a lake reclaimed from a salt lagoon, and marshes. Some of the oaks are now 467 years old." Sawyer whistled. "Some of them reach fifty feet high, and their canopies spread 100 feet."

"You're pretty passionate about this place," Sawyer said.

"I'm passionate about the history of a place, or people," Dani said. "You were right, earlier. I have been hard on Anya. But Nate and I—we have a history. I can't let Anya shatter that."

"By definition, darling, history is in the past. It would be like Sarah coming back to life and demanding her gardens back this instant."

"If that woman came back to life right now, I think we'd be smart to give her anything she wanted."

Sawyer roared with laughter. That made Danielle laugh, too. It felt good.

"You're the Ghost of Christmas Past," Sawyer said.

"Technically, yes. But what if I'm also the Ghost of Christmas Future?"

"What if you stop being a ghost and just live your life?"

"Because Anya has my life!"

"That's where you have a screw loose. Anya has her life. With Nate."

"I want a future with Nate. The one I always knew we'd have."

Sawyer must have given up on his lecture for he turned and looked out the window instead of throwing any more wisdom her way. "Is the mansion still here?"

"Unfortunately, no. The Corbett family bought the property next and dismantled it when it became too much for them. They built their own house, but sold sixty-seven acres to New Hanover County. And that's when Airlee Gardens came to be." Sawyer clapped. Dani gave a half bow from the car seat. "And at Christmastime a light show transforms it into Enchanted Airlee. You'll soon see why." Dani couldn't help but smile.

Sawyer smiled back and shook his head. "You're lit up yourself, darling. And this time it's not from rum and whiskey."

"I just—used to love Christmas so much. It's been a while since I could enjoy it again."

"That's a shame. Joy suits you."

"It's magical here."

"You can say that again."

Dani could feel it, that heat between them again as he stared at her. She looked away and started to get out of the car. Sawyer hurried around, opened her car door, and offered her his arm.

"Aren't you the gentleman?" Dani said.

"All this talk about the past. Makes a fellow want to bring back chivalry."

They headed for the entrance. "It's just hard for me to come here without imagining Sarah strolling the grounds."

"I wonder if any of the guests accidentally dropped their gold watches or diamonds on the lawns," Sawyer said.

"Now you're thinking," Dani said. "Keep your eyes peeled, Mr. Chivalry."

Enchanted, Airlee-on-the-Sound certainly was. Every tree was adorned with lights. The giant oaks had white streamers, appearing and disappearing among the branches like fireworks. Archways of lights formed tunnels to walk through, and entire fields beckoned with trees sparkling in every color. Lights formed flowers on the grounds. The grape arbor was dazzling. Look to your left, there was Santa and his sleigh. To the right, towering palm trees were aglow. Every path led to a new excitement. In the distance was a barge, with seven swans pulling a sleigh. Christmas carols played from speakers hidden about the place. Dani was thrilled when they came upon giant flip-flops and sunglasses all lit up on the ground.

"Now this is very Southern," Sawyer said as his camera snapped.

"Don't forget the palm trees, and the crabs," Dani called.

"Crabs?" Sawyer said.

Dani laughed and pointed to a light display of crabs crawling around wooden crates. "All I got for Christmas is crabs!" she said.

Sawyer laughed, snapping and flashing his camera nonstop. In almost every one, he insisted Dani get in for a photo. Sometimes she could tell he was taking her picture on the sly. She wondered if he did this with all the staff writers. She had a feeling he didn't. She had a feeling that he had feelings for her. She didn't know what to think about that, and she hated to admit how good it felt to know that someone, someone very, very attractive, had a little crush on her. She liked him. All that sparring between them had been because of her. Because she didn't want to admit that she had a little crush on him, too. But she wasn't going to let a little crush determine her future. Besides, they called it a *crush* for a reason. She wasn't going to hurt anyone else like she hurt Nate. She was here to make up for all of that. When Sawyer was done taking her thumbs-up next to the crabs, he pointed to a white tent set up on their left. "I can take your picture sitting on Santa's lap."

"Oh my God," Dani said. She grabbed Sawyer's hand.

"I was kidding but if you're that excited about it, let's get in line." He squeezed her hand gently.

Dani pulled away and pointed. "It's Nate," she said. He

stood just a few feet away under a pine tree that looked as if it were on fire with crystals. He was sandwiched in between Anya and Ruth.

"Let the games begin," Sawyer said under his breath.

"No," Dani said. "I'm going to be nice. Just like I promised you."

"Does that mean you're no longer going to try to snatch him away?"

"I'm going to trust in fate," Dani said. "I'm going to believe in Christmas miracles."

"What if you're granted one but you don't recognize it?" Sawyer said. And there it was, written all over his face, an explicit acknowledgment. He was hers for the taking. And with the lights glittering all around them, the warm breeze, the Christmas carols playing—she was tempted. Tempted to bridge the small gap between them and just see what it would be like to kiss him. Not like the kiss she gave him in front of the ice cream shop, but a real kiss. One where she would let him kiss her back. There was probably mistletoe hanging above their heads anyway. Dani glanced up, just to see if she was right, but Sawyer's eyes remained on her. "We don't need it," he said as if he knew exactly what she was thinking. Instead, she turned away.

"Come on," she said. "You won't get more Southern than Ruth Hathaway. We should feature her in some of the photos." Dani took off across the lawn before he could confuse her any more.

Nate looked so handsome in a black leather jacket and maroon dress shirt. Where were his T-shirts and jeans? He used to dress more like Sawyer. Anya was dressed up, too. Dani imagined she never wore jeans or sweatpants. She was more like Ruth than even Ruth would ever want to admit.

"Well, hello, there," Dani said. "I'm so glad you could make it." Dani made note of the fact that Ruth was standing in between Nate and Anya, preventing them from touching.

"Darling," Ruth said, uncharacteristically cheerful. She broke out of line to hug and kiss Dani on each cheek. It was something the woman had never, ever done previously.

"Hello, Nate," Dani said as their eyes met. "Anya," she said quickly, so as not to seem rude. It was so strange, so wrong! How many times had Dani come to Enchanted Air-lee with Nate? Since they were kids. Maybe just being here together would bring back all those wonderful memories. "Isn't this the most beautiful place you've ever seen?" Dani said to Anya.

Anya looked at Dani. "It's lovely," she said. There was a lot of hesitation in her voice. "Very . . . quaint."

Nate laughed. "Anya finds Wilmington a bit underrated compared to London," he said. "You must feel the same way about New York?"

"Actually, she doesn't," Sawyer said. Dani jumped. Shoot. How rude. She'd forgotten all about Sawyer for a moment. Was that the definition of insanity? Plotting to kiss someone one moment, forgetting he existed the next?

"How's that?" Nate said. Dani had to admit, she loved watching Nate take in Sawyer. Was he jealous?

"Dani hasn't stopped gushing about this little town since she arrived. Give it time, Anya, a few minutes in this girl's presence, and you'll see it through magical eyes." Sawyer held eye contact with Anya, treating her to his best, seductive grin. Nate frowned. Nope, he definitely didn't like Sawyer. Was he jealous because Sawyer was with her, or because he was flirting with Anya? Sawyer was certainly taking his role seriously, laying it on thick. Dani didn't like how his eyes seemed to twinkle when he looked at the Brit. Then again, it could have been from all the lights.

"Nate, I'd like you to meet our talented staff photographer, Sawyer Drake," Dani said.

"You think I'm talented?" Sawyer said. He turned his charm on Ruth. "First I've heard her say it, ma'am," he said.

Ruth Hathaway let out a startling sound. If Dani wasn't in her right mind, she would say that Sawyer had just made the matriarch laugh. Soon, Anya joined in. Nate's and Dani's eyes met. There he was. Her Nate. Dani gave a little smile. Nate smiled back.

"I need a couple of models for my photo shoot," Sawyer said, offering each woman an arm. "Would you mind?"

To Dani's astonishment, Ruth took his arm right away. "Come along, my dear," Ruth said to Anya.

Anya flashed Nate a look. He smiled at her and nodded. "Very well," Anya said. "Lead the way." Sawyer didn't even glance at Dani as he guided the two women toward the grape arbor. And just like that, Dani was alone with Nate.

"Shall we?" Nate said. He began to walk toward the marsh. *He wants me alone,* Dani thought. *Away from prying eyes.* She followed with her heart thumping in her chest, resisting the urge to turn and see what Sawyer was up to.

"Remember when we were kids and we would hide behind the trees?" Dani said.

"We were convinced they would never find us," Nate said.

"But they always did."

"He's a character," Nate said.

"Sawyer?"

"Nanna seems smitten."

"He does have a way with the ladies."

"Does that include you?" Nate stopped abruptly and turned around. Dani almost ran into him.

"What exactly are you asking?"

"You told me you loved me. That you wanted me back."

"I do."

"Yet you're here with another man?"

"We work together," Dani said. "That's all." Oh no. Why

was her voice cracking? It wasn't her fault that Sawyer was so good-looking. Dani held her breath. Didn't it mean something that he was jealous? Finally, Nate gave a nod, then continued walking. They stopped at the creek and looked out at the sailboats in the distance. Ghost trees towered just behind them, their stark branches backlit by the lights from the grounds. A twenty-foot pier jutted out along the creek. Nate continued to lead Dani away from the crowds. Her stomach was in knots as she watched his broad shoulders. He looked good all dressed up. Toward the end of the pier he stood and put his hands on the railing. So many memories of Nate. She always thought they would have time. To work things out. At least a second chance.

"You've really messed me up, coming here," Nate said quietly. Tears sprung instantly to Dani's eyes. He still had feelings for her. There was still a chance.

"I'm not here to cause trouble," Dani said carefully.

Nate turned his beautiful green eyes on her. "It wasn't easy for me to actively ignore all your calls, and texts, and letters," he said. "And I didn't do that to hurt you, either. But you ended it, Danielle. You ended us."

"I postponed us."

"I didn't see it that way. Heck. The whole town didn't see it that way."

"I know. I know and I'm sorry."

"I'm not the same man I was two years ago."

I know, she wanted to shout. You're more like the man I wanted. The man willing to leave Wilmington for love. "I had to try. Before it was too late. I had to tell you that I still love you. If I could take that night back—I would have said yes. I would have stayed here and—"

"And what, Dani? Write articles for *Star News* or *Encore*?"

"Sure. Why not?"

"Because you're too good. Not that our local papers aren't good. But you deserve a much bigger audience."

"What?"

"Your articles. They're very, very good."

Dani hadn't expected this. It made sense, of course it did, that Nate would read her articles. But somehow, because of the walls he'd put between them, she just assumed he hadn't even thought of her, let alone read her articles. "You read them?"

"Of course."

"It's kind of just a fluff magazine—"

"But your work isn't. I can tell you're pushing the limits as much as they'll let you. I really liked the piece on the homeless vet and his dog."

Perry, and Boots. She was proud of that one. She wrote about how that dog was a better human being than most of the people who stepped around them. The dog loved unconditionally, without judgment. Sawyer was with her on that one. His pictures were absolutely beautiful. They captured the humanity of a man and his best friend, sticking it out on the streets. "I can't take all the credit," she said.

"The photo," Nate acknowledged. "That was his?" Dani nodded. "You always did like the artistic type," he said.

"I told you. There's nothing going on between me and Sawyer."

"It's none of my business."

"Nate. I can't tell you how happy I am that your art is taking off. Anya was right about one thing. I would never do anything to stand in the way of that."

"I know you tried to tell me I needed to go somewhere with a bigger audience," Nate said. "I guess part of me thought you were just biased."

"But Anya was different," Dani said. "Because she's an art curator."

"We didn't start out romantic, of course. It was a fluke she was even here. They were filming a period piece and they needed her expertise with the artwork featured in it. She happened upon me on the beach, believe it or not."

"Building one of your sculptures," Dani said. Oh, she could believe it. She could picture it.

"I really threw myself into my work after you left. To be honest, some of what I was doing was quite dark. I guess women go for that kind of thing." He laughed. Dani laughed along with him, and they continued laughing until they looked at each other and it came to a dead stop. A sense of shame invaded her. Just a few minutes ago she had been thinking about kissing Sawyer. Now she wanted to kiss Nate. She was too deprived of affection. She'd better not sit on Santa's lap. What was wrong with her?

She knew exactly what it was like to kiss Nate. He was a little hesitant, a little polite, but not at all a bad kisser. Why, he had to be good. They had done it many, many times. Why couldn't she do it right now? Why did this woman, who had only known her Nate—what?—a year? Less? Why did she get to claim the boy Dani had loved her entire life? Why couldn't she just take a few steps forward, put her arms around his neck, and pull him in for a kiss?

Nate looked for a moment as if he might not resist it. Then, he suddenly looked up, and Dani heard laughter.

"There you are," Anya sang out. Sawyer and Ruth were at the far end of the pier, but Anya was running toward them at a sprint. It was as if she knew another woman had been about to kiss her fiancé. Anya grabbed Nate's hand. "Come. Let's have a photo in front of the swans." She began to pull Nate along the pier. Dani didn't realize she was holding her breath until Nate looked back. She waited to feel that spark. A rush of warmth, anything, as Anya pulled him away. She held a smile until she felt someone concentrating on her. She looked up to see Sawyer watching her. He didn't look happy. And it made her feel ashamed. And then angry. This was her life. Her future at stake.

"If you can't say anything nice—"

Sawyer nodded, mimed zipping his lips shut, then took a mock bow. Dani huffed past him. She'd never met someone so infuriating in her entire life. Just when she thought she was out of reach, Sawyer grabbed her arm and swung her around. She slammed into his chest, and before she could think, let alone talk, his lips were crushed on hers, and he was kissing her so hard he took all her breath away. An intense hunger ripped through her, and Danielle began to press harder against Sawyer and really kiss him back. Just as suddenly as he started it, he stopped. He stepped back and gently pushed her away as if she had made an unwanted advance on him.

"What was that?" she said, trying to sound offended, even though inside she was reeling. She had no idea a kiss could literally make her dizzy.

"The Ghost of Christmas Present," he said. "Just thought you two should meet. Before you do something incredibly stupid. Something you can never take back." There it was again, that intense look, almost a warning. *I like you. I'm right here. But if you go after Nate too hard, you're going to lose me.*

"Fine," Danielle said.

"Fine," Sawyer said.

This time he let Danielle stalk away. She just prayed it wasn't obvious as she tried to walk a straight line that she was shaking. Absolutely vibrating from head to toe.

Chapter 9

"A sailboat? Nonsense," Ruth said. "You'll stay with me."
They were standing by their prospective cars outside Airlee
Gardens. It felt odd to Dani that she would be getting into a
rental car and driving herself back to a sailboat instead of getting in Ruth Hathaway's Mercedes with Nate. Ruth, to everyone's surprise, loved to drive. She was putting on her black
driving gloves as she spoke. She never got in her car without them. Nate would be in the passenger seat with Anya
all alone in the back. That used to be Dani's place. And it
used to drive her crazy. She and Nate used to get in little ar-
guments about it. *Why can't you sit in the back with me?*

*Because then my grandmother would feel like a chauf-
feur!*

But I feel like a child with my parents riding up front!
She wondered if Anya minded. For once it was nice to note
something that she didn't have to put up with anymore.
And not only that—she couldn't get her mind off Sawyer
and that kiss. And how she wanted to do it again. Strictly as
a point of research. She'd never had a kiss that electric. Her
curious mind wanted to know if it would happen again. She
just wanted to see whether or not it was a fluke.

"Did you hear me?" Ruth said to Dani. "You're staying with me."

"But you said the guest rooms were getting made over, Nanna," Nate said to his grandmother.

"I did?"

"And that's why Anya's parents couldn't stay with you?" Nate gazed intently at her.

"Oh yes. I did." She turned to Anya with an apologetic smile. It looked extremely pained.

The reporter in Dani kicked in as she watched the exchange, fascinated. Ruth had turned away Anya's parents. She suddenly felt ashamed for using the British stuff against Anya. Sawyer was right. It was prejudice, plain and simple. And Dani couldn't remember Nate ever correcting his grandmother. He didn't want Anya's feelings to be hurt, and he was taking Anya's side. Dani waited for the hurt to come. Strangely, it didn't. She was actually kind of proud of Nate. "It's all right," Dani piped up. "The sailboat is kind of nice. And large. It has several very separate bedrooms." She glanced at Sawyer. He gave her a sarcastic thumbs-up.

"Grandmother's right. It's not appropriate—" Nate started to say.

"Appropriate?" Dani said. "In what way?"

Nate glanced at Sawyer, then looked away. "I can try to find another place for Anya's parents so you can have your house back," he said.

"But they checked into every option," Anya said. "And they're settled in the house."

Dani put her hand on Anya's arm. "Of course they are," she said. She turned to Nate. "I'm telling you, I'm fine on the boat." Nate didn't get to marry Anya *and* get jealous over Dani!

Ruth stepped in again. Apparently, she didn't like Dani with Sawyer, either. "It's just that I think the maintenance on the rooms may be finished. I didn't have the room ready for a couple, but I think I can squeeze in little Danielle.

Why she takes up no space at all. And she's hardly a guest, she's more like family." Ruth held her arms toward Dani as if she was going to rush into them.

"Actually. Staying on a boat is part of the article," Dani said. "It offers a unique perspective."

"She is very dedicated to her work," Sawyer said without missing a beat. "A true professional."

"Well, I'd love to see this sailboat," Anya said. "Maybe the four of us could have a nightcap and you could give us the tour? Unless you'd like to come along, Mrs. Hathaway?"

"Don't be silly. You young people have fun. I'm sure Nate and Danielle have a lot of catching up to do." Ruth's gaze slid from Nate to Dani and back again. All that was missing was the bat of her eyelashes.

"Good night, Nanna." Nate kissed her on each cheek.

"Danielle, will you and Sawyer be joining Nate and Anya tomorrow night for 'A Stroll Through Christmas Past'?" Ruth called out before getting into her car.

"Oh, we wouldn't miss it," Dani said.

"That's wonderful. I've volunteered as one of the tour guides."

"That's perfect," Dani said. That was the tour where Ruth always got worked up about how the "English Invaders" had "almost destroyed Wilmington." How would Anya react to that? Dani couldn't wait to find out. She forced herself to stop smiling.

"We're entertaining now?" Sawyer whispered to her as Nate and Anya got in the back of the rental car.

"It's the South," Dani said. "Get used to it."

They stopped at a market and bought a couple of bottles of wine. Nate got out his wallet to pay and then Sawyer stepped up to the plate and the two of them argued about who would pay until Sawyer bought another two bottles. Were they fighting to impress Dani, or Anya? Dani knew it was childish, but she so hoped they were fighting over her.

"We're going to get absolutely blotto," Anya said. Her eyes lit up and she clapped her hands. Danielle peered at her to see if she was joking. Miss Prim and Proper get blotto? So much for it being a shotgun wedding. Maybe Dani had judged her a little too hastily.

Nate was right, the cars were back and it was difficult to find parking. Dani finally had to settle for several blocks away. They walked toward the river. Sawyer and Nate were having what appeared to be a discussion ahead of them, and Anya and Dani strolled pleasantly behind. It was as if they were on a double date. Many of the little boutiques were lit up, staying open later to catch holiday shoppers, and lights glowed from within restaurants. Dani loved all the little decorations: wreaths on street lamps, Christmas trees in store windows, and even a red plume on the horse pulling the carriage. And for a few seconds, it felt normal. That Anya was with Nate, and Dani was with Sawyer. *I like Sawyer,* Dani thought to herself, trying it out. *I'm with Sawyer.*

"What are you getting Nate for Christmas?" Dani asked. She was curious. She had always bought Nate a T-shirt and a CD. Last Christmas she planned on greeting him in a sexy little Santa outfit, with a copy of the Kama Sutra. That probably would have been a disaster. Sawyer, on the other hand, would have loved the gift. Immediately she saw herself on the sailboat with Sawyer. In the Santa outfit. A red lace bra and thong, and a Santa hat. And the red heels, don't forget those. She imagined Sawyer sitting on the sofa. She, standing in front of him, hands on hips. His grin would light up the block. But every time she wondered what Nate would have thought of the gift, she couldn't picture it. She could only see him grabbing a blanket from the sofa and covering her up.

Making love with Nate had been nice, very nice, but even though she didn't have the field experience to back it up, Dani was worried that their lovemaking was not as passionate as it should be. Nate was so . . . quiet. And quick. He had a beautiful body and she loved touching him, and kissing him, but more often than not, he seemed to think it was something best to get over with, like brushing your teeth. And, she hated admitting this, but Nate had poor circulation. So his hands and even lips were always cold. Sometimes it was like kissing an ice cube. Which might have been nice if he had liked exploring her body with it, but he was rather shy in that department, too. Everything they did was so—clean. And she'd been too young to tell him how she really wished it would go. That she wanted clothes torn, and hearts hammering, and sheets sweaty. That she wanted to scream out, and thrash about, and maybe even do it more than once in one evening. That she wanted him to hunger for her. That she wanted to see a certain look in his eye—

Oh. The look Sawyer could give her from across a room. She liked that. Even if she got back together with Nate this evening, there would be times, for sure, that she would close her eyes and imagine Sawyer giving her that look. Just to remember what it felt like, knowing someone desired you so much that one lingering look from him could raise your body temperature to a feverish degree.

That couldn't have been why she turned down Nate's marriage proposal, could it? Oh God. Was she secretly some kind of sex maniac? Nate was the only lover she'd ever had. There were opportunities in New York, of course, loads of them. But she had always felt as if she'd be cheating on Nate. Even when he wasn't speaking to her. She felt ashamed and deathly curious to know what Anya and Nate's sex life was like. She couldn't imagine Nate any other way than he was with her. Maybe Anya liked it quiet and quick. Keep Calm and Carry On.

"Come on." Anya grabbed Danielle's hand. "I have to

show you," she said. She threw her arms up in the air and
waved at Nate and Sawyer even though they were way
ahead of them. "Oh lads!"

Sawyer glanced back, caught Dani's eye, and smiled. And
Nate's eyes sought out Anya's. Dani smiled back at Sawyer. *I like you,* she said silently. *Okay?* This was crazy.
Was it just the Christmas wreaths and the gentle glow coming from the restaurants that was giving her a sense of
buoyancy? How was it that she didn't feel jealous of Nate
and Anya?

"I'm taking Danielle on a little detour. We'll see you
lads back at the boat."

"All right," Nate said.

Sawyer caught Dani's eye again. "Be nice," he said.

"Yes, Santa," Dani said. *Although something about you
makes me want to be very, very naughty.*

Danielle and Anya stood in Nate's studio. They were in
the back room standing in front of an easel. A white sheet
covered something propped on the easel. Anya whipped it
off. It was a sixteen-by-twenty framed photograph. Anya on
the beach. The wind was slightly blowing her hair back. Her
head was tilted, her eyes sparkling, and her mouth open in a
smile. She was holding a starfish across her engagement finger.

"Wow," Danielle said. Was this girl in love with herself
or what?

"This was me a few moments after Nate proposed and I
said yes," Anya said. "He said this was the happiest moment of his life."

"Oh," Danielle said. "Wow." There was a giant lump in
her throat. Instantly, she was back on the boardwalk, begging Nate to tie his shoe, pretend he wasn't kneeling on the
ground to ask her hand in marriage. What was she doing?
She didn't deserve a second chance.

"You must think I've gone mad," Anya said.

"No. It's lovely. Nate will love it. I'm sure of it."

Anya grasped Dani's hand. "I hope so. I can't wait until our flat is filled with photos of the two of us. That's how you know you're a couple, isn't it? When the mantel is filled with lovely photos?"

All these years with Nate and Dani suddenly couldn't remember them in any photos together. Not romantic ones anyway. There were group photos, Nate and Dani at the galas throughout the years, things like that. Nothing Dani would want to frame and put on a fireplace.

"Sawyer is an excellent photographer," Anya said. "Does he only do commercial work, or does he have an artistic bent, as well?"

"I don't know," Dani said. "He's never mentioned it."

"And you've never asked?"

Although Anya's tone was genuinely curious, Dani suddenly felt like such a rotten person. She had been totally self-absorbed. She didn't know much about Sawyer at all. Except that he was sarcastic, and frustrating, and sexy, and a hell of a kisser.

"We'd better head back," Dani said.

"Do you want to see my wedding gown?" Anya asked. She pointed at a closet door. "It's just in there."

"Maybe another night?" Dani asked. The lump in her throat had spread to her stomach.

"Of course. I'm sorry. I'm just so excited, and my girlfriends aren't here to share it with."

"Wouldn't you rather get married in London?" Dani asked. "With all your mates?"

"All my mates?" Anya laughed. "We're going to have a huge celebration in London. I'm going to wear my gown again and everything. Tradition is much more important to Ruth, so we wanted to at least give her that."

"But why rush it? Why not wait a year or so?"

"Why would we do that?"

"Look, it's none of my business. But you haven't known Nate very long."

"When it's right, you don't need to wait. When it's right, you can't wait to begin your life with the person you love."

They walked back in silence. Dani couldn't get the wedding dress off her mind now. She was dying to know what it looked like. Was it anything like the dress she would have worn? Dani would have gone with something Southern. Satin, and lace, and a long train.

Once on the boat, Nate handed each of them a glass of wine. The girls gravitated to the deck while Nate and Sawyer retreated to the cabin. Danielle wondered what on earth they would find to talk about. Then again, she was wondering the same about her. Getting to know Anya might mean getting to like Anya.

"I don't think Ruth likes me," Anya said, barely a sip into the wine.

"Ruth can be intimidating," Dani said. "I didn't think she liked me at first, either."

"Really?" Anya said.

"Really," Dani said.

"How did you finally get her to like you?"

"You got engaged to Nate," Dani blurted out. Anya's eyes were as wide as saucers. Dani couldn't believe she just said that. Then, Anya burst into laughter. Finally, Dani did, too.

"I can't believe it," Anya said after they calmed down. "Even after you . . . Sorry."

"Even after I publicly broke Nate's heart?" Dani could tell from the look on Anya's face that that was exactly what she almost said.

"It was in poor taste to mention it. Forgive me. I just get this feeling—she's trying to stop the wedding." Anya paused, then looked at Dani. "What about you?"

"What about me?"

"Are *you* trying to stop the wedding?"

"I didn't know you were getting married so soon. I must admit. I'm taken aback."

"You didn't answer my question."

"What do you want me to say? I've loved Nate my entire life."

"I can't believe this. I hoped there was something between you and the photographer." Was it that obvious? Why hadn't Dani ever admitted it before? "You must know how he looks at you?"

"Come on." Dani was dying to hear how he looked at her. She thought there was a spark whenever he did, but could others actually see it?

"I'm quite serious. He watches you all the time." For a second Dani wanted to tell her about the kiss. Like they were girlfriends reliving every exciting moment. But they weren't friends. And Dani was still confused. She loved Nate, too, didn't she? And even if she didn't end up with Nate, he was her friend. She had to make sure he was getting a good woman. "Why Nate?" she said. "There must be loads of men in London lined up to date you."

"I fell in love. That's it."

"And then you just said, 'Hey, Nate, let's move to London,' and what? He just said, 'Sure!'"

"I realize this is quite a sore spot for you."

"I want to know how you talked him into it. That's all."

"If you must know, it was his idea."

It felt like a physical blow. "It was his idea? It was Nate's idea to move to London?"

"Yes."

"I don't believe you."

"Did I outline the opportunities that could be there for an emerging artist? Yes. Do I want to move to London? Yes. Was I the one to bring the subject up? No. He's ready to explore the world. I know he wasn't two years ago when you were ready, and I'm sorry for you. Love is all in the timing, as they say."

"As they say."

"But here's the difference. I would have married Nate whether we stayed in Wilmington or moved to London. Two years ago you couldn't say the same."

"I couldn't live in London, I'm not a citizen." Anya laughed and playfully pushed Dani. *I could playfully push her back,* Dani thought. *Right over the side of the boat.* "He's always going to be a grandmother's boy, you know," Dani said.

"I know that. Ruth is welcome to visit anytime she likes. It's because of her that we're having the wedding here."

"If you really want her to like you, you wouldn't take her only grandson off to London," Dani said.

"Then we'd be living our lives for her and not for us," Anya said.

"I haven't heard you mention Loretta and John," Dani said. "When do they arrive?" Nate's parents moved to Florida the year before Dani left for New York. The last time she'd seen them in person, she'd been Nate's girl-friend. Ruth was John's mother. Dani was surprised they had been "allowed" to move out of Wilmington. Of course John was in his late fifties, finally old enough to stand up to his mother.

"They're here," Anya said. "They've been here."

"Since when?" Dani said.

"A few weeks."

"I see," Dani said. Loretta and John always said they loved her like a daughter. But they hadn't answered her let-ters or calls in two years, either. And surely they knew she was in town by now. Heck, they probably knew the moment she landed at the airport. Small towns thrived on gossip. Yet she hadn't heard from them. Hurt welled up in her all over again. Sawyer was right. Everyone had moved on but her. And, apparently, Ruth.

"You know, the more I drink, the more I like you," Anya said, pushing Dani again.

"Bottoms up, then," Dani said. She glanced at the sky. It was getting colder, and it smelled like rain. That might make their dreams a little choppy. She had to admit, the thought of sleeping in close proximity to Sawyer was making her insides light up.

"Now, what can I do to make Ruth like me?"

Dani was feeling a little tipsy. And a little annoyed that Anya kept pushing her. Why had she let Sawyer almost stop her from what she came here to do? She came here to get Nate back. Besides, if she didn't at least try, she wouldn't have an article to write, now, would she? "If you want Ruth to like you, she has to respect you. The only way she's going to respect you is if you show some pride in where you come from. Just like she does."

Anya took another sip of her wine, then staggered back. "How do I do that?"

"How many glasses have you had?" Dani asked.

"One and a half," Anya said. "I'm blotto!"

"One and a half glasses?"

"I don't normally drink," Anya said.

"So why are you?"

"Because you've been making me nervous. The fact that you're even here, so close to my wedding, is making me nervous."

"I thought Europeans drank a lot," Dani said. *Note to self: Anya cannot handle liquor.* Dani wondered how she would react after a couple of Dark and Stormys. A few of those and she might really cause a scene. The type of scene that Nate would loathe. The type he probably thought his prim and proper fiancée would never cause.

"You seem to have a lot of preconceived notions about us Europeans. Don't you?" Anya said.

Why not? Dani thought. *Were the French the only ones allowed to look down their noses?* "You know what? You're right. I do. Ruth does, too. So what you need to do—that is if you want her to respect you—is show her who you really are."

"You mean, open up and show her my vulnerable side?"

"God, no. Ruth hates vulnerability. I just meant you should incorporate some of your British traditions into the gala. Don't you guys wear silly paper hats, and open Christmas Crackers, and whatnot?"

"Ruth would go mental if I tried to do anything like that."

"How about a British flag? You could hang it on her front porch."

"You're trying to get me in hot water," Anya said. She tried to point at Dani but her finger kept weaving.

"If you showed a little pride in who you are and where you come from, she would respect you. And then admire you. And finally, like you."

"Do you really think so?"

"I know. When we tour the Burgwin-Wright House, you can add your two cents about the British in Wilmington."

"Oh. To be honest I'm not quite up on it."

"Google it. General Craig, Cornwallis—there's a world of history at your fingertips."

"Do you really think it will do any good?"

"If you act like a pushover, she'll treat you like one."

Anya sighed, then leaned over the rail and looked into the depths of the river. "She wishes you were marrying Nate instead."

"I'm made in Wilmington. You can't change that. But you can show her what you're made of."

Anya straightened up. "I suppose I could try it."

"Just don't shy away from it. If you're going to do it, go all the way." What was Dani doing? Ruth would have a heart attack. And wasn't Dani just thinking that she liked

Anya? Wasn't she lusting after Sawyer? And oddly, wasn't it true that she didn't feel the same pull toward Nate anymore? She felt friendship, but she wasn't thinking about ripping off her clothes. Still, she was a bit annoyed at Anya, and tired, and maybe a little tipsy. Besides, Anya probably wouldn't go through with it. Stiff upper lip and all that. Her idea of making a scene was probably nothing to worry about.

"Thank you, Danielle."

"Don't mention it."

"Now, would you like some advice?" Anya was in Dani's face.

"Definitely not," Dani said.

"If I were you, I'd be all over that photographer boy of yours."

"Oh, you would, would you?"

"I bet he's worth the shag."

"Anya!" Dani and Anya whirled around. Nate was standing at the doorway. From the look on his face he'd definitely heard her last comment.

"I'm so sorry," Anya said. "I've had one and a half glasses of wine."

Chapter 10

"I don't think I can take her back to her parents like this," Nate said.

Anya sprinted down the short hall to the main bedroom and threw herself on the bed. "We're having a sleepover!" she shouted.

Nate stared at Dani. "I'll sleep out here on the sofa," Dani said.

"You can have my bed," Sawyer said. "I'll sleep out here."

"I'm sorry," Nate said. "She's not usually like this."

"She's fine," Dani said, stopping short of admitting she liked her better like this.

"I'll even make us breakfast in the morning," Sawyer said. "Texas style."

"There you have it," Dani said. "It's settled."

"Well, good night then," Nate said. He was looking at Sawyer.

"If you're looking for me to go to bed, the two of you are standing in my room," Sawyer said.

"Truly, I'm fine on the sofa," Dani said.

"I don't know how they do things in the South that's not really the South, but where I come from, if anyone has to sleep on a sofa, it's the man."

"The South that's not really the South?" Nate said.

"Long story," Dani said.

"Nate," Anya sang at the top of her voice. "I'm lonely." Nate turned visibly red. He stepped closer to Dani. "Are you sure you're okay?"

"Perfectly fine."

"Because we can leave."

"I insist you stay."

"I'm sure she'll be passed out in no time," Nate said. He glanced at Sawyer again. "Well, good night then."

"Good night."

"I often get up to get a glass of water. I'll try not to wake you if I do."

Sawyer crossed over to the little kitchen, opened the cupboard, and took out a glass. He whistled as he filled it with water then handed it to Nate. "Keep it by the bed," he said. "Problem solved."

"I'll just keep my bedroom door open," Nate said.

"Oh, don't do that," Dani said. "Please."

"I'm just in here if you need me," Nate said.

"Is there a problem here?" Sawyer said.

"I just want her to know—"

"Nate, I'm totally fine. I've worked with Sawyer for the past six months. He's a good guy."

"Except for when I'm not, right?" Sawyer said.

"NATE!"

The yell from Anya startled Nate and he jostled his water. Then, with a nod at Dani, he hurried into his room. Seconds later, Anya jumped off the bed and slid their bedroom door shut.

"Well, well, well," Sawyer said.

"Can I just get a pillow and blanket from your bed?" Dani said.

"Why don't you just sleep in the bed with me, Bright?" Sawyer said. He put his hands up. "I'll keep 'em to my-self."

"I'm sure you—"

"Unless you don't want me to."

He was looking at her again, in a way that made her tingle down to her toes.

"I think the sofa is fine," Dani said.

Just then, it began to rain. The boat rocked, and the drops began hitting the roof, sounding like little pellets being dropped on the boat by naughty elves. Dani suddenly felt a drop of water.

"Owner said this might happen if it rains." He reached under the sink. "Here it is. Didn't even need to go to the grocery store." He brought out a bucket. The leak was right over the sofa. He placed the bucket on the seat. "At least the other sofa is—" He glanced over to find the ceiling above it was leaking, too. He grabbed a towel from the bathroom, and a pan, then placed it on the other sofa. He glanced at his bedroom door.

"Okay," Dani said. "But definitely hands to yourself."

"Ma'am." Sawyer tugged on his imaginary cowboy hat. "Is now a good time to tell you I sleep in the nude?"

He was snoring, softly. But instead of being turned off, Dani found herself inexplicably attracted to Sawyer's snoring. Despite his declaration, he was actually wearing sweat-pants and a T-shirt and so was Dani. This had to be the strangest evening she had ever spent. When they first crawled into the little bed, Sawyer had knelt down next to it like a little kid, and put his prayer-hands on top of the bed.

"What are you doing?" Dani asked.

"Praying you sleep in the nude," Sawyer said. Dani laughed so loud that Sawyer had to shut his door, too. "Don't want Nate storming in here to see if we've each got one foot on the floor," he said.

"He did seem rather upset with the sleeping arrangements, didn't he?"

"Don't tell me," Sawyer said. "You're thinking that means something. That it's a positive sign."

"Well, isn't it?"

"He's a man. Men get jealous. Doesn't matter if he dated you four years or four hours. We're territorial around other men."

"Gee, thanks."

"If you want to get your hopes up, be my guest. I'm just telling it like it is. If you think he'd be any happier if I jumped into bed with Anya—"

"Do you want to?"

"Do I want to what?" He was on the bed now, on his side, his elbow propped up, his face resting on his chin. Dani lay on her side facing him. It was so intimate, and so polite. So strange. Because it felt natural. Very, very comfortable. No wonder she fell asleep on him on the plane. God, he smelled good, too.

"Do you want to sleep with Anya?"

"What kind of question is that, Bright?"

"I'm just curious. She is beautiful."

"If you like her type."

"What? Gorgeous and educated?"

"No. Sloshed after a drink and a half."

Dani laughed and swatted him. Sawyer caught her hand and held it. Dani's heart was beating so loud there was no way he couldn't hear it. She half-expected Nate to come barging in. What was the meaning of this? Why wasn't she crying about the fact that Nate was in bed with another woman? Why was her entire body on fire? Why did she feel as if she was doing something she wasn't supposed to be doing? Sawyer slowly turned her hand over and kissed her palm. Dani had to clamp her mouth shut to keep from moaning. She prayed Sawyer didn't know the reaction he'd caused by that one little kiss. Then, he let her hand go, and immediately turned away from her. Seconds later, he was snoring.

And she was wide, wide awake. Aware of every little inch that separated him. Aware that all she had to do was slide her hand over, and bridge the tiny distance, and be touching him. Aware that he would probably take very little persuading to make love to her. Right? Then how was it he could be so fast asleep and she was so miserably awake? She should have gotten a glass of water. The rain was still coming down and the boat was bouncing gently on the river. "I like you," Dani whispered in the dark. And then, she, too, turned away, hugged the pillow, and finally fell asleep.

She was so comfy. Resting against something so warm. One leg ran the length of his body, the other was thrown up and over, straddling him. Both arms were near his neck. Oh God, oh God, oh God, she was lying on top of Sawyer! What was wrong with her? She was going to have to slowly, slowly, slide off so that he would never, ever know, and then she was going to have to make sure she was never in this kind of proximity to him again, ever, ever, ever. She gently lifted the leg that was thrown over his body. Then she brought in her arms. Finally she rolled off him to the left. She stood, and crept to the door. She slid the door open.

"Morning, Bright," Sawyer said behind her. She whipped around. Oh, the grin on his face! He definitely knew.

"Morning," she mumbled and stepped into the main cabin as fast as she could. Anya and Nate were up on deck, standing as far away from each other as possible.

"And there she is," Anya said. "Hasn't even been hacked in pieces."

"Pardon?" Dani said.

"Nate was very worried about you. Unusually worried about you."

So that was it. They were arguing over her. Shouldn't Dani feel a jolt of pleasure? Instead, she felt bad. "There was a leak in the living room," Dani said.

"You don't owe anyone an explanation, Bright. You're a grown woman," Sawyer said, stepping onto the deck.

"And you're an engaged man," Anya said to Nate.

"Sawyer, didn't you say you were going to make us breakfast?" Dani said.

"Did I?"

"Yes."

"You said, 'Texas style'," Anya volunteered.

"Big and spicy," Sawyer said.

Like you? Dani wondered.

"I'm not hungry," Nate said.

"I'm absolutely famished," Anya said. "A good breakfast will help me soak up all that alcohol."

"I'll need to go to a grocery store," Sawyer said.

"Why don't we just go to George's," Nate said. "You love sitting by the window, Danielle."

George's used to be their Sunday brunch destination. A lifetime ago. "That's a great idea," Danielle said. "You'll love it, too," she said to Anya. Dani couldn't be sure, but she thought she heard Anya mumble, "I wouldn't be so sure about that."

* * *

Dani was relived to be sitting in the restaurant on the river, mainly because it was only seconds before she had a nice hot cup of coffee, and a mimosa. Christmas carols were playing and lights were strung above the wall of windows facing Cape Fear River. A tree glittered in the corner of the restaurant. Sawyer was whistling, and Nate and Anya looked just as miserable as they had on the boat.

When their dishes came, Sawyer photographed the grits. "Maybe I should get a picture of you eating grits by the Christmas tree, Bright," Sawyer said.

"Bright," Nate said. "I take it you think it's, what? Charming to call her Bright? Like the two of you have some kind of flirting intimacy going on?" It was the first words Nate had spoken since they sat down.

"Flirting intimacy?" Sawyer said.

Anya clanged her silverware down on her plate. "Are you still in love with her?" she demanded.

Was he? Dani wondered. He certainly was jealous, there was no doubt about that. The same panicky feeling that hit Dani when Nate was going to propose was thrumming through her body now. Sawyer was right. There was a very good reason she had turned down Nate's proposal. Her body knew she didn't want him, instinctively it had been trying to tell her at every turn. Just like her body had been gravitating to Sawyer every chance she got, even though she protested it when awake. Who knew that her body had a mind of its own? She'd better speak up before things got out of control. "Of course not," Dani said. "He's just being overprotective. Like a big brother."

"A big brother?" Nate repeated.

"An incestuous big brother," Sawyer added. Dani kicked him under the table. He seized the opportunity and wrapped his leg around hers. If she wanted to pull free, everyone at the table would know what was going on. She was going to let him have it later.

Anya stood up. "You had better let me know right now, Nate. I am not, nor will I ever be, someone's second choice. Although I'd think carefully if I were you, because Danielle had at least three glasses of wine last night and here she is drinking again!" Dani wanted to protest, but if Anya thought a glass and a half was getting drunk, maybe she had a point. Dani was already bummed that she probably wouldn't be ordering a second one now. Sawyer slid his mimosa over to her, and Dani grabbed it before anyone else noticed.

"Of course you're not second best," Nate said. "Dani's right. I guess I am being a bit like an overprotective big brother."

"Or maybe it's just a horrible idea to hang out with your ex no matter what the situation," Sawyer said.

"That is an excellent point," Anya said.

"But we still have to go to the Christmas gala," Dani said. "Our article depends on it."

"The Christmas gala?" Anya said. "You're calling my wedding a Christmas gala?"

Dani had forgotten all about the wedding. How was that possible? More proof that she wasn't in love with Nate, or was it that she just couldn't imagine anything usurping Ruth's holiday extravaganza? Probably a little bit of both. Either way, they had to attend. It would cinch the article. She had to smooth things over with Anya. "I have to use the little girls' room," Dani said. "Will you join me, Anya?"

"Very well. If that's how they do it in America," Anya said. Nate and Sawyer took up a staring contest as Dani headed for the bathroom.

The minute they entered, Dani confessed. "You were right. I did come here to win Nate back."

"I knew it!"

"It's even part of the article I'm writing."

"I thought it was 'A Southern Christmas'."

"Well. That's the backup article. The real article is—'All I Want for Christmas' and it's supposed to document step-by-step how I went about getting Nate back and making up for that humiliating Christmas two years ago."

"He's marrying me." Anya already had tears in her eyes.

"I know, I know. I get that now. I really get that."

"You think I'm going to fall for that?"

"It's true. Believe me, I'm just as surprised as you are, but I swear. It's true."

"You've only been here, what? A couple of days? You're telling me you fell out of love with Nate in a couple of days?"

"Not exactly. It's just become obvious that there are certain truths I didn't want to admit." Sawyer was right. She partly came here just to get the story. And maybe it was her heart that spoke up two years ago. Her heart that knew Nate wasn't meant for her.

"I knew it," Anya said, pointing at her. "You're in love with that Texas lad."

"Shhh," Dani said. "Don't say that out loud!"

Anya took Dani's hands. "I told you. He's gorgeous."

"Keep away. You're engaged, remember?" Dani pulled back and playfully punched her on the arm.

Anya rubbed her arm and frowned. "You're sure you're not just saying this so that I won't be on my guard?"

"I'm sure. Which is why I have something else to confess."

"Go on."

"I gave you terrible advice last night. About Ruth's tour tonight. You do not want to start mentioning anything pro-British."

Anya stood up straight and lifted her chin. "I beg your pardon?"

"Oh, you know how Ruth is. British imperialists and all that."

"British what?" Anya looked truly shocked. Was it possible she had no idea how prejudiced Ruth was against the Brits? Dani wanted to cut and run, but Anya was blocking the exit.

"Ruth's old-fashioned. That's all I meant."

"Oh no, it isn't. She actually says *British imperialists*?"

Among other things. "You didn't pick up on that when she wouldn't let your parents stay in her house?"

"She said she's getting her home ready for our wedding."

"Right," Dani said. "Right." This time she did try to squeeze past Anya and out the door.

Anya grabbed her arm. "You're saying it was a lie? She has room at the inn but didn't want my parents to stay?"

Dani put her arms up. "I can't say anything for sure. But if it is true—kind of appropriate for this time of year, no?" Anya didn't crack a smile. "No room at the inn?"

"I knew it. I knew she hated me! Nate said I was imagining things."

"I'm sure he just wanted to spare your feelings."

"That big, fat liar!"

"That's a little harsh, don't you think?" Dani said. Anya stormed out of the bathroom. Uh-oh. "Uh—Anya?" Dani hurried after her, calling her name in a loud whisper, but Anya refused to turn around. She made a beeline for the table.

"Dani told me everything!" she shouted. Behind her, Dani tried to signal Nate, but she didn't know enough gestures for "I told her your grandmother hates the British."

"What?" Nate said. "What's everything?"

"Your nanna hates me because I'm British."

"Oh," Nate said. "That." He looked relieved. Dani wondered what he thought she had said.

"Oh?" Anya mimicked. "That? Are you quite out of your mind? You think it's nothing?" Nate tried to touch her. Anya backed away. "What about you? Do you think we're imperialists, too?"

"Well, historically—"

Dani and Sawyer both shook their heads violently. Nate caught on. Unfortunately so did Anya. Her flames of anger erupted into a five-alarm fire. "Your grandmother had plenty of rooms for my parents to stay, but she didn't want them under her roof!"

"Anya, I'm sorry. I'm sorry," Nate said. "What did you want me to do?"

"Stand up for me. Just like I should have done." Anya swiped her purse from her chair. "I'll see all of you at the Burgwin-Wright House tonight. I can't wait to take your advice, Dani." She stormed out of the restaurant. Nate tried to follow but Sawyer held him back.

"Probably just needs a bit of space," Sawyer said. Dani could tell that Nate wanted to argue, but he also knew Sawyer was right.

He gave a brisk nod, then turned to Dani. "Advice? What advice did you give her?"

Dani froze. "I, uh. Last night, after a little wine, I may have, uh, told her to feel free to, you know, chime in any bits of British history during the tour."

Nate looked worse than angry. He looked as if he didn't think she was a good person. "That's really low, Dani. Really, really low."

"I was a little tipsy. That's all. But I took it back. Just now. In the bathroom. I told her not to do it!"

"What you did is wind her up even more by telling her my grandmother hates her!"

"Okay, that's what I did. But it isn't what I meant to do."

"You know what's obvious, Danielle?" Nate said. Dani winced, knowing something really bad was coming.

"What?" she whispered.

"It's becoming incredibly obvious that publicly humiliating me two Christmases ago was the best thing you could have ever done for me." He headed for the door, stopped, and looked at her for a long time. "And to think. For the briefest second there, you had me wondering if I was making a grave mistake in marrying Anya."

Chapter 11

"I'm going to fix it," Dani told Sawyer. "I have to fix it."
They were at the Cape Fear Model Train Show. Sawyer
was snapping pictures of the Christmas villages and sleek
model trains while Danielle trailed after him, pleading for
him to agree with her that she could fix this.

"You should stay out of it," Sawyer said. "Or you might
end up making things worse."

"I can't just walk away. It's my fault they're fighting."

"That's your problem, Bright. You can't just walk away."
Great. He was mad at her, too. Danielle sighed and watched
the miniature ski lift ascend while below the sleek black
engine blew its whistles and disappeared into a tunnel. The
world looked so perfect in miniature. Sawyer zoomed in to
capture a family skating on an ice pond. Wouldn't it be
nice if life were as easy to arrange?

"I like Anya. I have to make this right."

"I have one question for you, Bright." Sawyer didn't
look at her when he spoke; instead he continued to take
pictures.

"Okay."

"And I need one hundred percent honesty."

"I swear on Santa."

"How did you feel when Nate said that because of you he'd had second thoughts about marrying Anya?" Sawyer looked at her now, and waited.

"I felt as if someone had poured a bucket of ice over me."

"I'm not sure how to interpret that."

"I was terrified to hear it. Not happy to hear it, okay?"

"You sure about that?"

"I love Nate," Dani said.

"Here we go—"

"Like a brother. And not, as you so rudely piped in at the restaurant, in an incestuous way. You were right all along. I turned down Nate's proposal two years ago because deep down I knew he wasn't the guy for me. I may not have believed that then, but I sure as heck know it now."

"Okay." Sawyer glanced away.

"It's the truth." Dani stepped up, touched his face with her hand, and gently turned him so he was looking at her again. "I'm not in love with Nate," she said when she had his full attention.

"I think I have all I need here," Sawyer said. He gently removed her hand from his face. She followed him out to the car. Interesting. Suddenly he didn't want to talk about them. And obviously he didn't want to kiss her, either. Typical. She opened her heart to him and he shut her out. Was it all a game? Did he only like her when he thought she was in love with someone else? Or worse yet, had he been on some kind of mission? Had everyone at the magazine taken bets on whether or not the great Sawyer Drake could seduce her? Or was she just being paranoid and he simply needed time to process everything? Whatever. She wasn't going to think about it right now. She'd had all the drama she could take for an afternoon. And she wasn't going to put up with him sulking, either.

"Do you like Christmas, Sawyer?" she asked.

"What kind of question is that?"

"A very simple one. Some people don't like Christmas."

"I love Christmas," Sawyer said. "Always have."

"Do you have a big family?"

"Yes, ma'am. Seven brothers and sisters."

"Seven brothers and sisters?" How did she not know this? "Wow. Don't you all get together for Christmas?"

"This is the first year I won't be home," he confessed.

"Why?"

"Because I'm on assignment, Bright."

Dani spotted The Ivy Cottage just ahead. She suddenly felt like shopping. So far they'd spent all their time taking pictures for the article. But for the first time in two years Dani didn't want another Christmas to go by uncelebrated. "Have you done all your Christmas shopping?" she asked Sawyer.

"We usually draw a name and just get something for that person. Otherwise, it's too many people to buy for."

"Let's get all your brothers and sisters a present!"

"What?"

"Adel is making us work on Christmas. But she also wants it to be authentically Southern, doesn't she?"

"Uh-huh."

"And she gave us the company credit card, didn't she?"

"For expenses related to the article."

"Then bring your camera, and the credit card, and we'll show the world how Southerners like to shop." Dani took a left and parked.

"The Ivy Cottage?" Sawyer said, reading the sign.

"There are actually three cottages and a warehouse," Dani said, pointing to the other buildings. "I agree they should just stick an *s* on the end of *cottage* and be done with it." She winked and finally Sawyer cracked a smile. "It's the largest consignment shop in the South. You would not believe the treasures in these three buildings. And the best part is the prices. They're so good that I was kidding about using the company credit card. I bet I can help you find everything on your list for next to nothing. I'll even help wrap and mail them."

"You're nuts."

"I'm in the Christmas mood." They held eye contact and a surge of lust ran through her. "I think it's all your fault," she said softly.

"All right." Sawyer grinned and slapped his thigh. "Let's do it. What about your family?"

"I'll get something for them, too." Dani and Sawyer had just stepped into the first cottage when he took her hands and pulled her aside. "What if we get a little gift for each other, as well?"

"Really?"

"From the looks of it, we'll be spending Christmas Day together. I'd like to have something to open. How about you?"

"Yes," Dani said. "Yes I would."

"Great. Under twenty dollars?"

"Unless we use Adel's credit card," Dani joked.

"Uh, no. She's not getting credit for my genius gift-giving."

"Genius, huh? Those are pretty high stakes."

"So we'll shop together for family and friends and if we both are buying something for each other in the same cottage, we'll have to take turns."

"Got it. And save your appetite because after we shop, we're going to Indochine."

"Where?"

"It's a Thai and Vietnamese restaurant just behind the third cottage. The food is to die for, and wait until you see the outdoor gardens." Dani stopped. "That is—do you like Thai?"

"I like anything that makes your eyes light up like that," Sawyer said. Danielle turned away before he could see that she was thoroughly flushed from that statement.

It was fun going through the shops. They marveled over

Asian pottery, played with the Christmas villages, sat on antique sofas, and debated their most and least favorite oil paintings. When they reached circus toys that appeared to be from the '40s or '50s, Sawyer slowed and took his time examining them. Dani didn't dare ask if he liked them; she wanted to pick his present based on his reactions, and she didn't want to ruin the surprise. What fun to buy someone circus toys for Christmas. She filed it away as a possibility. She also tried not to drool over the expensive jewelry. There was a blue-topaz necklace she especially avoided. It would look amazing with her blonde hair and blue eyes, but she was afraid to even glance at the price tag. Instead she murmured how nice a pair of teacups were, especially since they were only eight dollars apiece.

Finally it was time to go their separate ways. Of course they had chosen the same building, so Sawyer said Dani could go first and he would run back to the first building and look around. Dani made a beeline for the circus toys. There were three animals: a tiger, a giraffe, and an elephant. There was a circus train. And there was a circus tent. God, how fun. A few shopkeepers helped her bring them up to the counter. While they were wrapping each piece in tissue paper, she quickly ran over to the jewelry counter to look at the blue topaz necklace. It was the size of a quarter, surrounded by tiny diamonds and pearls. The chain was platinum. She touched the glass above the necklace, then declined when she was asked if she wanted to try it on. Best not to get too attached. She hurried back to the counter and paid for the circus gifts. Only forty dollars. She went slightly over the limit but that was Christmas, too. What fun. Maybe she'd stop in at one of the kitchen shops at the Cotton Exchange Downtown and also buy him a few Texas products. They had hot sauce from all over. He could put it on his cheesy biscuits, eggs, and country ham that she planned on making him for Christmas breakfast.

She was humming as she went back to the car, and still

humming after she put the presents in the trunk and headed into the first shop to tell Sawyer it was his turn.

"What's that you're singing?"

"'It's Beginning to Look a Lot Like Christmas,'" Danielle said. She hadn't even realized it. For the first time in two years she could hum her favorite song without being struck by guilt at humiliating Nate. He was happy. He had fallen in love. And maybe, just maybe, she was falling in love, too. Of course, she had to make sure Nate and Anya patched things up. Despite Sawyer's warning, she couldn't possibly carry the guilt of being the one to break them up. Besides, they had to go to the Burgwin-Wright House and take pictures of it decorated for Christmas anyway. Maybe it wouldn't hurt to have a heart-to-heart with Ruth Hathaway while she was at it. Since Danielle no longer had to worry about being her granddaughter-in-law, she was no longer afraid to speak her mind.

Sawyer was done in a flash. He was allowed to hide his package under a coat in the backseat. She was pretty sure he had bought her the teacups. She would treasure them.

They had lunch at Indochine. It was too cold to eat in the gardens, but they still strolled through them. Dani loved the little bridge and the koi pond, and Sawyer snapped pictures of goddess statues hidden in leafy enclaves. Inside, they both ordered the curried chicken noodles and Thai iced tea. They ate and drank in a comfortable silence.

When their empty plates were taken away, Sawyer reached across the table and took her hand. Dani became so still, she could hear her heart beating. "I really, really like you, Bright," he said. There was a catch in his voice. It dawned on her that this wasn't any easier for him to admit than it was for her.

"I like you, too," she said.

"So what exactly are we going to do about it?"

Danielle grinned. "Why, Sawyer Drake. Are you trying to have a conversation about *us?*"

"I sound like a girl, don't I?"

"No way, cowboy. A girl would never be so stupid."

Sawyer chuckled and removed his hand. A blush worked its way up his neck. "There it is. The Bright I'm used to."

Dani felt as if she were soaring the skies in a hot air balloon. "We work together," she said, aware that it was a bit risky to start poking the balloon with a stick.

"I'll quit."

"Very funny."

"I'm dead serious."

"You would quit just to go out with me?"

"First of all, no. I would quit to be with you. Not just go out with you. You still with me or should I stop now?"

Dani reached up and took both his hands. A tingle went through her as he squeezed her hands gently in his. "I'm still with you," she said.

"Good. Second of all, we both hate that magazine. I think we should finish the article, hang around to see if there's a Christmas bonus, and get the heck out of there."

"Then what?"

"Travel."

"Travel?"

"Why settle for visiting gardens at a Thai restaurant when you can actually visit gardens in Thailand?"

"I've always wanted to go to Thailand. And a million other places."

"So why don't we?"

"Is it really that simple?"

"Yep. I could take photographs, you could write."

"How in the world could we afford it?"

"If we both get a Christmas bonus and our back pay, it's a start. We can find odd jobs wherever we go."

"Europe?"

"Sounds as good a place to start as any."

"Could we?"

"Of course."

"Let's not start with London. They might think we're following them."

"So you're in?" Sawyer's face looked so relieved, and joyful. He'd been thinking of this for a while.

"I'm so in!" They half-stood in their seats, leaned forward, and hugged each other across the table. When she pulled back, Sawyer was coming in again, this time for a kiss.

"But first I have to patch up Anya and Nate," Dani said as quickly as possible.

"You mean you're going to meddle in their lives again."

"Yes. But just so we're clear. Around here it's known as Southern hospitality."

Chapter 12

The path leading up to the Burgwin-Wright House was lined with flickering candles. A trolley hummed at the curb waiting to take patrons between it and the Bellamy Mansion. A group of Christmas carolers sang quietly from the side gardens. Wreaths adorned the banisters and hung on the iron gates. Inside, the tour guides would be dressed in colonial dresses and suits. Refreshments would sit upon the tables. Wreaths and greenery would abound on most surfaces and in the nine fireplaces. An enormous Moravian star hung from the front porch. There were even five animals from a petting zoo, all dressed in festive halters. A llama, a donkey, goats, and a cow. Apparently, Rudolph never came this far South. "If there had been an alligator, I would have been golden," Sawyer whispered in her ear. "Do you think Adel will accept a llama instead?"

"She'd be crazy not to," Dani said.

Ruth Hathaway was dressed in a red velvet colonial gown. Dani thought she looked like a slim Mrs. Claus. She began her tour on the front porch by telling the small group that the Burgwin-Wright House, built in the year 1770, was one of the finest examples of Georgian architecture in all the state, and that John Burgwin meant it as a gift for his wife.

"Makes my Christmas present kind of suck," Sawyer whispered in Dani's ear. She burst out laughing. Nate, who was standing with his arms crossed, glared at them. Beside him, Anya was too busy glaring at Ruth to notice. Danielle had meant to arrive early to try and straighten a few things out, but had totally lost track of time. *Time flies when you're falling in love.*

Enough. She had to stop smiling. This was about patching up Nate and Anya. Then they could go home. Danielle didn't even care about the Christmas gala or the wedding anymore. She just wanted to make things right with Nate and Anya and then start her life with Sawyer.

"This grand townhome is the epicenter of the events surrounding the end of the Revolutionary War. It predates the Declaration of Independence, and within these walls the battle between domination by the British imperialists and our struggle for independence was waged." Ruth Hathaway's eyes took on a passionate glow. "During the Revolution this home served as a command post and prison for the occupying British Army. Inside you will notice the heart of pine floors. Look for the nicks and cuts in the wood. Those were made by axes. Savage blows by British butchers!" The crowd murmured and twittered. Dani had a feeling Ruth was straying from the normal Christmas tales she was supposed to be telling.

"Where was John Burgwin from?" Anya called out.

Ruth looked startled by the question. "I believe he was Welsh," she said.

"Oh no. I believe he was English," Anya said.

"Perhaps," Ruth said. "Anyway—"

"It's so nice that my people could give you such a wonderful gift," Anya said. Danielle tried to catch Anya's eye, but she was purposefully not looking at anyone other than Ruth.

"That's not quite accurate, my dear," Ruth said. "John Burgwin married a *Southern* woman, by the name of Margaret Haynes. It was her *Southern* father, Roger, who owned this land. John Burgwin only acquired it through marriage."

"But if his bigoted brother would have had his way, there never would have been a marriage, and thus, never this exquisite home." Anya smiled at everyone in the group except Danielle and Nate.

"His brother?" Ruth was finding it hard to disguise her annoyance.

"Yes. His older brother, James. He inherited the family estate. Do you know what he had the nerve to tell John?"

"I have the feeling you're going to tell us," Ruth said.

"He said, 'If you ever marry an American, neither yourself nor your family will ever inherit a single shilling from me.'" Anya put on a theatrical voice and practically shouted it. "Can you imagine such hatred?"

"From the English?" Ruth said. "Why, I believe I can." Dani's head snapped from Ruth to Anya. It was impossible to look away.

"From anyone," Anya said through gritted teeth. "Although one might understand it back then. But surely not today."

Don't call me Shirley, Dani imagined Ruth saying.

"John went on to become an American citizen," Ruth said. She did not acknowledge Anya's last declaration but she did begin to speed up, as if trying to rush through before Anya could interrupt again. "He made North Carolina his home. He is buried in North Carolina. Unlike some people who seem as if they can't wait to get back to their fancy, imperialist lives!"

Anya gasped and pointed at Ruth. "She admitted it, Nate."

Nate looked flustered, and then began to clap. "Bravo,

bravo," he said. "I love the reenactment. With a modern-day twist!" Soon the small crowd joined in with an appreciative applause. Ruth gave a forced smile, and Anya frowned. Nate took his grandmother by the arm and together they stepped into the elaborate foyer. The small group followed, everyone but Anya looking at each other. Anya was too busy shooting daggers into the back of Nate's head. This was not good. Danielle knew she should do something but she had no idea what to say.

Ruth, still speaking quickly, explained that all the furnishings, although not the original pieces for this house, were true to the time period. And in the spirit of Georgian architecture, every feature in the house had a twin—if there was a window in the front, there was a matching window in the back. Each room had an equal size room above it, and if there was a sconce on the left, there was a sconce on the right, and so on. She paused to allow everyone to appreciate the symmetry. Then they started in the room to the left, which used to be a sitting room designed for a suitor and the girl he was courting to sit and get acquainted. A curved mirror near the ceiling assured that there could be eyes on them at a moment's notice. Here Ruth was forced to talk about various British officers, and how Lord Cornwallis occupied the Burgwin-Wright House in 1781, commandeering it as his headquarters. "Shortly before the British army was defeated for good," Ruth added quietly. Danielle prayed Anya wouldn't say anything else. Especially since this was usually the time when Ruth would tell stories of how horrifically Cornwallis behaved while in the house, including supposedly once exclaiming, "Death and destruction to all the Americans!"

Maybe Dani would cheer Anya up later by informing her that Ruth had left this bit out. They headed upstairs to a dining room, and a front parlor room that consisted of formal seating, and a piano. Usually unattended, for this occasion a pianist sat at the piano playing Christmas tunes. Most of the furniture of that time was made so that it could easily be rolled out of the way if guests wished to dance. Many famous and prominent politicians and families had been entertained in this very room. From here windows on three sides offered a remarkable view down Market Street. Danielle had taken the tour many times and could always imagine what it would have been like in the past. At the time this was built, it was the only house in town, for literally at the end of the long, dirt street was the town market. Ruth often pointed out that it would have been fairly noisy up on the second floor, not to mention the smells of a city from that time period. Sometimes Danielle felt as if she could actually hear the *clop* of horses, and smell the scent of tar, and manure. Not very glamorous, but it still seemed romantic to her. She glanced at Sawyer, to find that he was looking at her. She felt flushed with joy, and then guilt. Nate and Anya still looked miserable.

"Isn't this your favorite room, Danielle?" Ruth said.

"Yes, it is," Danielle said. She couldn't believe Ruth remembered that. She never thought Ruth had heard anything she had ever said.

"Danielle and Nate were childhood sweethearts," Ruth announced to the group. There was a murmur of "Awwww."

"I'm gobsmacked," Anya said.

"But now Nate is engaged to this lovely lady," Danielle said, stepping over and linking arms with Anya.

"Was engaged," Anya said.

"Is engaged," Nate said. He stepped forward, extracted Dani's arm from Anya, and put his arm around her waist. To Dani's relief, Anya didn't resist. Danielle wandered away from the group as Ruth explained how the Wrights came to own the house, and then William McRary and his wife, Martha, and finally, in 1930, it was purchased by the National Society of Colonial Dames of America in North Carolina.

The tour ended in the basement. Everyone got a chance to look down into the cellar that used to be a holding cell for prisoners who had been condemned to death. Dani could only imagine how they felt.

Anya stepped forward, then grabbed Ruth in a hug. "You were wonderful. I'm so proud to be your future granddaughter-in-law."

Dani gasped. She had never seen anyone hug Ruth in public, not even Nate. The most affection she'd ever seen Ruth give anyone voluntarily was a simple pat on the hand. Nate must have been just as horrified, for he stepped in to pry them apart.

Anya cried out as Nate ripped her away. "I'm trying!" she said. "Why can't you see that I'm trying!" With that, she turned and fled out the back door.

The back door emptied onto a porch and beyond it, a brick courtyard enclosed by ballast-stone walls. The stones had been shipped in from the West Indies, and even the ferns covering them were thought to be from seeds on the same journey. A small stone hut against the back was the original kitchen where the slaves prepared the meals, and above it, up a set of stairs, were the original slave quarters.

Danielle, Sawyer, Nate, and Anya stood in the back, near one of the two outdoor jail cells, while the rest of the participants had a look at the dungeon where horse thieves and murderers used to be kept until sentencing. Why they even bothered with the ritual, Dani didn't know, for any person who had been tossed into the dungeon was always condemned to die. Horse thieves were considered more heinous than the murderers. Visitors weren't actually allowed to go into the dungeon, rather they had to look down into it through a glass panel cut into the wood floor. Dani often wondered why Burgwin decided to use the old jail as the foundation for his home. Most likely it was too costly to dig up, but there was something terribly eerie about living among the remnants of the past. And when she looked out to the manicured lawn, she could easily see the gallows, and tried not to imagine men hanging. Anya, on the other hand, seemed almost giddy to be inside an old, outdoor jail cell. The jails and the dungeon dated back to 1740.

"Is this where you and Dani used to make out?" Anya said.

"It was hardly making out," Nate said.

"You told her?" Dani said.

"Ruth told me," Anya said. "I'm surprised she didn't announce it to the entire group."

"What do you say, Sawyer?" Anya said. "Should we make out?"

"What?" Dani said.

"Enough, Anya," Nate said.

Anya grabbed Sawyer, who was already grinning, and planted a kiss on him. Sawyer wasn't the instigator, but from what Dani could tell, he wasn't exactly pushing her off. Anya finally came up for air.

"How does that feel, Nate?"

"It feels as if my fiancée is so childish, so jealous of something I did when I was a teenaged boy, that I'm starting to wonder if I haven't made a grievous error in judgment."

"And how do you think I feel when your grandmother spews her hatred and you do nothing but stand there and take it?"

"She's been giving this exact tour for the past twenty years. It's history, Anya. What do you want me to do—rewrite history?"

"She hates us!"

"She hates the North, too, if it's any consolation. My grandmother would erect an impenetrable shield just around Wilmington and the beaches if she could, stick a flag in it, and never let another soul in."

"She was out of line today and you just stood there! How could I marry a man like that?"

"I'm moving to London for you. If that doesn't prove how much I love you, then nothing ever will."

"You're moving to London for me? For me?"

"Of course. Who else? If I had wanted to move out of Wilmington, I would have gone to New York with Dani."

Danielle tried to sink further into the jail cell but she hit the wall. Sawyer joined her. "If you've got a bobby pin," he whispered. "I might be able to dig us a way out." Dani slapped her hand over her mouth; it really wasn't a good time to laugh.

"I thought we were moving to London for your art career. I thought you were excited about moving to London."

"I was excited about being with you. I didn't care where we were. I like to make things. With shells, and driftwood, and stones. Where am I going to find those things in some crowded city?"

"I told you—you can make street art. People in the city toss out the strangest things. Broken glass, and shoelaces, and what have you."

"Garbage? You're comparing garbage to seashells?"

"We can fly to a beach anytime we want!"

"Would this wedding still be on if I told you I wanted to stay here in Wilmington?"

"Is that what you're saying, or are we being hypothetical?"

"Just answer me."

"I will not. I will not answer you unless you are truly saying you wish to stay here, and you are asking me a serious question."

"I'm sick of living in fear that yet another woman is going to get cold feet and find some way to sabotage our marriage."

"And I'm sick of hearing what brutes the British are.

Blah, bloody, blah! I'm starting to think I don't want to be chained to a Yank for the rest of my bloody life, either!"

Anya stormed off, exiting through an iron gate in the back and to the left.

Nate turned and glared at Dani. "Congratulations, Dani, you've done it again. I hope the two of you will be very happy." He took off after Anya. Dani and Sawyer stood in the jail cell, looking at each other. Sawyer started to whistle, and then stopped when he received a glare from Dani. He lifted his head and looked out to the distance. From the side yard the donkey brayed.

"Where did you say the gallows were?" Sawyer asked.

Sawyer and Dani stood on the boardwalk. Sawyer paced as he considered her request. "I thought you would have learned your lesson by now," he said. "You're still meddling."

"This wouldn't be a Southern Christmas if I wasn't," Dani said.

"What if she won't come with me? If I knew how to get women to do what I asked them to, then we wouldn't still be here."

"You're a photographer. Tell her you want to see her Christmas present to Nate. Then show her the picture I sent you." Dani couldn't believe she was actually letting someone else see that picture. It was taken right after Nate proposed. A close-up on her face. Horrified. She wasn't sure why the person sent her the picture. Perhaps they thought it would be good for her to see what the expression on her face looked like just in case she ever had any doubts that she had done the right thing. Too bad that didn't work or they might not be here now. "If that doesn't melt her heart, then just pick her and the present up, and carry them to Ruth's house."

"Pick her up and carry her."

"Yes. Sling her over your shoulder like a sack of potatoes. Are you a real cowboy or not?"

"Should I come galloping in with her on a white horse?"

"If you can pull that off, it would be lovely."

"You are totally off your rocker, Bright."

"And you are free to run screaming into the night. After you deliver Anya to the Jewel of Wilmington."

"The Jewel of Wilmington."

"Sorry, that's what they call Ruth's home."

"They must be talking about the home because I've met the matriarch and the title doesn't fit."

"It's a lovely home," Dani said. "It was once owned by Captain Harper. A steamer captain."

"I'm starting to think that 'A Southern Christmas' is just another way of saying that you're all certifiably insane."

"Now who's being bright?" Dani walked up to him, wrapped her arms around him, and pulled him in for a long kiss. "If you pull this off, you won't believe how appreciative I can be."

"Using sex to get your way."

"Is it working?"

"Has it ever not?"

"Thank you, thank you, thank you."

"Kiss me again." They kissed, only parting when it became obvious that any further and they wouldn't be able to stop. Dani didn't want to make love to Sawyer until Nate and Anya were back together. "Let me practice throwing you around like a sack of potatoes," Sawyer said.

"Try it and I'll have a go at your crown jewels," Dani said.

Ruth Hathaway's jewel of a home was situated up on a hill on South Front Street. The sea-green Queen Anne Victorian was built in 1902 and had undergone extensive restorations after Ruth and her husband purchased it some fifty years ago. Nate's grandfather had long since passed away, and the eight-bedroom home was more room than she needed, but Ruth considered herself a steward of the property and couldn't bring herself to leave. Gardeners maintained the expansive grounds surrounding the home, taking special care to prune the magnolia trees, and only lightly trim the crêpe myrtles in the front yard. Too many of Ruth's neighbors went too far with their trees, Ruth thought, turning them into crêpe murders instead. Ruth Hathaway liked everything just so, and nothing exemplified this more than her annual Christmas gala. And this year it was going to double as a wedding, that is if Sawyer could deliver the bride.

Danielle wished Sawyer was with her as she stepped into the foyer. He would love the dramatic entrance. Mahogany, and cut-and-place English oak floors were in gorgeous contrast to rich dark walls, and Flemish ceilings with exposed beams. A built-in bench imitated the curve of the windows. The elegant wood door was framed by beveled glass. The middle of the foyer was currently taken up by a twelve-foot Christmas tree, with white lights, crystals, and white ribbons adorning it from head to toe. It looked like a wedding tree, but if the festivities were off, it could serve just as well for Christmas. Dani wondered how it was going with Anya, and she was dying to get to Nate and let him know that the cavalry was on the way.

Danielle thought she was early, but several guests were already milling through the exquisite rooms. To her right, the parlor room, and beyond it, separated by parlor doors, the living room. The parlor doors were open, allowing guests to flow from one space to the other, and later, for dancing. Each room boasted a fireplace with its own hand-cut colored tiles, mantel, and decorations. The parlor room's tile was cream, the living room, a gorgeous emerald. Fires danced in each. Original oil paintings competed with detailed crown molding, chandeliers, and antique furnishings for attention. In the parlor room, two young girls dressed in gowns played Christmas carols on the violin, accompanied by a pianist at the baby grand. Dani passed the curved staircase leading to the second and third floors, and paused to look in at the dining room.

Each room had a lovely color on the walls, but the dining room was Dani's favorite. It was a sea-blue. The chandelier was from France, the size of a small tree, with crystal droplets as big as leaves. The dining table was fit for a king. Dani was thrilled to see her favorite centerpiece: a large white swan pulling a red sleigh. Dani realized, with a bit of guilt, that she had been more in love with the promise of the lifestyle Nate offered than she was with Nate. She wasn't entirely aware of it at the time, however, and she was grateful she had followed her heart. Speaking of heart, she couldn't wait to see Sawyer. And truthfully, she couldn't wait for Sawyer to see her. She was wearing a silk gunmetal-gray gown. It hugged her figure in the right places, and came down to the floor. She had a light sheer shawl and a black crystal necklace and matching earrings. Her blond hair was piled on top of her head with a few tendrils hanging down. Given the added glow of the candles flickering in nearly every corner of the home, Dani knew she looked gorgeous. She relished the thought of Sawyer thinking so, too. At Sawyer's suggestion, the framed photograph of Anya had already been delivered. It was sitting on an easel in the living room, near the fireplace. This was where the small ceremony was to be performed. A perfect choice given that it was situated between a set of double Corinthian columns. A smaller pair of Christmas trees flanked the columns, also decked out in white and blue lights and little white satin bows. Dani imagined Anya and Nate saying "I do." It didn't hurt in the least. If she had tears in her eyes, they would be tears of joy.

She found Nate in the back gardens, pacing. "Hey," Dani

said. He stopped, looked up, nodded, then continued pacing. Dani hurried over to him. "She's coming," she said.

Nate's head snapped up. "How do you know?"

"Because Sawyer is going to bring her here no matter what."

"No matter what? As in he's going to throw her over his broad shoulders and carry her here?"

"If he has to."

Nate suddenly took Dani's hands. "What if I'm making a mistake?" Dani thought of the photograph. Anya's beaming face when Nate asked her to marry him.

"Close your eyes," Dani said.

"What?"

"Just do it." Nate closed his eyes. "Family. Happy. Love. Children."

He opened his eyes, stared at Dani. "Anya," he said quietly.

"Exactly," Dani said. "But I think there's something you're going to have to do?"

"What?"

Dani turned Nate around and pointed in the window. Ruth was standing, staring out at them. "You have to stand up for your wife. You have to let your grandmother know, in no uncertain terms, that Anya deserves her rightful place."

"I've been a bit of a coward, haven't I?"

"It's time to stop being afraid of your grandmother and start being afraid of your wife instead."

Nate laughed. "Thank you." He kissed Dani on the cheek. "And I'm sorry."

"For what?"

"For ignoring you for the past two years. All you did is make the best decision for you at the time, and I punished you for it. I really am sorry."

Dani nodded and then glanced at the window again only to see Sawyer standing there smiling and giving her a thumbs-up. "I think it worked out for the best," Dani said. If she hadn't thought she wanted Nate back, she never would have fallen in love with Sawyer. Love worked in mysterious ways. She took Nate's hand. "I think your bride has arrived. Let's go."

Sawyer was holding court in the parlor room with at least six women from six to sixty surrounding him. Peals of laughter rang out. He was wearing a tuxedo. He looked absolutely gorgeous. Dani was a little stunned and forgot all about wanting him to see how good she looked. But he did anyway. He stepped out of the estrogen circle and looked her up and down appreciatively. Then, he gave her the best compliment a bad boy could. He didn't say a word. He just let out a low whistle. Dani grinned, then before she could stop to mind her Southern manners, she kissed him full on the lips. When they pulled away he kissed her neck just so he could give a low growl in her ear.

"Is Anya here?" Nate asked the minute they parted.

"She's upstairs," Sawyer said. "She said she wanted to change."

"Is she—still marrying me?"

"Well. That's probably going to be up to you," Sawyer said.

"What do you mean?" Nate said.

"There's good news and there's bad news," Sawyer said.

"Please. Spit it out," Dani said.

"She's hammered," Sawyer said.

"She had one and a half glasses of wine?" Dani asked.

"Look. She wanted to talk. So we went to the Duck and Dive again—and I might have mentioned how you had three Dark and Stormys—"

"Oh no," Dani said.

"And so she had to have four."

"Four?" Dani said. "Four?" She couldn't believe Anya

was still walking and talking. They were twice the punch of a glass of wine.

"What's a Dark and Stormy?" Nate said.

"Nate," Dani said. "Find the priest. Reschedule the wedding."

"Not until I talk to Anya," Nate said.

"Whiskey, dark rum, and who knows what else," Dani said. "They're lethal."

"Is she sick?" Nate said.

"Actually she's just—rather—bubbly so far," Sawyer said.

"TOODALOO!" It sounded like a battle cry, and it rang out from the direction of the foyer. Dani, Sawyer, and Nate all rushed in. There, at the top of the stairs, was Anya posing in a bright yellow gown with tons of crinoline. She was carrying a yellow parasol. She looked like a cross between Big Bird and Little Bo Peep. Nate's mouth dropped slightly open, too, as Anya made a show of coming down the stairs. Behind her, her sister, Victoria, tripped after her, trying to hold up the train. Partygoers, sensing an entrance, began to gather and stare at the phenomena. When Anya reached the bottom, she held her hand out for Nate to kiss. He seemed frozen in place.

"You look . . . you look . . ." he said.

"Southern?" she said.

"I guess so," he said. He finally took her hand and kissed it.

"Y'all are so kind," Anya said to the crowd in a fake Southern accent.

"My word," Ruth said, stepping into the foyer. "What is this?"

"I made Christmas grits!" Victoria said. She thrust up a container.

"What in the world is Christmas grits?" Ruth asked.

"Grits with red and green M&M's," Victoria said.

"Please, everyone, do spread out and mingle," Ruth said, trying to herd her guests back into the parlor room.

"Is there dancing?" Anya asked, grabbing Nate's hand and pulling him into the living room.

"I think I need a drink," Dani said.

"Way ahead of you," Sawyer said. He handed her a flask. She stopped short of telling him she loved him and took a swig.

"Ruth," Dani said. "Any chance there's a pot of coffee on?"

"Coffee," Ruth said. "If we want to sober that girl up, we're going to need charcoal." The music picked up in tempo. Anya was leading a dance. Despite Ruth's horror, the guests loved her. Soon they were gathered around her and Nate as they danced, clapping in rhythm. Ruth stood on the outside of the circle, fuming. Dani stepped up. It was now or never.

"Ruth?" she said.

Ruth turned, her mouth in a grimace. "It's not too late," she said. "My wedding dress is upstairs. Put it on, and I'll grab Father Mike. You and Nate can get married and—"

Dani grabbed Ruth's hand and pulled her over to the photograph on the easel. She reached in her little clutch and pulled out her phone. She brought up the picture of her after Nate proposed, the one with the look of horror, and showed it to Ruth. "That's my face after Nate proposed," Dani said. Ruth studied it, then searched Dani's face. "And this is Anya's face after Nate proposed." Dani discreetly lifted the covering on the photograph, slowly exposing Anya's beaming face. "I want you to look at each photograph, and think carefully, Ruth. Honestly. Which face do you think has the best chance of bringing you great-grandchildren?"

Ruth clasped her hands under her chin and pursed her lips. She looked to the ceiling. Then looked at the photos again. "Do you think they'll have a British accent?"

"I'm sure Nate's Southern drawl will give them a run for their money."

"She does seem to be a hit with the guests." Just then Anya's laughter boomed through the room. Ruth paled.

"Keep Calm and Carry On," Dani said. "Keep calm and carry on."

Victoria suddenly popped up from behind them. "Off with her head! Mind the Gap! Blimey! Gobsmacked." She grinned at Ruth. "Criminey, it's balmy in here," she said. She held up her purse. "Do ye mind if I put Christmas Crackers and Crowns on everyone's plate?"

Dani waited to see if Ruth would spontaneously combust. Instead, she looked at the photograph of Anya, then back at Victoria. She grabbed a paper crown out of Victoria's parcel and put it on her head.

"Follow me," she said.

If anyone had told Dani that everyone would be sitting at the table wearing colorful paper crowns and opening Christmas Crackers, including Ruth Hathaway, well, she would have thought he or she was on crack. But showing Ruth the photographs and mentioning the word *great-grandchildren* had certainly seemed to do the trick. Dani just wished she'd had time to tell Anya that she could stop acting like a crazy person. Dani didn't realize how crazy until she realized the swan was missing from the middle of the table. At first she thought it had been cleared to make way for the platters heaped with ham, and roast, but soon, Anya's arm movements gave it away. The swan was in Anya's lap and she was cooing at it and stroking it like a kitten.

When the salads were cleared, Ruth stood and lifted her glass of champagne. "I'd like to propose a toast," she said. "To Danielle—"

Anya let out a growl. Nate pushed back his chair. "I have to stop you there, Nanna," he said. "You shouldn't be toasting Danielle. She's only here on assignment."

"A Southern Christmas," Dani answered when everyone stared at her.

"The British are coming!" Anya shouted as she thrust her fist in the air.

"Hear, hear," Victoria said. From down the table, their mother, Margaret, shushed them.

"Nathaniel," Ruth said. "I—"

"Grandmother, do let me finish," Nate said. "Anya is the woman I'm going to marry. Although I must announce that we have decided to wait until the new year and have a proper wedding in a proper church."

"Nathaniel, I think that's—" Ruth said.

"Frankly, Grandmother, I don't want to hear what you think right now. Dani is simply here for 'A Southern Christmas'—"

Anya stood. "Oh, bloody hell. That's not the real assignment. That's just her cover story. The real story was on how to get your ex back. You, darling, were all she wanted for Christmas." Besides swaying and slurring her words, and molesting a swan, Dani was impressed that Anya hadn't passed out yet.

"What?" Nate said.

"Let's not worry about that," Danielle said. "That was ages ago. You're in love with Anya, and I'm in love with Sawyer." She gasped, then slapped her hand over her mouth. It was the first time she'd said it. "Damn," she said under her breath. Sawyer started to chuckle. This was worse than falling asleep and drooling on him. She was never going to hear the end of it.

"Nathaniel, what I was going to say—" Ruth started once again.

"What?" Anya yelled. She stood up, clanked the swan down at her place setting, and swayed. "That you won the war?"

"It is true, we did win the war," Ruth said. "Just like we should have won the War of Northern Aggression."

"Grandmother," Nate said. "That's all in the past."

"The War of Northern Aggression is just as important now in the year 2014 as it ever has been. However—"

"Did you bring our tea, Mother?" Anya shouted down the table. "Perhaps Ruth would like to dump it in the bathtub."

"Oh please, do it," Sawyer said, snapping pictures. "Please, please, dump tea in the bathtub." Dani stepped on his foot.

"I love you, too," Sawyer leaned down and whispered. Dani lit up like a firecracker. The violinists were still playing, and as the noise level at the table increased, they moved in closer and played louder.

Ruth began to strike her fork against her champagne glass until everyone quieted down. "Do let me speak. This is still my house. Nathaniel, you will sit down."

"I love Anya!" Nate shouted. Anya yanked him back into his seat and nodded at Ruth.

"To Danielle," Ruth said. "Who helped me realize that Anya Pennington was the woman my Nate should marry."

"What?" Anya said.

"She did?" Nate said.

"Hear, hear!" Mr. Pennington said.

"Dear," Ruth said, "you are welcome in my home, and I have no designs whatsoever on your ghastly tea. Or your Christmas grits for that matter."

"More for me!" Victoria shouted.

"What about the lanterns on your porch?" Anya asked. "Will you take them down?"

"Let's not push it," Ruth said. "Merry Christmas." The table stood, thrust their glasses in the air.

"Merry Christmas!" they said as one. Dani leaned in to kiss Sawyer when something nailed her on the head and dropped at her place setting. She picked up the swan, and looked at Anya.

"Thank you," she said, hugging it to her chest.

"Merry Christmas," Anya said.

"Pass the Christmas grits!" Victoria shouted.

The food kept coming. Dani had to taste a bit of everything. Roast, and ham, and buttery biscuits. Turkey with corn bread stuffing, and gravy, and cheesy potatoes, and green bean casserole. "Save room for the red velvet white chocolate cake," Dani whispered to Sawyer. "It's to die for."

"I'm going to need a stretcher to carry you home," Sawyer whispered back.

"I thought you brought the horse," Dani said. Sawyer tried to wrestle the swan out of her arms, but she held on to it with an iron grip. The two started to laugh, and it took a long time to stop. After dinner and before dessert there was a chorus of crackles as guests popped open their Christmas Crackers. Dani's contained a large, fake diamond ring. Sawyer shook his head as she placed it on her finger.

"Setting a really bad precedent," he said. Dani laughed, then felt another rush of joy as his meaning sunk in. She tucked the swan in her lap, and waited for the red velvet cake. "Oh my God," Sawyer said after he took the first bite. "Oh my God."

"Right?" Dani said. "Right?"

"I'm really starting to like the South," Sawyer said.

Shortly after dessert, leaving the other guests to their dancing, Dani and Sawyer stepped out onto the wraparound porch. At the bottom of the hill, the horse and carriage could be heard coming down the street. It stopped in front of the house and waited. Sawyer held out his arm. "Madam," he said.

"For me?" Danielle said.

"For you," Sawyer said. Together, they skipped down the steps toward the waiting carriage. Stars glittered overhead. The horse whinnied. There was a smell of cookies baking in the air. Dani lifted her head to the sky and searched for reindeer. It was beginning to look a lot like Christmas.

Chapter 14

Dani and Sawyer stood in the sailboat, next to the bed. It had been a long night, but Danielle was charged with desire. All her senses were on fire. Sawyer looked so handsome in his tux, especially with his bow tie taken off and the first couple of buttons undone. "You're beautiful," he said.

"So are you." He took her hand and kissed it. She slid her arms around his neck and pulled him down for a real kiss. Soon their bodies were pressed together, mouths and hands hungrily exploring each other. When Sawyer touched her breasts she felt a tingle all the way down to her toes. After a bit of teasing, he stopped to kiss up and down her neck. She groaned, grabbed his shirt with both hands, and tore it down the center. "Woman!" he said. "It's a rental."

"Don't call me woman."

"You're going to pay for that." He playfully threw her down on the bed and straddled her.

"Please don't rip my dress," she said.

"Wouldn't dream of it." She smiled, then rolled over and let him unzip her. Soon she was out of her dress and he his pants. She told him to keep his ripped shirt on. He laughed and tipped a fake cowboy hat. "Ma'am." He admired her black lace bra and panties, gently outlining every bit with his finger. She wrapped her legs and arms around him, and whispered every little thing she wanted him to do to her. He was happy to oblige. She was already thinking ahead to next Christmas. She would definitely break out the naughty Santa outfit. He was going to love it.

On Christmas morning they awoke to the sound of seagulls. Dani was once again draped over Sawyer, but this time they were skin to skin. She stirred and then a few seconds later his hands began to rub up and down her body. In less than a minute they were making love again. They couldn't get enough of each other. They did it again in the tiny shower, after laughing, and kissing, and knocking each other into the walls. Then it was coffee and donuts up on the deck, each back in their sweatpants and shirts. The sun was beaming on the water, causing it to glitter like gold.

"Chocolate eclairs and coffee," Sawyer said. "Very Southern."

"A mouthful of amazing," Dani said.

"You can say that again," Sawyer said, coming in to lick a bit of chocolate off of her bottom lip. "Should we open our presents?"

"How about we take a walk on the beach first?" Dani suggested. "We can open them there."

"Perfect."

The roads were clear, and they cranked Christmas carols on the radio as they drove to Wrightsville Beach. They found primo parking and soon they were standing with their toes in the sand, watching the waves crash onshore.

"I hope you're not thinking of the Russian nanny," Dani said.

Sawyer threw his head back and roared with laughter. "I lied about her," he said.

"Good."

"She's actually Polish." Dani pushed him, then he grabbed her around the waist and spun her around. Then they sat on the sand and exchanged gifts. Dani made Sawyer open his first.

"Circus toys!" he exclaimed. The delight in his voice was real. He examined each piece carefully. The tiger. The giraffe. The elephant. The circus train and tent. He set them all up in the sand and gazed at them. "I love them," he said. "Thank you."

"You're welcome."

"Maybe we'll go on safari and see them for real." It sounded amazing. "Your turn." He handed her a box that was too small to be teacups.

"I thought you got me teacups," she said.

"There's no more tea," he said. "I dumped it all in the bathtub."

Dani was laughing as she opened the box. She stopped when she saw the gorgeous blue topaz and diamond necklace glittering back at her. She gasped. She'd forgotten how beautiful it was. "How did you know?"

"How could I not know? It was meant for you." He took it out of the box and went to put it on her.

"I couldn't," she said. "It was a small fortune."

"I put it on Adel's credit card," he joked.

"I love it." She held her hair back as he clasped it around her neck. Soon, he was kissing it.

"Thank you," she said, putting her hands on the side of his face. "You gave me Christmas."

"Y'all come back now, hear?" he said in his best Southern accent.

"That's terrible," she said.

"I'll work on it," he said. They lay on the sand and listened to the waves. "How about a Texas Christmas next year?"

"Hook 'em horns," Dani said.

"Don't ever say that again," Sawyer said. They laughed, and then kissed, and then played with the tiger and the giraffe in the sand.

CHRISTMAS IN MONTANA

CATHY LAMB

For Karen Calcagno

Chapter 1

I am, currently, the manager for the hard-rock band Hell-fire.

I am quitting tomorrow. My boss, front man Ace Hell-fire, real name Peter Watson, son of a pastor, will be un-happy.

It's going to be a sticky situation, but it doesn't change my mind.

I have been traveling the world for ten years with Ace, his band, and crew. I have listened to more eardrum-splitting concerts and head-banging rehearsals, and been witness to more temper tantrums and wildness than I ever wanted to see. My nerves are shot, my exhaustion complete. I don't think I want to travel again unless it's to a remote cabin in the woods.

I love to sew, but I haven't sewn in years. I love to em-broider, but I don't know if I remember the cross-stitch. I love to cook, but haven't followed a recipe in way too long. I love to ski, garden, and ride horses, but I never do any of those things.

I have lived out of suitcases for much of every year, my

outfits a collage of color, but now I want to find a home, stay in it, and set up a sewing room.

I am a country girl from Kalulell, Montana, who has been working with hard-core rock musicians out of Los Angeles and I am done. I am headed home for Christmas, and then I will figure out Plan F, the F standing for my Future.

I miss small town life. I have always missed it, especially during the Christmas season. I did not miss, however, what happened on a snowy, dark night on a curvy road. It still haunts me.

Some might say I ran from small town country life, that I wanted the twinkly lights of the city and the excitement.

They would be wrong. I was never running from it. I loved it.

I was running from him.

"You what?"

"We sold the house, Laurel." My mother smiled, fists up in victory.

"And the land." My aunt Emma smiled, then high-fived my mother across the rolled sugar cookie dough. "The feminists are free."

I leaned back in my chair at our eighty-five-year-old wood table, in our cozy kitchen, in the home that my great-granddad and great-grandma built by hand, and did not smile. I felt the blood leaving my face. "Are you kidding me?"

"No, sweetheart, I'm not," my mother, Ellie, said.

"No joke," Aunt Emma said. "We've established our financial independence until we're one-hundred-year-old Montana women."

"But . . . but . . . I don't understand." My voice squeaked.

"We sold because we needed the money," my mother said, wielding a red cookie cutter.

"You needed the money?" I felt sick. I ran my hands

through my hair. It's brown, with red highlights. My mother says the red is from the temperamental Irish in me, via her family. She and my aunt have the same thick hair, only theirs is shot through with white. "What do you mean?"

"We mean that our apron business makes us some money, but not what we need," Aunt Emma said, tossing dough from hand to hand.

My mother and aunt were wearing matching aprons with Rudolph the Red-Nosed Reindeer on the front. Rudolph's eyes were crossed and he looked like he'd drunk too much spiked eggnog. It was one of their best sellers. Obviously it wasn't selling enough.

"Why didn't you tell me? I would have given you the money for anything you needed or wanted. Anything."

"The day I take money from my beloved, hard-rocking daughter is the day I want to be dropped from a plane without a parachute."

"You are not our parachute, golden eyes," Aunt Emma echoed.

"But—" I was going to cry, I knew it.

I stared at the Christmas cookies, red and green sprinkles covering four-leaf clovers. We always decorate St. Patrick's Day clovers to honor our Irish ancestors. "You're not sick, are you?" I felt faint.

"Heavens to Betsy, no," my mother said. "We want to travel around the world. Before it's too late."

"We're going to become traveling ladybugs," Aunt Emma said. "First stop: Ireland. The homeland."

"Ladybugs!" My mother flapped her wings. She had flour on her chin. "Society told us we had to be a certain way when we were younger. We had to be ladylike. We never bought in to that hogwash nonsense, and we're not buying in to it now, so we're going to call ourselves ladybugs and travel into our old age. We want adventures."

"And, darling," my aunt said, laying down a row of Red Hots, "we need to think of the future. Sewing aprons is fine for now, but what if we get sick in twenty years and can't sew? We both have a touch of arthritis in our hands. We need a nest egg for security."

"So you sold the house and all twenty acres?" I could hardly speak. "When are you moving?"

"We're not," my mother said, twirling a clover cookie cutter on her finger. "We're going to become world wanderers, but here's the gift. When we get home from globe skipping, we're staying right here."

"Here," Aunt Emma said. "Until we're both"—she pointed up to the blue Montana sky—"up there."

"If we make it," my mother said. "We may get naughty on our world travels. As strong women, we will do as we please."

"Naughty, naughty," my aunt said, and they both laughed. "We might end up"—she pointed to the floor—"down there."

Oh, they thought they were funny.

"I don't understand," I said, trying to find my way through this crooked conversation. "You've sold the house and the land, but you're not moving."

"Right-o, dearie-o," my aunt said. "It's going to be his land, but we're going to stay in our home."

"What? Who owns it?"

My aunt and my mother lost their cheer instantly, and my stomach took a nosedive out my toes. My mother put an arm around one shoulder, my aunt put an arm around the other, their drunken reindeers ogling me.

Oh no. I knew who it was. I so knew. I swayed. I closed my eyes.

"We went to him, honey," my mother said. "He did not come to us."

"We brought him a Christmas cake in the shape of a Thanksgiving turkey because we are grateful."

"It took us all day to bake and ice in red and green," my mother said. "The feathers were tricky. He made us an incredibly generous offer. More than what it's worth."

"We couldn't turn it down. We know you don't want the house, Laurel."

"I do want the house. I always have."

My mother's and aunt's faces betrayed their shock. "But your work . . . you live in Los Angeles . . . we thought you were never coming back to Montana . . . you said many times you would never live here again."

That was because of *him*. "I could have bought the house from you. I would have liked to. You could have stayed forever."

My mother opened her mouth, but she couldn't speak. My aunt said, her voice wobbling, "Dear girl. I am so sorry."

"Sweetheart," my mother said, her eyes filling.

I took a deep, shuddery breath. "Who owns it?"

"Josh, honey," my mother said, holding my hand tight, her face crushed. "Josh owns it."

That night, tucked up in my pink childhood bedroom, fighting back grief, I thought about our home.

Carrick and Mabel Stewart built our light green farmhouse when they arrived here in Kalulell from Ireland in 1925 as a young couple. It's rambling, two stories, with a huge rock hearth to combat chilling Montana winters. The dining room is now our sewing room, filled with fabrics, sewing machines, tables, and jars of buttons, rickrack, and lace for my mother and aunt's apron business.

Our home has the original trim, a curling banister, wide front porch, dormer windows, and wood floors. We remodeled the kitchen again three years ago, adding a nook and French doors, but kept its traditional style to respect our past.

We recycled old lathe board, used it for cabinet doors, and painted them blue. We used bricks from a crumbled garden wall my grandma built to cover the entire wall behind the woodstove. We used my great-grandma's white kitchen hutch for linens and my grandma's light blue apothecary chest with multiple drawers for the silverware.

We hung up my grandma's kitchen utensils to honor her, along with black-and-white photos of all the grandparents. My great-grandparents' daughter, Dorothy, was born here, as were my mother and aunt. My late grandparents gave the home to my mother when I was born, with a half ownership for my aunt, who was still married to her husband at the time.

My aunt Emma's husband died when he fell off their roof when I was ten. She said she didn't miss him because he constantly criticized her. When she moved back in with my mother she had to re-find her voice, she told me, as it had been smothered, and she vowed to never let it happen again. "I became a feminist then. Being a feminist means you believe in equal rights and opportunities. That's it. I wanted an equal right to live a peaceful life. That's why I won't marry again."

I thought with the apron money, and a fully paid for house, that they did fine.

Clearly, I was wrong, as our home was no longer ours. Another wave of grief hit me like a wrecking ball. For a second in my pink bedroom, I couldn't breathe.

I knew every stream, meadow, rock, and tree on our twenty acres. We have five horses and two furry mutts named Thomas and James and a difficult, old gray cat named Zelda who scares the poor dogs to pieces.

This is our home.

Correction: It *was* our home.

I would get it back.

Oh, my poor beat-up heart. The blond giant was more knee-knocking gorgeous than ever. He was taller, broader, and tougher. The true difference, though, was in his light green eyes. He used to look at me with gentleness, kindness, indulgence, humor, respect, and an abundance of "I want you naked now," which set me on fire about twenty-four hours a day. All that was gone. His eyes were . . . neutral. Normal. Polite. A little friendly, not much.

"Hello, Josh."

He smiled, but it was a bit restrained. He walked down the porch steps of his home. I couldn't move. My feet wouldn't budge.

"Hello, Laurel. Good to see you again."

"You, too." Ah heck. What a voice. Deeper than before, it seemed. I had waited three days to call him after my mother and aunt told me about the sale. I hadn't been up to confronting him, to seeing him, and asking if we could talk. I could feel my courage for this meeting fading rapidly, but there was anger there, too. Josh knew I loved my home. How could he have bought it, even if my mother and aunt asked him to, without asking me first? "How are you?"

"Fine. And you?"

"Fine." Sort of. That was a semi-lie. I was wiped out. Felt empty. I'd been dragging loneliness around with me for a long time. Christmas was always hard. Being near him was killing me. Jab a stake in my heart and twist. *Get a grip,* I told myself. Self-pity is about as attractive as snakebites. "What have you been up to?"

He didn't answer for long seconds, studying my face. "You mean for the last twelve years since I saw you?"

"Yes. I mean, no. Yes." I closed my mouth. Yes, I wanted to know what he'd been doing for twelve years; no, I didn't want to sound desperate or stalker-ish. "But what are you doing now?"

"Right now I'm talking to Laurel Kelly."

"Yes. Okay. Well." I felt myself blush. It was like I was a teenager again, blushing around my boyfriend.

"Why don't you tell me first, Laurel? What have you been doing the last twelve years?"

"I've been chasing a rocker around the world. And you?"

"I've been chasing a business."

"How is your business?"

"Chased down."

He was always clever with words. The cowboy boots, the jeans, the cowboy hat, they could not hide the fact that the man had a top-notch brain, had top-notch grades in college, and had become a top-notch Montana businessman. He owned a number of businesses and buildings downtown.

"Good for you, Josh." My words came out soft, emotional. I blinked so my suddenly hot eyes would stop being hot. "I knew you would."

"Did you?"

"Yes, of course."

He took another step toward me. We were standing way too close. I saw those light green eyes travel over my brown slash reddish hair. I had brushed it before I came, my hands shaking at the thought of this very encounter. Still, it's generally untamable. The ends have pink streaks on the bottom two inches, done when I was in London last month.

I had tried on six different outfits, three pairs of boots, and had finally settled on a shirt that looked like it had been painted by Monet. It was slightly tight. I also wore jeans, fancy cowboy boots with pink leather flowers at the top, and a puffy pink jacket with a collar and belt. My ears are double pierced, and I was wearing two sets of silver hoops and a red knitted hat with a fluffy camellia on it. I like color.

"This is your home?" It was a dumb question. Of course it was his home. Whose home did I think it was? Mrs. Claus's? An elf's? Josh didn't make fun of me, though. He never had.

My mother had given me his address. His home was about ten minutes away from ours, private, on the river, surrounded by land, sixty acres, which attached to ours. It was about five years old. Craftsman style. Huge windows. Wide deck. A view, like ours, of the sweeping, bluish-purple Swan Mountains.

"Yes."

"It's absolutely stunning." I looked straight ahead, which set my gaze right on that Paul Bunyan chest. I had lain on that chest a hundred times . . . and more. One graphic naked image after another chased its way through my sizzling brain.

"Thank you. Come on in, and we'll talk."

And that was that. I walked beside the man that I had run from years ago.

Say yes, Josh, please, I thought.

I mean, yes to the house. Not yes to me.

Because I would say no to yes to me.

I think.

"Josh, thanks for seeing me."

"Anytime." He handed me a cup of coffee. I took it and tried to hide the fact that my hands were shaking. He sat down across from me at his kitchen table, and for a moment I stared straight out his windows and watched the snowflakes flutter down.

His home, if it was possible, was even more incredible on the inside than the outside. The ceilings went up two stories, and the windows framed the Montana mountains and meadows, now covered in snow. They were right there, as if they were a part of the house, only they were freezing cold and we were warm.

He had a two-story fireplace, the fire roaring, with towering bookshelves on both sides. There was leather furniture, wood floors, and a kitchen with everything I'd always wanted—granite counters, two ovens, and open shelving for my collection of cookbooks. *Not your collection of cookbooks, Laurel,* I said to myself. *Sheesh.*

I noticed that he did not have a Christmas tree. He and I used to love Christmas. We always exchanged ornaments and little gifts, as we were both broke. I made him Christmas cookies.

After more shallow chitchat, I put the coffee down and laced my fingers together before I looked up into those familiar green eyes. "My mom and Aunt Emma told me that they have sold their house and land to you."

"Yes."

"They said that you're going to use their land, but they can stay in the house until, Aunt Emma says, 'They're flying high in heaven, if they get there.'"

"That's right." His gaze did not waver.

"I didn't know they needed the money."

"You haven't been home in a while."

"I come home, Josh, but you're right, not enough. That doesn't mean I don't talk to them. We call, we Skype, we e-mail. I didn't know. They didn't share it with me. They don't have a mortgage on the home, and they said the aprons were selling well."

"Your mom and aunt will be fine, Laurel." His eyes, for the first time, softened. "If the house needs any repairs, I'll pay for them. In fact, I'm having a new roof put on in the spring. I had the front porch and back deck repaired already."

"I noticed. They look a lot better. They sound a lot better, too. No cracking. Thank you."

"They like being outside, so they need the decks. When a pipe burst, I had it fixed, too. I'm not going to let the house fall down around them."

"I know. You would never do that." Our gazes locked. I saw a lot in his I didn't want to see, felt a coldness I didn't want to feel, a remoteness, a wariness . . . I didn't blame him. "Anyhow, Josh. I wish they hadn't sold it to you. I'd like to buy the land and the house back from you."

"You want to buy it back?"

"Yes. I'll pay you what you paid my mother and aunt, plus, say, fifteen percent?"

"No."

I felt like he'd pushed me, which he would never do. "No?"

"That's right. No."

"Why . . . why not? It's pure profit for you."

"Because I need the land."

"Why?"

"I'll use the land now, but I plan on eventually donating it to a charitable trust here so that it will never be developed."

"I have no plans to develop our land. I just want the house and the acreage. It's been in my family for generations."

"I know, and I understand."

I felt my temper start to take off. "You apparently don't. This is my family's land, Josh, it's not yours."

"It is now."

And there it was. Josh's strength. His indomitable will. He had always been kind to me, consistently, but even when we were younger, I knew it was there. I saw it in the way he played sports, how tough and relentless he was, how he skied. I heard it when he told me his plans for his life, for his business. I saw it in the way he stood up to kids who were bullying weaker kids, and how fast his fists flew, to protect them.

Josh had come from a broken home. His mother died when he was six and his father decided to be a real man and deal with that grief by binge drinking and bullying Josh. Josh had moved out of his home the summer before his junior year of high school into a small apartment above his football coach's home. He worked twenty hours a week at the grocery store to pay for his expenses and his car. And now that boy was a hard-driving man.

I tried to stay reasonable. "I'd like it back."

He nodded. "I'm sorry."

"Please, Josh."

"No."

"You are still so stubborn."

"This is business, Laurel. It's not personal."

"How can you possibly say that? It's my home. It is personal. It's personal to me." I could tell he was not moving.

"I told you, Laurel. I want the land."

"And I want the house." *Oh, Josh,* I thought. *I have missed you, but now I'm getting pretty dang ticked off.* "It's my mother's, my aunt's, it was to go to me when they—" I couldn't even say it. I loved my aunt and mother from here to the moon.

"You live in Los Angeles. You work for Hellfire. Why would you want a house in Montana? They told me you had no plans to return and live here, ever."

"It's our home, Josh. And I love that home. It's part of me. Part of who I am. Who my grandparents were, who their parents were."

I did not want to tell him that I had quit my job and was trying to figure out where to live and what to do, also called Plan Q, as in Questions. I couldn't live here, that was for sure, but I could return for vacations. I think. If I avoided seeing this man, right in front of me. "I love Montana. I want to be able to return and stay here sometimes."

Josh unexpectedly leaned across the table and wound his finger around my hair. Even though he did not touch my skin, I felt his touch like a blaze of sexy heat. That heat was still there after twelve years. I was not surprised. I thought I was going to catch on fire in his driveway looking at him.

"I like the pink," he said. "And I like that your hair is as soft as I remember it."

Yep. I was going to heat up so high I melted. *Control yourself, Laurel!*

"You're more beautiful than you were twelve years ago, Laurel."

I blushed. I am a band manager. I yell at the men in our band now and then, including Ace. When we're performing with other bands, sometimes I yell at those guys, too. I know how to get them to work together, how to get them sober quick, and how to get the stage up and ready.

I handle a thousand details and a lot of employees. I know about lighting, sound, videos, everything that goes into a head-banging concert. I can move a hundred people at a time to one hotel after another, competently, quickly, and get the ones who need to be on stage, on stage.

And Josh made me blush.

"You still blush." I heard his low chuckle.

"No, I don't."

"Yes, you do."

"Okay, I do." I laughed. I suddenly felt young around him, even though he was making me mad.

He tilted his head, studied me, then slowly smiled. I knew he felt that crazy attraction, too.

"Josh, please reconsider." *I really want to kiss you even though I'm ticked off.*

"Do you know how much I paid your mother and aunt?"

"Yes," I told him.

"And you're able to pay me that?"

"Yes." I had been paid well to manage Hellfire and I didn't have a life, so I didn't spend money.

He smiled. "I always knew you would be a massive success in whatever you did, Laurel. But I'm sorry, my answer is still no."

I pulled back so my pink-tipped hair fell from his fingers. I wanted to throw something. In the end, all that my family had owned for almost ninety years would be gone. Out of our family. "It's my family's. You know that. How can you do this?"

"They asked me to."

"And I'm asking for it back." I was upset. I couldn't believe our home was not ours.

"I don't like hurting you, Laurel, you know I don't—"

"I don't know anything about you anymore."

"I don't want to hurt you."

"Did you think this wouldn't hurt me?"

"I assumed you knew."

"I didn't."

He was immovable. He'd made his decision and that was it.

"I feel like throwing something at you," I said.

"I can tell. Try not to throw the coffee. It's probably still hot."

"I want to buy it back, Josh."

"I know, and no."

I thought of our light green farmhouse. The small parlor with the red toile wallpaper that I read books in every day as a kid, next to books my great-grandma read. I thought of my pink bedroom with the two dormer windows that used to be my mother's, the long wood farm table, scarred and nicked from generations of my relatives using it, the two rocking chairs built by my granddad, the stairs that creaked from generations of feet, and the red barn that had been restored by my granddad.

Gone. It was all gone.

We argued more, but nothing I said moved him.

"Then, I guess that's it. You own *my* home." I stood up and walked out before I started snuffling like a baby. I did not want him to see my tears. It would be too embarrassing. I was also afraid I might try to tackle him and hold him down until he acquiesced. I would not be successful. He was a former football player and still looked it.

I heard him call my name, soft, and I heard his boots behind mine, but I kept walking. I heard him again as I hurried down the driveway.

"Laurel—"

"Go to hell, Josh," I said.

"I think I've already been there."

"Then go back."

"I'd rather not. I don't like it there. Drive careful."

I whipped around and glared at him. Those two words about undid me. Josh had always said that to me, every time I'd gotten in a car. "Drive careful." Then he'd given me a hug and a kiss. A tall, tough kid, who told his girl-friend to drive careful.

I slammed the door to my car, reversed fast to show some immature rebellion, and kept my head at an angle so he couldn't see the tears streaming down my cheeks.

The tears weren't only for the house.

I took a detour on the way home, probably to torture my-self further. Snowflakes fell, light and fluffy, as I drove along the same road where it happened.

I stopped at the curve and climbed out of my car.

The river rushed by, snow covering the banks and road like white blankets, exactly as it was that night.

I don't remember all of it, but I remembered enough.

I remembered the words, the skidding, the echoing crash, the cold, the blackness, the fear.

I remembered what happened next.

I sat back on my ankles and let my tears loose.

Chapter 2

I stood and stared at our farmhouse when we finished decorating it the next afternoon. It had taken hours, and the snow, fortunately, had held off. My aunt Emma and mother blared Christmas music from their newly fixed porch. "Jingle Bells." "Santa Claus Is Coming to Town." "Frosty the Snowman." We sang along.

Our home—which was no longer ours—was all lit up with Christmas lights. The weekend before Thanksgiving, every year, all the lights and decorations went up.

My aunt and my mother, to my acute embarrassment when I was a teenager, could not be normal with their Christmas lights, as they couldn't be normal when they decorated the five Christmas trees in our house, either.

An electrician friend had been paid to build an eight-foot-tall frog with green lights, blue lights for the eyes, and a red bow. "It's our Christmas frog, Gary."

"You've named the frog Gary?"

"Yes," my mom said. "We met a sanctimonious, misogynistic, sexist man named Gary recently, so we thought the name fitting, although it is rather insulting to our frog."

In front of the frog was a five-foot-tall giant dragonfly in pinks, reds, and yellows. The frog had a red tongue pointed at the dragonfly. "The dragonfly's name is Tilge."

I didn't even ask.

There was another display with a seven-foot-tall ginger-bread house. It would have been a sweet Christmas display except for the green-faced witch on top, à la *Hansel and Gretel*.

The house was lined with colorful, twinkly lights, as were a few trees.

My mother grabbed champagne.

"Merry Christmas, Laurel, darling," she said.

"May you live your life as you wish it, not as anyone else wishes it," my aunt said.

"May you always hold your chin high, like the strong woman you are," my mother said, "and follow your dreams."

My mother lit a firework.

Each year they light off two fireworks to celebrate the season. It's an odd July 4th–Christmas tradition. They like to blend their holidays.

My mother kissed my cheek, between explosions. "The family will love the lights."

"What?"

"Everyone's coming here for Christmas Eve this year."

My jaw dropped, I'm sure, to the snow. "Everyone?"

They both turned to me. "Everyone."

I picked my jaw up. "All the wives, the kids, Dad?"

"You bet," my aunt said. "I hope we all survive."

"Should be exciting," my mother drawled. "Hopefully there will be no serious injuries."

"You'll have to serve hot buttered rums then," I muttered, as my mother lit another firework. "Because I'm going to need a bunch of them."

* * *

Ace called. He begged. He was emotional, a "nervous train crashing track jumping wreck," his words. I tried to calm him, comfort him. He hardly heard me.

That night, staring out one of my dormer windows at the giant Christmas frog named Gary, I thought about Christmas Eve. I would refer to it now, until I recovered from it, as the Kelly Family's Chaotic Christmas. Who knew what would happen?

My father would be there along with his three ex-wives, his current wife, and a noisy gang of kids, most related to me via my father, but not all.

With Wife Number One, Amy, my father had two twin daughters, Camellia and Violet. Amy remarried after my father. Her husband's name is Richard. His last name is Longer. One can understand why he gets irate when anyone calls him Dick Longer or Longer, Dick. Camellia and Violet are about two years older than me and each have a five-year-old and a three-year-old. The toddlers are miniature hurricanes who talk, as they have inherited the Wild Bone of the Kelly family, as we call it.

My father left Amy six months after she had the twins. I know. Nice guy. Amy says living with my father was like living with an immature monkey. He met my mother, Wife Number Two, six months later and I came ten months after that. My mother and Amy get along fine, always have, strangely enough, so Camellia and Violet and I grew up together.

I am my mother's only child. She said she never wanted to remarry again because she didn't need Male Stress. She only needed Male Company, now and then. And yes, she made sure I knew she was capitalizing those words.

With Wife Number Three, Chantrea, who was raised in Cambodia and met my father there on one of his exotic plant and flower research expeditions, my father had three sons. The sons' names are Oakie, who is 19, Aspen, 20, and Redwood, 22. They are tattooed and pierced, and are, now and then, arrested for mischievous things, because they, too, are afflicted with the Kelly Wild Bone.

Chantrea has a temper. She periodically throws things at my father's head, so we all make sure we are on the floor when she pitches a fit. Chantrea left my father, then immediately remarried. She divorced recently. Chantrea has another son, with her second ex-husband, named David. David is six. He has an odd fascination with the galaxy and insists we are living in something like a hologram in a fake 3-D setting. He's brilliant. He's confusing.

After Aspen was born, my father quit traveling at Chantrea's fiery insistence and he and Chantrea opened a Cambodian restaurant in town, which she received in the divorce. It's delicious.

Wife Number Four, is named, and I'm not kidding, Velvet. It is not her given name. Her given name is Betsy Elaine Warbinger. Velvet is five years older than me, which makes the whole thing creepy, but predictable. She and my father have a four-year-old girl named Daisy and a three-year-old boy named Banyan.

Velvet also has an eleven-year-old son, whom she named William Robert Rhodes, from a fling she had with a governor of another state, William Robert Rhodes, who was, unfortunately, married at the time. His wife did not appreciate Velvet, who may have, or not, been a successful stripper called Velvet Glove.

Their affair hit the headlines, especially since the governor always touted his "family values," and his new son was his namesake. The governor's wife divorced him, fleeced him, and he did not run for office again. William Robert Rhodes, senior, now lives in Alaska in a village. It is rumored his beard is quite long.

You might have noticed something odd with my father's biological children's names. You are right. We are all named after flowers or trees. My father was a botanist who wrote humorous books and magazine articles about his travels and semi obsession with plants. He's been all over the world and was gone a lot during his first two marriages.

Some people in my family like each other. Some don't. Personalities clash and collide and love on each other. They fight about silly things, like who makes the best pecan pie, Velvet's provocative attire, Chantrea's temper, and the next generation's Wild Bone.

It gives me a Santa's sleigh–sized headache to think of the drama at our home on Christmas Eve.

I simply hope that open warfare will not be declared, as the turkey carving knife will be out as will the hot gravy.

On Tuesday evening, as warned, my twin sisters, Violet and Camellia, came to get me. Violet is blond and tall; Camellia's a brunette and curves. Except for having dimples, like me, they hardly resemble each other. "We're going to Taylor's Bar and Grill," they said.

"We're going that crazy?" Taylor's Bar and Grill had a reputation. The music blared. There was a bucking bronco you could ride in the center of the ring, there was karaoke, and fist fights.

"We need the excitement," Camellia said. "I'm smothered in laundry and mommy-ness. I used to be cool. Look at my hand. Tad bit me."

"Those are impressive bite marks. What is he, part vampire?" I asked.

"No." She seemed miffed, then her face fell. "But he does have these unusually long eyeteeth. They're fang-ish."

"And he's stubborn once he bites down," Violet said, snapping her jaws together. "Like a pit bull."

"As if you should talk about pit bulls, Violet," Camellia

huffed. "Your daughters keep getting kicked out of pre-school. Didn't Lizzy empty all the glitter bottles on some-one's head the other day? And what about Shandry? She took the lizard out, put it down her pants, and tried to leave preschool with it."

"They were playing glitter monster, and Shandry was bringing the lizard home to let it go because she doesn't like to see animals locked up. Don't attack my daughters."

"Then don't criticize my vampire child!"

The twins got into it for a second, then they both, as if on cue, reading each other's minds, grabbed my elbows and pulled me out the door.

At that second, James and Thomas, the mutts, zipped around the corner, tails wagging. They surprised old Zelda, who doesn't like surprises. She clawed the air and let loose with a spine-tingling meow. The dogs yelped and leaped behind the couch.

"They need to man up," I said.

"Your cat runs the place," Violet said, tugging me out.

"Bye, Aunt Ellie, bye, Aunt Emma," they shouted.

"You girls behave," my mother called out. "I do not want to see the sheriff pulling up in his car again with you three in the backseat."

That was a night about two years ago on one of my quick trips home. There was a misunderstanding with a rude, crude man at the bar and Violet let him have it. With her purse. Perhaps Camellia and I jumped in to defend her, too, also wielding dangerous purses. Perhaps the rude, crude man needed stitches.

"Lord, have mercy, neither do I," Aunt Emma called out. "But if it happens, ask if you can ride with Lieutenant Janes. He's a hunk and I'd like to have him in for some dessert."

We agreed to request Lieutenant Janes.

* * *

Taylor's Bar and Grill was packed.

I don't like bars. I don't like being crammed in, I rarely drink, and I don't like the pickup scene. If Violet and Camellia hadn't wanted to recapture their youth as their "mommyness" had worn them out, I would not have come.

The three of us have always been colorful dressers, like my mom and aunt. It's a bonding thing. Camellia was in a burgundy velvet halter, red jeans with a silver buckle, and black heels. Violet was in a purple sequined tank top, jeans, and purple knee-high boots with silver studs. I had my hair in a ponytail, pink tips swinging. I wore a white shirt with all sorts of embroidered flowers on it from Mexico, jeans, and red cowgirl boots.

"You're getting on the bull first," Camellia shouted at me through the high-octane din of country music and talk. She handed me a drink.

"Heck, no," I said. I took a sip of the drink. I would have one drink to get Josh the Edible Cowboy out of my head.

"Heck, yeah," Violet said. "Are you scared?"

I took that as a challenge. The more I rode that buckin' bull, and the more sips of my drink I had between rides, the funnier it became. Camellia and Violet rode, too. On my third ride, I looked up, right into Josh Reed's (otherwise known as the Edible Cowboy) bright, light green eyes, his jaw sporting a five o'clock shadow, his broad shoulders encased in a light blue shirt.

He was a manly, muscled man.

I flew right off that buckin' bull and landed straight on my face.

I heard Camellia and Violet shrieking, "Ride 'em, cowgirl!" and laughing. I laughed, too. What else to do? When I saw Josh, I felt like crying. Laughing doesn't hurt so much.

* * *

"Josh," I said to him, about fifteen minutes later, when he threaded his way through a crush of people to our table. Violet and Camellia gave him a hug, the traitors, although I don't think they knew about him buying my mother and aunt's house.

Violet said, "I suddenly have to powder my nose," and Camellia said, "And I have to powder my ears."

"What?" I said. "You two don't powder anything. The only powder you two know about is gunpowder from your army years."

"Then I'm going to go use my gunpowder on my nose." Violet pointed to her nose.

"I heard it clears the complexion." Camellia patted her cheeks.

They turned away and I was stuck with Josh, the hard-talking, land-taking, house-possessing cowboy.

"Laurel, nice to see you." He sat down beside me.

"I wish I could say that to you, but currently I want to shake you." I crossed my arms over my embroidered flowers.

"Yes, I know."

His face was serious. He was a lot more serious than he was when we were dating as teenagers, and when we were dating in college until that bleak night. It was as if part of his humorous side had dropped out of him. "Who are you here with?"

"Jason Aster, Chuck McDonnel, and about five other men."

"I remember them. What are they doing now?"

"Jason is a part owner of the ski resort and Chuck's a high school science teacher."

"And you're out for guys' night."

"Yes. A friend of ours named Miles Zell is getting married tomorrow. Bachelor party."

"No strippers?"

"I would not be at a party where there were strippers,"

Josh said. "Neither would Jason or Chuck. We're here having beers, that's it. I don't like the bar scene, but Miles is a good friend so we're here."

"I don't like the bar scene, either."

"I noticed you rode the bull." The corner of his mouth tilted up in a smile. I told myself that I did not want to kiss that corner.

"Yes, Camellia and Violet, the terrible twins, forced me and I was actually having fun until I face-planted off it."

"It was graceful."

"Funny." I reminded myself that he owned our green farmhouse, our red barn, and our meadows, rocks, and visiting deer. Plus our purple and blue view of the Swan Mountains. "I don't like you very much right now, Josh."

"I'm aware of that."

He was so calm, unruffled. He watched me closely.

"I am so mad at you."

"I'm aware of that, too."

"You've changed."

"Yes, I have. So have you. It's been twelve years. We're different people."

"But you're hard now. You're too tough. It's like you've lost your heart and your emotions and your humor. You're a wealthy landlord type of man who likes to own things, control things. I think you like knowing that I want my house and land back but you won't sell it to me. It's a power trip for you, isn't it?"

"No, it's not." His voice was clipped, and that jaw tightened right up. "I don't do power trips, Laurel, and I don't appreciate you telling me the type of man that I've become when you don't even know me."

"I know enough."

"You know nothing, Laurel, nothing, of who I am. Do you have any idea how offensive it is for you to call me a wealthy landlord, and to tell me I want control over something you want? And thanks for your judgment about not having a heart or emotions. As if you are one to judge me. I should ask you, what happened to you? What happened to that super-smart, interesting, adventurous, happy girl? Who loved sewing and skiing, baking and fishing, reading books and horseback riding? Who are you now, Laurel? You seem pretty hardened up yourself. Where did the other Laurel go?"

"What do you mean by that? How do you know she's gone?" But he was right. She was gone, gone, gone. Long gone.

"You're a woman who took off for years, hardly ever came home, and then on a rare visit is angry that her mother and aunt came *to me* to ask me to buy their home and land so they could have money to travel, money to live off, money for their future, and still live in the house."

He had done them a huge favor. I got it. I still wanted it back. "It's my family's home and land and you should sell it back to me."

"My answer is still the same. No."

"You're a jerk, Josh, do you know that? There's no give in you, no gentleness, no compassion, no laughter anymore, is there?"

"Yes, there is, but I believe you told me loud and clear twelve years ago you didn't want to see it anymore."

Low blow. That hurt. The pain radiated straight out from my heart.

"Then you went to Los Angeles and became an ungrateful, demanding, angry woman who throws a temper tantrum when she can't get her own way."

I wanted to throw my beer in his face, but I wouldn't. That wasn't me. I did, however, need to get away from him before I kicked him with my red cowgirl boots. Hot tears were burning my eyes. A hot blush was burning my face, and my hot temper was triggered.

I did not want to fight with Josh. I did not want it to be like this. I could feel my chin tremble and I wanted to smack myself until it stopped.

"Laurel," his voice softened. Deep and soft. It ran right through my body.

I turned away, embarrassed because I knew he knew I was about to dissolve into sniffly tears, grabbed my purse, and went to look for my gunpowder-dusting sisters.

It was my way of running from him. Again.

I could say that I don't know what got into me that night, but I do know: Josh got into me. Into my head and heart.

I don't drink much alcohol, probably because I've been around it way too much on tours with Hellfire. Violet and Camellia hardly ever drink now, either. They're mommies. We used to when we were teenagers, we fed that Kelly Family Wild Bone, and we did stupid stuff.

But that night, Camellia said, "I've called my hubby. Told him I'm drinking martinis. He said he'll come and get us in two hours."

"Hi ho, Silver, and gallop away," Violet said. She'd already had three drinks. "Because I need a night off. I need to dance and sing and be a Rockette."

"A Rockette?" I asked.

"Yep. Like this." Then she climbed up on the wooden stage near the bar and did the cancan. Everyone cheered. We knew many of the people there.

"Go, momma!" I shouted.

"Kick 'em high!" Camellia said.

And that started us off on a slippery slope of Kelly Family Wild Bone trouble.

We ordered more drinks. That was a bad idea that became badder.

The three of us ended up on stage singing karaoke. We screeched out, "It's raining men." Then we chortled along with *Saturday Night Fever*'s hit, "Stayin' Alive, Stayin' Alive." We ended with, "We are family, I got all my sisters with me," in which Violet hit a high C for a long, long ear-blistering time and Camellia decided to do a handstand and I did a cartwheel.

A bunch of people we knew from high school joined us and we sang love songs, one about muskrat love. I later took another face-plant off the bull, danced with Camellia and Violet, but not Josh, Edible Cowboy, and laughed 'til my stomach hurt.

I laughed so I wouldn't cry.

"I'll take Laurel home."

"What? Nope and nope," I said to Josh outside Taylor's Bar and Grill. I shook my finger at him as the earth seemed to tilt. "You are not taking me home, mean landowner."

Talo, Camellia's husband, a college professor, had a gentle arm around Camellia's waist. She was nibbling on his ear. "Thanks, Josh, that'd be great."

"Hold on tight, hi ho, Silver," I said. I held my head. My. What a rush! I would blame it on the bull. Or my head-stand on stage with Camellia and Violet upside-down be-side me. Nah. It was the alcohol. "I'm not getting in a car with this here"—I tapped my finger on Josh's chest—"this here snow monster man. No way in Montana." I swayed. Josh put an arm around my waist, and I leaned against his chest. "It's raining a man. Bad man." I sang a verse from the raining men song.

"You can tell by the way I use my walk," Violet sang out, walking a crooked line, hips swinging. "I'm a man's woman, no time to talk."

Talo settled the ear-nibbling Camellia in the car after she trilled, "How deep is your love, how deep is your love?" Talo shut the front door, then guided Violet in. Violet warbled, "I'm stayin' alive, stayin' alive. Ah ah ah ah! Stayin' allliiivve!" She hit another high C and I laughed 'til I bent over.

I sang/shouted back to both of them, "We are family. I got all my sisters with me."

They stuck their hands out the window and waved and yelled, "I love you, Laurel!"

"Thanks, man," Talo said to Josh. "If you don't mind."

"Not at all. I'm ten minutes from her house."

"Muskrat love," I said. "I will not ride this cowboy like a bull." I poked Josh in the chest again. My, it was fuzzy and swirly out here.

Josh led me toward his black truck. I wobbled beside him. "I'm not going with you because of your King-Kong size and because you stole my house and put it on Santa's sleigh and now it's at the North Pole and you are not getting any presents because you were a bad boy this year."

"I can't change my King-Kong size, I did not steal your house and put it on Santa's sleigh, and I am not surprised about Santa's decision."

"Why are you mean to me, Josh Josh?" I said, looping an arm around his waist. I stared deep into those green, cold cowboy eyes. "Yep. You still have gold in your eyes mixed in the green. And you still have a lot of blond hair, but you don't have a smile anymore. I think you lost your smile. Maybe it's at the North Pole with my house on Santa's sleigh."

"I think I lost my smile about twelve years ago. Let's go, Laurel."

"I no go with Sam I Am."

"That's right. You're going with Josh I am."

I went with Josh I am.

* * *

The cool air rushing by my face when I hung my head out Josh's truck's window sobered me up a tad, but not enough.

I told Josh I was drunk for the first time since he and I got drunk together one night on a canoe when he was more of a friendly elf than he was now. I told him he did not actually resemble King Kong and I hoped it didn't hurt his feelings but I thought he was intimidating now because his eyes were frosty cold, like Frosty the Snowman. Was he related to Frosty the Snowman? No? Are you sure?

I further told him that I would not get naked with him again like a snow angel because he was not Santa Claus and fat and jolly and friendly, no, he was more like the Grinch and did he think bah humbug for Christmas, I bet he did. I said he might own my house and my land in the North Pole but he did not own any part of my privates, so there.

Finally I told him he was a sexy reindeer. Then I slung my head as far out of his truck's window as I could because I thought I was going to be sick.

I do not remember him carrying me past my mother and aunt and upstairs to my pink bedroom. My mother and aunt told me what happened in the morning. They seemed to think the whole thing was hilarious.

I only know I woke up with the most miserable headache of my entire life and I felt like a damn muskrat love fool.

The drama for the Kelly Family's Chaotic Christmas Eve started the next day, via e-mail, which only increased my brain-splitting hangover headache.

Dear Laurel dearie,
Greetings!
About Christmas Eve dinner at your place. We hope a family tizzy war is not imminent. Between you and me, a

secret, I was hoping you could run a tiddly bit of interference for me. Last year, Chantrea's sons kept making fun of Richard because his last name is Longer. Old Swedish name, he thinks.

Remember how Oakie, Aspen, and Redwood made up that phallic song and wiggly dance about Dick Longer? I told Chantrea that her boys sounded like braying donkeys and she threw that butter dish at me, which was uncalled for, goodness me.

I can't have the boys making fun of Richard again. If they do, I think he's going to punch them. He's a former boxer, and he does not appreciate being made fun of. Can you talk to Chantrea for me? You're the only one she and her ballistic nature listens to, and I can't have a butter dish flying at my ole' head again.

I love you. Tell your mother and aunt I said tra la la hello. I will bring my mother's hash and onion casserole and meat-loaf balls for Christmas Eve.

Tootles,
Aunt Amy

To Laurel:
I no can stand that Amy. She say mean lies about my good boys. They are not troublemaker; they make little trouble, but they good boys. Judge say they have that probation but not the jail time for the borrowing of that friend's (who not a friend) car and drive fast and judge say next time jail, but not time now. They serve community. They community servers. Like servants. Good boys.

Okay, so if Amy come to your house for Christmas, not me. I no come and talk to her and her Longer Dick husband. He get mad at my good boys for singing nice song. That no sense. She say I throw butter dish at her. No. She lie. Not butter dish. Small flat plate. I shoot to miss.

You my angel girl. Glad you back in this cowboy cowgirl town. Me, I miss Cambodia.

I bring Cambodian ginger catfish to Christmas dinner and I bring Beef Lok Lak. You come see me again at restaurant soon and come my house for dinner on Wednesday.

Kiss to you. Kiss kiss. Love to you. (Not that Amy)

Chantrea

Chapter 3

It took us almost all day to get the Christmas trees decorated. We drank eggnog and ate St. Patrick's Day clover leaf Christmas cookies while we did it.

As usual, the trees were as eccentric as my mother and aunt. The parlor tree was decorated only with high heel ornaments. The tree in the sewing room, The Feminist Tree, was decorated with women-power types of sayings on red paper. The small tree in the kitchen was decorated for Valentine's Day because they love love, and a fourth tree in the entry was covered in shamrocks and leprechauns to honor our Irish heritage.

The tree in the family room was ten feet tall and covered with all our other ornaments, red ribbon, colorful lights, gold beads, and a two-foot-wide gold star at the top that had to be wrapped in wire and attached to the trunk. It still tilted.

In the middle of it, James and Thomas skidded in, tongues flapping, Zelda hissed and shrieked, and they headed straight back out, whimpering.

"They have to learn to stick up for themselves against Zelda," I murmured.

"We've talked to them about that," my mother said. "Merry Christmas to three women who know and speak their own minds at all times."

"Let no man ever squash us," my aunt said.

"Cheers to that," I said.

We clinked our eggnog glasses.

I thought about Josh. He had never squashed me.

I was twenty. It was snowing and icy. It was cold enough to freeze a dog's tail off. I was home from college for Christmas.

I told him what I thought of our relationship, of him as a man. "I hate you," I said.

I cried.

He cried, too.

It was a sad, destructive conversation and when he went for a handkerchief to hand to me, we hit a slippery patch on that deadly curve.

It all came to a head that one snow-blasted night.

I blamed myself.

I still do.

I will never stop blaming myself.

"Tell me about your apron business." I cut the reindeer fabric on the long dining room table my granddad built in the sewing room, while Elvis Presley sang "Blue Christmas" on a CD.

"We're sewing Christmas aprons as fast as we can. Glad you're here to stitch and sew, honey," my mother said, talking around two pins in her mouth.

"If you have any new apron ideas, you go right ahead and whip them up," my aunt said, running poinsettia fabric expertly through her sewing machine.

My aunt and mother made aprons for a number of businesses across Montana. I had helped them make aprons from the time I was about six. Usually, they made the old-fashioned type—a bib and skirt, pockets, ruffles, pretty trims and piping, large bows in back. They would use at least two different fabrics for each apron, often more. They also liberally used lace and unique buttons. There were no "plain" aprons. They didn't believe in plain. Every apron had to be, in their words, "Montana spectacular."

What they created was apron art, in my mind. I've never seen aprons anywhere near as well-sewn, decorated, and original as theirs.

"I'm a little rusty," I said. "But it's coming back."

"Nonsense," my mother said. "Your seams are as straight as ever, your fabric choices compatible and charming blends."

I had slid back into sewing as quick as I slid into my pink wool socks this morning, red jeans, and a purple sweater. My sewing machine felt like my best non-living friend. I'm a sewing geek, I know it. It's genetics. I sew, my mother and aunt sew, their mother sewed, her mother sewed, all the way back, I'm told, to Ireland.

There were three sewing machines on the table, one for each of us. The rest of the table was piled with Christmas fabrics, pins, patterns, threads, and sketches of aprons. Above us were two twinkling chandeliers my late grandma bought when she was sixty. It was a gift to herself for "surviving Montana winters."

There was a wall of shelves for other sewing supplies, including buttons, trim, rickrack, tape measures, a collection of antique thimbles, and sewing books.

The sewing room was filled with color, light, and a sense of purpose. That my ancestors had all laughed, sang, cried, and danced in this room made it even more special. I tried not to have a mini-breakdown when I thought about how our sewing room wasn't truly ours anymore.

I decided to use fabric with candy canes on it as trim for the apron's skirt.

"A woman needs a pretty apron when she's cooking and enjoying the pleasures of the kitchen," Aunt Emma said. "Or, when she wants a little ooh la la from her man, she can wear an apron with nothing underneath and enjoy other pleasures."

"You've done it before, right, Laurel?" my mother asked. "Made dinner naked, wearing only one of our aprons?"

"Do we need to talk about that, Mom?"

"I'd like to know, too, dear." My aunt winked at me. "What was the end result? Did our aprons contribute to a successful evening?"

I put my hands over my face as a picture of me cooking chicken tacos for Josh, naked, wearing a pink frilly apron skittered through my mind . . . another time I made spaghetti for him in a red and white flowered apron *only* . . . once I wore a black ruffled apron over my birthday suit and we hadn't made it to the meal. . . .

Stop thinking about him, I told myself. *Stop.*

"Now, let us live vicariously through you and your radical rocker man, Ace Hellfire," my aunt said.

"Tell us more stories about the fire-breathing rebel," my mother said.

I laughed out loud thinking about "radical rocker man, Ace."

They did, too.

"I should have known you would be here," I muttered.

"How about, 'Nice to see you, Josh.'" Josh raised his eyebrows at me and handed me a glass of wine.

"No, thank you. I'm not drinking."

"You look beautiful."

"Don't say that."

"Why?"

"Because I said not to. You look intimidating."

My best friend from high school, Kristi Lellenstein, had an annual Christmas party.

Kristi shot off a rocket on a Wednesday afternoon in the cafeteria in eighth grade. She pulled the fire alarm when she wasn't ready to take a math test, and she painted, with her considerable artistic talents, a bottle of beer on a school hallway in the middle of the night.

Now she had four kids, a balding husband, was head of the PTA, and her house was dripping in Christmas trees, wreaths, mangers, and Santa collections.

She pushed her blond bob of curls off her face when she saw me, gave me a long hug, and said, "Brace yourself. I've become totally boring. I had spit-up on my left boob ten minutes before the party. Now give me the guts of your life. How many women has Ace slept with? Is he as sexy as he seems? Are you two together?"

"I can't tell you the number of women Ace has slept with because I don't know." Slight lie. I did know. "He's quite sexy on stage." He didn't look that sexy in his kitchen in jeans and a pink shirt stirring pancake batter when I last saw him, but what the heck. "Ace and I are not together, never have been." No. Never.

When Josh walked in, it was like the whole room turned. Several men scooted up immediately and shook his hand. I saw two women fluff their hair. One actually pulled on the vee of her Mrs. Claus sweater so more cleavage spilled out. I rolled my eyes.

Josh laughed and I felt that laugh deep inside myself. It made me lonely. That laugh was not for me anymore. That man was not for me.

"Dang it," I whispered. I'd been at the party for almost two hours and I figured that was long enough. I darted through the kitchen, down the hallway, grabbed my purple coat and faux zebra print purse, and tried to slink like a snake out the door.

And there was Josh.

"You're not headed out already, are you?" he asked.

"Yes."

"Why?"

"Because I need to go home and sew aprons. Stack spools of threads into towers. Poke myself with knitting needles."

"Ah." He got it. "Don't go because of me, Laurel."

"I'm not."

"Yes, you are."

"Okay, I am. I would rather run my sewing machine over my finger than stay here. Have a pleasant evening. I hope you don't choke on your beer." I headed out the door and he followed me down the driveway, the music, the noise, and chatter gone when he shut the door.

"What are you doing, Josh?" I pulled my hood up, the snow gently falling. I was wearing a black dress, black lace tights, and red knee-high boots. I was trying to get in the Christmas spirit with the boots. Didn't work.

"I'm walking you out to your car."

"I can get there by myself."

"Yes, you can. I also wanted to tell you that your pink bedroom hasn't changed much."

"If you think I'm going to thank you for carrying me up the stairs to my bedroom, I'm not going to."

"Okay. I did notice that you have a new bedspread. I liked the flowers. It looked soft."

"It is soft and we're not having this conversation."

"I think I could still climb up that tree, if I was invited."

"You're not invited. Climb up that tree and I'll cut it down." No, I wouldn't.

"It brought back a lot of memories." He smiled, slow and loose.

"Well, you can shove those memories straight out of your head."

"Can't do that, darlin'."

I whirled on him, angry but hurting. I remembered those tree-climbing times, too. "Stop talking, Josh. Go back to the party."

He stopped, he waited.

"I know what you're doing," I said.

"What?" Smile, smile.

"You're waiting for me to talk. Okay, I'll talk. I can't believe where we are." I threw my hands in the air and tried not to cry. Last time I was drunk; this time I was sober and I would not allow myself to turn into a crying hyena.

"What do you mean?" Slow and loose smile now gone.

"I can't believe that after not seeing you for so long, I come home, and we're in this." I waved my hands.

"Mess?"

"Yes. And it could be fixed so easily."

"If you had your way."

"It's not about my way, Josh, it's about my home."

"I know. I missed you."

"What?" I was confused. Thrown off. His words and being that close to him threw me. "We're not talking about that. We're talking about my home, and why did you say that?"

"Because it's the truth. I missed you."

"Don't be truthful then, I don't want to hear it." *Yes, I did.*

I bent my head. He was inches away. He smelled delicious. Like pine and snow, and all things seductive. I wanted to run my hands through that blond, longish hair. I wanted to put my hands on his cheeks, then kiss that square jaw, the high cheekbones, and the scar across his eyebrow, courtesy of his father.

I didn't mean to lift my head, but I did. I didn't mean to stare at his mouth, but I did. I didn't mean to tilt my head to his and step forward, but I did. On instinct. Out of habit. Because I wanted to.

That's when his mouth came down on mine, warm and

seductive, and his arms wrapped around me and my purple coat and pulled me close. I should have pulled back but I didn't want to. I linked my arms around his shoulders and molded myself to his body, to that hard chest, and I clung to him.

All the years dropped off . . . everything dropped off . . . except for Josh and his mouth and his hands and how protected I felt, like I had never felt with anyone, and how right it felt, and how the sweet, steaming passion I thought was buried forever came flaming to life, as if there were no lonely years or wretched heartache between us. I sighed and held him closer, kiss for kiss, stroke for stroke. I wanted to strip my clothes off. . . .

And then, panting embarrassingly hard, I pulled myself away. I pushed at his chest. I fumbled for my purse and my keys.

He said, "Laurel, wait," and I didn't say anything, my whole body on fire, craving him and his touch and that fun, tight friendship we used to have.

"Don't leave," he said, following me, his boots crunching the snow. "What the hell—"

I climbed in my car, shut the door, didn't look at him, and drove home. I said a string of bad words, and tried to keep the tears in my eyes.

It didn't work.

Josh and I started dating during our junior year of high school. We had math class together. I was too intimidated to speak to him at first. He was the athlete, the popular kid, tall and handsome. He played football, basketball, and baseball.

I played sports, too, but I also spent a lot of time at home sewing aprons with my mom and aunt, helping them with their business. On the flip side, I also spent time with my half sisters and we often got into trouble.

We were the Kellys.

Camellia and Violet were known for living fast, driving fast, and partying. Unfortunately for all the parents in town, my sisters believed in "the more the merrier" and invited everyone to all sorts of rendezvous: midnight parties at the lake, or in a deserted barn, or in the middle of the football field. When the police came, it was not unusual for a hundred kids, including me, to make a hilarious run for it.

My father drove a hearse he'd painted pink and had elk for pets. Chantrea had started her Cambodian restaurant with my father but was known to tell customers off when they irritated her. She served one rude man a live, flopping fish on his plate. She spelled out a common expletive with slices of radish for another difficult customer. She dropped a bowl of noodles on one man's head who was drunk and later told him he'd done it to himself.

My mother and aunt were raving feminists, which I was proud of, but they also wrote inflammatory commentary for the newspaper on various women-centered topics that had some people cheering and others in a tizzy.

Josh and I started with a smile, then notes passed between us, and within a few weeks we were dating. He was funny and fun. He explained my math homework to me, helped my mother and aunt around the house with fixing things, and called to talk every night when he was home from practice or work.

He did not seem to be embarrassed at all that I was part of the semi-notorious Kelly clan, all stricken with a Wild Bone. In fact, he hugged me in the middle of the hall, held my hand, and kissed me in plain sight. He would come over and I would cook him dinner. He frequently brought me flowers he picked and little gifts. I brought him homemade cookies every day.

We talked about our futures. He wanted to own a business. Since we fished together, he would call the business Salmon Fly, as I had suggested one afternoon on the river.

I wanted to be a nurse. We both wanted to travel the world and we spent tons of time looking at *National Geographic* and making a list of the countries we wanted to visit together.

Josh also climbed up quick to my bedroom via the tree outside my window. We used birth control, brought by him. We were very bad. We enjoyed being bad. We were totally, completely in love. The first time he told me he loved me, our junior year, we were in a canoe on the lake fishing. I told him I loved him, too. We both teared up.

He told me that his grief over his mother's death and his drunken father gave him the fierce aggression he needed for sports. "I take my anger out on the court or on the field, Laurel." His bullying father, who was a contractor when he was sober, whom Josh worked for until he left home the previous summer, never even came to any of his games.

I, however, went to all of Josh's games, as he went to my soccer, basketball, and softball games where my competitive streak came roaring out, too, partly stemming from my anger and hurt with my own father.

Josh received a full-ride scholarship to our state university for basketball. I was accepted there, too, and off we went. He had nailed the SAT and had won rifle shooting and rodeo competitions. He was my stud.

As in love as I was, as passionate as we were together, it never occurred to me that we would be together for life. My father had left me. He had left his first wife and his second wife, my mother. I refused to talk to him most of the time, and he seemed way too busy with his new wife, Chantrea, the restaurant, and his boys. I had huge abandonment and trust issues, and I assumed that Josh would leave me, it was only a matter of when.

I also believed that Josh would find someone better than me. Prettier, smarter, more like him. My self-esteem issues were a direct result of my father not being around enough to tell me, and show me, that he thought I was "enough."

I made a decision to be with Josh as long as I could, to grab life and ride it, as my mother always told me to do, and deal with the despair later.

Who knew it would be me who would make the decision for both of us after a skid, a roll, and a plunge?

Ace sent a Christmas bouquet the size of an elf and a note. He begged, he pleaded, he said he couldn't go on. I consoled and reassured. He hardly heard me.

The e-mails about Christmas Eve dinner kept rolling in. . . .

Dear buckin' bull-riding sister Laurel,
(I was so proud of you at the bar! Whip it, lady!) I can't imagine all four wives and our gang of kids mashed together for Christmas Eve at your house, but hopefully everyone will be in a non-combative Christmas spirit and we can sing carols together and forcibly separate Chantrea and Velvet if we have to.

They had a fight recently and are currently not speaking. Something to do with Velvet dressing too sexy in front of Chantrea's boys and that's why they want to go to Dad's all the time. Ugh. Well, Velvet should keep those big girls of hers in her shirt if you ask me.

I can't believe this! Lizzy was suspended again for two days from preschool for painting another girl with a paintbrush. She used green this time. Shandry was also suspended for two days when she let the mice and the rabbit out. Whose kids get suspended from preschool? This is embarrassing. They have the Kelly Wild Bone.

At least I don't have vampires for sons like Camellia. They sure have chompers.

I am bringing eggplant lasagna to Christmas Eve dinner because, as you know, dear Italian husband had that every year growing up and I don't want to disappoint him.

I'm also bringing banana bread because I like it. Stay in Montana, please. I miss my little bronco-riding sister!

Violet

Sister Laurel,

Mom says you and your mother and aunt are organizing Christmas Eve this year at your house. For one, thanks, pal. Way to take one for the team. For two, just so you know, I am not coming if Velvet is coming. She can take her rock-hard fake boobs and stay home and practice sliding up and down her stripper pole. We're going to have a Merry damn Christmas but not if she's there.

I am tired of her constant jabber about the benefits of vegetable cleanings on the bowels. She's gone from stripping to organic health queen. What's that all about?

I don't even think she can cook. Dad didn't marry her for her brains. (Duh.) I think he was attracted to the same thing the governor was attracted to. By the way, her son, William, is her exact opposite. Which means he's smart. He likes wearing suits. Nice attire here in Montana.

I will bring a pecan pie and a chocolate silk pie. You think my pecan pie is the best, right? Velvet said hers is. No one makes a pecan pie like me.

Love you, girl. Thanks for coming over the other day. Sorry that Teddy bit you. Doesn't look like it will scar, though.

Love, love, (again),

Camellia

I was up late sewing Christmas aprons. We had a whole shipment due out tomorrow. I was using pink fabric with pink, red, and white Christmas trees and would attach three

Christmas wreath buttons down the bib. A wide ruffle at the hem of the skirt would add the frill that all our aprons had.

As I sewed I sucked on a candy cane and thought about Josh. I was still mad. And hurt. He knew I loved my house. I was also mad at myself for being in a befuddled mess about him.

We had grown and changed the last twelve years. We were not the same people. And yet . . . all that passion was still there. It came roaring on up until I couldn't think. Maybe it was simply because of memories. Time spent together when we were young, he was my first, nostalgia, blah blah. That was it. That was all it was.

I took the candy cane out of my mouth and ate a Christmas cookie. The cookie was in the shape of a Halloween pumpkin, decorated with green and red sprinkles.

I sniffled. I couldn't believe the house wasn't ours. I loved it, loved the land. I knew where the deer hid. I knew where the elk congregated.

I knew where my great-granddad and grandma's initials were carved in the cement on the foundation. They had walked up the same stairs I walk up every day and admired the same views of the majestic Swan Mountains.

I ate a second pumpkin Christmas cookie.

I had learned to bake apple and pumpkin pies with flaky crusts on the kitchen table he built and how to sew stockings in front of his hearth. My grandma had shown me how to make Irish truffles on the island in the kitchen. She had also taught me how to shoot a rifle. My granddad had taught me how to rope cows, ride horses, and drive a tractor right outside our front door. In my room hung my grandma's mirror and my granddad's old holster.

It was our home. This was where we decorated Christmas trees with high heels, feminist sayings, leprechauns, and Valentines.

I had to get it back.

And as soon as I stopped thinking about Josh's kiss, how I fit right back into his arms, and how warm and strong and yummy he was, then I would devise another plan.

Yes, indeedy, I would.

I would call it Plan H and L, as in Laurel, get your house and land back!

But that kiss . . .

I put the candy cane back in my mouth.

Chapter 4

Wow.

Josh owned the whole building? Obviously, he did. It was called the Reed Building, and it was in the middle of downtown Kalulell. It was brick with green canopies, old and traditional, with white trim and dental work, but clearly restored. There were busy ground floor businesses, a restaurant, a café, an art gallery, and two stories above that with offices.

The lobby had been remodeled and the floors gleamed. Christmas trees, decorated with shiny red ornaments, graced either side of the doors to the elevator.

I tried to settle down as I stared at my reflection in the silver doors of the elevator. I'd brushed my reddish/pink-tipped hair down, but the wind had swept it around. I was wearing black cowboy boots, woolen black tights, a black skirt with a lace ruffle to my knees, a flowing red and pink silk tunic, a striped red and orange scarf, and two pairs of gold hoops. I was also wearing a thick red coat.

I looked pale. I looked worried. I looked ill.

Don't kiss him again, I told my reflection. *Restrain yourself.*

The elevator swooshed up two floors and I stepped out into the office. The old, traditional feel to the building was there, with the open wood arches to the ceiling, the white trim, and crown molding, but it was modern, light, welcoming, and bustling.

I stopped at the receptionist's desk and stared. "Mrs. Alling?"

"Yes. Oh, it's lovely to see you, Laurel!" She stood up and gave me a hug. She had been my and Josh's favorite English teacher in high school. We caught up, I heard about her four children and eight grandchildren. We talked about Hellfire, she liked their music, Ace was a true musician, wasn't he? How tall was he? Was he married? His voice, to her, sounded smoldering. Was Ace always smoldering? It took us a while.

"Here, dear. Come with me." I followed her back to Josh's office. She knocked, then opened the double wood doors to Josh's office and announced me. I walked in and stopped. Josh's office was so Montana-y.

His windows offered a view of the ski slopes up the mountain and the Main Street of town. His desk was huge, with an exquisite leaping salmon carved into the front of it. I had flashes of all the fish we'd caught and released . . . and ate with butter and dill. There was a leather couch and two chairs in one corner and a long table by the windows.

"Hi, Laurel." He stood up, smiled at Mrs. Alling, who then left and shut the door.

"Thanks for seeing me, Josh." *Don't kiss me again and don't make me think of kissing you.*

"Anytime."

His voice was so . . . deep. Always had been. It was like he had gone from being a kid to a man overnight.

"Have a seat." He indicated the couch and chairs, and I chose the couch and sat in the middle of it. He, too, chose the couch. I shifted over and saw him try to cover a smile.

I studied him for a second. He seemed tired, a bit strained.

"I wanted to know if you had reconsidered selling my mother's and aunt's land and house back to me." I knew he hadn't.

"I have not."

"Would you consider a new offer?"

"Probably not, but what is it?"

"How about if I buy from you the house and five acres?"

"No."

Shoot. I could tell he was not budging on that one. I went to Plan D, as in D for Desperate.

"What about the house and one acre?"

"No."

I felt like I'd been kicked. I told him what I would pay him. It was more than generous.

"No."

"You're kidding. Why not? You'll have the other nineteen acres." I felt cold, inexplicably lost. "Why would you want that house when you already have one?"

"It's not the house, Laurel, it's the land the house is on. That acre has a stream on it and access to the road. I told you, I'm going to use it, then donate it."

"I'll donate my part of it. I'll sign any contract. It'll go to whichever organization you want after my death."

"Don't talk about your death. And no again." I saw his face tighten, then he leaned forward and stared at his clasped hands.

I blinked hard. I would buck up and not cry like a wimpy wuss. "Please, Josh. It's my family's land."

He stood up and walked toward the windows and stared out, his hands on his hips.

I wiped a few frustrated tears that snuck out, glad he had not seen them, then dug in my purse for a tissue and wiped up my wet face. I took a deep breath, and waited.

"Ten dates."

"What?"

He turned around. "Ten dates. You go out on ten dates

with me. You let me take you to dinner, or skiing or a movie, ten times, and I'll sell the house and five acres of land back to you."

Ten dates? With him? Alone with him? I pictured him naked.

Do not do that.

I wondered how his chest had changed over the years under that blue shirt.

Knock it off.

He was so tall, built like an ox with a flat stomach.

You are not going to make love to the ox again.

I pictured making love to him, his cowboy boots hitting the floor.

That's it. No!

"You want to go out with me? Ten times?"

He walked over and I stood up. When we were younger, I would have grabbed those muscled-up shoulders, his arms would have gone around my waist, and we would have talked like that.

"Yes."

"But . . . why?"

He didn't say anything for long seconds, those sharp green eyes analyzing me. "Because, Laurel, I want to know who you are now."

Who I am now? Who was I? I'd quit my job. I didn't have another one. I was tired. I was tired of being tired. I was tired of feeling like I didn't have a meaningful life. I was tired of feeling guilty about that snowy night. I didn't know where I was going to live, what I was going to do.

I didn't even know me anymore. How could I let him see what I didn't know?

"I want to know why you broke up with me. I'm not mad at all. I know we were kids, but I would like for you to tell me what was going through your head at that time."

I couldn't tell him that.

"I want to know . . ." He closed his mouth.

What else did he want to know? Did he want to know if I thought of him when we were apart?

Yes, I did.

Did he want to know if I regretted breaking up with him?

Yes, I did. But I wouldn't have changed it, either.

Did he want to know if I was still that naïve, sweet, angry, sometimes trouble-oriented, not-too-bright girl?

I was not. She was long gone. She left on that icy curve in the road.

"You want to know what?" I asked.

"I want to know . . ." He shook his head and I knew he'd changed his mind about what he was going to say. "I want ten dates."

Could I do it? Could I be around him? On a date? Ten times? Could I resist? Did I want to? Would I get hurt all over again? Smashed to smithereens?

"Yes or no, Laurel," he said.

"Once you go out with me, I highly doubt you'll want to go out another nine times." No, I am a pretty damaged woman.

"I will."

He was totally serious, his eyes never leaving mine. Intimidating, smart, formidable Josh.

I thought of our creaky, light green farmhouse. My great-grandma's white kitchen hutch. My grandma's parlor with the red toile wallpaper and her blue apothecary chest. My mother's and aunt's sewing room.

I could do it. I might need a little Christmas magic, but I could do it. Right? I could control myself. I wasn't a teenager going for a ride in a clunky car and parking by the lake anymore. "Yes."

I saw his eyes widen, and he smiled at me. "I'm going to hold you to it, Laurel."

"I'm going to hold you to it, too, Josh. You'll sell the house and five acres back to me after the tenth date."

"I will."

I knew we didn't need a contract. Josh Reed was as good as his word.

"I'm already looking forward to it," he drawled.

And I am scared to death. Don't make me fall in love with you again, Josh. That would not be fair. And leave my clothes on.

As if he sensed what I was feeling, he said, his voice gentle, "Don't worry, Laurel. It'll be fun."

It won't be if I get my heart all mangled up again. "Thank you, Josh."

He nodded at me. "You're quite welcome."

I turned to leave.

"Oh, and Laurel. One more thing. I want you to bake me cookies. Please."

"Cookies?"

"Yes. Christmas cookies." He grinned. It made him seem less intimidating. "You make the best Christmas cookies I've ever tasted."

I tried not to smile, but my Christmas cookies were pretty darn good. I used to make yummy peppermint bars, fudge, gingerbread, lemon meringues, stained-glass windows, and butterscotch crunches.

"And Laurel?"

I turned around again.

"Your Irish truffles that your grandma taught you to make."

"Okay, Josh." Now I was feeling a smidgen too pleased with myself.

"Thank you. And beer cheese soup. I'm begging you. I loved it."

"And beer cheese soup. My momma's recipe."

He rocked back on the heels of his cowboy boots for a second. He looked happy.

Ten dates. With a man who was still pulling my heart as if it were attached to his by the reins of Santa's sleigh.

But what would my hurt heart do at the end of the ten dates?

When I sewed an angel with white wings on the bib of a red apron that night, I thought about Josh.

I would be with him ten times.

It would take all I had to resist whipping off my Christmas apron and leaping, naked, into his arms. That would be Plan L. No leaping.

Maybe I would sew a Christmas apron with a chastity belt attached. I'd wear it around Josh and make sure I threw away the key.

That would be Plan C. For chastity.

I groaned.

My father, Ian Kelly, had insisted that I come to dinner at his new home when I was on Christmas break during my sophomore year of college. "I have not seen you in weeks, sweet Laurel. Please. I miss you."

"Fine," I agreed, but with much more sulk than enthusiasm. My relationship with my father had hit the skids when he left my mother and me when I was six. He had not had an affair, he simply wasn't happy with my mother, and she wasn't happy with him. That doesn't matter at all to a child. All I knew was that my father was gone, my world shattered, my family broken. I cried for months.

He was thrilled when he fell in love with Chantrea in Cambodia on one of his expeditions and brought her home. I was not thrilled. I was devastated to have a wicked stepmother. Three sons in quick succession made me feel abandoned three times over.

He picked me up that snowy night for dinner in his pink painted hearse, cheerful, patently glad to see me. He had tried to be in my life, but in the last few years I often lashed out and refused to see him. I was busy with school, sports, and Josh, my father busy with his kids, Wife Number Three, and the restaurant. Too busy for me, at least that's what my temperamental teenage mind believed.

We drove to his place, about five miles from ours. I was sullen, quiet, bracing myself.

Chantrea, the wicked stepmother, hugged me. My brothers, Aspen, Oakie, and Redwood, hugged me. Their home was warm and cozy, and messy, the fire blazing, Chantrea's Cambodian touch in the décor. Everyone was happy. My father had made me my favorite dish: pasta primavera.

Chantrea had made me my favorite Cambodian dish: Cambodian French bread with beef.

The kids had made me my favorite dessert: chocolate mint ice cream pie.

It was not enough.

Their home was a *family* home. Kids, dogs, a cat, a mom and dad. There was a towering Christmas tree and red stockings decorated with glitter. There was even a stocking with my name on it and the names of Camellia and Violet.

But I was an outsider, at least that was how I felt. I was not a member of *this* family. My father had left our family and now it was only my mom, aunt, and me. This house, the stockings, the Christmas tree, this should have been us. The three of us. My anger seethed, the anger born from searing hurt, rejection, and loneliness that only my father could have fixed.

It was that hurt, that rejection, that loneliness, and my immature sulkiness and raging temper that caused what happened next.

"I love making Christmas cows and chickens," my mother said.

"I love making Christmas grizzly bears," my aunt said.

"And I love eating the cows, chickens, and bears," I said.

My mother was using six-inch cookie cutters in the shapes of farm animals. They would later be iced in red and green and decorated with Red Hots and sprinkles.

My aunt was using grizzly bear cookie cutters. She would ice the bears in purple, red, and green, then make Christmas wreaths around their necks.

I was making traditional sugar cookies—Christmas trees and ornaments—because I am a dull traditionalist and someone in our family had to be normal. Plus, they were for Josh.

"I was thinking about your aprons," I said. "And how you said you wanted to sell more."

"Yes," my mother said. "Then we'll take the apron money and run off to Greece."

"I want to see Greece before my arthritis takes over my femininity," my aunt said.

"Right," my mother said. "We don't want our arthritis down there."

They are so blunt, and funny. "What about a Web site for your aprons?" I used a cookie cutter to make six Santas. "We could sell aprons through a Web site."

"We don't know how to do a Web site," my mother said.

"We know e-mail!" my aunt said, triumphantly. "And I know grizzly bears. Look at this pink bear. Does she look properly individualistic to you? I don't want a wimpy lady bear."

"She does," I said. "I could have a Web site set up for you."

"You could?" my mother asked.

"Yes. Then we could reach a wider group of people."

"How do we work the Web site?" my aunt asked.

"It's easy. I would show you. Customers would order

an apron on the Web site, pay for it online, the money would be routed to you, and you'd sew the apron and mail it out."

My mother dusted flour off her hands. "But how would they know about our Web site?"

"We'd advertise. Go to the local media, the newspapers, the TV stations, see if they'll come and talk to you." I paused, feeling insecure. "Only if this is something you would like to do."

We had ourselves a good old-fashioned business meeting.

At the end of our talk, my mother said to me, waving her floury hands in the air, "This is bucking my imagination. We could sell more aprons and travel the world once a summer with our apron money. We could save the money Josh gave us for when we're old and can't sew anymore and need to pay handsome male nurses to come in here and give us our baths."

My aunt cackled, wielding the rolling pin. "I want someone tall, dark, and handsome."

My mother tapped her fingers on the table. "I think you might be on to something, Laurel."

My aunt said, "Me, too. She has a smart brain."

My mother said, "Got it from her grandma."

"She broke horses, had a clean shot, and could build a fence in an afternoon. She was empowered."

"Plus," my mother added, "she handled Granddad. He kept going to the bar after working in the mines early in their marriage. She slammed into the bar one night, dragged him off his bar stool, and clocked him in the head."

"She did. Whopped him," my aunt said. "Grandma said to Granddad, 'You can drink or you can have me, but not both. I'm pretty enough to get a new husband, but you're too ugly for another wife, so which is it?'"

"He dusted himself off, said good-bye to his friends,

and walked out," my mom said. "Never drank again. I came along nine months after that, then Aunt Emma twelve months later."

Granddad wasn't that good-looking of a man. His nose had been broken a few times, he had a wide forehead and scars. He was towering tall, like a crane. He was the kindest man I'd ever known.

"Do you want me to set up the Web site then?" I asked. I hoped I was doing the right thing. I hoped I wasn't bringing stress into their lives.

"Yes, indeed," my mother said. "We'll be on the computer and we'll be famous. We can share ways for women to have power through their aprons. Apron independence!"

"Famous," my aunt said. "Maybe we'll get a date. Two brothers."

"And all we would wear would be Christmas aprons," my mother said.

"I'll sew a red apron," my aunt cackled. "Red lace. My buttocks are still firm."

"And my bosom is—" my mother started.

I jumped in before I heard more than I wanted to. "What do you want to call your business?"

"That's simple," Aunt Emma said.

"It is?"

"Yes," they said, together. "We're The Apron Ladies."

The Apron Ladies it was.

This time Ace sent Maine lobsters. Scallops. Clams. He cajoled, he listed all the reasons why I should stay. I declined. I told him all would be well. He didn't believe it. He said he was having an anxiety attack that was my fault and hung up.

*   *   *

I called a friend of mine, Josy, who lived in Los Angeles and developed Web sites, mostly for musicians. She liked the sound of developing an apron Web site. "I've done hard rockers and country crooners. Bring on The Apron Ladies."

We had a long chat. "Start taking photos, Laurel," she told me. "If you can photograph Ace like you do, and Scotty Stanford and Leroy Stemper, and that bang-up drummer of Hellfire's, you can photograph your mom and aunt in their aprons."

I had taken most of the photos for the band's Web site and production over the years, after intensive lessons from Ace's brother, Darrin, a kindergarten teacher, who was a photographer on the side. I was pretty comfortable with what I could do, especially since my mom and aunt wouldn't be striding back and forth, smashing a guitar or swinging a mike.

"I think we need to sell my mother and aunt, Josy," I said. "The aprons are darling, but those women are the key. Independent, strong, resourceful women who believe in cooking well and looking pretty while you do it. Feminism and happy baking, mixed. . . ."

"Remember this is Date One," Josh said, winking at me. "I don't want you to get the count off."

"I'll remember." I turned my skis and stopped at the top of the slope, Josh beside me. It was a clear blue day. Montana stretched below us, like a white, bumpy quilt, punctuated by snow-covered trees.

"Perfect day for skiing," he said.

The blond ox seemed even taller on skis. "Yes, it is. Only I haven't skied in about twelve years."

"You're kidding."

"No." I pulled on the strap of my helmet.

"But you love skiing."

"I know. I've missed it." I've missed a lot of things. "I'm still mad at you."

I thought I saw a flash of sadness. "I know you are, Laurel."

"I feel like taking my ski off, wielding it over my head, and chasing you with it." Why did he have to look so delicious in his black ski jacket and black pants?

"I would like to see that." He smiled.

"Stop smiling at me with that smile of yours."

He tried to stop smiling, then he laughed.

"I can't believe . . ." I gripped my ski poles, then pointed the tips at his chest, like I was preparing to spear him. He did not seem daunted by my ski pole weaponry. "I can't believe you own my home. How would you feel, Josh, if I owned your home?"

"If you owned my home and we lived together, I think I'd be okay with it."

"Very funny." But it wasn't funny. I thought of us living together, me making Christmas cookies in the kitchen while he hung out and talked to me. I thought of us hosting Christmas Eve dinners with my chaotic, crazy family. Then I saw a bunch of happy kids running around who were exact replicas of Josh, which hurt like I'd stuck myself in the gut with my ski pole.

"You cook better than anyone I've ever known, Laurel, better than any restaurant, so you cook and I'll do everything else."

"I haven't cooked much in years, but thanks for the flattery. It's not taking away my desire to give you a little push."

"Maybe skiing will."

"Maybe. Probably not. I may run you over with my skis."

"That's not friendly."

"I'm not in the mood to be friendly." I pulled on the collar of my old red ski coat. Sheesh. My pants were too loose, but I didn't take pride in that. I didn't want to be bony. As my mother always said, "A woman should have curves to grip."

"What's wrong, Laurel?"

"What's wrong is that you own my home."

"What else?"

He could tell, couldn't he? He always knew. He could read me like no one else could. "Nothing. I'm in the ho ho ho Christmas spirit."

"Something is wrong, but if you don't want to talk about it, then we won't."

"Good. Because I'm not talking to a man who now owns my pink bedroom."

He smiled. Man, he was killing me.

"I remember all kinds of fun things that happened in that pink bedroom."

"Yes, I'm sure you do. I'm glad you never broke your neck on your way up or down the tree outside of it."

"I took a risk, but it was worth it."

"Stop talking about it."

"Okay. But now I'm thinking about that pink bedroom and you in it and thinking that I should climb up that tree. . . ." He skied close to me, his skis between mine.

"You're too close to me. Back off or I will use my poles to defend myself and you may end up less of a man."

"Please don't. I'd like to keep my manhood."

He was sexy. He hadn't lost an ounce of sexiness. In fact, he was more sexy than ever. Irresistible. Funny. Quick.

I moved my skis, pulled my goggles down, and took off down the slope. It would have made a cool "shove off" sort of statement, except that twenty yards later I caught an edge, fell, tumbled, rolled, lost a ski, and ended up on my stomach, facedown in the snow. It's hard to be cool when you're eating snow.

When I dug the snow off my face, Josh was bending over me. "I think if you skied with me you'd have better luck."

His smile was going to kill me a second time. I flipped inelegantly onto my back, packed a snowball, and threw it at him. He ducked, I missed. I threw again, missed again. A third time: missed. I lay back. We both laughed.

"I'll get your ski," he said softly. "Why don't you work on your pitch while I'm gone?"

I watched the blond giant ski down to get my ski, then walk back up, sideways. He helped me get it back on, then pulled me up. I tried not to smile, I tried not to heat up like a volcano. I tried not to let my head get all wrapped up in him again.

Josh was always protective. Caring. Always there.

And I'd run. Before that, I hid.

I pulled my hand out of his, but not until after I'd stood staring up at those green eyes for far too long.

I would run again. It was only a matter of time.

That night my whole body ached. My muscles were no longer used to skiing, and I felt like I'd been eaten by the ski slope and spit back out. I peeled off my clothes, turned off the lights in the bathroom, dumped in amber rose bubble bath, and settled in.

"Groan," I said out loud. "Oh, groan."

Amidst the bubbles, and screaming muscles, I thought of Josh. We had skied all day.

We'd laughed. I crashed three times. He pulled me up each time, my body against his, his arms around me. We rode the ski lift. We stopped for lunch and hot chocolate in the lodge in front of the massive fireplace.

"Tell me about your job," he said, the flames warming our hands.

"It's busy." It *was* busy. I wouldn't tell him that I'd quit and was currently jobless.

"How did you come to manage a rock band?"

"When I was in college in Los Angeles, studying to be a nurse, I had a roommate, Dani Shriver, and we became best friends. Her father, Leonard Shriver, was managing the Don Steiger Band. We interned for him one summer, followed the band around the country to their shows, worked constantly, and we loved it. After college Don Steiger hired us.

"I met Ace when Hellfire was opening for Don Steiger before Hellfire had their first hits. We met backstage, started to talk. Ace and I had a common interest in cooking, actually. When Don Steiger took a break, I went straight back out on the road with Ace, as did Dani, and then we stayed on with the band. They soon had hits and I helped to organize their first national, then their world tours, with Charlie Zahn as my mentor, a great man who retired three years after I came along to go fishing."

"What do you do for Ace?"

"I see myself as the headache manager. I'm the organizer behind the music and the hard-rocking men, including rehearsals and concerts. I work with the band and crew. I get them from one place to another, and figure out what the concerts are going to look like, including lighting, special effects, stage antics, song choices. I work with the agents, and the people at the record label. I arrange interviews with the press. When I'm out on tour, I work about sixteen hours a day. By the end of the tours I could not tell you my name or if I was a human or a baboon."

"Definitely human, lovely Laurel."

I tried to shrug that off. Couldn't, so I blushed. I only blushed in front of Josh. "I manage all the trouble that comes up, whether it's personal or professional. For example, one of our band members had too much tequila and decided to start throwing bananas out the hotel windows in

Tokyo. Couple of people were hit in the head. Another time two of our band members, a little drunk, took all the hotel room furniture out of their penthouse suite, including their beds, and decorated the hallway. They fell asleep in the hallway, too. Not in the beds."

I fell into the conversation with him as if we'd never been apart. He asked questions. He listened. He laughed with me. He asked what I'd liked about my job and what was hard. "I liked Ace, his band and crew, and a lot of their music."

"Was there anything you didn't like about working for Hellfire?"

"Yes. I was never home. I didn't even have a home. When I came home from the tour the first time, I moved into Ace's guest house in the hills above Hollywood and stayed there."

"Are you dating Ace?"

"No. I've never dated Ace. Never wanted to."

"Good." He looked so pleased, and relieved. "Where have you traveled to?"

"All over." I told him about our stops. "Eastern and western Europe. Canada. All over America. South America. Southeast Asia. Australia."

"You loved the traveling, didn't you?"

"I did love it, often. New countries, people, cities, food, culture. Sometimes I didn't." *I thought of you everywhere I went, Josh. I imagined you with me.* I shut those thoughts out because they shredded my heart. "Even though I'm friends with the guys in the band and crew, and Dani, it could be . . . lonely."

"I'm sorry. But I understand."

I could tell by those green eyes that he was sorry, and he did understand. "I think everyone gets lonely sometimes."

"I do," Josh said. "Part of life. Not the best part, but it's there. I would like for it not to be, although loneliness does make you examine your life, the people in it, and you become more compassionate, I think, for others."

That was one of the things I loved about Josh: his honesty. His introspection and thoughtfulness. Tough guy, yet I could sit down, talk about something serious or tell him my problems, and he could always handle it. He always knew what to do, what to say, or to simply be quiet and hug me.

"I think, sometimes, it's about managing the loneliness," he said.

"How do you manage the loneliness?" *I have never been able to manage my loneliness for you.*

"Staying busy. For me, building a company. Work has taken up a lot of my time. When I have time off I ski. Fish. Hike. Full days."

"Yes. Full days. Like today. Skiing 'til you hurt."

"But I don't feel lonely now, lovely Laurel, at this moment."

I smiled at him. "Glad to hear it."

"Since you came back, in fact."

"You're flirting a little." *Oh, stop it. Or I might fling myself at you.*

"Yeah, you're right. I am. It's that huge smile of yours and the dimples. And the pink hair on the ends. I am liking the pink hair on the ends."

Dang. That was one more thing I loved about Josh. He had always flirted with me. He never flirted with any other girl. He always made me feel like I was the special one.

"Try not to flirt with me, Josh."

"Impossible. Flirting with you is wired into my DNA. Want to go up again?"

"Sure." I had to get out of the warm lodge and into the cold air to cool off.

On the ski lift up he tried to hold my hand. I pulled it away. He laughed.

Why did we have to be tumbling right back into our relationship, as if we'd never left it? I thought that high school sweethearts who broke up and came back to their ten-year reunion were supposed to look at each other, find they had nothing in common, and say to themselves, "Whew! That was a close call! I could have been stuck with him/her my whole life. I would have been a wreck. We would have been a wreck. Lucky me."

I stole a peek at Josh on the ski lift, those snowflakes falling down around us, the mountains covered in white, the sky now purplish blue.

He turned his head and saw me studying him. He winked.

Dang.

I gave Josh the Christmas cookies I'd baked him after we tossed our skis in the back of his truck. I had put the peppermint bars, fudge, gingerbread, lemon meringues, stained-glass windows, and butterscotch crunches in a red tin with an 1800s scene of two women in long dresses, bustles, and flowery hats in front of a Christmas tree. It was feminine, which was so not Josh, which made me laugh.

"Ah, Laurel." He lifted the lid. "Now I'm completely, totally happy."

I blushed. *Stop blushing!* That would have to be Plan B, for blushing.

Chapter 5

"Get your smiles on, ladies," I told my mother and Aunt Emma. "I need to take photos of you two for the Web site. The farmhouse, the land, the animals, your aprons, and your sewing room. And Zelda, if she'll cooperate."

"Photos. Like we're models." My mother elbowed my aunt. "I'm going to lie across our sewing table on my side with an apron on. Prepare to be a model, Emma."

"Are we doing naked modeling?" my aunt asked. "I'd do it. I'm not embarrassed. A body is your vessel on earth, it's not your character. It's not your personality. My scars and sags have come from a life well lived. Some of that life has been easy; some of it made smiling again a struggle. But I'm still here, in one piece, and I'm proud of my body."

"Women definitely get better as they age," my mother said. "There's more freedom in your life and freedom in your head."

My mother and aunt do not bother with makeup, but they did brush their auburn/white hair before we headed out. I studied both of them in their jeans and jackets. They were beautiful. Slender physiques, elegant cheekbones, peaceful blue eyes.

Out on their deck, newly rebuilt by Josh, I took photos of them in their aprons. Many of them were Christmas designs, candy cane fabric, Santas, gingerbread houses, reindeers, stripes and ruffles, polka dots and pockets, but I photographed them in the day-to-day aprons they sewed, too.

They pulled out the apron skirts, twirled around, arms out, then wrapped an arm around each other. I took photos of them posing in front of the snowcapped Swan Mountains, their tractors, the farmhouse, and sitting on the fence talking.

I took photos of them in our rocking chairs, riding their horses, and cooking lasagna and cinnamon rolls. I took photos of all the Christmas cookies, the colorful grizzly bears with the wreaths around their necks and the Christmas farm animals. I also took photos of our five decorated trees, the giant Christmas frog, Gary, the gingerbread house witch, and the dragonfly, Tilge.

I photographed the cat, Zelda, paws scratching the air, mouth wide open, the dogs cowering in fear in a corner. I took photos of their colorful sewing room, sewing machines, the stacks of fabrics, the reams of lace, and their jars of buttons, rickrack, and thread.

I sent Josy photos of my great-granddad on a black stallion, and my great-grandma looking saucy as she leaned against a fence post. I sent old black-and-white photographs of the women in our family in long skirts and bonnets, then in flapper dresses, then my mother and aunt in their hippie outfits in the sixties with long hair, tie-dyes, and peace signs.

I grabbed my great-grandma's and grandma's personal recipe collections and took photos of the pages, the recipes written in their flowing script.

I sent all the photos to Josy, the web designer, then wrote copy for the Web site.

It would be interesting to see what she would come up with.

And the Christmas Eve e-mails kept coming. . . .

Hey girl,

You're a brave but insane woman to host all these loose cannons for Christmas. Man, if I did it, I'd end up getting my fine butt handed to me in a sling, if you know what I mean.

Last year I thought that Longer Dick was going to box Chantrea's boys for their song and dance.

Chantrea sure had her panties in a twist. Could have konked someone clean through with that butter dish she sent sailing across the room.

But, moving on, quick as a bottle of whiskey. I know you were here a few days ago, but can you come over and visit the kids again? Daisy and Banyan would love to see you. They love all the souvenirs you send them from around the world. They wore the stuffed snakes around their necks for a week and whoa! I mean, the shark teeth necklaces and dinosaur models were, like, kicking. They loved them. They also loved the posters of that art museum with the triangle glass thing in front in Paris and whatever they call that big bridge in London.

Anyhow, I'm bringing pecan pie and carrots and slew for Christmas. I got the carrots and slew recipe from a friend at the Strip and Click in Nashville. Sounds bad, but it'll make your tongue hang out it's so tasty. Heavy on the brandy. We're gonna need brandy at your place, I'm telling you.

I don't want to compete with Camellia over the pecan

pie, but mine is kick-butt special. My grandma gave me
the recipe before she had to do a stint in the state prison
for running over her cheating boyfriend's leg. I don't know
why Camellia thinks hers is better. Her pecans are always
dry, and the crust tastes like plastic, like silicon. Silicon
pecan pies. I know you won't say I said that or a hissy-fit
war will break out.

    See you soon, insane one.

    Love,

    Velvet

    Laurel, dude,

    Thanks for taking us all skiing last night. You are a sick
sister. Radical. Sorry you fell so much, but you'll get the
hang of it again. Don't worry about losing your ski over
that hill. Those skis of yours are, like, antiques. You need
new ones. You skied sick on one ski, though.

    We three ski bums had a beer-busting night with you,
old sister.

    Thanks for taking us to lunch on Wednesday, too. We
love steak. Makes us manly.

    So, Mom says we have to cook something this year and
bring it to your house for Christmas Eve. To, like, partici-
pate. We're bringing hot dogs and mustard because that's
what we like to eat. And fries. We're going through the
Burger Cow before we come and we'll get a huge bag of
fries. Ketchup.

    We love you, old sister. We wished you lived in Mon-
tana. Thanks for getting us each an autographed T-shirt of
Hellfire and the band. That was sick.

    Be cool, cool one.

    Oakie. Aspen. Redwood.

    PS Get ready for a new song we made up about Longer
Dick, Amy's dude.

In between sewing aprons, and talking to squabbling family members about Christmas Eve, I thought about Josh.

He hardly left my thoughts. When he called two days after we went skiing and asked me to dinner for Date Number Two, I figured if I had a tail, I would be wagging it.

Maybe it was Christmas joy, but I could not wait to see him.

And it had nothing to do with getting the house back.

On the way home from my father's house on that freezing night, driving through snow that blew sideways, I exploded at him like a mini human bomb. I told him what I thought of him moving out years ago. "You left us. You broke up our family." I told him what I thought of him as a father and as a man. "You're a crappy father. You left your first two kids, you left me, you'll probably leave Chantrea, too. A real man would not break up two families." I went on and on. "I hardly even think of you as my dad." I saw him wipe tears from his cheeks, then he handed me a tissue for mine.

That's when he skidded on the ice. There was no guardrail, and we pinwheeled right off the road, our car bumping and rolling down the embankment and splashing into the water. I remember watching the brackish, icy water rush in through the broken front window. My head banged up, my panic swiftly rising, I unstrapped my seat belt and turned toward my father, but I couldn't see him through the waterfall. I screamed his name, but heard no answer, and swallowed water.

I couldn't find the door handle, couldn't get out. I took in another gulp of water and coughed it out. It was pitch-black, the car tilted, and I hardly knew which way was up. I screamed for my dad again, swallowed water, heard a crash, then felt his hands on my arms. He pulled me out as the water went straight over my head.

I woke up on the side of the road, my father leaning over me. I later learned he'd done mouth-to-mouth resuscitation. He was yelling my name.

I spit up water, coughing, choking, and he pulled me up, tilted me over, and hit my back with his open palm. More water spurted out, then more again. In the distance I heard the ambulance's siren, called by a passerby.

He held me close to him, rocked me back and forth, his cheek on mine, our bodies shaking with shock and cold. "Laurel, hold on, please, the ambulance is coming, breathe, breathe, honey, I love you, baby—"

I held on to him, so relieved to be holding him, that he was alive, that I was alive. I started crying, remembering what I'd said, how I'd treated him. The ambulance came, slowing around the corner, but they still skidded sideways. My father saw them spin and picked me up and ran, his feet hardly getting traction, but enough to get us out of the way.

The ambulance missed us by about six feet, turning a full one hundred eighty degrees, heading down the road sideways. The paramedics, who looked shaken themselves, quickly had me on a stretcher and bundled up. They cut off my clothes as we rode through the snow in the ambulance, dropped heat packs on my body to prevent hypothermia, and buried me in blankets. We slid twice and my father never let go of my hand.

I was as overwhelmed with guilt as I was overwhelmed with that chilly water flowing over my head. *I had caused the accident.* "I'm sorry, Dad," I rasped out, my whole body trembling uncontrollably. "I didn't mean it. I'm so sorry. I love you."

"It is me," he said, crying, his head bent, those gold eyes, like mine, flooded with tears. "It's me who is sorry. So sorry, Laurel. I have hurt so many people. This is my fault. Everything you said is true."

And then, on that ice rink–like road, disaster struck.

Again.

* * *

"Tell me about your company, Josh. It's called Salmon Fly?"

"Yes. I liked your idea for the name, and it stuck."

I bent my head. I was so touched that he'd named his company Salmon Fly. I remembered that day on the river with our fishing poles. I sniffled.

We were at an Italian restaurant eating ravioli and lasagna. Shadowy. Candle-lit. Pictures of Italy that I couldn't help wish I had visited with Josh. "Start at the beginning, would you?"

"During my junior year of college, I took all the money I had and bought a run-down house for next to nothing. I was working half-time for the athletic department. My father's skills as a contractor were the only positive things I gained from him. Anyhow, I lived in it and fixed it up and sold it for a profit. I bought two more homes, same thing. I kept flipping homes, then I used the money to buy the building I have now. It was completely run-down, a sweet deal, but I fixed it up to the period, provided office space upstairs and room for cafés, art galleries, and businesses at the street level. We still buy, fix up, and sell homes and buildings, or we lease them out."

"You have a lot of people working for you."

"But my favorite employee is Mrs. Alling." He winked.

"She's one of my favorite people on the planet. I'm impressed, Josh, with what you've done."

"Thank you, but don't be. It's only business."

"What do you mean?"

"It's my job. It's my career."

"It's what you always worked for, what you wanted."

"It's what I wanted professionally, Laurel, it's not what I wanted personally."

It hurt, but I said it. "I thought you would be married with five kids by now, Josh."

"I did, too. That was in the plan. The right girl ran off."

I didn't want to presume. I'd heard he'd been engaged. I didn't even want to think about that annoying, dreadful woman. "I heard you were engaged."

"My engagement was a mistake. I feel terrible about it still. Lavina was a great lady. Smart. Fun. Kind."

"So what was the problem?"

"Old story, Laurel. A cliché. She wasn't you."

And I have never met anyone like you, Josh. Never.

"We were engaged for about two months and I broke it off. It hurt her. I hurt. It was awful. I felt like a horrible person. She's married now, three kids. Lives in Las Vegas."

Stupendous news. Dreadful fiancée was out of sight.

"You were the right girl."

"I wasn't the right girl." So not right. He had no idea how not right I was after the accident.

"Yes, you were."

"How would you know that, Josh? You sound so sure." And I'd been so lost. "We were young. I hardly had a brain in my head. I was geeky and wild and caused trouble and stopped seeing you when I had to help my father."

"Because I knew." He stared straight across that candle-lit table at me. "I've never felt happier with anyone than I did when I was with you."

"That was uncontrolled lust."

"Do you honestly think that's all it was?" He shook his head. "It wasn't like that for me. Yes, I liked the passion between us. I was a teenage boy. But I loved you, as a person. You were my best friend. We had fun. We talked."

"I'm not that girl anymore."

"I know, I can tell. But I'm not the teenage boy you knew, either."

He was . . . and he wasn't. "You're the same in some ways. You're incredibly smart, Josh. You have a business, your own building, employees, exactly as you planned as a teenager. I remember you telling me what you were going to do. You're ambitious, focused, determined, that's still there."

"I think I need to hang out with you more, Laurel. You're outstanding for my ego."

"You don't have much of that. You're a macho he-man stud, but you don't suffer from an ego. You're more . . . measured now. Confident. More reserved, maybe. Tougher, for sure. Decisive. I used to talk your ear off, but I still have the feeling I could talk and talk and you'd still listen." I shut my mouth. I was being way too honest.

"You never talked my ear off." He shook his head. "I always loved talking to you. I didn't have the easiest childhood, as you know, but you were my light. You brought the laughter, the relief, the friendship. You wanted to talk to me. You wanted to be with me. I was not getting that at home." He paused for a second, breathed deep. "You needed me, and I needed you. I would leave my house and my dad would still be passed out on the couch. Sometimes he'd throw a punch. Or he'd yell, he had that raging temper. We got so many eviction notices I couldn't even count them. He'd get it together, but only when he had to."

"I remember. He scared me."

"I was scared, too, as a kid, and so lonely for my mom, but I stopped being scared when I was bigger and stronger than him. He decked me that one night and I hit back, twice, and he was on the floor. Never hit me again, but that's because I soon moved out and into Coach's upstairs apartment."

"Oh, Josh." I ran a hand over my face. "I'm sorry. My mother and aunt wanted you to move in with us, but they didn't allow it for obvious reasons."

"I think they were right. I would have been living in your pink bedroom, pushing aside the stuffed animals."

"What a drunken jerk your miserable father was. It makes me want to cry thinking of a kid living like that. You had to support yourself at only sixteen, alone. I didn't understand the magnitude of that when we were dating."

"When I have children they will not live as I did. They'll

work, I believe that kids need jobs to teach them the value of money, but they will never have to be a teenager working a job so they can buy groceries." He sounded bitter, and I didn't blame him.

"Where is your father now?"

"He moved to Arizona."

I could tell he did not want to talk about him.

"I didn't have a sober, calm father, but I had you, Laurel, and that made it all easier. I'd work an eight-hour shift at the grocery store but knew I'd be climbing up that tree outside your window and that got me through. Or, I knew that I'd see you in math the next day or that you and I and our friends would have lunch together. And every day you'd give me a hug and a kiss and a bag of cookies."

"I loved to bake those cookies for you."

"I loved to eat what you baked." He looked down for a second. "Laurel, the cookies weren't just cookies for me. They were a lot more than that." He held my hand and brought it to his lips. He kissed every one of my fingers. I watched his mouth. I could hardly breathe.

"Josh. You are not to try to seduce me. It's against the Ten Date Rules."

"What?" He pretended to be outraged. "I didn't know anything about the Ten Date Rules. I didn't agree to that." He laughed, deep in his chest. "Could I seduce you if I tried?"

"Yes, handsome one. So don't."

He knew I was serious. "Okay, Laurel, I won't."

"Thank you." Did I mean that?

"It will be my honor to let you seduce me."

My mouth dropped. He laughed again and so did I.

My. That cowboy was a smoldering son of a gun.

Ace sent me a Christmas tree. Full-sized. Decorated in gold. My aunt and mother clapped their hands. The card said, "Rudolph misses you already. He is sad." But I had made up my mind. My answer was still no.

Josy sent me a draft of the Web site.

I called her while staring out the window at Gary, our Christmas frog, and the gingerbread house witch. "I can hardly speak."

"Okay. Tap once on the phone if you like it."

I tapped. "I love it. You totally nailed it."

She actually giggled. "This is one of the funnest Web sites I've ever done. I love the photos of your mom and aunt throwing hay in the hayloft in their aprons and when your mom is pushing your aunt in the wheelbarrow. Your grandma holding the rifle is my favorite. Same with your granddad on that bucking horse. Did you like the photo of your aunt and mom as little girls holding hands next to the photo of them now holding hands?"

When people clicked on The Apron Ladies, the home page of the Web site showed a photo of my mother and aunt, wearing fluffy, ruffly Christmas aprons, one with Santa on the bib, one with Mrs. Claus. They held pitchforks on either side of them, the snowy Swan Mountains in the distance.

Josy had used old-fashioned blue toile wallpaper and antique lace around the edges of the Web site on each page. Down the right column were photographs of their aprons.

The navigation bar had different tabs: The Apron Ladies. Our Aprons. Our Home and Land. Family History. Grandma's Recipes.

Each page was filled with colorful photographs and the text I'd written.

I showed my mother and aunt.

"Whoee! We're The Apron Ladies," Aunt Emma said. "Mature models."

"A smart woman is proud of her body and grateful to

still be in it and not"——my mother pointed to the sky——"up there."

"Or," my aunt Emma said, "down there." And she pointed to the floor.

Date Three with Josh was snowshoeing. I brought the beer cheese soup, bread, hot chocolate, and salad for our lunch. He was thrilled; his whole face lit up.

Date Four was a trip to Glacier, the park covered in snow, pure white and silent. I brought my grandma's Irish truffles, as Josh wanted. That don't-mess-with-me face lit up again.

Date Five was a party at a high school friend's ranch. Afterward, we drove around the lake, watching it shimmer under the white rays of the moon, people's colorful Christmas lights reflecting off the snow.

We talked and talked, a whole range of subjects. We were quiet, too. I was dating the new Josh. Somehow, in all the years apart, we'd grown together. We were different from our life experiences . . . but we were still Josh and Laurel.

Josh didn't kiss me, but I felt him every second. I had to force myself not to make an awkward lunge onto his lap. I wanted to reach my arms around him and hug him. I wanted to pull his head down to mine and kiss him until I couldn't think, which would take about one second. I wanted to knock off that cowboy hat, strip open his shirt, and yank down his pants. Then I wanted to push him back onto a bed and straddle the man.

That same gut-wrenching, desperate passion for Josh, which I knew was buried in my soul, was still there.

It had never left.

But I had left . . . and I would leave again.

* * *

Date Six was different. Josh and I had dinner at my house, my mother and aunt out at Feminist Book Club. I made salmon, his favorite fish, baked potatoes, a shrimp appetizer, and chocolate cake, also a favorite.

"Laurel, thank you so much. That was incredible."

Maybe it was the heartfelt thank-you. Maybe it was my long years of feeling lonely and alone, even through the frantic busyness of my life. Maybe it was that face of his, hard and angled, familiar and dear.

I stepped toward him, and smiled, I know I did. He smiled back and took charge, his arms pulling me in. I lost myself in that kiss. *Poof.* All rational thought gone. I didn't let myself think, only feel. And what I felt was Josh, those lips knowing exactly what to do, those big hands knowing exactly where to go, those arms holding me so close I thought we were one person.

I undid the buttons on his shirt as I was kissing him, then ran my hands straight up his chest, loving the warmth, the muscles. I heard him inhale, felt his heart pounding like mine. He untied my red and white ruffled Christmas apron and dropped it to the floor, then my sweater went flying over my head, followed by my purple bra.

We were skin to skin, hands flying, lips meeting, our lips only parting when they moved lower.

Later, I would have to blame Zelda for breaking up my free-flowing lust. I heard her shriek-meow at the dogs. The dogs weakly barked back, then scampered up the stairs. At the bottom of the stairs, Zelda let loose again with a murderous scream, paws clawing the air. The dogs whimpered.

I pushed at Josh's chest, his hands pulling off my jeans, my breath coming in unattractive gasps. "Okay, stop, Josh, please."

"What?" He pulled back. "Stop?"

"Yes, please. I'm trying to resist you, Josh."

"Please don't." He bent to kiss me again and I gave in for another minute because he is delicious.

"You're ruining my resisting," I gasped.

"Happy to hear it, honey." He ran his hands up my naked back, then back down to my waist while kissing me.

"Don't honey me." Ah, he was a scrumptious, manly man.

"Okay, darlin'." He kissed my neck. He was still breathing hard, like me.

"Don't darlin' me, either, you seducer." He laughed as I turned shakily away and grabbed my bra, which had landed on the Rudolph cookie jar. His warm hands fell away. I tried to snap my bra, but my hands were trembling and I couldn't.

Josh did it for me, but said, "Poor me. I wish I wasn't doing this." Then he kissed my shoulder.

"Thank you."

"You're not welcome. I would rather you kept it off. I like the purple."

I reached for my sweater, which had landed near the coffeepot, and pulled it on. Unfortunately Josh did not button his shirt, so I was forced to feast my eyes on that chest again.

"You are the most beautiful woman I've ever met, Laurel," he said, his voice soft. "Outside and inside."

"I don't feel that way."

"Why do you say that?"

"Because I know who I am, Josh."

"I know who you are too, Laurel." He put one hand on either side of me on the counter, then bent to look me straight in the eye. "When you want to talk, when you want to tell me why you don't feel beautiful inside, I want to hear it. I know something is making you unhappy, and I want to know what it is so we can work it through."

"There's nothing to work through."

"Sure there is."

His voice was low, strong, and confident. Josh was a true man. Masculine and chivalrous, a take-charge type, who had always let me be myself, but the man had a gentle side.

I wanted to wrap my legs around his waist and forget everything.

"Can I have one more kiss?" he asked. "Just one."

Oh no. I'd be a goner. I'd have him up in my pink bedroom within seconds. "No way, cowboy."

"I'll take a hug then, cowgirl."

He held me close. I could live in that hug the rest of my life.

Zelda screech-meowed at the dogs again. The dogs whined. Poor things.

"Those dogs need to toughen up," Josh drawled.

My mother and my aunt's Web site launched. We loved it.

That evening, I checked to see if we had any orders.

There were two. I was not surprised. No advertising, no marketing.

My mother and aunt, however, were thrilled.

"We're modern ladies," Aunt Emma said. "Building our own, independent online business."

"We make aprons for feminists who love to cook for those they love," my mother said.

"Women power in the kitchen," my aunt declared.

Chapter 6

Josh came by our house two days later.

My aunt Emma spotted his black truck coming down our driveway toward Gary, our Christmas frog.

"Laurel," she said, "I'll give you three guesses. He's not tall, dark, and handsome; he's tall, blond, and reeks of a sexually adventurous man."

I didn't need three guesses.

"I'll be back in a minute." I fairly flew out of that sewing room.

"Hi, Josh." I stumbled out to the porch and shut the door. I could feel my face heating up. Why did he have to look so seductive without trying?

"Hi, Laurel." He handed me a huge Christmas bouquet with carnations, red roses, white chrysanthemums, and red and gold ribbons.

"Oh. Oh my." It was lovely. My voice wobbled. "Thank you."

"You're very welcome, ma'am." He tipped his cowboy hat at me. "I wanted to thank you for dinner the other night and for letting me take off your sweater."

"I can't believe you said that."

He grinned. "And your purple bra. I appreciated that."

I could feel myself blushing. He took two steps closer, then kissed me. Didn't take long for that kiss to take me to a better place. "I . . . we . . . it's . . ." I pulled back an inch, tried to get control. "It's the same, isn't it?"

"Yes, it is, darlin'." His voice was low, and deep, and yummy. "It's the same."

"Together we . . ."

"Get out of control. It's fun. I like it."

"I don't know what to do. You're overwhelming and messing up my plans."

"Plans are meant to be messed up sometimes, honey."

I tapped his cowboy hat. "Don't do this, Josh."

"Don't do what?"

"Don't be so darn sexy."

"Okay. I'll try my hardest." He snapped his fingers. "I've got it. I'll put on a long blond wig and a dress next time. That should smash the lust."

"It won't because underneath I'll know you're still Josh."

"That would be hard to change. I believe you owe me four more dates."

Yes, I did. I would need a bunch of Christmas elves to go with us so I wouldn't let him strip off my clothes.

He held up a hand. "I promise I won't take off your shirt this time."

"Thank you." I didn't mean it. I wanted to take off my shirt right now so I could feel his hands on me.

"I'll wait until you take off your own shirt. Then I'll let you take off mine."

"Josh." I had to laugh. It had always been like this between us. So hot, and yet, we were friends, we laughed, we joked. "I don't think—"

"You don't need to think about this too much, Laurel," he said. "Come out with me tomorrow night for dinner. I know of a new lodge with a restaurant overlooking Blackfish Lake. You'll love it. Candlelight. White tablecloths. Crystal. Your style."

My style. Josh always made me feel classier than I knew myself to be.

I hesitated.

"Do it for the house and five acres." He dropped a kiss on my cheek. "Or do it so that I don't go out of my mind sitting at home alone thinking about you and your purple bra."

I didn't want to sit home alone, either, not when blond King Kong was ten minutes away. I looked down at my Christmas bouquet. Josh was such a kind man. So masculine and sexy, but comforting. I could not fall in love with him again. I could not risk that heartbreak. I could not live through it a second time.

"Yes."

In the ambulance, on that icy, disastrous night, my body shaking from cold and shock, my father's hand in mine, the other covered in blood, he had a stroke.

His face collapsed on one side, his eyes went blank, and he pitched straight over.

"Dad!" I yelled. "Dad!"

The paramedic grabbed him and began care, starting with an oxygen mask. I panicked again. It took a while to get to the hospital because of the ice, but we finally made it, the doors whipping open as doctors and nurses took us both in separately.

The wicked stepmother, Chantrea, cried over my father. She hugged me tight, her tears flowing down my cheek as I lay in the hospital bed after my X-rays. My mother, after getting the call that I was in the hospital and had nearly drowned, was near hysteria. She and my aunt flew over. Aunt Amy rushed in, her face pale, along with Camellia and Violet.

Josh was there within minutes after Camellia called him. He kissed me full on the lips and I clung to him, but then I remembered what I'd said to my father, what I'd done, what I'd caused, my shame, my mortification, and pushed him away. I saw the confusion in his eyes, the hurt.

My father had managed to get out of our sinking car. He went up for air, over the roof, and down to my side. He slammed his fist into the window and broke it. He'd pulled me out, then up on the bank.

He was not conscious for twelve hours after his stroke and the doctors did not know if he was going to live or what type of life he would have if he did.

I fundamentally changed during that twelve hours. Who I was on that slick road and who I became while waiting for my father to wake up, to breathe, to talk, was a different person. I went from a rebellious, mouthy, immature teenager who had almost drowned, to a young woman who almost died from guilt.

The next day when Josh came to sit with me at the hospital when I was sitting with my father, I hardly spoke to him. He was kind and gentle and hugged me but I couldn't respond. I was shut down hard, depressed, panicked that my father would die because of me.

When my father woke up, his left side was paralyzed.

I bent over his chest and cried. I saw his right hand move slowly, oh so slowly, to stroke my hair. "I'm sorry, Daddy," I whispered. "I'm so sorry."

The tears flowed out of both his eyes. His left side was immobile, his face drooped, but the left side of his mouth was frozen in a slight smile. He looked friendly, welcoming.

I did not leave his side at the hospital, except when it was my turn to babysit Aspen, Oakie, and Redwood. My older sisters also took time to babysit, as did my mother. In fact, my mother moved the boys into her house several times so Chantrea and I could concentrate on my father.

My father had saved my life even though my meanness, my inexcusable rant, had made him take his mind off the road, which caused the crash, which caused the stress, which caused his stroke. He might never be the same again, and he had three young boys, plus my sisters and me, to take care of.

My despair was complete.

I had almost killed my father, *our* father.

I deserved nothing in life, including Josh. I could never be happy again. If my father died, I was the reason for it. That was the night I started to hate myself.

I cried until I couldn't.

I loved The Apron Ladies Web site.

It was unfortunate that the orders were trickling in.

I called the newspapers and the media and sent photos of the aprons via e-mail. I put tags on all our aprons advertising the Web site. I took out ads in the local newspapers.

But most of the time I sat around and sewed aprons and thought about Josh.

What did I like about him?

Everything.

"Have you traveled, Josh?" The restaurant overlooking Blackfish Lake was classy. It was decorated for Christmas with a wreath made of branches on the stone hearth and a towering tree in the corner adorned in silver ribbons and ornaments. There were white tablecloths, candles, and crystal. It was a far cry from the sack lunches with anemic sandwiches and baggies of cookies we used to share.

He nodded. "I have. I've traveled every summer for the last seven years. About sixteen days, total, each time. It's all I can take off."

"Where have you gone?"

"Scotland and England, one trip. Turkey. Kenya. Greece. Thailand and Cambodia. Chile, Belize. I know we planned to travel when we were kids, and a few years after I started my company, I decided to go. I planned the trip to Cambodia and Thailand, loved it, was surprised at how much I loved it, came home, and planned another one. After my first trip I realized how much travel changed a person, made them grow and learn. It gave me a whole different perspective."

Our conversation took off then, happily, with great excitement, as we had been to many of the same countries.

"I loved seeing new cultures, new places, meeting people," he said. "But when I come home to Kalulell, I'm glad to be home. I'm a Montana man, and I love it here, love my land, my business, my life here."

We had seen the world as we'd planned as teenagers. Our *National Geographic* talks worked, but we'd traveled separately. I thought of us in Greece together, on a ferry to the islands. In England, at a pub. In Scotland, watching a dance with men in kilts. How would Josh look in a kilt?

"Do you consider Los Angeles to be your home now, Laurel?"

"No."

"Kalulell?"

"I don't know anymore."

"I wish it was. It's a Laurel place to live. Skiing . . . the lake . . . hiking . . . fishing."

Why did he have to smile at me like that? A few snowflakes clung to the windows of the restaurant. Outside the trees were lit up with white lights for Christmas. "I wish it was, too, sometimes."

"How about all the time?"

Those green eyes, I swear, they were twinkling at me. Twinkle, twinkle. I wanted to cuddle up on his lap.

"You're impossible, Josh."

"Thank you. I missed you, too."

I missed you. And you are going to melt my Josh-lusting heart.

"Don't try anything on the way home," I told him, before he closed the door of his truck.

He climbed in. "Sit right here beside me, honey." He patted the seat.

"Tempting, but no."

"Please? Think of it as a Christmas present for me."

I pretended to sigh. He sighed back. We both laughed and he pulled me into his arms quick as a hopping reindeer and I hopped on that passion train.

He knew exactly what to do with that mouth.

This time I kept my clothes on. I was wearing a mocha-colored dress with a ton of blue buttons down the back and blue knee-high boots.

"You're killing me, Laurel," he said, as I pulled away. "And I don't like the looks of all those buttons."

"Why do you think I wore this dress?" I tried to get my breath, darned if it wasn't hard to start breathing right again. "It's like a button chastity belt."

He groaned. "What color bra tonight?"

"Burgundy. With black lace."

"Torture me further." He touched my pink tipped hair. "You're my Christmas elf, Laurel."

"I'm a Christmas elf who's keeping my clothes on."

"For now. But you might want to take them off, soon." He looked outside, the snow falling steadily. "It's awfully hot out there."

He held my hand and kissed it, three times. I swear I felt those kisses going straight to my heart.

I put new red thread into the sewing machine. I loved the apron I was working on. My mother had made the pattern. There was a vee neckline, crisscross back straps, and three different fabrics. I would add white lace.

I studied our "feminist Christmas tree" with the women power sayings. I thought of my mom and aunt's comments about romance and aprons and naked cooking.

Pretty, unique aprons for independent women.

Cooking aprons. Bedroom aprons.

Aprons to be naked in.

Sexy aprons.

Ruffles. See through. Cleavage. Fun. Frilly. Lacy. Role playing. Chiffon and silk. Not cooking aprons. Bedroom aprons.

"Mom," I said. She turned to me.

"Aunt Emma." Aunt Emma turned to me.

"This idea came from both of you. It's all yours. I wasn't taking it seriously at first, but . . ."

They clapped their hands when I told them.

"Bravo!" my mother said. "I've always wanted to be a porn apron star."

"This way I can show off my figure . . . tastefully," Aunt Emma declared. "Nudity is about class. It's about the human form, with all my curves. A woman's curves are physical art, nothing to hide."

We planned. We drew designs. We made patterns. We chose new materials. We laughed.

"We're naughty!" Aunt Emma said, taking off for the fabric store with my mother.

"Naughty as can be. Mrs. Claus would be proud of us!" My mother kissed my cheek. "And most proud of you, dear daughter."

I received two letters in the mail with pictures of Christmas trees, an ant wearing a red bow, and a skinny rabbit with five feet.

Dear ant Laurel.
I bite good.
For Christmas I want vampire teef.
I love you ant Laurel.
Teddy

Dear Ant Laurel,
I no can go to the preschool for two days becauze I let
the rabit out the windo he wants to be by the flowers and
son.
When Im home from the preschool you come over to
make the Crissmas kookies.
I lovee you.
Teddy bit me.
That bad.
I bited him back. There blood.
Love Shandry

Our eighth date was at Josh's house.

I arrived and parked in front of his home at seven
o'clock. I sat in the quiet of my car before I climbed the
steps. I pictured him inside, warm and snug in one of his
sweaters, his shoulders packed in, his jeans packed nice, all
cowboy Montana-y.

Ah, Josh, I thought. *I lost you once when I kicked you*
out of my life. I don't know if I can lose you again without
falling apart, piece by piece. That was not part of Plan NL,
as in, new life.

I thought of our green farmhouse. If it wasn't for the
house, I would not risk ten dates with this man and getting
hurt again.

Or would I?

Was it still all about buying my great-grandparents'
house back again?

Nah. It wasn't.

Truth can be hard.

I wondered if I'd show him my red bra. It had a nice push-up.

"This is Date Eight, Josh," I told him, after he'd made me a steak, potato, and salad. We sat on his couch, in front of a blazing fire. I love a gas fireplace, but there's something about a crackling fire that warms the soul up.

"I know, honey. Come sit with me." He lifted me onto his lap, quick as could be. I felt his warmth, his muscles, that smiling, oh so enticing mouth inches away. I felt myself go limp, which would have been mildly embarrassing, had I had a brain cell left in my head. I touch the man and I go limp? Ah, but that's how it was.

"What do you say to a kiss, Laurel?" he murmured.

He smelled yummy. Like spices, wine, and chocolates, and Josh, safe and snuggly. "I say that if I kiss you I'm gonna be lost."

"Lost in a good way?" He cupped my face with his hand.

"Yes, in a good way and a bad way."

He grinned. "I want to get lost with you in a good way, baby, not a bad way."

I did not have time to reply, as his mouth came down firmly on mine. I linked an arm around his shoulders, my chest against his, and slid into . . . us. I slid into Josh and me.

All restraint and "what the heck am I doing" and worries . . . gone. All brain cells . . . gone.

Delicious passion takes the place of thought when I'm with Josh every . . . single . . . time.

* * *

My night with Josh and our delicious passion did not end well.

We went from kissing to stripping, in not too many seconds. I took off my pink silky shirt, then I took off his, as he chuckled, exactly as he had predicted. My red bra went flying, his hands went north, I unbuckled his belt, he tugged at my jeans. He picked me up and carried me across the room to his bedroom. We rolled on that huge bed of his, the headboard carved with a blue heron in full flight.

I reached for him, held him close and tight, his mouth only leaving mine to forge hot trails down my body, which was precisely why mine left his, too. I could hear my own panting, and his, my legs wrapped around his hips, all clothes off and out.

And then, in mid-arch, in mid-kiss, in mid-mind-blowing passion when I knew we were going to consummate all this in another blaze of crazy lust . . . I froze.

"Oh no, Josh, no." I could not do this. What about tomorrow? The next day? After the holidays when I wasn't here? I couldn't walk away after making love to him. . . .

"What?" he panted, his lips hardly leaving mine.

I wanted to cry, I wanted to run, I wanted to make love to him. "No," I choked out.

"What . . . why, honey?" His voice was tight, his mouth an inch from mine.

"Don't call me honey." I felt my heart clench. His face, planes and angles and kindness and confusion, about killed me.

"Laurel—"

I pushed at his chest and he didn't move.

"What's wrong?"

"Everything is wrong with this." I pushed again and he lifted up.

I saw him clench his jaw, breathing hard, like me. He bent his forehead to my chest, then looked me in the eye. "We'll wait. I'm sorry. It's too fast, I shouldn't have—"

"Josh, please, don't blame yourself. It's me. It's always been me."

"What do you mean?"

"Can you get off before I grab you again and change my mind?" I was close to tears. Close to making a fool of myself. He got off and I grabbed a blanket he had folded at the end of the bed and wrapped it around myself. I don't know why I did that; he'd seen everything.

Josh flopped straight back on the bed, rubbed his hands over his face, and took a long breath in.

The whole scene made me sad and sick.

I went searching for my clothes. I grabbed my white negligee, which was over the back of a chair, searched for my pink silky blouse, which had somehow hooked onto the door handle to his back porch, picked up the rest of my clothes, and went to the bathroom and dressed.

I realized I did not have my red bra, but I was not going to look for it now. I'd grab it and go. I shook as I dressed, then ran my hands over my messy hair. When I opened the door to the bathroom, hoping to make a quick getaway so I could get to my car and cry my eyes out, he was standing in the kitchen, jeans only.

"What is it, Laurel?" He was serious, and sad, like me. "Tell me."

I folded the blanket and hurried it back into his bedroom and put it on his bed. "I don't want to talk about it. Do you see my bra?"

"No, I don't." His eyes were firmly on mine. "What's going on, Laurel?"

"Josh, I'm not . . . I'm not here to get . . . to get involved with you again."

His face moved back, as if I'd slapped him. "Why not? Everything we had before, we still have."

"No, we don't." We have my memories and my damage and my abandonment issues and I don't even know where I'm going to live.

"We do. I don't know what happened here tonight. I don't know why you pulled back, but I'd like to know." He walked over to me, stood too close. "I want us to start over."

"Start over?"

"Yes. I've wanted to start over with you since I saw you the first day. I didn't tell you, because I knew you weren't ready to hear it. I'm not willing to play games here anymore. I don't need more of"—he waved his hand toward the bed—"this. We certainly don't need to make love now, you can have all the time you need, but I want you to know where I want to go from here and I need to know how you feel."

Start over. With Josh. I couldn't. It had almost killed me to push him out of my life last time.

Maybe you wouldn't have to push him out again? I asked myself.

No, I would. "I don't think so, Josh."

"Why not?"

"Because I'm not staying here, in Montana. I'm leaving after Christmas."

"Give us some time, Laurel."

"No."

"Please."

"I can't."

"Why? And don't tell me you don't want to talk about it. That's not working with me. Don't shut me out."

"Josh, it's simple. We were together years ago. I'm here temporarily." Maybe. "I'll leave and go back to LA. I don't fit in up here," I don't think I fit in anywhere, "and I'm sure you don't want to live in Los Angeles." I sure didn't.

"I would if I had to."

"You would?" He would do that for me, for us?

"Yes. Is there someone else?" He didn't like that idea, I could tell. Not one furious bit.

"No. I'm leaving." I turned. I would leave without my red bra. I snatched up my purse on the way out.

"Laurel, don't go. Please. Talk to me. Tell me what's going on. Don't do this again—"

I pulled on the door.

"Are you kidding me?" he said, his deep voice so ticked. "You're leaving, you're running *again,* you won't talk this out?"

"Yes, I'm leaving." I yanked open the door, he pushed it shut. I turned around to yell at him, then saw the tears in his green eyes, frustration and sadness mixed. He had never been afraid to show emotion. He pulled me into his arms, kissed me hard, and gentle, possessive and loving, until both of us were breathing hard and I was blubbering.

"Damn it, Laurel, sweetheart. Stay. Please. Talk to me."

"No. I'm not staying," I sputtered out, wiping at my tears.

This time, when I opened the door, he didn't stop me, but those high-octane emotions followed me right out to the car. I could feel them, feel him.

"Drive careful, Laurel."

Why did he have to say that? It brought on the water-works. I had never been able to get that man out of my head and heart. He was stuck there. He always would be.

But I would leave Montana.

Wouldn't I?

Chapter 7

Two days later, when my mother, aunt, and I had ten completed aprons for our new "Naughty Aprons for Naughty Women" line, I said to them both, "Get your cowgirl boots on, grab your cowgirl hat, and let's go outside."

The snow shimmered. The red barn rose from piles of pure white. The fence posts were covered, icicles hung from the roofline, and the horses' breath created white puffs. We had ourselves a winter wonderland, perfect for, as my mother said, "a soft porn apron photo shoot."

My mother and my aunt, The Apron Ladies, were naked beneath their colorful, but sexy, aprons.

"Shoot quick, honey," my mother called out.

"Glad I have my cowgirl boots on," my aunt said, "but every other part of me is getting frostbite. Including my ya ya. Here we go, Laurel. Snap away."

The new aprons we sewed were flat-out sexy, flirty, and fun. One had a red silky bib and a red lace skirt propped up by layers of white gauze. We called it, "Red Hot Mrs. Claus." My mother modeled it with her black cowgirl boots and a Santa hat.

Another apron, with red and green hearts, had two holes

where, when tied in back with a red velvet bow, a woman's bust would push through. This was called "The Bust Out Apron."

A third apron had a pink heart for the bib with a black silky skirt. MY ANSWER IS YES, SANTA, was embroidered on the bib.

I took tasteful photos. For example, I did not take a full frontal of my mother when she modeled the apron with her bust busting through. She held up two red apples, strategically placed.

My aunt modeled the lacy Rockin' Your Reindeer apron holding sprigs of mistletoe in front of her chest, the horses in the background.

My mother and aunt modeled the other aprons on hay bales. They lifted a cowgirl boot onto the back of a snowy fence post. They posed on their tractors. They leaned against the barn, their cowgirl hats pulled low. They sat on their horses, Trixie and Lee Lee, wearing only their "Seductive Elf" aprons and boots and hats.

I also took photos of them in their old-fashioned farmhouse kitchen, cooking. As with the outside shots, they held cookbooks, mixing bowls, and giant wooden spoons over key areas.

"What will the neighbors say?" my mother said, then she and her sister laughed until they howled. They couldn't care less what the neighbors said about them. Ever.

"How will we control the men now? They'll beat down our door," my aunt said, wriggling her bottom in a black frothy apron we called "The Strip Tease." "It's hard enough as it is!"

I downloaded all the photos and we chose our favorites. The photos showed my mother and aunt's curves and smiles, but they were classy, daring, sweet.

"We don't look perfect, but we're perfectly beautiful," my mother said. "I'm glad to be alive, glad to have a body, glad to be a Montana woman."

"A body is a gift, not something to self-criticize," my aunt said. "And The Apron Ladies are delighted to be showing off their gifts."

I studied the photos later. My mother and aunt were in their sixties. They weren't shy about posing; they weren't shy about their bodies. They were proud. Their strength, humor, and courage came shining through. I wiped my eyes. I loved my aunt and mother and their lust for life and living as they wanted to live.

I sent the photos to Josy, the web designer.

Josy called me fifteen minutes later, sniffling. "Your mom and aunt . . . the expressions on their faces . . . I love it, I love them, their house and barn and the horses and the beautiful aprons. I love their lives in Montana. Get ready for the orders, Laurel, they're going to come rolling on in."

On Monday Josh called me. I did not call him back. My heart squeezed up tight, and I felt despair start to swirl. I should call him. I couldn't. I should. I didn't. There were so many things stuck in the middle between Josh and me and I couldn't seem to move them.

After our car accident, which I knew I had caused, and his stroke, which I also knew I had caused, I fell hard into a guilt-driven depression. All I felt was black around me. A total loss of hope. I couldn't see the light around my father's shaky right hand, the paralyzed left side of his body, his wheelchair, his helplessness.

The first five weeks were slow going for my father. There were many medical problems, many trips back to the hospital, some through the emergency room. We cried together. I wiped his tears and nose.

He could only grunt at first. He would wink to spell out words. One wink was an *A,* two a *B,* and so on.

When we were alone I said I was sorry a hundred times. He responded with love and kindness. When he could write again he wrote, in wobbly letters, "Not your fault. Mine. All mine. . . . Lousy father to you. Will be better father soon. . . . I love you, my Laurel. . . ."

I did not return to college. I moved into my father's house when he was in the hospital and in the rehabilitation center to help Chantrea and babysit the boys.

Wicked stepmother Chantrea, who was no longer wicked, was so grateful she broke down. Chantrea had to keep the restaurant going. They could not lose the restaurant, the income, and the health insurance they had through it.

I got the three boys off to school, visited my father at the hospital or rehab, then worked in the restaurant as a waitress for the lunch shift. I cleaned and cooked at home.

When my father came home from rehab in his wheelchair, I took care of him all day, and the boys after school. I took him to therapy, gave him his medicine, dressed him. Chantrea told me, repeatedly, that I was, "the best daughter. My good daughter. You"—she pointed to her heart—"you here forever. Heart daughter. Me and you."

My mother helped, as did my aunt Emma, and Aunt Amy, all resentments and anger toward my father over their divorces long gone. Camellia and Violet helped, too, when they came home from college, both telling me they felt so guilty for still being in school.

I said, "You don't need to be here, I do. He saved my life." I didn't tell them the truth, about the fight, the unforgivable things I said, how I'd distracted him from the road, I was so ashamed.

Josh came to see me often at my father's home. He helped with the boys. He brought me flowers and tried to interest me in *National Geographic* and other travel magazines.

I pulled my hand away from his. I pulled out of his embrace. I was cold. I hardly spoke. I could hardly look at him.

I had almost killed my father. He had saved my life. I would now save him. I would do everything for him. There was no room around my crushing guilt and debilitating remorse for Josh. I hated myself, and when you hate yourself you cannot be in a healthy relationship.

I finally told Josh not to come by again.

His eyes filled with tears. "Damn it, Laurel. What the hell is going on? I know you're upset about your dad, but I'm right here. I'm trying to help you."

"You don't need to help. I can do it myself. I don't have time to be your girlfriend, Josh. I don't have the energy."

"What do you mean, you don't have the energy? I'm coming to you. I'm trying to make things easier."

"You're not making anything easier."

He looked both stricken and frustrated. "Sorry, Laurel, I'm trying."

"Quit trying." I hated how mean I was to him, which told me, once again, that I was a hateful person who didn't deserve him. "I'm not going back to college because I'm going to stay here and take care of my dad."

"Laurel"—he shook his head, stunned—"you have to go back to college."

"Why? For you, Josh? So you can have me there to sleep with?" I cringed at my own words. I knew they weren't true.

He looked like I'd slapped him. "No, Laurel. Not so I can sleep with you. For *you*. For your education." We argued and it became more and more heated until we were yelling at each other.

"Why do we have to break up because you're not going back to college this term, Laurel? Because you're going to be here? We can call, we can e-mail. I'm only two hours away. I'll come up."

"No, we're breaking up now." I was so filled with pain already, it was simply one more swipe to a battered, deadened heart.

"What? Why?"

"I don't think that you and I should be together anymore. Find someone else. Play basketball. Be in your rodeos. Start that Salmon Fly business you're always talking about. I can't be with you."

Josh was moving on and moving up, like I'd always known he would. He was an excellent athlete and student. He was tough. He would end up with his engineering and business degrees and become someone.

I might very well never get to college, much less finish. I was a girl who had been so mean to her father she damn near killed him. I was young, devastated, emotional, and exhausted. I was in no shape to continue our relationship.

I didn't deserve him. I didn't deserve anything.

He argued with me, I argued back. He cried. I didn't.

Then I lied, because he kept arguing. "I don't love you anymore, Josh. I'm sorry. I've changed my mind."

"You've changed your mind?" His rolling anger covered his hurt, but I could see it. He lost color in his face, swore up a storm, we fought and yelled, then he left, his truck peeling out of the driveway.

I experienced such a profound feeling of loss that I lay down on my stomach, in the driveway, and cried.

Before he went back to college, he came over to my father's one more time. When I saw him I wanted to drop into hysteria and stay there. The boys were running around, and I was feeding oatmeal to my father, whose mouth was still frozen in that half smile. I was wearing a messy sweatshirt and saggy jeans. I didn't have makeup on, and my unwashed hair was held in a ponytail.

I was sleepless, as my father needed care during the night. I was pale. I was gaunt. Depression had landed like lead.

Josh was kind to the boys and my father. He looked like he'd lost weight, too. He looked miserable. I was shut down so hard from losing the man my father used to be and from losing Josh that I could hardly breathe.

He hugged me and said good-bye. I left my arms at my sides, unresponsive. "Can we be friends, Laurel?"

Friends? With Josh? That would never work. "No."

"E-mail me, Laurel, or call. Or visit. We need to talk."

I nodded.

"You're not going to call or e-mail or let me visit, are you?"

I shook my head.

"We're not going to talk, are we?"

I shook my head again.

He swore, said, "I can't believe this," and then, "If you change your mind, Laurel . . . I'm here. Anytime." He kissed me, on my lips, hugged me tight, one of his tears hitting my cheek, then turned on his cowboy boots and left in his truck.

He was headed back to college, off to a life I used to share with him. A life where I went to his basketball games and we met for meals in the cafeteria and walked around campus, hand in hand, and snuck into the library late at night and made love between the stacks of books. We also made love in his dorm room, in the locker room of the gym, and in the basement of the science building. We had friends together and English lit. A life.

It wasn't my life anymore.

I went back into my father's house, yanked up my jeans, and finished feeding my father his oatmeal through his crooked half smile. He patted my hand with his good hand, then wrote, "Go with Josh."

I shook my head. "No, Dad. I'm here with you."

"Go."

"No."

I wiped a tear from his cheek, then from my own.

* * *

On Wednesday Josh e-mailed, asking to meet for lunch. I lay down in front of our towering Christmas tree with the gold beads and red ribbons, hands over my face. James and Thomas lay on me, moaning, as Zelda the frightening cat had just scared them.

My despair over Josh kept swirling.

Our Naughty Aprons for Naughty Women grabbed the attention of our local news team and newspaper, then the state newspaper.

We arranged a date and time and the photographers and journalists all came out to the farmhouse. I told my aunt and mother that the local paper was not the place for them to make their "naked apron debut."

My mother argued. "A woman's body is something to embrace, not hide." She sewed a straight line down a silky black apron with a sassy skirt that would barely cover a nude bottom. The top half looked like something a stripper would wear.

I argued back. As I could not control them and their antics, or how they would look in the newspaper and online mostly naked, and those photos are forever nowadays, I tried to be convincing.

"But we're all about being proud of our age," my aunt said. "And not letting men define what is beautiful."

"We'll let you win this one," my mother finally agreed. "Because the photographs they take won't be near as good as yours, honey. You know how to work the shadows so nicely, too."

Oh, that I did.

When the reporters and photographers arrived, I stood back and let 'em go. My mother and aunt were hilarious in their flirty aprons, jeans, sweaters, and cowgirl boots and hats.

A few of the things they said on camera and to the newspaper reporters: "All naughty women need a naughty apron to get through the holidays."

And, "Make cooking seductive and sweet, and remember, you're in charge of your kitchen and your bedroom."

And, "Life is too short not to be sexy in the kitchen!"

The photographers and reporters laughed and wrote. We handed out bags of Christmas cookies as they left.

"I would have trusted that handsome photographer with the blue eyes and long hair to photograph me naked in an apron," my mother said later.

"Oh, me, too," my aunt said, waving a hand to cool down her suddenly warm face. "Let's invite him back for a private viewing."

I saw Josh on TV playing basketball for our university once when I was walking my wobbling father to the bathroom in his bathrobe after his stroke. He was having an incredible season. I noticed he never smiled after he made a basket, though, like he always used to. I refused to watch another game.

He called, and I didn't take his calls. He e-mailed several times. I did not respond. When he came home for spring break, we sat outside on my father's picnic table, the conversation devastatingly painful, stilted. I could hardly speak. Seeing Josh re-broke my already broken heart. I still felt dead with guilt because of my father's frozen half smile.

After some small talk and silences he said, "Can I take you to dinner, Laurel?"

"No, Josh. I've already said no."

"Lunch?"

"No."

He wiped his eyes. He tried to hug me. I pulled back.

"I still love you, Laurel." His voice cracked. "I still want to be with you, plan trips around the world together. . . ."

I did not respond. I looked straight ahead, then pushed my messy hair off my forehead and pulled my messy T-shirt down over my messy too-big jeans. I felt so ugly, inside and out. I didn't even want him to see me. I walked back into the house.

He left in his truck.

My guilt ate me further as my father continued to have setbacks that landed him back in rehab or the hospital, but through sheer will and determination, my father healed.

He had forgiven me. In fact, his exact words were, "It is not me who needs to forgive you, it is you who needs to forgive me, darling. I will be a better father."

I would never forgive myself.

The Christmas Eve e-mails continued. . . .

Daughter,
You made my old soul cry with joy when I saw you again yesterday. Every time I've seen you these past weeks, my soul has cried with joy. Joy! I wish you would move here permanently. Nothing to do in Los Angeles. Dusty. Flat. No fishing. No deer in the front yard.

Daisy and Banyan had a heck of a time putting together the puzzle of the Tyrannosaurus Rex you brought them and they wore the hats with the bats to bed.

Velvet already told you that she'll be bringing carrots and slew for Christmas dinner? She got the recipe from the Strip and Click in Nashville. I'll bring the wine. Her food will go down better with jugs of wine.

Velvet's afraid that people are not going to eat her pecan pie, in favor of Camellia's. Recipe from grandma, the convict.

Oakie, Redwood, and Aspen are trouble. They're wild and out of control. They have the Kelly Wild Bone. I am trying to work with Chantrea, but she does not want to think the boys are trouble. Thinks the hellions are only slightly shy of being angels and the police are out to get them. I suppose it was the police who made them attach a long, plastic penis to the plastic Santa in the middle of town on Saturday night.

   Ah well.
   See you on Saturday for lunch, right?
   I love you, Laurel.
   Love you,
   Yours,
   Dad

   To Laurel
   From Daisy a flower
   I like flowers. do you like flowers? I am a flower Daisy.
   I am four years old how olds are you? I like frogs. do you like frogs? I like bat hat.
   I sees you soon.
   Santa say I good so I get a presents. Mommy likes carrots.
   Love Daisy Kelly
   A flower

   To seester Laurel
   This picktur I drew is bat. They fly. I want to be bat. I like my bat hat from u.
   I luv you luv Banyan Kelly

   "Oh my goodness," I breathed, two days after the TV station aired their report of The Apron Ladies and the state and local newspaper articles appeared. "Mom, Aunt Emma." Both of them hurried over to my computer, my mother with fabric with gingerbread houses tossed over her shoulder. "Look."

My mother's hand flew to her chest. "I think Naughty Aprons for Naughty Women is successful."

"Power in the kitchen, power in the bedroom," my aunt added.

Sheesh.

We were bombarded with orders.

I sewed aprons like a speed demon and also kept track of, and mailed out, the aprons. Every apron we sold was wrapped in red and green tissue, this being Christmas, and tied with red and white ribbons. On the ribbon was a gold, oval sticker that said THE APRON LADIES.

It was now chaos.

I was delighted and worried. I was not planning on staying in Kalulell. I had hoped to increase The Apron Ladies' sales, so my mom and aunt could make more money and travel.

They would need a manager for their business, someone who understood money, Web sites, orders, business . . .

My head spun.

I had managed a rock band, but I could sell aprons. . . .

If I did, though, I would have to stay here.

In Kalulell.

Near Josh.

Could I?

I had two more dates with Josh. At the end of it, he said he would sell me the house and five acres.

I knew he would. The problem was that at the end of those ten dates, I'd probably be totally lost and in love with Josh again.

Then what would I do?

*   *   *

On Friday Josh called. Our conversation did not go well.
"What's wrong, Laurel?"

"What's wrong is that I don't want to talk to you right
now." Zelda hissed at James and Thomas. They both leaped
into my lap for protection, eyes wide.

"Okay, when?"

"When I can figure this out." James whined in my ear.

"You mean us?"

"There is no us, Josh." Thomas hid his nose in my
shoulder.

"I think there is, honey."

For how long? "No, there's not. There's ten dates, then
you sell me my house and five acres back, and I return to
Los Angeles."

"How about this? There's ten dates, I sell you your house
and five acres, and we go skiing together?"

"No." I petted the trembling dogs. Zelda shriek-meowed.

"No? How about you tell me what's going on in your
head? What you're thinking?"

"No to that, too. I have to go, Josh." I hung up.

I don't know what to do about Josh. I do know I don't
like myself right now at all.

I hugged James and Thomas. They were so scared.

Chapter 8

On Thursday afternoon, I drove to downtown Kalulell to go to the fabric store. The fabric store was visible from Josh's office. I hoped he wouldn't be looking out the window. I darted in, bought three bagfuls of Christmas fabric, and darted back out.

Josh was leaning against my car. "Hey, Laurel." He stood up straight, cowboy hat dusted with snow, those awesome legs packed into blue jeans.

"Hello, handsome cowboy." I sighed, unlocked my car. He took the bags and put them in the backseat for me.

"How about Date Nine right now?" Josh said.

I burst into tears. He gave me a warm bear hug, and I hugged him back, my wet face on his shoulder, right in the middle of downtown Kalulell.

We took his truck and drove around the lake and stopped at our favorite place. It was private and quiet, snow covering all the trees surrounding the lake like cotton.

"What do you want to do, Laurel?"

"I don't know." That was the truth. "I don't live here

anymore. I live in Los Angeles." Los Angeles had no appeal to me anymore, if it ever had. I had lived there for work. I'd had an exciting job. I traveled. I didn't want to live there again. I didn't want that head-banging job.

"I don't fit in here. I have pink-tipped hair. I wear odd clothes. I like colors and patterns." I was wearing red jeans and a flowing, sari-like shirt from India with tiny mirrors underneath a black and white checked coat. I was not going to change that part of myself. But why did I think I needed to change in the first place?

"My family is crazy. All those wives. Half sisters and half brothers and stepbrothers. The dynamics. The Wild Bone. Fighting over pecan pie." I thought of all of them. Noisy. Cantankerous. Periodic run-ins with the law. My latent guilt when I'm around my father.

"I don't have a job here." Oh yes, I did. The Apron Ladies needed me. "There isn't a beach nearby. No beach."

We sat in silence in his truck. Years ago we would have been naked by this point. He turned to me. "Laurel, you do live in Los Angeles, but you could move back to Montana. You do fit in here. You always have. Everyone likes your clothes and your pink hair, and who cares if they don't? You like it. For what it's worth, I like it. I like you the way you are. Your family is crazy. Whose isn't? At least they're interesting. They love you. The Wild Bone does seem to be in every generation, but it is what it is. When Aspen, Redwood, and Oakie recently made a snowman in the middle of the square and put three joints in his mouth and tucked a bottle of rum in his stomach, I laughed out loud."

I laughed. The snowman made the front page of the newspaper. He was called "The Inappropriate Snowman."

"You do have a job here; you can manage The Apron Ladies. Sounds like business is booming. Or you could do something else. Start another business. Or can you manage Hellfire from here when they're not touring? You could fly in and out of Los Angeles. Tour the world, then come home.

Or if you want me to hang out with you, I'll move to Los Angeles."

"You said that before. Are you kidding?"

"No."

"From Montana to LA?"

"Yes."

So he had meant it. "You would hate it, Josh. No land, no stunning home with a view of the blue and purple Swan Mountains, no elk and deer in your yard, no endless acres, no fishing, no river, no business."

"Where you are, I'll be happy. If you decide to stay here, as far as the beach goes, I promise I will fly you to Oregon or southeast Asia to visit a beach anytime. Open a *National Geographic* and pick a place."

"You . . ." I snuffled. "You would?"

"Yes."

I was a mess. I had been afraid to go out with Josh ten times because I thought I would fall in love with him again. In love with those green eyes that had softened up these past weeks. In love with the way he listened. In love with the way he talked to me about his business, asked my opinion, cared about my day, my mother, my aunt, The Apron Ladies, my work with Ace Hellfire. In love with how funny he could be, how calmly cheerful, as if he was inviting me to enjoy life with him, he and I in a bubble where only Josh and Laurel existed. In love with his kindness and his toughness. And what if he decided he didn't love me, want me? Then what? Heartbreak.

But I hadn't fallen in love with Josh again when we started our ten dates. I was already in love with him. I had never fallen out of love.

How would he feel when he found out that I had caused my father's stroke with my unrelenting harshness? I was so shamed by that, so humiliated by what I'd done.

He reached across the seat and gently grabbed my hand. He brought it to his lips, then pulled me over onto his lap.

"I want us to be together. I don't know what's going on, Laurel, but I'll wait until you figure it out."

I put my forehead on his neck and he hugged me.

"While you're figuring it out, I'm going to kiss you, honey."

And, ah, he did.

I laughed when I came home and found a box on the front porch. My aunt, mother, and I unwrapped it. It was champagne, the expensive stuff. I called and invited Ace and Scotty to Christmas dinner. He said he couldn't bear to see me, he was going to have another anxiety attack. I tried to calm him, comfort him. He sniffled. He heaved a sigh.

"The menu is set," my mother said to my aunt and me the next afternoon in our sewing room. My mother was sewing an apron that looked very much like a 1920s flapper dress, only it was sheer purple and had a gold bow.

"Christmas dinner will be delicious," Aunt Emma said. Her sewing machine was whirring. Her Christmas Super Snowwoman apron with a white furry bib and skirt was proving to be quite popular.

"Yes, delicious," I drawled. "We have the traditional turkey, gravy, and stuffing. Then we have Beef Lok Lak, Cambodian ginger catfish, eggplant lasagna, banana bread, hash and onion casserole, meat-loaf balls, carrots and slew, which is a recipe from the Strip and Click, and a pecan pie war. We'll have a house full of possible trouble with four wives, siblings, half siblings, and two step-siblings. Velvet and Chantrea aren't speaking because Velvet dresses suggestively in front of three innocent boys, Aspen, Oakie, and Redwood, they of the inappropriate downtown snowman who was smoking not one, but three joints."

"A song about Longer, Dick will set Boxing Richard off," my mother said.

"If Velvet feels that her pecan pie is not appreciated, we're going to hear about it," my aunt said.

"Watch out for Camellia's boys," I said. "They're biters."

"Chantrea and Amy are not getting along, either. Hopefully no butter dishes will be thrown again, at least not any of Mother's," my mother said. "I'll put an old one from Goodwill at Chantrea's place setting, just to be safe."

"Merry Christmas," I said. "Make sure all the guns are locked up."

"Merry Christmas!" my aunt and mother said. "Guns are already locked."

Zelda hissed and clawed when James peeked in the door. He barked once, unconvincingly, and darted out.

"It's going to be a heckuva dinner," my aunt declared. "The Kelly Family Christmas. Unpredictable. Are other families like this?"

I invited Josh to my house for dinner for Date Ten. My aunt and mother were out at a friend's house. They had hired a hypnotist to bring out their inner women's strength.

I pictured inviting Josh over.

I pictured the trouble I could get into, alone with Josh in my house.

"Come on over, Josh. It's Date Ten. Name your dinner."

"Really?"

That low voice, that gravelly, happy voice, got to me. I put a hand to my heart. "It's your menu, Josh." I knew Josh would keep his word. I could buy the five acres and the house back from him and save it for my family.

"Laurel, you make the best chicken tacos. I love them. And I love your pumpkin pie. Odd combination, but that's what I'm thinking of. Too much work?"

"Not at all." I smiled into the phone. I loved that he loved my cooking.

There would be trouble tonight.

Sometimes we all need a little trouble.

After many worrisome medical disasters, my father finally recovered to about 90 percent of where he used to be. The left side of his smile was permanently tilted up, and his left leg dragged some, which was a constant, crushing reminder to me of my role in it, but he was intellectually all there.

I left for college in Los Angeles in the fall. It was at my father's insistence and threats from my mother and Aunt Emma and Aunt Amy to banish me to a remote village in Siberia if I didn't leave. Chantrea did not join the clamor for me to go, I noticed and, in fact, cried. I didn't blame her. We had grown so close.

Ironically, after that disastrous argument in the car before the crash, born from not feeling a part of my father's life and new family, I now felt welcomed and loved. Chantrea always told me, "You! My angel. Heart daughter. I love you." The boys loved me, loved playing games and running around outside with me, and my father clearly enjoyed my company, his eyes lighting up whenever I was with him.

But college called. There was a family meeting with all three mothers, my aunt, and my father: The loud, vocal opinion was: Go, Laurel, go.

Except for Chantrea, who could only bring herself to whisper, "Go, Laurel, go." I hugged her. She cried.

I went.

I did not return to the state university because I could not face Josh. I had hurt him. I didn't deserve him. He surely didn't love me anymore, and to see him with another girl would send me into a downward spiral.

At the end of my first year in college in Los Angeles, I heard that Josh had a girlfriend. Her name was Tracy. Of course I hated her. Two years after we left with Hellfire on tour, on a trip home to Montana, I heard from my sisters that Josh was engaged. This girl's name was Lavina. I hated her, too.

"I'm sorry, Laurel," Camellia said, hugging me.

"Me, too," Violet said, hugging me. I pretended I didn't care; they knew I was pretending because I sobbed like a dying warthog.

I went to bed for three days when I returned to Ace's guest house in Los Angeles and cried all the tears out of my body. It felt like I'd died. Josh and I were on our separate paths. I would make sure they didn't cross.

Soon after, Chantrea and my father split up. I thought it was fallout from the accident, and the stress of it all on their marriage. I had broken up a family. I took on more guilt.

When I later heard from Violet that Josh was no longer engaged, I was so relieved I cried for three pathetic days again. I hadn't heard from Josh in years. He surely wouldn't want to talk to me anyhow, much less be with me.

Hellfire was headed out for another world tour and I couldn't wait to get on a plane and go. The job was exhausting, nonstop, and earsplitting, which I wanted. Then I didn't have to think.

Over the years I loved working for Ace and Hellfire because the job allowed me to run.

I ran.

"I know we were young," Josh said, after the chicken taco dinner, which he ate with gusto, "and I know it was a long time ago, but why did you push me away when we were younger, Laurel? What did I do that made you think we shouldn't be together?"

"I almost killed my father, Josh." I told him what happened that night. I told Josh what I said, my exact words, my hands over my face. I rocked back and forth. "I was so mean and he became distracted. I made him cry. I caused the accident and I caused his stroke."

He wrapped his strong arms around me. "You can't blame yourself, Laurel. You were twenty. You had felt rejected by him since he'd left when you were a girl. He hurt you, he hurt Amy and Camellia and Violet, he hurt your mother. He was gone all the time for work. Then he married another woman and had three kids, a new family.

"It was an icy street. You said yourself the ambulance slid and almost hit you. You slid on the way to the hospital. Your father smoked for over twenty years and drank too much sometimes. He was overweight and out of shape. You didn't cause that stroke, you didn't cause that accident."

Was he right? Could I lift some of the burden? "I've always believed it to be my fault. It's never left me. After the accident and stroke, I was so unbelievably depressed, Josh, I thought the guilt was going to kill me. My poor father, his left side paralyzed, hardly able to eat, to move, in and out of the hospital." I told him about those terrible months. "I didn't see myself with you because I wanted to save my father. I didn't think I deserved you, deserved us, deserved to be happy, either, after what I'd done to him. I know my issues of being left, by you, were there, too. My father left me, why wouldn't you?"

"I never would have left you, Laurel." He cupped my face with his hand.

"Josh, I am so sorry."

"I am, too, Laurel. I should have fought harder for you."

"No, you did all you could." He had called and e-mailed. He had tried to heal us. I wasn't healable.

He leaned over and kissed me and I kissed him back. It did not take long for things to get heated. He stood up, pulled me into his arms, and we ended up on my bed in my pink bedroom, me on top, then him on top of me, and one time we rolled right off the bed, which made both of us laugh until we cried.

We climbed back onto the bed, Josh pulling me close, and we made love as if there hadn't been twelve years between us, and miles of pain and grief. I completely lost my little ol' mind. All I could feel, taste, and hear was Josh.

He had always been an inventive, creative lover, and he outdid himself, as usual. It was like being thrown off a sex cliff.

"I'm glad I don't have to crawl out the window," Josh said, kissing me. "It's cold out there."

"Me, too, Josh. Me, too."

I fell asleep in his arms, woke up in his arms, and we made love again, that bright Montana moon shining through.

We smiled at each other and snuggled back in again.

Josh left for work after sitting down and eating scrambled eggs and bacon with my mother, aunt, and me. They fluttered and flittered and declared me a "liberated woman" who had chosen a "fine man who will embrace your independence and life's goals."

Josh gave my aunt and mother a hug before he left, kissed me full on the mouth, then picked me up off my feet and gave me a huge hug and another kiss.

My mother and aunt laughed and clapped and said, "A feminist still appreciates romance," and "equal rights, equal love." My mother pointed to our Valentine's Christmas tree. "See? Love."

They waved enthusiastically at him from the porch.

"Come again!" they called out. "You're always welcome, Josh," and "We have an apron here for you!"

I handed him a box of Christmas cookies.

I knew what it meant to him.

My cell phone rang. It was Ace Hellfire, real name Peter Watson, son of a pastor, and my former boss.

"Merry Christmas, Laurel." He was snuffling. "I bet you've reconsidered and will come back and work for me next year . . ."

"I haven't, Ace. I'm so sorry." We talked, he did some more begging. I thanked him again for the champagne and the gold Christmas tree and asked how his panic attacks were. "Where is Scotty?"

"He's here. We both miss you."

Scotty Stanford, devilish, outrageous, long-haired bass player, and Ace's partner, unbeknownst to their millions of fans, grabbed the phone and whispered, "Crimeny. He's a total mess, Laurel."

"I know."

"We're both wearing your aprons. The ones with the apples. Red and green. We're making pies."

My mother and aunt make Hellfire about fifty aprons a year to give out as gifts. Ace puts bonus checks in the pockets for the employees.

Ace Hellfire, hard-core rocker, infamous for his on-stage antics, and off-stage hell-raising, was the most domesticated man I knew. His image of an out-of-control, law-breaking rebel was only that—an image that we cultivated, as we did with Scotty, who had read almost every classic ever written. Favorite: *Pride and Prejudice*.

They loved to cook and bake and garden. Ace and Scotty both periodically call my aunt and mother for recipes.

"Could you please put your mother on the phone, Laurel?" Ace grumbled. "I'm having a terrible time with my meringue."

"Here ya go, honey. These are the papers for your house and the five acres," Josh said. We were at his house, in front of his fireplace, after eating the mushroom and avocado hamburgers he'd made.

Before he flipped the burgers, we took a tumble in his bed. I'd walked in, he'd smiled, I'd smiled, he'd kissed me, I set the banana butterscotch cream pie I'd made on the floor, and we headed to his comfy bed with the blue heron carved in the headboard.

We'd finally eaten. It was late by then.

"Sign on the line and we're done, Laurel. Thank you for the ten dates."

I laughed, leaned over, and kissed him. "You're welcome. Thank you."

I took the papers from Josh. Much of it was in legalese, but I saw the price of the house and the land.

"You're kidding me," I said. I felt about twenty emotions hit at once, all colliding and crashing into each other.

"No, I'm not."

"We agreed on the price for the house and five acres. Your cost plus fifteen percent."

"I changed my mind," Josh said, his tone unbending.

"I will pay you what I told you I would pay." I tossed the contract back to him. "Write up a new contract."

"No."

"You're making me feel like a hooker. I sleep with you and you do this?"

"You are no hooker, Laurel. You slept with me because we both wanted to."

"This makes me feel like it." My voice rose.

"I didn't mean to make you feel like a hooker. We had a deal. Ten dates. You met the deal."

"Did you read the numbers you have on this contract? I sleep with you and I get this?" I flung my hand out. "I hope it was worth it."

"It was worth it, Laurel. But that's not why I wrote the contract up as I did."

"Why did you?"

"Because it's your land and your family's home. It's your legacy. I should have called you before I bought it from your aunt and mother. I assumed you knew what they were doing, and I shouldn't have assumed that and I'm sorry."

I stalked over to my purse, whipped out my checkbook, and wrote a check for the initial amount. I gave it to him. He wouldn't take it. "Take it, Josh."

"No."

I slammed it on the table. "I won't sign that contract then."

"Then you don't get the house and the five acres."

"I don't like that . . . that . . . *tone* of yours."

"What tone? The one that says you're not getting your way? Why are you so stubborn?"

"Because I am, Josh. I am not going to take this from you. I don't want to owe you. I don't want to feel like I'm indebted to you. I don't need this hanging over my head whenever I see you."

"You're not indebted to me—"

"Yes, I am—"

"It's a business deal."

"It's a rip-off."

"The house and land is yours. How is that a rip-off?"

"It's yours until you take my check."

I would not be controlled in any way by a man, and this smacked to me of control. I was independent, I worked, I made money, I saved money, I would pay for the house and land at our agreed-upon fair price—whether or not I'd stripped and popped into bed with him.

We argued, and I ended up grabbing my faux cheetah purse and my silver jacket and stalking out of his house.

I heard him swear once, then yell, "Laurel—" He followed me out.

"Call me when you can agree to what we already agreed upon."

"What the hell are you doing? Are you going to run again? Shut me out?"

"Maybe, Josh," I shouted back. "I haven't decided yet because you've ticked me off." I ignored a little voice in my head that said, yes, I was running, again. "We don't need to talk until you change that contract."

"Fine." The blond King Kong stalked after me through the snow. "We won't talk. Come back in and we'll eat the pie in silence."

"Not funny, Josh."

"We can have breakfast in silence, too."

"You can have breakfast in silence by yourself or you can talk to one of your elks."

"I want to have breakfast with you, Laurel. It's a gift. Take it as a gift."

"I don't want any of your gifts, Josh. There are too many strings attached."

"There are no strings."

I turned my car around in his driveway, visions of that contract dancing through my head. I was furious. What did he think I was, some weak damsel in distress? Some helpless woman?

$1.00.

That was the amount that Josh wanted for five acres and a house.

$1.00.

"Drive careful," I heard him shout.

I was so steaming mad I hit my steering wheel with

both hands and said a bad word. Was he trying to buy me with that? Make me everlastingly grateful? I wanted an equal relationship, not this.

Dates and sex for a house and land, from a wealthy man, that was how it felt to me, and I did not like that one bit.

I fell into a dark pit, like I had the first time I lost Josh. I was surrounded by our odd Christmas trees with four-leaf clovers and feminist sayings, Gary the Christmas frog, the wicked witch on the gingerbread house, and Christmas aprons, but I was not in the Christmas spirit.

Every day was worse than the last. The despair didn't swirl; it settled in.

I couldn't sleep. I'd get up at night and wander the house, hold Zelda the screecher on my lap, or pat the dogs. I'd watch the snowflakes fall and get lost in them.

Josh did not call, e-mail, or come by.

Camellia and Violet and their kids visited, as they often did, and I could hardly speak. Camellia and Violet hugged me tight when I brokenly told them Josh and I weren't dating anymore. Aspen, Oakie, and Redwood, visited, too, and were later arrested for pushing the car of the mayor, an unpopular man, to the middle of a city park and dropping a toilet on the hood. My father came by to talk. He patted my hand, the left side of his smile tilted up. "Go to Josh," he told me, as he'd told me years before.

I called the bank. Josh cashed my check. I knew he did it for me, not him.

I thought about my own fears, my guilt, my pretty strong commitment and abandonment phobias, and the running I'd done. I thought about Josh. I was crushed by what I'd done to him in the past, and now.

My mother and aunt had some honest, blunt words for me, in the midst of me beating myself up.

"A strong woman knows when she has to put her fears

aside to grow. . . ." And, "Courageous women understand that life is not always going to be perfect, but they grab the perfect man when they find him." Finally, "You love him. He loves you. Go get him."

I had been a scared, untrusting, guilt-ridden fool.

"I need you to stop running, Laurel."

"I'm not running anymore, Josh." I leaned against his kitchen counter, my hands trembling. "I'm sorry I did. I truly am, Josh."

"You pushed me out of your life." Josh's jaw was clenched. "Again. Why can't you talk to me?"

"I will. I am. I should have before." My knees started to tremble, too. "You gave me the house and five acres for a dollar. I told you I would pay full price. Why did you do that?"

"Because I love you, Laurel." He was angry, and frustrated. "It's that simple. I wanted you to have your house and your land."

"You love me? After all this, all we've been through?"

"Yes. I have loved you since we met when we were sixteen. I will always love you." He looked miserable. Resigned. "We went off on separate paths for many long years."

"Many long, lonely years," I said.

"Yes. Many long, lonely years." His broad, huggable shoulders bent, as if he'd about had it, and I thought I would cry.

"Laurel." Those tired green eyes met mine. "I want to be with you forever. I will never leave you, I will never abandon you, but I need to know what you want. I can't go on as we are. I can't handle being in a relationship with you, making love to you, laughing and talking with you, holding you, and then have you run off, or have you push me away and out of your life for years on end. You're in or you're out. We work things through or we quit. We're a couple, or we're not."

"I'm in."

"You are?"

"Yes," my voice broke. "I am so in, Josh."

"I'm glad to hear that, honey." He looked away, blinked rapidly, then back to me. "I wanted to give you the five acres and the house as a gift. I never meant to insult you. I never meant it as a control type of issue. I never meant for you to think you were being paid to sleep with me. I never wanted to hold it over your head. I wanted you to have it because I love you and you love the house and the land."

"I understand. I do. I'm sorry, Josh. I overreacted. I ran, again. I shut you out, again. I feel terrible about it." I told him what I had been thinking about the past days, the tears I'd cried, the hopelessness, the harsh realizations about myself, and how I wanted to start over with him, this time, for forever, if that was what he wanted. "I love you, Josh, and I am so, so sorry. I could not be more sorry than I am."

Those bright green eyes filled with tears, like my gold ones.

"I have missed you every single day for twelve years, Josh. I tried so hard to not think about you and all we had and all I'd lost. I flew all over the world to forget about you and it never worked. You followed me everywhere in my head."

"It's been the same for me, sweetheart. It's always been you."

"By the way, I've already quit Hellfire."

"You have?"

"Yes." I told him how I'd had to quit, my brain too fried, my soul too tired. I stepped forward, he stepped forward, and I wrapped my arms around his neck. "I'm a head case. I know it. But what I know even more is that I want to be with you every day. I want you. I need you. I love you. I can't be happy without you."

"I'm not happy without you, either, Laurel. You are not a head case. You're thoughtful, interesting, fun, smart, and funny. You make the best cookies. How about if we start over for the last time?"

"That'll work for me, cowboy."

"For me, too, cowgirl, for me, too."

His mouth came down on mine.

He is delicious.

Chapter 9

The Kelly Family's Chaotic Christmas Eve began in the light green farmhouse my great-granddad and grandma built. My mother had the hot buttered rums ready.

Aunt Amy brought her momma's hash and onion casserole and meat-loaf balls. The scent of the hash and onion casserole about knocked me over, but my smile did not waver when she kissed me and said, "Merry Christmas to my third daughter. I love you."

Her husband, the former boxer, Richard Longer, hugged me, too, then whispered, "Sorry about the casserole. Trust me, it smelled worse at home, like a dead rodent."

A truck roared up the drive, way too fast. I saw Oakie at the wheel. He stuck his head out and yelled, "Sister! We comin' to you, girl! We comin'!"

My two other half brothers, Aspen and Redwood, sons of my father and Chantrea, were in the back of the truck. As the truck slowed, they both stood up and waved, each of them with a six-pack of beer in their hands. "Merry happy beer Christmas!"

Oh, they were trouble. Oh, how I loved them. They leaped out of the truck and hugged me, then because they are big and strong and funny, they lifted me up in the air horizon-tally, and walked me back into the house like a Cleopatra queen. I would have objected but I was laughing too hard.

When they set me down in the family room, everyone was laughing.

"Okay, okay," Aspen said. He has a mop of black hair and spends most of his time on the ski slopes. He has a tat-too of a Tazmanian devil on one arm. "We've got a song."

"It's for you, Dick Longer," Oakie said, running a hand over his mohawk. He, too, spends most of his time on the slopes. One of his tattoos is a pair of handcuffs. He'd told me it was to remind him to stay out of trouble. "We been workin' on it."

"This year, we have a melody," Redwood said. He is the third black-haired ski bum. He recently got a tattoo of a leopard on skis. "You know, like a symphony or a rock concert."

All of them have a tattoo on their right arm that says, "Kelly," and "Three brothers."

The girls are crazy about them, their tattoos, ski bum-ness, and their piercings.

"No," Aunt Amy said. "No singing."

Richard stood up, bull-like chest out, and said, "You can sing the song, and then we'll go for a round in the back-yard. Three minutes each?"

We all knew what Boxing Richard meant.

"Hmmm." Oakie put his fist under his chin. "That doesn't sound pleasant. Sing a song, then I get my pretty nose bashed in."

Aspen swallowed hard. "With you being a boxer, it does appear that the outcome would be poor for me."

Redwood said, "I can't let you hit me, because then I'll get a black eye and it'll turn the girls on too much. You know, bad boy gone badder. They like that."

"We have a decision then," Richard said. "Let's forget about the song and all sit down and have a beer."

The boys cheered and tossed him one.

My mother and Aunt Emma and Aunt Amy sighed with relief.

We were distracted when Camellia and Violet burst in with their husbands and Camellia's two vampire boys and Violet's two girls who keep getting expelled from pre- school. I went straight up to hug them. The vampire boys were actually wearing vampire teeth.

"I like your teeth," I said to them.

"Mommy said we wear the teef until we no bite the peo- ples anymore," Tad said.

"I a biter so now the teef stop me," Teddy said.

"It's best not to bite people," I said, hugging them. "They might bite back."

Tad's eyes grew huge in his cute face. "That ouch."

"I don't yike that," Teddy echoed. "No teef bite."

I hugged Violet's girls, Shandry and Lizzy. "How's pre- school?" I asked. Violet sighed. Her husband said, "Who gets expelled from preschool? Our kids. It's that Kelly Wild Bone. Your side of the family, Laurel."

"Preschool fun," Shandry said, throwing her little hands in the air. "I let animals free. Bye-bye, hamster!"

"I like to paint kids at the painting time," Lizzy said. "Rainbow. You want me paint you, Aunt Laurel?"

The kids ran around the house to pet Zelda, Thomas, and James. "Keep their teeth on when they're around the cat," I told Camellia. "It's a safe bet Zelda will bite back."

Camellia looked worried and took off after the boys, dropping her pecan pie, which she knew was better than Vel- vet's, and a chocolate silk pie, on the counter, followed by Violet's eggplant lasagna for her Italian husband and banana bread because she likes it.

I went back out to the front porch. An elegant car came next, and Chantrea stepped out. She had her fourth son, David, with her, who was actually carrying what appeared to be a four-foot-tall galaxy with him. There were colorful wires, marshmallows, and something that looked suspiciously like a large firework. "Hi, David." I gave him a hug.

"Greetings, from a scientist." He bowed, then adjusted his large glasses. Some scientific table fell out of his front pocket and he tucked it back in.

Chantrea was dressed in silk and high heels, even in the snow. She doesn't dress like that when it's only she and I. I think she's threatened by Velvet.

She was carrying her Christmas Eve Cambodian ginger catfish and Beef Lok Lak dishes.

I grabbed the catfish dish, then hugged her. I had remembered to put the Goodwill butter plate at her table setting so we didn't lose one of Grandma's if she threw it. The Goodwill plate was quite pretty. China. Blue flowers. I hoped it lasted the dinner.

"You see my boobs?" she asked. "Bigger now."

I eyed her chest. Whoa. Boob job. "They are splendid."

"Yes. Splendid. See?" She put the Beef Lok Lak on the ground and flashed me. "Ya. Much better. No one call me flat pancake girl Chantrea no more."

"I've never heard anyone say that about you, Chantrea." I saw beneath the bravado. She was scared. She was coming to Christmas dinner with two ex wives and a current wife. The current wife was younger and had two children with her ex.

"I got the big knockers like Velvet," Chantrea said. "But mine better. I show her tonight at dinner. Mine better."

"I'm so glad you're here."

"Ya. Me, too. You keep that Amy away from me, too. She say my good boys not good. They good. I learn to fight in Cambodia and I can do here in America."

"I understand. But no plate throwing."

She gasped, outraged. "No, not a plate I throw. That wrong. Butter dish. I throw butter dish."

"Keep it safe. It's Christmas."

"Merry Christmas. You my angel."

"Merry Christmas. You're mine, too, Chantrea. I love you."

"I love you more, heart daughter."

She headed to the house as my father, Velvet with her controversial chest, and their two little kids, Daisy and Banyan, arrived, along with Velvet's boy, William Robert Rhodes II, the son of the governor who had the affair with Velvet. I am told that the governor, William Robert Rhodes, senior, pays $3,000 a month in child support from the Alaskan village in which he lives with his long beard.

I don't know Velvet well, but my father is totally in love with her.

"Hello, Velvet," I said.

"Merry Christmas, insane one." She hugged me. She was carrying the carrots and slew made with the recipe from the strip joint, heavy with brandy, and the pecan pie. I knew she believed it to be better than Camellia's.

"I don't want my fine butt handed to me in a sling tonight, Laurel, if you know what I mean with this family of yours, but I'm happy we're here with the loose cannons anyhow."

"Merry Christmas. I'm glad you're here, too." I think she still had Chantrea beat in the chest department. Chantrea would not be pleased. However, Aspen, Redwood, and Oakie would be, which would irritate Chantrea.

"You look lovely, Laurel, as always." My father hobbled over, his left leg dragging a bit, the left side of his smile up higher than the right. My guilt rushed straight at me, hard and fast, as usual, but then he wrapped me in a hug. When he pulled back, he wiped his eyes. "It lifts my soul to see you. Every time. Never changes. Merry Christmas. I love you."

"Merry Christmas, Dad. I love you, too."

I hugged my half siblings Daisy and Banyan. Daisy, four years old, was wearing a princess dress, the shark-tooth necklace I gave her, and an army helmet. She jumped up and down when I said "Merry Christmas" and told me that Santa had brought her a doll for Christmas Eve. "I take doll head off, like this." She turned around and dug in her pink backpack. "See now doll head a baseball." She threw the doll head baseball, then ran after it, army helmet bopping.

Banyan, three years old, was wearing a miniature hunting outfit, the stuffed snake I gave him around his neck, and he was carrying a plastic spatula and a wooden fork.

"Are you going to cook?" I asked him.

He seemed confused, then he grinned and waved his utensils. "New toys!"

"He likes to play in the kitchen," my father said.

Banyan banged the spatula and spoon together. "Bang, bang, bang!"

William Robert Rhodes II, eleven years old, stuck his hand out and shook mine. "It's a pleasure to see you again."

"It's a pleasure to see you, too."

He was wearing a suit. "I like to dress for the occasion."

"You look very handsome."

"Thank you. Do you have a chessboard here? Or backgammon?"

"I don't think so. We usually play poker on Christmas. Don't be afraid if people get angry when they lose."

"Poker?" He arched an eyebrow. "That's acceptable. Your father taught me. No one can ever read my expression, so I do have some expertise in that area. It can be a gentleman's game, as I'm sure you're aware."

"I'm aware. And a ladies' game. I wish you the best of luck in your endeavors tonight."

He adjusted his tie. "Do you like the symphony, Laurel? If you had to choose between Beethoven, Dvorak, or Strauss, who would be your favorite? Mine would be Dvorak."

"William!" David, Chantrea's son, called from the front deck, holding his science experiment up. "I brought it. Come on in, I need you to look at some of the wiring and routing systems."

"Excellent. I'll be up straightaway."

My father sighed.

You can always tell which children are not biologically related to him.

When I was boiling the gravy on the stove, Josh walked in, to much fanfare. My family hugged him, told him it was "the best" to see him. He finally made his way over to me and gave me a hug and a kiss in my red ruffled Christmas apron. Everyone clapped. I blushed.

"The accident we were in was such a blessing for me, Laurel. I felt terrible about the impact on you, *terrible,* but for me, it was a blessing."

"Dad. What?" *A blessing?*

"I realized"—he wiped his eyes—"that I was an incredibly selfish man who ran away at the first sign of adversity, of trouble. I left Amy and your mother when they made reasonable demands on me as a father and husband. When we were in the car together that evening, and you told me how you felt, I was devastated. You were so young, yet you knew more about life, loyalty, and love than I did. In the months that followed I understood, finally, the emotional damage I had done to you kids and to your mothers. I was a self-centered donkey's butt."

I felt the beginnings of forgiveness. Forgiveness for myself. Finally.

"After my stroke, I had time to think about how I was as a man and a husband and father. On all counts, I failed. It broke me down, I'm telling you, honey, it did. It's odd, isn't it, how sometimes the best lessons in life come at the worst times. Family is what's most important to me. You kids, your mothers." He sniffled, he blustered, he wiped away tears.

CHRISTMAS IN MONTANA 395

"Twelve years ago I had a second chance to make things right, and look at our family now."

It was actually funny, and ironic, what came next.

Chantrea asked my mother, "You think my good boys go jail because that funny joke snowman in town with plastic private? I think no."

Oakie put a beer can on his head and shouted, "Shoot it off my head, someone, I dare you!"

Daisy and Banyan streaked in without their clothes and yelled, "See, Daddy! We naked mice!"

William Robert Rhodes II stood on a chair in his suit and said, "Let's take a moment to turn on Mozart and be quiet within our own spirits."

I heard an explosion in the backyard. I figured it was David's science experiment. Yep, it was. I heard a whoop of glee.

Tad took off his vampire teeth and bit his brother, who bit him back. They both screamed, outraged.

Camellia and Violet clinked their champagne glasses too hard together and they shattered.

Velvet said, "This carrots and slew will make your tongue hang out."

Zelda the cat screeched, paws scratching the air, as the dogs tried to sneak down the stairs. They scampered back up. Ah, family.

What a mess.

I turned and saw Josh wink at me. He smiled, sweet and loose. I smiled back.

Ah, Josh.

He was Plan J.

What a love.

We drove to Josh's house in his truck after I helped clean up the kitchen. We did not arrive until after midnight.

When we turned the corner onto his private lane, I gasped. "Oh my gosh. I can't believe it. It's gorgeous!"

The trees on both sides were decorated with white lights, the glow glistening off the white sparkle of snow.

"I thought you might like a few lights since it will be our first Christmas together in twelve years."

"A few lights? Josh . . ." As we made the last turn, his home came into view. "You outdid yourself, Santa."

He laughed.

"Mr. Claus will not have a hard time finding your house."

"I haven't been in the Christmas spirit for a long time, Laurel, but you've definitely brought it back."

"You've done the same for me, cowboy."

When I stepped into his house I had another surprise. Josh had a towering tree in his living room. It, too, was covered in lights. There were only four ornaments.

I stepped closer. "These are the ornaments I gave you when we were dating."

"Yes, they are."

One ornament was Mr. and Mrs. Claus holding hands. Another was two reindeer kissing. A third was of two polar bears on ice skates, and the fourth was a boy and girl elf, the girl elf perched on the boy's back. "I'm so glad you kept them, Josh. I kept mine, too."

"Then we'll have to hang them up. Merry Christmas, Laurel."

"Merry Christmas to you. Sit down. I have presents for you."

He lit a fire, we turned off the lights, except for the lights on the Christmas tree, and he opened his gifts. I bought him an ornament with two moose, male and female, on skis. I gave him two aprons, matching, so we could wear them together while we cooked, a cool cowboy hat, a box of Christmas cookies, and a fishing pole.

He seemed to love the gifts. I got a long kiss for the fishing pole. "I can't wait until we can fish together again."

He had bought me a Christmas ornament, too. It was two bears in Santa and Mrs. Claus outfits. He bought me a box of lingerie, a new ski jacket, and a pink ski hat.

Then he handed me a ring box. "Will you marry me, Laurel?"

I sniffled and snuffled and couldn't talk, those darn tears getting to me again.

"I love you," he said, threading our fingers together. "I want to be with you my whole life. I don't want us to be apart again. I promise I will do everything to make sure that you're happy, that we're happy, that our family is happy."

"Yes. I will, Josh Reed. Yes." I kissed him, wiped my tears. "This is the happiest moment of my life. I love you so much."

"Me too, baby." He leaned over and kissed me, put the sparkling diamond on my trembling finger, and we started the smiling and stripping routine.

"You are the best Santa Claus in the world," I told him, my breathing heavy, as usual during our naked antics.

"Ho ho ho. And Santa wants to take you up to bed for a special gift, Mrs. Claus."

"Sounds perfect, Santa. Mrs. Claus says yes."

And it was.

Perfect, that is.

UNDER
THE MISTLETOE

LISA JACKSON

Chapter 1

Christmas Season

Don't ruin the holidays. Whatever you do, Meg, wait. It's Christmas. The kids will be home. You need to be patient.

Megan Johnson fingered the divorce papers she'd helped prepare. For herself. To end a marriage of over twenty years. Tossing her car keys onto the counter and leaving her briefcase on one of the kitchen chairs, she walked into the living room of the house she'd lived in most of her life. She couldn't say she was happy about the idea of divorce, not at all. Never had she thought she'd be single again. Never would she have believed that she'd pull the trigger on the divorce. Never had she thought it would be she to break up their once-happy family. But there it was. Despite the heartache and, yes, the fear of an unsteady future, she was relieved. She and Chris had been separated for months and, really, had been drifting apart for the past two years, ever since Lindy, their youngest, had taken off for college.

Chris had said he'd meet her here. After work. But he was late. And that ticked her off. He couldn't even show up on time to this, their final meeting before she actually did the deed. *Typical.* She checked her phone again, expecting that she'd missed a call or text, but no, he hadn't tried to contact her.

That was part of the problem: communication.

Yanking off her gloves, Megan stepped through the archway to the living room, where stairs ran up to the second story and the house had been decorated for the holidays.

It was as if she and Chris were adrift, that the kids had been their anchor. When Brody had left home, Megan had sensed the tides of her marriage turning. Two years later, while Brody was still serving in Afghanistan, Lindy had decided to go to school in New York, and, once their son had been discharged from the army, he'd returned home briefly. His stay was short-lived. Brody was now in Boston, also in college, and Megan and Chris had been left alone. Their marriage had faltered, neither partner understanding the sudden change in their relationship.

And, if she were truthful with herself, Megan would admit that when Adam Newell had joined the staff of her law firm as a senior partner, things had gotten worse. *That* not-so-little complication had been her fault, of course, and she had to fight a crushing guilt.

Now, it seemed, as she snapped on a couple of table lamps, her marriage was over. Not finishing the paperwork had just been putting off the inevitable, which, all things considered, was unlike her. She'd always been organized, a doer, and couldn't stand lack of decision-making on anyone's part, especially her own.

But divorce. That was different. So final.

Eyeing the Christmas tree positioned in the bay window she felt an overwhelming sadness. Trimmed in white, silver, and bloodred, a few of the old hand-me-down ornaments from her parents adding spots of color, this tree stood where one had during the winter holidays for all of her thirty-nine years. She'd grown up here, in this part of Connecticut, in this very house, only moving away for col-

lege when she and Chris were first married. In this Cape
Cod–style house, her parents had raised their two daughters,
and they probably would have lived here forever, had things
been different. Megan's mother's struggle with and loss to
cancer had changed all that.

When Carol Simmons had passed, everything had changed.
Everything. The cluttered rooms filled with a lifetime of
memorabilia, the echoing, empty hallways, and the lack of
life had proved too much for Megan's father. No longer was
there the sound of Carol's off-key humming as she baked,
or her deep laughter, or even the scent of her perfume un-
derlaid with the odor of a cigarette to waft through the
rooms. Barely six months after laying his wife of a quarter
of a century to rest, Jim Simmons had packed up and
moved to Arizona where, to Megan's mortification, he'd
found a woman twenty years his junior. He'd married Lara
after a whirlwind courtship of less than three months. In
less than a year from the time he'd buried her mother, her
father had started a new life.

Meg had met Lara several times, of course, over the
years. Still, she couldn't say she was a fan of her stepmother, and though she tried to "get over it" and "be happy"
that her father wasn't grieving any longer, it had seemed
false and taken her years to accept.

*Who are you to judge, Meg? What do you think your
own children will think when you tell them that you're fil-
ing?*

Something within her withered, and she told herself it
wasn't as if she wanted to make such a final, irrevocable
move, but she felt she had to.

The upshot of her father's move to Arizona, other than
his giddiness at his May-December marriage, was that he'd
sold this house to Chris and Megan, so they as a young couple had returned to the one place in the universe she considered home. And she still did. She flipped a switch and
hundreds of tiny, clear lights, like stars in a dark sky, winked

on. She should have felt that same tingle of anticipation she'd always experienced when the tree was lighted, but tonight . . . nothing.

She stared through the window. Outside, snow was falling, the late evening seeming serene and peaceful, the lawn covered in a thin blanket of snow beneath which was a slick layer of ice, from last night's storm. The area was supposed to be blessed with a white Christmas if the weatherman was to be believed, and a dangerous one as the roads had yet to be cleared. On her way home, she'd slid a couple of times, narrowly missing a struggling minivan as it tried to climb the hill leading to this street.

Frowning, she glanced at the clock, her mother's, still mounted on the wall. Six twenty. She'd been home nearly half an hour, and Chris was late.

For the first time since arriving home, she was starting to worry. Again, she pulled out her phone, and this time she called, but when Chris's voice answered as part of his voice mail message, she cut the connection.

He'd be here. He knew that it was time, and what she wanted.

Still . . .

Craning her neck, she looked past the yard and along the street to the corner and half expected to see familiar headlights turning toward the house. Instead, the darkness settled deeper. Nervously, she ran her fingers along the window frame.

She saw her pale reflection in the glass, an image she'd noticed before, though always before, at this time of year, there had been a sparkle in her eye, a smile upon her lips, and the watery image seeming young at heart. Odd, how things turned out, she thought now, standing in the house where the soft hum of the furnace was the only noise to break the silence of the coming night. Here, where there had been parties and laughter, and . . . Oh, God, now there was nothing.

And whose fault is that?

Walking to the fireplace where the grate was cold and the framed pictures on the mantel of her once-happy family stood at attention, every sunny smile seeming to mock her, she couldn't help but wonder what would happen to the place. The thought that she would have to sell the family home bothered her, just as it nearly broke her heart to be considering divorce.

But there it was, in plain black-and-white, she thought, glancing down at the pages, all neatly typed, ready to be signed and filed, clutched in her hand.

Come on, come on, Chris. Let's just get this over with.

Feeling a chill, she didn't bother taking off her coat and walked to the hallway where she adjusted the thermostat up a few degrees. From the corner of her eye, she caught a glint of something silvery on the hardwood floor, just beneath the tree. Upon closer examination, she discovered that an ornament had fallen off a branch, and, as she picked it up, her throat tightened. The ornament was really a tiny silver picture frame that surrounded a picture of Chris and Megan at their wedding twenty-odd years earlier. How fitting that it had fallen, she thought sarcastically, but surprisingly the glass hadn't cracked, and the etching along the silver frame, OUR FIRST CHRISTMAS, was still legible. Her heart grew heavy as she stared at the faded photograph. How long ago it seemed. She started to put the ornament onto a branch again, intent on tying the fraying red ribbon over an empty limb, but she hesitated and instead slipped the small frame into the pocket of her coat, all the while wondering if Hallmark or whomever ever came out with an ornament for OUR LAST CHRISTMAS.

"Sick," she told herself, and sighed. She had to go through with the divorce and move forward with her life. It would be best for everyone, she rationalized, though a bit of melancholy burrowed deep into her soul and begged to differ. She'd told herself she would wait until after the first of the year, let the kids get back into their routine at their colleges, and—

Her cell phone jangled, and she slid her hand into the pocket of her slacks to retrieve it. Finally. About damned time. Still scanning the documents, she hazarded a quick glance at the screen, expecting to see Chris's number and bracing herself for an excuse as to why he was running late. Instead she spied a number she didn't recognize, but she figured it was a client who needed a little handholding after hours. She could do that.

"Megan Johnson," she said automatically as she came to the page with the division of property.

Over background noise she couldn't immediately identify a deep male voice said, "This is Officer Ben Sheldon, Connecticut state police, Mrs. Johnson."

Her heart leapt to her throat. *The police?* This couldn't be good. In a heartbeat, she thought of her kids.

"Are you the wife of Christopher Johnson?" he asked, then rattled off their street address.

Oh, dear God, what had happened? "Yes." But Chris didn't live here anymore, she thought, he'd moved out months ago. . . . Oh, God. He'd never changed his ID that she knew of; his driver's license would still list her home as his residence. A sick feeling grasped her stomach. "Where's Chris?" she asked, starting to panic. "What happened to him?"

"I'm sorry to tell you this, Mrs. Johnson, but your husband was involved in a multiple-car accident."

"What? No!" She felt her knees buckle, and she fell against the back of their couch. There had to be some mistake. "Involved?" she repeated, trying to make sense of what the policeman was saying. "What do you mean? Is he all right?" Her heart was hammering; her usually steady voice barely a croak.

"He's being life flighted to County General."

Oh. God. "But . . . but he's alive?" she said, fear and re-

lief battling within her. "You're telling me that he's alive?"
Otherwise they wouldn't bother with *life* flight. In desperation, she clasped both hands over the phone. Her divorce
papers fluttered to the floor, scattering under the forgotten
Christmas tree.

"He was alive when the helicopter took off."

"Thank God. I'm—I'm on my way to the hospital."

A pause. "Mrs. Johnson?"

She'd already started searching for her keys as she walk-raced for the back door. "Yes?" she shouted, now running
toward the back door.

"You'd better hurry."

County General was a madhouse.

Ambulances and helicopters had brought the injured,
and police and emergency workers were dealing with the
ensuing chaos. Several news vans were parked near the front
entrance of the hospital, reporters already standing outside
the brick building, snow blowing around them as they spoke
into microphones and looked steadily into the eyes of cameras held on the shoulders of crew members.

After circling the parking lot twice, Megan found a spot,
slid into it, cut the engine, and sent up a quick prayer for
Chris's life. Then she locked her CR-V and dashed through
the snow to the wide glass doors that opened automatically
to a vestibule, where a second set of doors whispered open.
She saw the information desk wedged between the emergency room and the admitting area and skirted a huge decorated tree as she made her way to the desk where, amazingly,
there was only one man in a business suit standing in line.
As she approached he was already walking away. "I'm looking for Chris Johnson," she said to a harried-looking woman
manning the phones behind the desk. A bit of a thing with
kinky gray hair, she glanced at Meg and held up a finger,
finishing a call that had come in to her headset.

Meg stood on one foot, then the other as another woman came up behind her to wait her turn. When the receptionist finally said, "Thank you for calling," Megan said again, "Christopher Johnson. The police told me he was in an accident and brought in here via life flight . . . and . . . and I have to find him, to find out he's okay." Then realizing she hadn't identified herself, she added, "I'm his wife. Megan Johnson." She was frantic, her heart pounding in dread, fear that he might not make it sliding through her like a ghost.

"Just a second." The woman, whose name tag read Betty Hilgaard, held up a finger again.

Meg wanted to scream as the tiny woman talked into her headset again, answering another person's inquiry about a patient. It was all she could do to keep her cool. To distract herself, Meg scanned the room; every chair in the lobby was occupied, and people were standing in the hallways. The ER was filled to overflowing, patients wheezing and coughing, a toddler crying, a muted TV mounted high on the wall with pictures of the accident site visible.

Her heart nearly stopped.

On the way to the hospital, she'd listened to radio reports and found out there had been a twenty-three-car pile-up on the interstate. According to the information she'd heard, a truck loaded with Christmas trees had hit a patch of ice, skidded across two lanes of traffic, and jack-knifed. The vehicles near the huge truck had either run off the shoulder or slammed into each other or had been smashed by the falling bundled trees that had somehow been torn loose of their bindings and, like torpedoes, had sailed and dropped onto the icy pavement and any vehicle in their paths.

To her horror, now, as she stared at the screen, she thought she recognized Chris's sedan, a white Ford with a crumpled front end, broken windshield, and mangled quarter panel. The roof had suffered horrid damage, collapsing deep into the interior, the entire interior caving in. Anyone riding in the car would have been seriously injured if he or she had survived. "Dear God," she whispered, horrified. *Not Chris, not Chris, not Chris.*

But someone. Someone who is loved by someone.

Her heart twisted.

Chapter 2

"Johnson? Isn't that what you said?" the woman behind the desk asked.

Startled out of her reverie, Megan caught her breath and blinked back tears of worry. "Yes, yes, Chris Johnson, the police said that he was life flighted from an accident scene and—"

"He's in surgery," Betty Hilgaard said, eyeing a computer screen in front of her. "Third floor. OR 7. There's a waiting room for family members near the nurses' station up there."

Alive! He's alive!

Tears gathered in her eyes. "Please, can you . . . can anyone tell me how he's doing? What're his injuries?" Dear God, this was a nightmare.

The little woman offered a patient, practiced smile. "There are volunteers on the third floor," she said. "Someone there can help you. I'm sure there will be paperwork to fill out, and a doctor will talk to you."

Damn the paperwork.

Megan just needed to know that her husband would survive, to be assured that he would survive and be all right. As another couple joined the woman behind her in the line to the information desk, Megan tried to get a grip. Ms. Hilgaard pointed to an alcove tucked near the admitting area. "The elevators are just over there."

"I know," Megan said a little more curtly than she'd intended. "Thank you." Her nerves were strung tight, her heart a drum as she half ran to the bank of elevators, her boots clicking a sharp tattoo on the floor. She'd been in this hospital often enough. Both her children had been born here, she thought with a pang, remembering barely being able to get to the delivery room as Brody, true to his nature, had come fast, hurrying to be born, just as he'd barreled headlong into the rest of his life, moving quickly, with a high pain threshold that would make him a threat on the football field and a fearlessness that caused him to join the army barely after he'd turned eighteen.

How eagerly she and Chris had anticipated their son's birth. Megan's throat tightened as she remembered seeing Chris in the delivery room, his eyes shining with tears of happiness, his hands so large as they cradled a screaming, red Brody for the first time.

She nearly stumbled at the memory. Oh, God, Chris had to be all right.

At the elevators she slapped the call button and paced, seconds stretching endlessly before one of the elevators landed, doors opening, a hospital worker pushing an elderly man in a wheelchair, oxygen tank attached, into the hallway.

Once they passed, Meg slipped inside before the doors closed again and impatiently pounded the button for the third floor. The car was detained as two teenaged girls, both in skinny jeans, one holding a bouquet of pink roses and a helium balloon in the shape of a baby rattle, entered and pressed the button for the second floor, where the maternity ward was located. Megan thought she would go out of her mind as the balloon nearly got caught in the doors, the rattle floating back into the hallway, the teens thinking it was so damned funny they both giggled and laughed. Meg held her tongue and onto her rapidly fleeing patience as they reeled in the balloon and the car finally moved upward.

Pink roses. Pink balloon. A girl.

Megan's heart nearly tore from her chest as she remembered Chris holding Lindy as he had their son, just after cutting the umbilical cord. How he'd said, "She's perfect," and had beamed, again tears sheening in his eyes. And now . . . now . . . She couldn't even think the worst, wouldn't let her mind go there.

And yet less than an hour ago, you were intent on divorce. Angry with him for being late to read over the papers.

She felt a jab of guilt, but buried it. Chris, after all, had been the one to move out, to initiate the separation.

The car stopped, doors whispering open, and the two girls, talking and joking, blissfully unaware of the crises happening in the ER and surgery rooms, stepped onto the second floor. The doors closed, and with a jolt the elevator car moved again. Within seconds, Megan was on the third floor, glancing at the signs mounted on the hallway walls, making her way quickly to the waiting area for patients in surgery and bracing herself for the worst.

She wasn't alone. The room was filled, most chairs and one small couch occupied. A coffeepot stood empty, ready to be refilled, in one corner; magazines were strewn across tables. An oversized computer monitor mounted on one wall displayed an Excel-type program listing patients by numbers and colors, which indicated where each was in his treatment: Beige was pre-op; blue indicated the patient was in surgery; and green denoted that he'd been transferred to a recovery area. In each box, along with the ID number, was a tiny digital clock indicating how long the patient had been involved in his or her procedure. After speaking with the attendant, showing her ID, and filling out a release while handing over insurance information, Megan was handed a slip of paper with Chris's hospital ID number.

"Can you tell me how he's doing?" she asked, desperate. "All I know is that he was in an accident, a bad accident— the one on the interstate—and that he was life flighted and . . . and now he's here." Her voice faltered, and she fought tears again.

"I'm sorry. This is all the information I have," the attendant, around sixty, with kind eyes behind rimless glasses, said. "I'll try to find a doctor or a nurse, someone from ER who might have admitted him. In the meantime you can follow his progress." She offered a smile, then motioned up to the computer screen mounted on the wall.

"Thank you." Megan, shell shocked, found the colored rectangle on the screen dedicated to her husband, a glowing blue square. According to the glowing chart he was still in surgery, the timer indicating that so far the procedure had gone on for one hour and seven minutes. Since no one could give her any more information, Megan found a seat in the waiting room, clung to the paper with his number, and stared vacantly at the computer screen as the digital timer continued to add seconds to the length of his procedure. Or procedures, she reminded herself when she recalled the picture on the television, just a flash of the horrifying image, the mangled vehicle she thought belonged to her husband.

Sooner or later she would have to call her children. They had the right to know that their father was battling for his life. She'd only hesitated because she'd hoped before she made those calls that she'd have a more complete report on his condition, understand more what had happened to him, would be able to give them the extent of his injuries and, of course, be able to assure them that their father would be fine.

But that wasn't going to happen for a long while, if at all.

Please let him be all right, she thought, sending up a prayer while a tight-lipped woman in her thirties said, "So what's with the coffee? Hey! Does anyone care that we're outta coffee over here?" The Thirty-Something was glaring at the woman at the desk where three people were waiting, and, ignoring them, held up the empty pot.

Everyone in the waiting room stopped what they were doing to stare at her, and she finally got the hint. "Hey! I'm just sayin'. They offer coffee in this place, then they'd better take care of it, you know what I mean? It's not like we're not payin' for it. Ever seen a bill? Out-effin'- rageous!" She replaced the pot, looked up at the screen, then headed through the door. "I'm goin' to effin' Star- bucks!" she proclaimed as if anyone cared, her high-heeled boots ringing sharply down the hallway.

"Bully for you," a man muttered. Slouched in one of the chairs near the doorway, a baseball cap covering his head, he was reading this morning's sports section of the local paper and hadn't even looked up at the woman's dramatic exit.

Within seconds, it seemed, a hospital worker rolled a cart into the room and exchanged the empty pot for two carafes, then refilled all the baskets containing stir sticks, sweeten- ers, and creamers.

"So there is a God," the guy in the cap said as he folded his paper and made his way to the counter with the fresh pots. "And he's got an effin' sense of humor."

Meanwhile, Megan stared at Chris's rectangle on the chart.

One hour. Sixteen minutes.

No change in status.

She couldn't put it off any longer.

It was time to call the kids.

Bracing herself, she pulled the cell from her purse, ready to speed-dial Brody. Her phone jangled in her hand.

She looked down at the tiny screen, and her heart sank. The heart-wrenching situation took a turn for the worse as Adam Newell's name and number flashed onto the display.

Chapter 3

"I just wanted to make sure you were okay," Adam said after she'd stepped into the hallway and answered. A nurse pushing a rattling cart of medications walked by. Megan glanced up at a sign mounted on the wall. **No Cell Phone Use** had been posted in bold red letters, and a circle with a line drawn through it was painted over the image of a flip phone.

Perfect.

"I'm fine." She was moving quickly, around a gurney where a man, covered in sheets and with an IV attached to him, was being wheeled along the wide, glistening hallway; the attendant rolling the cart glared at her. "I can't talk now. Hold on a sec."

She found a stairwell, hurried to the first floor, and walked through the lobby to the parking lot, where the temperature was far below freezing and falling snow was dancing in the bluish light from the security lamps.

"You still there?" she said as she pressed the phone to her ear again.

"Of course I am."

"Good, good," she said.

"Look, there's been a bad accident on the interstate. It's all over the news. I knew that you'd been working late and was worried that you might have been involved."

She closed her eyes for a second to gather herself. Her life was such a mess right now, such a disaster, and Adam Newell, Chris's cousin and now her boss, was squarely in the middle of it.

"I'm fine," she said, seeing her breath fog in the cold air.

"Thank God."

"But . . . but not Chris."

"Chris? What about him?" Concern edged Adam's voice.

"He was in the pileup somehow. I don't know the details, but he was life flighted to County General."

"Oh, my God."

"He's in surgery. I don't know what for or how he's injured, how bad it is, but obviously it's not good. I'm at the hospital."

"Jesus, Meg." He sounded devastated.

Quickly, she filled him in on the sparse details, then finished with, "I have to get back inside to check on him, and then I need to call the kids." She watched two more cars that were circling for spots and noted that most of the emergency vehicles had left. No longer were ambulances, their lights flashing, taking up space under the canopy of the emergency room entrance, and only one news van remained, two people cradling coffee cups visible through the windshield, no reporter or cameraman braving the elements.

"I'll be there in half an hour," Adam was saying as she walked through the first set of double doors of the main entrance.

"No, Adam," she said. "You don't have to—"

"Of course I do. Chris is my cousin, for God's sake. And you—" She stopped dead in her tracks and squeezed her eyes shut. *Don't. Don't say it.* "—well, you know what you mean to me."

She knew that he wasn't talking about the fact that he'd once been her brother-in-law, had been married to her older sister. At the thought of Natalie, Megan's heart twisted a little more painfully. "Adam, don't," she warned. "Please. No."

Click!

The wireless connection was severed.

Like it or not, Adam Newell was on his way.

"Is he all right?" Lindy's voice was an octave higher than usual. "Mom?"

What could Megan say? How could she reassure her daughter? "He's in surgery now," she repeated from a cell-phone friendly area near the hospital's cafeteria. "He's been in for over two hours, but I still don't know what's wrong with him or any details. I've asked over and over again, and they've promised that I can speak to some nurse in the ER, but it's a madhouse here." And that wasn't a lie. Though it was now close to midnight, the hospital was crawling with visitors, worried loved ones who, like Megan, waited for any kind of news. Not only had there been the massive accident on the interstate, but other emergencies as well. The one cafeteria that was open 24/7 was crowded and running out of food, benches and chairs in the open areas were filled, and through the wide glass windows, Megan noticed others talking or smoking in the parking lot, where the temperature had plunged to below twenty.

"I'm coming home."

"Not now, honey. Please. There's nothing you can do."

"I'm coming, Mom. I'll catch the next train."

"But you have finals and—"

"This is Dad, Mom. Dad! And I'm coming. You may not love him anymore, but I do!" Lindy clicked off, and Megan quietly counted to ten.

Though the separation had been a mutual decision, Megan had been blamed for Chris's moving out. At least by their daughter. "You never loved him enough," Lindy had said more than once. "He adored you, Mom, *adored* you. And you didn't love him." Lindy hadn't even realized she'd used the past tense when talking about her father's feelings for Megan. That adoration had been a long, long while ago.

"I loved him, love him . . . but you just don't understand."

"You're right; I don't. People who love each other don't get a divorce, Mom; they find a way to get over it, past it, through it, or whatever. You just have to try."

So easy for a girl not yet twenty to believe. Lindy was on the brink of womanhood, but still believed in Disney-like fairy-tale endings. There was nothing, in Lindy's mind, that love couldn't conquer. Meg, at Lindy's age, had felt the same. Now, though . . .

May as well make it a double, she thought as she stood in the hospital's hallway and speed dialed her son. No answer. She wasn't surprised. Brody lived in Boston now, was registered for school, but, Megan suspected, wasn't really attending. A few classes here, an odd job there. Brody had come back from the war a man, yes, no longer a boy, but seemed to have no real goals, not even a purpose in life. Whatever spirit and boyish charm he'd carried with him to Afghanistan, he seemed to have left there. He'd been a medic, seen far too much, and now was drifting. Hopefully, not for long.

She texted her son, asking him to call, then made her way to the third floor again, where, she discovered, there was no change in Chris's status. He was still in surgery, but now, the clock registering the length of his procedures was ticking off the seconds at over three hours.

She slid into one of the vacated chairs, glanced at the muted television, then at the scattered magazines, but nothing held her interest, and she couldn't help checking and rechecking Chris's status.

At least he was alive.

"Mrs. Johnson?" A female voice caught her attention,

and she looked up to see a nurse standing in the doorway. Tall, slim, and African-American, she wore her hair clipped short and a uniform of a blue hospital tunic with matching pants. She said again, "Mrs. Johnson?" to the waiting room in general.

"Yes. I'm Megan Johnson," Meg said, on her feet in an instant. "My husband is Christopher."

"Edie Brown, RN." Even though Megan's boots had two-inch heels, Nurse Brown was taller than she, with regal features and eyes that had seen it all. Edie shook Megan's outstretched hand. "Come into the hallway. It's a little more private there, and I do mean 'a little,' but all of the consulting rooms are full right now, and I've only got a few minutes. I heard you wanted to know about your husband."

"Yes," Megan said, trying not to sound as desperate as she felt. She followed the nurse to a quieter space near an alcove for vending machines. "How is he? What's wrong with him? I've heard nothing." She was panicking again, her voice rising, and with effort, she took it down a notch. "Sorry. I'm just . . . I'm just worried sick."

"I know. I apologize for any delay or confusion. Look, it's crazy tonight, but I was your husband's ER nurse, and I won't lie to you, his condition is serious. Multiple contusions, fractured pelvis, internal bleeding, head injuries." She hesitated a second while Megan processed what was being said. "From what I understand he had to be pulled out of his vehicle. Jaws of life."

Megan leaned against the wall for support. "Oh, God." For the first time she thought, really considered, what life would be like without Chris, how empty life would be for her, for the kids, if he didn't survive.

Her kids . . . oh, Lord, her kids would never get over it. Nor, she guessed, would she. The void would be so all-consuming. It was one thing to separate, to consider and decide on divorce, but another to be faced with the final and decimating thought that he would no longer exist. Her throat swelled so tight she could barely whisper, "Is he going to make it?"

The nurse's smile was patient if not reassuring. "We're doing everything we can. He's got a great surgical team with him, headed by Dr. Atwood. She's the best. And your husband seemed like a strong, fit man." She glanced down the hallway, then placed a warm hand on Megan's shoulder. "But, as I said, his injuries are severe. You might want to contact any other of his relatives, if you haven't already."

"Oh, God."

"Where there's life, there's hope," Nurse Brown said as a pager in her pocket went off. "Good luck. I'll check back with you before my shift's over."

"Thank . . . thank you," Megan whispered, her eyes flooding. God, she'd been a fool. All the fights, all the anger, all the pain . . .

Clearing her throat, she dashed her tears aside with the back of her hand. Now wasn't the time for recriminations. Feeling numb inside, she made her way to the waiting room, checked the chart, saw no difference in Chris's status, and fell into a chair. She texted a few people who were close to him, just saying he'd been in an accident and was in surgery and to call her—his folks, who spent their winters in Florida, and Natalie, across the Atlantic. Megan had known her husband since she was seventeen and to consider that he might not be around was . . . unthinkable. Sliding her phone into her pocket, she felt her fingers brush against something else, a sharp corner.

Frowning, she pulled out the ornament she'd slipped into her pocket at the house, the silver frame with a tiny picture of Chris and Megan at their wedding over twenty years earlier. She'd been young, about Lindy's age. And just as filled with dreams.

In the photo, she and Chris looked so fresh-faced, so full

of life, so ready to take on the world, even though, really, the ornament wasn't representative of their first Christmas together, just their first holiday season as a married couple. Nowhere on the silvery decoration was it mentioned that she had been barely nineteen and already three months pregnant. She still remembered how disappointed her parents had been, how they'd pinned their hopes on her finishing college, and even going further, to law school, her dream, all of which she'd managed to accomplish. With not just one baby, but two.

And Chris's unyielding support.

She bit her lip as the memories washed over her in an emotional torrent. Her first Christmas with Chris had happened two years earlier than the holiday captured in the photo. She'd been barely seventeen. At the time Megan had naïvely believed she was in love with the man who was marrying her sister, the man who even now was on his way to the hospital: Adam Newell.

God, she'd been a fool. An innocent, naïve idiot.

Glancing once more at the wall chart with its timer ticking off the seconds of Chris's life, Megan blinked against those same tears that had been her companion since she'd heard of his accident. As she clutched the ornament tightly in her palm, she remembered that first magical night when she'd met Chris, a night when he'd been bold enough to kiss her and in so doing had altered the course of her life forever.

Chapter 4

Twenty-two Years Earlier

With her fists clenched and her eyes closed tightly, Megan Simmons tried to erase the scene that was before her. But every time she sneaked a peek, the setting was the same.

White lace and satin whispered across the polished floor. Soft music filled the air. Glasses clinked over the sound of soft music. Friends and family smiled as the newly married couple finished the dance that was to be the first in a lifetime.

Megan's insides churned, and she forced a smile she didn't feel despite the tears she felt burning behind her eyelids.

Yes, she felt a jab of guilt. How could she feel this way about her sister? On Natalie's wedding day no less? But there it was: jealousy. Dark and deep and hideous, but burrowed deep in her heart. Megan had to be an awful person. Right? The whole situation was bilious. Yeah, that's right: bilious. She was a nerd, plain and simple. An A student who liked literature, band, debate team, and everything so UNcool she could barely stand herself. No cheerleading.

No modeling. No cool-crowd party invitations, but oh, watch out, she could ace a trig quiz with no problems whatsoever.

And look where it had gotten her: staring at her older, gorgeous sister now married to the man of Megan's dreams. It was sick and unfair, and she couldn't stand it a second longer. She made a beeline for the French doors leading outside, where she could get away from the sickening happily-ever-after scene.

Ugh!

She was at the doors, her hand on the lever, when she noticed the same tall, brown-haired boy observing her. What was he looking at? She felt as if he'd been watching her most of the night and wished he'd just dial it back. In the reflection of the doors, she caught another glimpse of Natalie, positively glowing, the train of her gown tucked up, her smile infectious, and Adam . . . Oh, God, Megan's heart twisted painfully. Elegant, almost regal-looking in his black tuxedo, he complemented Natalie perfectly. In pure white and striking ebony, they were the consummate image of a bride and groom.

Megan's stomach churned.

She had to get out of here! Outside, the wintry Connecticut landscape beckoned, snow piling on the stone veranda, an icy contrast to the warm interior decorated with thousands of tiny lights, candles, and poinsettias.

Yanking open the door, she heard her aunt's voice over the music.

"Look at you," Aunt Janice said.

Oh, yeah, right. Like *any*one would notice her. Well, except for the boy she hadn't recognized. He was still watching her and trying not to be too obvious. She wondered what his problem was.

Aunt Janice, always a little out of step, said, "You look fabulous."

"If you say so."

"I just did." She lifted a knowing eyebrow and glanced at Megan's hand, still poised on the door handle. "Going somewhere?"

"Not really," Megan lied.

"Hmm." Aunt Janice wasn't buying it. "It was a perfect wedding, don't you think?"

"Perfect." Would it be anything else? Come on, Aunt J.

"And Natalie! A beautiful girl, and she's never looked lovelier."

Megan couldn't argue that obvious fact. "Yes, she, I mean, they do look happy." Megan forced the words out, told herself to quit being such a horrid person. After all, she was the damned maid of honor. With a sigh she leaned against the glass panels of the door and stared wistfully at her willowy, dark-haired sister.

Why was it always that way: tall, beautiful Natalie, forever in the limelight, and smart Megan, always in the shadows? It wasn't so bad that Natalie had enjoyed all the fruits of being gorgeous in high school. Megan had survived when year after year Natalie had been a member of the cheerleading squad, or whatever princess or queen was in season. In fact, it hadn't really bothered Megan at the time.

After all, that had been over two years ago, and Megan had only begun high school the year that Natalie had graduated. Those days, Megan had even felt a rising sense of pride in her older sister. Secretly, she'd thought, well, maybe *hoped* was a better word, that some of Megan's popularity would rub off on her.

But then Natalie had graduated, and even though the two girls had still lived at home together, they had grown further apart, or at least it seemed that way to Megan. Of course then there had been Adam. All too clearly Megan recalled the day that she'd met him. She'd been at home studying, of course, when Natalie had come breezing into the house, announcing that she'd met some incredible, hot boy, someone "different" from all the other cool dudes who'd hung out at the house. Megan had hardly looked up from her homework.

Then Adam had appeared. And everything had changed.

At the sight of him Megan had felt her throat tighten and her pulse jump.

Tall and broad-shouldered, he'd had thick, kind of shaggy black hair and deep-set eyes that seemed to look right through her. And his smile was killer! The second that Adam had flashed Megan his faultless grin, she'd realized in horror that she could be falling in love. That had been silly, of course, but the idea had bloomed with each subsequent meeting. Far more mature than any of the other boys Natalie had dated, Adam had been the one with a purpose. Adam had been vocal about his intention of becoming the partner in a prestigious law firm one day.

Now, the music stopped. Megan nearly jumped when she heard Adam call her name.

"Hey, Meg, how about a dance with your new brother-in-law?" He took her hand and gently pulled her toward the dance floor.

Oh. God.

Megan wanted to refuse. But she couldn't. Not in front of all of the guests. Crap! As much as she had dreamed about being in Adam's strong arms, she felt it a grim sort of betrayal of Natalie. Megan gazed furtively around the room, but Natalie was nowhere in sight. The only person who seemed to be paying any attention to her was the mysterious lone boy, the one who was still watching her with unconcealed interest. She wondered what his problem was.

"I'm really not that good of a dancer," Megan protested, hoping Adam would take the hint and let her beg out of the dance.

"Neither am I."

"No, you don't understand," she whispered desperately

as she died a thousand deaths. "Really, Adam, this is a bad idea. . . ." *A really bad idea.*

"Quit stammering and dance. Ignore them." He gestured broadly at the guests circling the floor. "Pretend we're alone."

Inwardly she groaned. But she was stuck. Even though most of the crowd was involved in private conversations, Megan hoped that she could use Adam's remarks as an excuse.

"I know they're watching, and that's just the point! I can't dance in front of them. I'll be too embarrassed! I just can't," she pled as she tried to step away from him.

"The only thing you *can't* do is leave me stranded in the middle of the dance floor. Besides, you have to dance with me. You're the maid of honor and the sister of the bride. It's tradition. At least in my family."

"Who needs it? Look, I don't think that my making a fool of myself is expected by anyone."

"Oh, Meg. Just chill out." Adam looked down into her eyes, and she felt her heart bound with excitement. She couldn't even find her voice—she was just so stupidly breathless to be this close to him.

"So, come on, smile and act as if you're having a good time."

The small dance band was playing a slow tune, and Megan felt her stiff body begin to relax as Adam led her easily through the waltz. When she closed her eyes, she could almost feel that it was she, and not Natalie, who was his bride.

For a silly moment, she let her head rest against Adam's chest. She could hear the hollow sound of his regular heartbeat. She smiled to herself. If only this dance could last forever—She heard the click of a camera. Adam suddenly whirled her quickly. Her eyes blinked open, and she caught that same boy silently watching them, a deep furrow creasing his brow.

Who was he?

As if on cue, the music ended. "Thanks for the dance, sis. Maybe I'll catch you later," Adam said, then with a smile and a wink, added, "Next time, though, try to let the man do the leading."

Oh, God, she'd blown it again!

"Adam!" Natalie's voice called impatiently. "It's time to cut the cake. And then Mom insists that we have a receiving line over by the arbor."

"I thought we already did that scene," he grumbled.

"Yeah, I know. So did I, but Mother insists that we do it again because some of the guests didn't get a chance to meet you earlier. Also, the photographer wants to get some 'candid' shots." Natalie's large brown eyes pleaded with him not to argue. "Come on, Meg. Mom wants you there, too."

"Me?"

Natalie would not be put off. "Let's go! Mom and Dad are waiting over at the trellis." Natalie was off in a rustle of white satin.

Without further protest, Megan obediently followed Natalie over to the wooden archway covered with holly and mistletoe. She forced a smile and hoped beyond hope that it appeared sincere.

The faces of the people in the line seemed to blend into one: some old, some young, but for the most part all unfamiliar. Meg nodded vacantly as she automatically shook hands with the guests and all the while was caught up in her own misery. She felt as if she were the heroine of some Greek tragedy or romance novel or worse! If only this heart-wrenching night would end! She'd go home, eat a tub of ice cream, and burrow under the covers with a book so that she could forget—

"You haven't heard a word I've said." A male voice broke into her reverie, and she found herself shaking the strong hand of that same boy who had been staring at her all night. What the hell was his problem?

"What? Geez, I'm sorry," she said, her forced smile crumbling. She tried to retrieve her hand, but he held it clasped tight in his.

"I said," he emphasized, "I'm Chris."

She realized he was staring at her as if she'd met him before.

"I'm Adam's cousin. We moved from Boston last summer."

Megan had found her practiced smile and pinned it on. "I'm Megan. Meg Simmons, Natalie's sister."

"I know." His blue eyes were intent.

"You do?"

"Sure." He shrugged. "I like to know everything I can about all of the good-looking girls."

It figured. "So that's how you found out that Natalie had a younger sister." Sarcasm edged her voice. Of course. This Chris guy had checked out Natalie and had found out about Megan as a by-product of the investigation. Wouldn't you know? The same old thing: second fiddle to Nat, *again*.

"I guess I haven't seen you around school," she ventured, embarrassed that he hadn't released her hand and feeling like a complete dork. She was awful at this small-talk stuff. Thankfully, the push of the guests in the receiving line forced him to let her fingers slip from his. Good! She told herself she didn't like that little warm glow that his touch had evoked and was glad to release his palm before her fingers got all sweaty.

From the corner of her eye, she caught him glancing back at her, and she ducked her head and tried to ignore him.

When the receiving line finally broke up, Megan joined her parents and Natalie's new in-laws. Her father's eyes sparkled when he saw her. "You look almost as beautiful as Natalie does tonight."

Her father was always quick with a compliment, as if he understood how his younger daughter felt, always being outshined by her older sister.

"Thanks. I guess."

Her mother cut in, her smile as false as Meg's. She was nervous. Worked up. "Why don't you go back to the house and get started?" she suggested. "I'll be right along, but I might get caught up here, and I'd like things to be ready."

"Sure," Megan said, hiding her enthusiasm. Anything to escape. Even if it was because some of the family was returning to the Simmons house for an after-reception get-together.

"Thanks. I owe you, and so does Nat." Megan's mother let out a heartfelt sigh as her gaze strayed to the bride, who was talking and laughing, her arm linked to Adam's. "You know, you're really going to miss her."

Something in her mother's gaze made Megan aware that this was a hard day for her, too. Natalie was moving out of the house for good.

"Carol! Mrs. Simmons." The raspy voice of the effervescent photographer broke into their conversation. "How about a shot of you and the two girls, over by the arch . . . no, better yet, near the staircase? The paned windows and the snow would make a perfect backdrop. We'll try to make it look really natural!" He bustled off to the staircase.

"Doesn't he ever give up?" Megan whispered to her mother.

"He's just trying to do his job."

"I know, but he follows everybody around with his camera poised, ready to capture just the right picture. Kind of like some kind of creep!"

"What? No. It's not that bad. I'm sure this *must* be just about his last pose. At least I hope so." She chuckled. "I have to admit that I plaster a smile on my face every time I see him coming in my direction!" Mrs. Simmons laughed, and all of a sudden Megan felt better, just knowing that her mother was as uncomfortable about being on display as she was.

"Oh, there you are." Natalie sighed as she approached them. "I guess we need some more pictures. A million isn't enough." She rolled her eyes in the direction of the staircase. "Let's get it over with!"

"The sooner the better," Megan agreed.

Once the final photograph was snapped, Mrs. Simmons sought out her husband, leaving the two sisters alone for the first time that day.

"I have a surprise for you," Natalie told her sister.

"For me? What?"

"It wouldn't be a surprise if I told you," Natalie said. "Come with me, and I'll show you."

Megan followed Natalie back into the reception hall. "It's right here, in my purse, wherever that is."

"Maybe in the dressing room."

"Crap. Of course." Relief flowed across Natalie's face. "I can't believe I didn't remember. Disorganized, Mom always says. What would I do without you?" she tossed over her shoulder as she hurried to retrieve her small clutch. Returning a few seconds later, she held up the jeweled bag and rolled her eyes. "Right where I left it. What am I going to do when you're not around? I'll never find anything. Sometimes I wish I were more like you, Meg."

Megan felt another jab of guilt as her sister, her beautiful sister, actually praised her. Natalie snapped open the purse and retrieved a small package, which she handed to Megan. Natalie's diamond ring caught in the light, the gold band nestled close to it reminding Megan again that her sister was actually married. To Adam. Megan's heart twisted once more as Natalie, her eyes dancing, urged, "Come on. Open it!" Megan's throat tightened. She opened the little box. Inside was a lovely antique ring wrapped in white tissue paper. She found it hard to speak, but managed to say, "It's your ring. . . ."

"No, it's your ring now. It was Aunt Janice's ring, before she married Uncle Ned. Her first husband had given it to her. When she remarried after he died, she gave it to me. And now I'm giving it to you."

"Are you sure? What will Aunt Janice say?"

"She knows all about it! Come on; put it on. The only thing you have to worry about is who to give it to when you get married."

"If I get married."

Natalie laughed. "Hey. I never expected to get married so young. Then I met Adam, and the rest is history!" Her face lit with a mischievous air, and one dark eyebrow arched. "You know, I couldn't help noticing that Chris couldn't take his eyes off of you!"

"Who?"

"Chris Johnson, Adam's cousin."

"Really?" Megan said, as if she hadn't noticed, and cast a glance at the boy in question. His eyes were averted, but she'd sensed he'd been looking her way only seconds before. Was he really interested? Not likely. Maybe he was just surprised that she was Natalie's sister, as different as they were.

At that instant, Adam hurried down the stairs. His gaze landed squarely on Natalie. "What are you two up to?"

"Nothing!" Natalie insisted.

"Yeah. Right." He pressed a kiss to his bride's cheek. "Come on, Nat. The guests expect us to do a little more socializing and dancing before we head over to your folks' house."

"I guess I can't complain that my feet are killing me," she whispered.

"So take off your shoes."

"No way." Natalie acted as if he'd just asked her to commit hari-kari.

How could anyone be tired of dancing with Adam?

Megan wondered to herself as she watched the bride and groom head for the dance floor again.

It was about time to make good her escape and head over to the house, to get away from the celebration and clear her mind. She was wicked, that was it, for being jealous of her sibling, a sister she'd once adored. No, she decided, it wasn't Natalie who was the problem. Megan was mad at herself for being such a goody-two-shoes, as her mother had once pronounced, a kid who had colored within the lines and striven to do what was right, to the point of sometimes being boring. Oh, she had a wild side, but she'd tamped it down all the while she'd been in school.

And what has that gotten you? A 4.0 GPA and no boyfriend, zero social life. Again, through the mullioned windows, she saw the wintry landscape. All of the trees had lost their leaves, and they stood out as a dark reminder of the icy season. Even the glowing candles and the laughing guests with sparkling glasses of champagne couldn't warm the winter's chill for Megan.

Time to leave.

She wasn't paying much attention as she made her way around knots of guests to the dressing area where her own purse and keys were stuffed into a closet and found herself near the bridal arch. Woven wood slats had been braided with red-berried holly and occasional sprigs of mistletoe. The miniature lights winked as if they were tiny stars, and cautiously she stepped under the arch. From the corner of her eye she noticed a movement, and suddenly Chris Johnson appeared on the opposite side of the archway.

"Waiting for me?" he asked, a crooked smile playing on his lips.

"What?" she asked. Was he kidding? "Waiting? For you?"

"Yeah."

"No."

"But you're waiting for someone?"

For the first time she noticed how blue his eyes were, how they caught the light. "What are you talking about?" Megan couldn't stop a note of irritation from creeping into her voice. She was in no mood for games.

"I don't suppose that you know you're standing under the mistletoe?"

"Under the—?" She glanced at the center of the arch. Directly over their heads was a beribboned sprig. "Oh, geez. No, I mean I . . . didn't realize," she began. Her gaze collided with his.

"Sure you did."

"What? No!" She was shaking her head, but didn't step back. Her heart raced a little, and she felt bold, the wild child within her coming to the fore. She swallowed hard. What the hell was she doing? Before she could think twice, he leaned down and gently kissed her on the lips.

She almost kissed him back. Almost. And then, as quickly as he'd appeared, he vanished, stepping backward into the throng of guests to disappear.

Chapter 5

Megan wanted to die.

And as for that stupid "wild child" within her? A quick beheading would suffice, she thought as she lay on the bed, on top of the quilt, absently petting Madonna, the family's long-haired calico cat, who had followed her up the stairs. What had she been thinking? Okay, so it was only a kiss. No big deal, right? Except that it had happened under the bridal arch at her sister's wedding reception, and she was too young to make up some lame excuse about being drunk or something. So there it was—she'd let Chris Johnson, a virtual stranger, kiss her in front of God and everyone. Including Aunt Janice. And Adam.

Yep. Death would be a great alternative to joining the rest of the family downstairs. She'd made good her escape from the reception and helped her mother get things ready at the house, then had come up with a lame excuse of going upstairs to change. Of course she'd been hiding out ever since.

Chicken! Her brain nagged.

She couldn't hide up here all night. Unfortunately. The tinkling of glasses and sound of laughter filtered upstairs to her bedroom, so she'd have to go back down. After tonight, she wouldn't have to deal with her sister's wedding, at least not until the happy couple returned from their honeymoon.

Ugh. Megan should have changed her clothes and been back downstairs helping her mother by now, but she couldn't manage to get off the bed. She just wished that this wedding business would soon end and that she could relax. After all, this was supposed to be the start of Christmas vacation.

Rather than dwell on Adam, she thought about Chris Johnson. He had actually seemed interested in her, and if it weren't for her feelings for Adam, she would probably be attracted to him, too, even if he seemed like a boy when compared to Adam.

All too clearly she remembered the feel of Chris's lips on hers. The kiss had been a bit of a joke on his part, she thought. The way his eyes had twinkled devilishly. The curve of his mouth. Yeah, he'd been playing with her. Nothing more. Still, when she thought about the chance meeting in the archway she couldn't help but be intrigued. Kissed under the mistletoe by a handsome stranger! She had to admit it was kind of romantic. She wondered where he lived. Hadn't he said that he lived here now? Why hadn't she seen him in school?

A gentle rap at the door chased away her thoughts.

"Megan?"

Mom. Great. "Yeah?"

"Are you okay?"

"Fine." She sat up. "I, uh, I kind of fell asleep," she lied, cringing a little. "I'll be, um, I'll be right down." She threw on a pair of pants and a sweater, nothing fancy, but not her favorite pair of beat-up jeans, then shook out her unruly hair, getting rid of the French braid Natalie had insisted she wear. Megan hesitated, saw the little box Natalie had given her, and slipped the cameo ring onto her finger. It was really old-fashioned, but who cared? She liked it in its funky-grandma kind of way.

As she reached the door and the cat slunk under her bed, Megan wondered if Chris would be downstairs. He was, after all, now "family." *Great,* she thought sourly. As if it wasn't bad enough that she'd have to deal with Natalie and Adam, now she had another worry. *Get over yourself. It was one kiss. No big deal.*

So why then did she think Madonna, hiding under the bed, eyes glowing from the shadows, had the right idea?

As Megan descended the stairs, she eyed the living room, where family members had gathered. She was amazed at how many people were already in the house. Was it possible that between Natalie and Adam they had this many relatives? She scanned the faces of the crowd, but nowhere did she see Chris. Stupidly, she felt a pang of disappointment, which only convinced her that she was a bona fide cretin.

But of course there was Adam.

Perfect, handsome, mature Adam.

And he was waiting for her at the base of the stairs. "I wondered what happened to you."

For a second her heart leapt, then she saw the brotherly glint in his eye.

"Hiding?" he asked, guessing the truth.

"From what?"

"You tell me." One corner of his mouth lifted, and she noticed that his rock-hard jaw was already showing a bit of shadow.

"Adam?" Megan's father's voice reached them. He was standing near the open doors to the den as he searched out his new son-in-law. "It's time."

"Time for what?" Megan asked.

"To open a bottle of twenty-year-old champagne."

She nodded, knowing about the bottle that had been

bought the day Natalie had been born. Her father had talked about it for years. "I wonder if it's still good."

"Guess we'll find out."

Megan felt that she had seen enough traditions, ceremonies, and customs to last her a lifetime.

Just as Megan was stepping into the kitchen, Natalie came down the stairs. Her hair was pinned up, and she'd changed into slim black slacks with a matching jacket. Adam was at her side in an instant, and Megan tried to retreat into the kitchen, but Aunt Janice spied her.

"I hear Natalie gave you the . . . oh, there it is!" She spied the cameo ring. "Does it fit?"

"Perfectly," Megan said, which was a white lie as the ring slid a bit on her finger. She spied Chris Johnson as he entered the house. Her foolish heart soared slightly, which was just plain ridiculous. Natalie and Adam, who had apparently done the honors with the old champagne, descended on him in an instant. While he was unzipping his jacket he looked around the room, his gaze landing on hers for an instant before skating away.

Ridiculously she felt a little bit of disappointment.

What had she expected, she asked herself, then squared her shoulders. One stupid little kiss under the mistletoe was just that. Nothing more. No big deal. To hear some of her friends talk about it, kissing was nothing. Or at least just the start. Which made her curious.

And she thought about kissing Chris again. With a little more passion.

The wild child raised her head again, and Megan bit her lip. Why not? But she'd never been bold where boys were concerned, and maybe that was the problem. Time to grow up. If Nat could get married, to Adam no less, maybe it was time for Megan to step out of her sister's shadow and find out who she really was.

She found Chris standing near the Christmas tree, decorated in the colors of the wedding, shining brightly in front of the living room window. He, like she, seemed a little out of place. "Hey!" she said, and he looked up, his gaze finding hers again.

"Mad at me?" he asked.

"For?"

"You know what for." He jammed his hands into his pockets and actually looked away, as if he were embarrassed. For what?

"Happens all the time," she teased.

"It does?"

"Sure." She laughed then, and he relaxed a little. "So, I said I hadn't seen you at school. Did you just come here for the wedding?"

"Moved here last summer. I go to LaSalle," he explained, mentioning the private school across town. Ludicrously, Megan felt a little glow inside. At least he wasn't leaving the area after the wedding, though why she cared, she didn't really understand. She learned that he'd met Natalie several times and had heard about Megan, that Natalie had even shown him a picture of her younger sister. Weird, considering that Natalie had never once mentioned anything about Adam's cousin to Megan. Then again, Nat had been pretty caught up in the wedding. It seemed to Megan that it was all anyone had talked about ever since Adam had proposed nearly a year earlier and her parents had gotten over the shock of their eldest daughter's marrying so young.

Chris, the bold kid who had kissed her under the mistletoe less than two hours earlier, seemed suddenly a little shy, but finally summoned the courage to ask her out.

"I thought maybe you might want to come with me next Saturday night for the LaSalle sleigh ride."

"A date?"

He lifted a shoulder. "Yeah." His lips twitched as if he were trying to swallow a smile.

Megan surveyed Chris critically. His features were

even, if a little oversized, and although his smile wasn't perfect, it seemed genuine. With longish brown hair and intense eyes, he was good-looking and had a bit of charm to him. His jaw, while not dark with beard shadow like Adam's, was strong. He seemed smart and probably athletic, and he was practically family, so why shouldn't she go out with him?

"Sure," she finally said. "Unless Mom and Dad have me scheduled for some family thing. It can get a little crazy here around Christmas."

"There is a catch," he admitted, backlit by the tree. She felt a needle of disappointment.

"Which is?"

"You'll have to bring a date for my friend Ken."

"I *have* to?" she repeated. "Hook your friend up with a blind date?" What did she know about this guy really?

"Yeah."

"Or you won't go out with me?"

"I didn't say that."

"None of my girlfriends will go on a blind date, especially when I haven't even met the guy myself!" This wasn't a request, she thought; this was an impossibility!

"Oh, I don't know," he disagreed, his eyes growing a shade darker. "From what I can tell, the LaSalle sleigh ride is a pretty big deal around these parts."

"What? Some nerdy old tradition?" she threw back at him, though, of course, he was right. A lot of the girls at her school talked about it, not so much about the sleigh ride itself, but just about hanging out with the boys from LaSalle. The truth was a couple of her friends had talked about it, probably because Heather Winters acted like it was a really big deal.

"Look, if you don't know anyone, that's cool."

"I'll see," she promised.

He grinned, that sexy, slightly dangerous smile that caught her off guard. "So Adam was right."

"About what?" she asked, her curiosity piqued that Adam had said anything about her.

"He said you liked challenges. I like that in a girl."

"Oh, you do? Why?" How did they get on this stupid subject?

"I don't know. I guess it shows intelligence and imagination."

She wrinkled her nose. "Is that a compliment?"

"If you want it to be," he said, eyes glinting, reflecting the lights of the tree, and Megan realized they were kind of alone, most of the guests having wandered into the dining area and kitchen for drinks and appetizers. Intelligence and imagination weren't exactly in the same category as beautiful or gorgeous, but they weren't bad, and were much better than *nice*.

So maybe a date wouldn't be so bad, not so bad at all.

"Come on. It'll be fun," Megan pleaded the next day. She was flopped on the couch, hoping that no one in the house could hear her conversation, the cordless phone pressed to her ear.

"I'm just not sure. Why doesn't this guy—Ken—get himself a date? What is he? A real loser or something?"

Megan didn't know. In fact she didn't know a whole lot about Chris, either, though she wanted to know more—a lot more—and was checking through a friend whose brother had gotten kicked out of Central and landed at LaSalle, but so far she hadn't heard back.

"I would do it for you!" Megan pressed, not really sure she was telling the truth. Tail aloft, Madonna strolled in and hopped onto the couch, and absently, with her free hand, Megan petted her soft fur as the cat curled up next to her and began kneading the sofa's cushions and purred loudly.

"What does he look like?"

"I . . . really don't know," Megan said.

"You have seen him, haven't you?"

Ooops. "No, not exactly, but Chris told me that he was very popular and a great guy." That might have been stretching it a little.

There was an audible groan at the other end of the line. "Being popular at an all-boys school could mean that he's the class clown, or a real jerk! What do you know about him? Anything?"

"Not much," Megan admitted, though Chris had told her a little before leaving last night. "Uh, Ken's a . . . good student. . . ."

"Wonderful." Sarcasm dripped from Leslie's voice.

"He plays video games. . . ."

"Every guy does that. And it's BORing. Oh, wait. Don't tell me that he plays Frisbee. I don't know if my heart could stand all that excitement at one time."

"The only thing I know is that he *and* Chris are on the debating team," she said, recalling their quick conversation.

"Ugh."

"And that he is willing to go out on a blind date with *you.*"

"Sounding better and better all the time," Leslie said. "What a hottie! You know, I get that you're all into intellectual types, the A plus plus plus students or whatever, but, that's not me. I like something a little—"

"Jockier."

"I was going to say 'edgy,' but, yeah, jocks are cool." She paused, then added, "As long as they're cute. You know, like Ryan DuBois!"

Ryan was the star of Central's basketball team. And, in Megan's opinion, a real jerk. "Come on, Les. When will you ever get an opportunity to go on the LaSalle sleigh ride? They're talking about making the school coed next year, so who knows if they'll even have it again."

"I don't know—"

"You got something better going on?"

On the other end of the line, Leslie sighed. "You've got a point there. Okay. I'll go," she acquiesced, though she sounded less than enthused. "But if this turns out to be a disaster, you owe me. Big-time."

"Deal. Now, we're supposed to meet the boys down at the Hayloft around six thirty on Saturday. My folks will take us."

"You mean they're not even going to pick us up? This just gets better and better."

"They have to work on setting it up; they're part of the committee."

"I'm already thinking this is a bad idea. So how do we get home? Hitchhike?"

"Of course not! They'll bring us home!"

Leslie was certainly not making it easy. Besides that, she was reinforcing Megan's existing fears about Chris.

Leslie echoed her thoughts, in a careful voice. "Meg, just why are you so interested in this guy? Tell me it's not because he's Adam's cousin?"

She couldn't. And Leslie was the only person besides Megan herself who knew her feelings about her now brother-in-law.

"This is sounding incestuous," Leslie said.

"Ick!"

"I was kidding. But come on, Meg. Is Chris really all that interesting? I mean, to you. If he wasn't related to or close to Adam, would you be going out with him?"

Good question, Megan thought. One she really couldn't answer.

Later, at breakfast, things didn't get any better. Her mother, tired from all the wedding fuss, dressed in her favorite bathrobe, gave Megan the evil eye.

"Last night at the reception, you seemed a little quiet." Megan's mother had been rinsing her coffee cup in the sink, but turned to survey her younger daughter.

At the table, Megan averted her gaze from her mother's and reached for the glass of orange juice near her plate. "What do you mean?" she asked, though she already knew.

"I think you know." Megan's mom refilled her cup from the Mr. Coffee coffeemaker on the counter. "Enlighten me."

How could she even start a conversation about her feelings for Adam with her Mom? Megan stared at her scrambled eggs, toying with them with her fork.

"Does it have anything to do with Natalie?" Her mother took a long swallow of coffee as she looked at Megan over the rim of her cup.

Megan shot her a quick glance. "No."

Carol Simmons sat down and leaned back in her chair. "I know this is hard for you, Meg."

You couldn't. You just couldn't.

"We're all going to miss your sister. Believe me, your father and I tried to talk her out of the marriage, at least for now. We wanted her to finish college and . . . Well, it doesn't matter now. Natalie had her mind set, and you know how bullheaded she can be. So, what's done is done. But this has got to be hard on you, too." She cleared her throat, her gray eyes, so much like Megan's, clouding a bit, as if she were troubled. "You two were always so close. But lately . . ." She paused, her lips compressing, and it was almost as if she'd forgotten the coffee cup in her hand. "Lately, I've had the feeling that maybe it was more than that."

"Like what?" Megan nearly choked on her juice.

"Envy, perhaps?"

Megan remained silent, unable to answer her mother. To her absolute horror, she felt tears burning behind her eyelids and her throat becoming thick.

"Look," her mother continued. "I know that it's not easy for you. Natalie is so . . . outgoing."

"You mean she was popular in school," Megan clarified. "And I'm really not." She saw the denial cross her mom's face. "No, I know it. It's not a big deal." With a shrug she added, "Just the way it is. Or was. When she was at Central."

"Okay. But it never seemed to bother you before. You've always been happy just to be yourself."

Never! Megan thought. Then amended it. "When I was a kid. In grade school."

Her mother took a sip from her cup, then set her coffee onto the table. "She was the one who was envious, you know."

"Natalie?" *No way!*

"School comes easy for you. Easier than for your sister. And you're always so organized when she, well, you know, she was always losing things and running around like a chicken with her head cut off looking for her keys or lipstick or whatever."

"Big deal."

"It is. And more important, you, ever since you were old enough to speak, knew your own mind. She's stubborn, I know, but you . . . you, you're at ease with being yourself. At least you used to be."

"I'm okay, Mom," she said, as much to end this psychological probing and motherly advice as anything. "Natalie's been gone a long time." And that much was true. Ever since her older sister had met Adam, Natalie had placed one foot firmly outside the Simmons's front door. Megan carried her plate to the sink and dumped the rest of her eggs. "Don't worry about me."

"Impossible," Carol said as she got up and reached into the small drawer near the back sliding door for her ever-handy pack of cigarettes. "It comes with the territory of being a mother."

Chapter 6

"This might not be as bad as I expected," Leslie whispered as she appraised the two boys walking toward them in front of the Hayloft, an old barn turned into a restaurant, on the night of the sleigh ride. With thick red-blond hair and attitude written all over him, Ken was slightly shorter than Chris, a wiry guy, definitely *not* a basketball jock. Megan crossed her fingers in the pockets of her jacket, all the while hoping that Ken was a wrestler or maybe a soccer player or some kind of athlete.

"Hey!" Chris said, his grin stretching wide. "I was afraid you might not show."

"Really?" Megan asked, but he laughed.

"Nah."

"This is Ken Dickens."

And so the date began. And sure enough, though it started out well enough, it turned into a disaster.

The frigid December air chasing them inside, they headed into the restaurant, where weathered planking covered with old farm tools comprised the walls and fake kerosene lamps burned on tables surrounded by benches.

Chris led the foursome to one of the long tables already occupied by several couples who were passing out song-books for caroling.

"Ken and I will get drinks."

"Diet Coke for me," Leslie said. Though tiny, she was forever dieting.

"Regular," Megan said.

Chris nodded. "We'll be right back."

As Megan and Leslie slid onto a bench, Megan took a look at the other couples. Her heart sank. Every girl at the table was poised and beautiful and knew it. Shiny hair, bright smiles with perfect teeth, makeup applied as if by a professional, tittering laughter, and each and every one reminded Megan of Natalie.

A slim blonde cast a radiant smile in Megan's direction. "Hi, I'm Claire Wakefield. Welcome to the sleigh ride. It's a great night for it."

"Thanks. I'm Megan Simmons, and this is my friend, Leslie Baker. We're with Chris and Ken." Megan motioned in the direction of the two boys, who were still busy ordering drinks.

"Is this your first sleigh ride?" Claire asked. "I don't remember seeing you here before."

As Megan and Leslie nodded, she said, "You're not from Upland-Gable," the all-girls high school that was a counterpart to LaSalle, a private, exclusive school that was rumored to be merging with the boys' school if things worked out.

"We're from Central."

"Oh!" The tone said it all. The friendly sparkle in Claire's eyes died, and she turned back to her friends, effectively shunning the newcomers.

"They're giving me an inferiority complex," Leslie whispered.

"No way. You've already got one."

"Thanks."

"Of Freudian proportions."

Of course there was no reason for it. Leslie was short and cute and could hold her own with any of the girls from Upland-Gable.

Megan caught a sideways glance from Claire. The girl was whispering with her friends, just out of earshot as the restaurant was noisy, other customers arriving, pizza orders being shouted, music flowing from speakers mounted high in the rafters.

"Sometimes it sucks being the 'nice' girls," Leslie said, bringing up an old topic, one that always reared its ugly head whenever comparisons to the more popular girls were made.

"I know." At the moment Megan wasn't feeling very nice. At all. As a matter of fact she was feeling downright mean, which she effectively controlled as Ken and Chris arrived with a tray of sodas.

They got on pretty well, talking and laughing, comparing schools. Ken was funny, his sense of humor not as dry as Chris's, but conversation didn't lag. Megan was enjoying herself, though every once in a while she would catch sight of Claire looking her way.

Who cared?

Within a few minutes, the rest of the carolers had arrived, and the sleighs were waiting outside, parked near the entrance of the Hayloft. The ride consisted of ten sleighs crammed to capacity with carolers. Unfortunately, Megan and Leslie were split up as Ken and Chris had volunteered to drive different sleighs.

"How on earth are we all going to sing in unison?" Megan asked Chris as he helped her up to the front seat behind a huge black horse that was pulling at his bridle, snorting and pawing.

"We're not. As I understand it, each sleigh takes off five minutes after the one ahead of it, and we all sing at our own pace. When we converge at the park, we'll sing about four or five carols together and then return to the Hayloft. The senior class has rented it for the night, and the dance will be held there."

It sounded a little old school to Megan, but then it was all part of the LaSalle tradition. Chris helped all the passengers aboard. Unfortunately Claire and her date ended up in the same sleigh. *Great,* thought Megan. *Not only do I not get to be with Leslie and Ken, but I end up with Claire and Brad What's-His-Name, a loud basketball type.* But if she was worried about small talk, it was no problem. As Claire climbed into her seat, she managed to look right through Megan even though Brad gave her a quick head-to-heels appraisal.

Made for each other! Megan thought.

Chris got back into the driver's seat and tucked a thick plaid blanket around Megan before they took off. As the horse pulled the sleigh, Megan snuggled next to Chris, and together they sang the familiar old carols. Chris's deep baritone voice was more than slightly off-key, but he didn't seem to notice. Or if he did, he didn't care. Megan joined in wholeheartedly, and when either she or Chris hit a particularly bad note, she laughed. And all the while Claire's boyfriend talked, cracking off-color jokes and going on and on about his "awesome" last game, then pulling his own blanket high over the lower half of his face as if to ward off the cold.

Somehow Megan managed to ignore Brad, and, between songs, she and Chris talked. Chris told her of growing up in the suburbs of Boston, where he'd lived before moving to Connecticut. Every once in a while Adam's name would crop up in the conversation and, each time, Megan felt a sharp stab of pain. She tried to ignore it, telling herself that she didn't care that Adam and Natalie were wed. But that was a lie. She didn't want to think of Adam and Natalie, or the fact that they were man and wife. She wanted to enjoy the evening as the draft horse plodded through the snow, and the sleigh slid beneath the street-lamps, and snowflakes, continually falling, danced and swirled around them. Somewhere in the distance, she could hear faint Christmas songs and laughter from the other sleighs.

"Are you warm enough?" Chris asked.

She nodded her head in jerky movements to indicate that she felt fine, but her chattering chin gave her away. He hugged her closer, and it felt right.

All too soon, he said, "Here's the park," pointing in the direction of the trees. "Let's pull up next to the pond before we join the others."

Chris directed the horse over to the icy pond. Several wobbly-legged children and cautious parents were precari-ously skating by the streetlamp's light. The carolers were suddenly quiet, entranced by the scene. Even Claire's loud-mouth of a boyfriend had become still, at least for the mo-ment; then he ducked under the blanket again.

The black horse snorted; steam rose from his nostrils. He nickered softly, and somewhere close by, another horse answered. For a heartbeat it was as if she and Chris were captured in a magical dreamland. He reached under the blanket and took one of her gloved hands in his, and she didn't pull away.

"I'd like to spend some more time here, but I think that maybe we'd better join the others," he said.

She nodded her agreement, and he flicked the reins, al-lowing the anxious horse to trot off in the direction of the other sleighs and carolers.

When they joined the group, Megan and Chris caught up with Leslie and Ken. He had his arm around her, and they whispered together, laughing as if they'd known each other for years.

When Megan caught Leslie alone, the other girl said, "Okay, you win. I thought this would be a nightmare but

Ken . . . He's great." Leslie was actually blushing as she glanced over at the boys, who were talking with some others. "We had a great time. And the Upland-Gable girls were okay."

"Seriously?" Megan couldn't believe it.

"Yeah. Real friendly."

"But Claire—?"

"Is stuck on herself. And on Chris. That's what the girls in my sleigh said."

"She's with the basketball jerk—er, jock."

"I know," Leslie said, "but everyone said she's been interested in Chris since he transferred from Boston."

That explained a lot, and Megan felt more than a little bit of jealousy until Chris returned and hooked his arm around her waist. It seemed the most natural thing for him to do. As they sang a few more carols she told herself not to listen to Leslie's gossip, but that was before Megan, turning her head, caught Claire's frosty glare. Her blond hair glistening in the lamplight, Claire whispered a private joke to her date. Brad laughed out loud, then cast a sly, sidelong look in Megan's direction. Subtle, the basketball geek was not. Obviously Claire had made Megan the butt of some bad joke. She was an outsider, but then, that wasn't exactly a news flash.

When the caroling was finished, Chris once again began helping the kids into his sleigh. Megan couldn't help seeing the wistful looks that Claire cast in his direction and, when it was her turn to board the vehicle, Claire paused for a moment, letting her full weight rest on Chris as she stepped upward into the sleigh. She seemed to slip, and then caught herself by clinging to Chris's neck.

"Damn it!" she swore, her pretty face puckering. "It's these new boots. The leather is so slick in the snow."

"Be careful," Chris cautioned as he assisted her. "Are you all right?"

"I . . . think so," she said, looking into his eyes. Her

gloved hand slid and lingered across his shoulders, and Megan thought she might be sick. Claire's damsel-in-distress ploy was right out of some of those stupid romantic movies Natalie watched late at night, a move that seemed to be from the sixties.

Save me.

Chapter 7

"Here, Meg, let me help you down." Chris smiled as he held his hand out once the sleigh had stopped at the Hayloft.

With his help, Megan jumped lightly to the snow-covered parking lot, only to lose her balance when Brad, the athlete no less, stumbled into her as he slid from his seat. Scrambling, he nearly dropped a bag and quickly hid it back under his jacket, darting a look at the couples nearby.

"What the hell was that?" Megan whispered to Chris.

"A bota bag," was the terse reply. Chris's jawline hardened. He was watching Brad intently, as the basketball player snaked his arm over Claire's shoulders and trudged off in the direction of the main door of the restaurant.

"What's a bota bag?" Megan couldn't restrain her curiosity.

"You don't know?"

"If I knew, would I ask?"

"Okay, so you're ignorant," he teased, pulling her stocking cap over her eyes. "Or maybe naïve."

"I'm not—" She started to argue, then shut up. Okay, so she was naïve. A little.

"A bota bag is kind of like a purse, but it's a watertight container that can hold liquid, usually alcohol. It's got a thin strap that holds it neatly over your shoulder and a spill-proof spout. You have to squeeze the bag as you hold it to your mouth in order for the contents to squirt into your mouth." His blue eyes narrowed in thought. "I wondered why Brad kept hiding under the blanket. I guess we know now."

"I thought he was just showing off. You know, for Claire."

"I figured he'd been drinking, but I didn't think he was actually doing it on the sleigh ride itself. I thought that he had probably had a couple of beers before the ride began." He glanced to another sleigh where a young priest was talking with a couple of kids. "Let's just hope that Father Anthony doesn't catch wind of this, or we'll all be in big trouble."

"All of us?" Megan asked.

"Yeah, there's been a big stink at school lately about alcohol. Well, and drugs, of course. A few of the members of the basketball team were caught drinking and smoking weed a couple of weeks ago, and they're suspended. Off the team. Pending hearings, probably kicked out of school."

"Was Brad one of the players who was put on probation?"

"Somehow he skated. That's why he's still here."

"And didn't seem to get the message," Megan said.

"He's not exactly known for his brains."

"Hey!" Ken and Leslie joined them. "Guess what?" Ken asked. "You and I have just been volunteered by Father Anthony to take the horses back to the barns."

"Why us?"

"Dunno. But I wasn't going to argue. Besides, he picked a couple other guys, too." To Leslie, Ken said, "Can you two wait for us inside? We just have to get the horses back to the stables; someone else will take care of them and the sleighs."

Once inside, after they'd spent a few minutes in the small restroom, Megan purposely chose a table removed from the immediate friends of Claire and Brad, but Leslie kept smiling at the Upland girls, as if sharing a special secret with them.

"Can't you ignore Claire and her crowd?" Megan asked her friend.

"Relax, will you? I told you that the kids in our sleigh were really okay. And the boys should be back any minute."

"Let's hope so," Megan said.

"How long could it take to unharness a horse?" Leslie said, then giggled.

"I suppose that depends on where you have to take the horse to unhitch him. We aren't exactly in the middle of acres and acres of farmland, you know."

Leslie laughed again, as if Megan were hilarious.

While a DJ played requests, several couples ventured out onto the dance floor. For a moment, Megan pictured her sister Natalie shimmering in white, while floating in Adam's arms. Adam. Tall, dark, wonderful Adam, now married to her sister. Somehow it didn't hurt as much as it had a few weeks earlier. For now, she forced her thoughts back to the present.

A few minutes later Chris and Ken, along with a few other "volunteers," came clattering back into the restaurant, stomping snow off their boots and brushing it from their hair.

Megan's eyes wandered to the dance floor where Leslie had begun dancing with Ken. As if she'd tripped, she wrapped her arms around Ken's neck and was laughing loudly. Megan frowned. She had never seen Leslie warm up to a boy so quickly.

"Wanna dance?" Chris asked as he turned her face toward his with a gentle touch of his hand.

"Yeah." Megan nodded absently, letting Chris guide her to the dance floor. She tried to forget about her friend and her erratic behavior, but each time they danced near Ken and Leslie, it became more evident to Megan that Leslie was acting strangely. She was giggling and talking loudly. Every once in a while she would miss a step, and then break up into uproarious laughter.

"Chris," Megan whispered.

"Yeah."

"Do you think Leslie's been drinking? Or she's on something?"

Chris stopped dancing. "I don't know. . . . It's possible, I suppose. I did see her standing with part of Brad's crowd before the last time we came inside. Ken hasn't said anything to me about it, and he's not usually the kind of guy who would drink at a school function."

"Or slip her a Mickey?"

"What? No!"

Megan wasn't so sure, and she saw her friend trip and catch herself on Ken again. "I don't feel good about this." She was shaking her head, mentally struggling. She didn't want the night to end, but at that moment Leslie threw back her head and closed her eyes, almost as if she was going to pass out.

"But it's only ten thirty!"

"I don't care. Something's wrong." Megan chewed on her lip thoughtfully.

"All right, but it seems as if she's enjoying herself to me," Chris said. Then, to Ken and Leslie, "Meg thinks it's time to take the girls home."

"So soon?" Ken complained. "I thought you girls didn't have to be home until midnight."

"Yeah," Leslie said thickly. "What's the rush, Meg? I'm having a terrif . . . terriff . . . a great time." She giggled and staggered toward Meg. Had Ken not caught her she would have landed on the floor. "Oops, guess I lost my balance—"

Meg grasped Leslie firmly by the arm and propelled her to the checkroom.

"You've been drinking," Megan accused as she helped Leslie put on her coat.

"You could tell?" Leslie was incredulous. "I just had a little bit."

"What do you mean . . . a little?" Megan asked, her eyes narrowing.

"I only had a couple of sips." Leslie giggled.

"What else?"

"What'd'h mean?"

"Some kind of drug? Pills? Pot?"

"No—I just . . . just . . ."

"Great, Leslie. Just fricking great!" Megan shot Ken an icy glance as they walked out the door toward his car. "Did you have anything to do with this?"

"Nothing! I had no idea that she had been drinking. I don't even know where she got the stuff," Ken said indignantly.

"Oh, that was easy." Leslie giggled as she slumped into the front seat and Ken got behind the wheel. "One of the guys, that big basketball jock, he gave me a drink, or two. Right before we came in here."

"What was it?" Chris asked.

"Some kind of wine . . . I'm really not sure. The guy said it would warm me up, and he was right!" Leslie smiled as she laid her head on Ken's shoulder before Megan strapped on her seat belt.

"Are you sure you didn't know about this?" Chris demanded, staring at Ken.

"Look, Johnson, I told you I didn't know anything about it, and that's it!" Ken's fists clenched around the steering wheel.

Chris and Megan climbed into the backseat. Ken slammed his door shut and started the motor. The car roared out of the parking lot and slid on the icy streets.

"Hey! Take it easy, man," Chris shouted. "I didn't mean to accuse you of anything. I just wanted to know how Leslie got the drinks."

"Umm," Leslie mumbled as she nearly fell asleep. "It was Claire's idea. . . . She's . . . she's nice. . . ."

Not so nice, Megan thought. "What a surprise," she said, not bothering to hide her feelings.

"Hey . . . hold on a minute," Chris ordered. "You can't blame Claire."

"Why not? It's her fault, or at least that boyfriend of hers, Brad, his fault."

"No, it's not," Chris reiterated. "No one forced Leslie to drink anything tonight. She said so herself."

"But Leslie never drinks," Megan argued, heatedly defending her sleeping friend.

"She did tonight." It was a flat statement.

"She did it to be accepted by those stupid Upland-Gable girls!" Megan threw back at Chris. "How are we going to get this past my parents?"

"We'll come in for a few minutes," Chris offered, but Megan wasn't sure how that would play out. A few sips? Megan didn't think so. Her friend was acting like she'd downed five or six shots.

When they were in the Simmons's driveway, they tried to rouse Leslie. It was difficult, but with the aid of a little cold snow down her neck, she seemed to sober up a little. Though pale, she still looked reasonably presentable, and Megan hoped that her parents wouldn't notice Leslie's abnormally sluggish reactions.

Though angry with Megan for sliding snow under her sweater, Leslie finally seemed to grasp a bit of the gravity of the situation. Supported by Ken, she assumed a casual walk.

"Mom, we're home," Megan shouted in the direction of the den, where the flickering blue light emanating suggested her parents were watching television. To Chris she said, "I'll take it from here."

"You sure?" he asked, and then kissed her on the cheek when she nodded and started shepherding a teetering Leslie up the stairs.

At ten the next morning, Megan woke up. Leslie was sleeping in a bag on the floor. Madonna was curled up next to her, the cat's long hair ruffling with each of Leslie's deep breaths. Leaning over the side of her bed, Megan gave her friend a push.

Moaning, Leslie rolled over.

Madonna hopped onto the bed and then to the window-sill.

"Wake up. It's after ten."

"Too early," Leslie grumbled, wadding her pillow over her head.

"No, it's not! We've got to get up and act normally if we don't want Mom and Dad to get any more suspicious than they already are."

"Oooo . . ." Leslie said as she raised her hand to her forehead. "This must be what a hangover is all about. And I don't get up until one. Sometimes two." She blinked. "That would be p.m."

"Forget it. And as for the hangover, you earned it."

"Don't be such a goody-two-shoes . . . or is it three shoes? Something weird that Mom always says." Wincing, Leslie blinked again slowly as if testing to see if her eyes still worked.

"What the hell were you doing last night?" Megan insisted.

"Making new friends?"

"More like enemies."

"They were nice to me."

"They got you drunk."

"I got me drunk."

"You're lucky no one slid something else into your drink," she said.

"The whole blind date was your idea," Leslie reminded her.

No, it was Chris's, Megan thought, *and it had backfired.*

Megan's parents were waiting for them in the kitchen. Her father was reading the Sunday paper, and he glanced over the top of his glasses as the girls entered the room. Although he smiled at them, Megan sensed trouble. Leslie looked green at the sight of the scrambled eggs and toast.

"How did the date go last night?" Megan's father asked, scanning the open Sunday paper with his reading glasses.

"It was okay," Megan said, wishing the topic would just disappear. "We had fun, I guess."

"You don't know?" her mother said, her eyebrows pulling together.

Pale, Leslie nodded. "It's just that we didn't know too many people."

Dear God, she actually appeared green, like she might barf up anything she tried to eat, so Megan said, "We'll just have a little toast and take it upstairs, okay?"

Her mother's eyes narrowed, but before she could protest, Megan grabbed a couple of napkins and two slices of toast, then headed back upstairs. Leslie followed her, and as they reached the upper hallway, made a beeline for the bathroom. Great! If her parents had any idea what had happened, they'd be upset, maybe call the school and Leslie's parents. They could even drag Chris's family into it.

With one ear cocked toward the open staircase, Megan waited, then when a white-faced, shaky-legged Leslie reappeared, hustled her into the bedroom and shut the door. It seemed they'd escaped, thank God.

For now.

The few days remaining until Christmas passed slowly for Megan. Christmas itself had lost some of the wonder and magic it had once held for her. She could remember a few years ago, when early Christmas morning she and Natalie had raced down the stairs to catch a first glimpse of the tree with many presents displayed invitingly beneath its boughs. No matter how early the girls had arisen, their mother had always been up before them.

The lights on the tree would be glowing in the early morning winter darkness, and the girls would smell freshly baked cranberry bread. The sisters had hardly been able to contain themselves through the meal, knowing that there were hidden surprises waiting for them under the tree.

Best of all, there was always something unique hidden in the needles of the pine tree. Usually in a plain white box or a handwritten envelope, the special gift that Mom and Dad had planned all year long was the last one opened, after all of the gifts under the tree were gone. It was one last prize. One envelope had read "Bow Wow" and had contained a dog biscuit. That was the Christmas that Snow White, the funny little mutt of a puppy, had joined the family. Another Christmas, the envelope had said simply: "24 months or 500 miles, whichever is greater, WARRANTY." That was the now old ten-speed bike. It was strange to think that, this Christmas, Megan didn't feel any enthusiasm for the yearly ceremony.

Of course most of her restlessness was due to Chris.

It had been over two days since their date, and he hadn't called her. And she wasn't going to phone him. At least not right away. And, though she hated to admit it, her mother was right; the house did seem bigger and lonelier without Natalie. Megan didn't even want to think about Adam. Of course, Megan hadn't seen him since the wedding. Except for a quick e-mail from Natalie, no one in the family had heard from them. It was weird, really.

On Christmas morning Megan woke up feeling empty. Even the enticing scent of her mother's baking couldn't lure her down the stairs.

A lot of her ennui could be attributed to Chris, she supposed. She liked him; she liked him a lot. Not with the same deep feeling that she had felt for Adam, of course, but she did definitely think about Chris, which kind of pissed her off.

Then there was the other little irritation. Ken had called Leslie. He had even gone over to her house once since the sleigh ride. They seemed to be a couple already, and after less than a week Leslie was sure that she was falling in love with him.

As if! In love? After a single date? Leslie had always been a dreamer, but this time she had really gone off the deep end, and that pissed off Megan as well.

It was as if the whole world had conspired against her. And it had all started with Natalie's wedding. Yeah, Megan was in a bad mood, a real bad mood.

On Christmas morning.

Terrific!

Finally, Megan forced herself to get up. She threw on a

short skirt and a sweater, then brushed out her hair and attempted a bit of makeup. She stared at her reflection in the mirror critically. She was far from gorgeous like her sister, but she was okay—kind of. She played around with eye shadow and mascara and then gave up. She was a nerd, a "braniac" as Natalie had often referred to her. Despite her gray eyes and high cheekbones and thick hair, she was still "the girl most likely to run a major company by thirty."

Ugh.

Aunt Janice came over and, though everyone in the family tried to keep up their spirits, everything seemed off. Even Mom's Christmas turkey tasted bland.

Later, after dinner and when Aunt Janice had gone home, Megan was clearing the table when the telephone rang. "I'll get it," she shouted. Maybe it was Chris.

"Hello," she said.

"Hi, Meg! It's . . . so good . . . to hear your voice," Natalie said at the other end of the line. She was actually blubbering, sobbing into the phone.

"Nat! Are you crying? What's wrong? Is Adam all right?" Megan's thoughts leapt instantly to pictures of instant disasters—boating, swimming, scuba-diving accidents. What could have happened?

"No . . . no . . . Adam, I mean we're both fine. It's just that it's Christmas and I miss all of you so terribly." Natalie sniffed loudly. "How—how are you? How was Christ—Christmas?"

Megan imagined her sister dabbing a finger under her eyelids to swipe at the mascara running down her cheeks. "It was okay, but, you know, different. Without you."

"It's Natalie?" Mom said, waterworks flowing from her eyes, too, as she waved frantically to get the phone. "It's Nat," she said to her husband. "Get on the extension."

Another round of sobs from Natalie.

"I'll talk to you soon," Megan said, and handed the phone to her mother, who clutched the receiver in two hands.

"Merry Christmas, honey!" Carol Simmons said to her daughter who was, Megan knew, in the Bahamas. With Adam. And Natalie was crying? Homesick on her honeymoon? Well, it was Christmas, but Natalie had known that when they'd set their wedding date so close to the end of the year. Though Megan missed her, she didn't feel sorry for her older sister in the Bahamas with Adam. Megan pictured the two of them laughing in the sun as they ran in the sand. Their bodies were tanned and sleek, foamy waves chasing them. Megan imagined Adam chasing her sister, catching her and kissing her as they fell into the sand, still embracing as the tide rolled around them.

No, Natalie with Adam in paradise should *not* have been crying.

When the doorbell pealed, Megan, the only member of the family not on the phone, answered the door.

Chris was standing on the porch, his hair a little wet from melting snowflakes, his face ruddy from the cold. Stupidly, her heart soared a bit.

"Hey," he said, appearing uncomfortable.

"Hi," Megan responded, and then added, without thinking, "What are you doing here?"

"I don't really know," he said. "It seemed like a good idea to show up and say, 'Merry Christmas,' but now I kinda feel like a dweeb."

She laughed and stepped onto the porch, pulling the door shut behind her. "You're definitely *not* a 'dweeb.' Merry Christmas."

Relief washed over his features, and she noticed just how good-looking he was with his hair mussed and a bit of embarrassment still clinging to him.

"Come in," she said, then, glancing up at the sprig of mistletoe her father had tacked over the porch, kissed his cheek. "Payback," she said, pointing up.

His grin widened.

"Gotcha!" she said, realizing she was actually flirting

with him as she led him into the house. In the kitchen her mother, a tissue pressed under her eyes, was just hanging up the phone. "Sorry, I . . . didn't hear you come in," she said. "I was just talking to Natalie and Adam."

"Adam was on the phone, too?" Megan asked, and her heart dropped. She'd missed a chance to talk to him!

"Yes, Meg. Oh! He told me to give you his love."

She felt as if a thunderbolt had struck her. *His LOVE.* Oh. God. Then she blinked and realized it was just an expression, a greeting from her new brother-in-law. Still . . .

"He also wished you good luck with the debating team. You know your father," her mother said with a roll of her expressive eyes. "He brought it up *again!*"

Megan cringed. "I wish he wouldn't. I'm not . . . I'm not sure that I'm even going to try out." Now who sounded like a "dweeb"?

"Of course you are," her father, hearing the tail end of the conversation, said. He nodded at Chris and placed a hand on Megan's shoulder. "You're the one who said you wanted to become a lawyer, right?"

Megan wanted to wither through the floor even though it was kinda cool that her father was *so* proud of her. Inwardly she wondered if he, a little disappointed that Natalie had decided to marry so young, had turned all of his own ambitions toward his youngest. Megan had heard it whispered that at one time he, too, had hoped to become an attorney. Until he'd gotten married in a rush as Natalie was on the way. No one had ever admitted it, of course, but Megan had done the math and didn't buy the whole "premature" thing, as Natalie had been born at over seven pounds with a full head of hair.

Besides, it wasn't that Megan had changed her dreams; it was just that she wasn't sure she was ready to share all her deep, dark desires with Chris just yet. "Maybe a lawyer," she admitted, and her father scowled.

"Never give up on your dreams, Meg. Never."

Her parents exchanged glances that held stories Megan couldn't hope to understand, and her mother reached for her pack of Virginia Slims sitting on the counter.

"No 'maybe' about college or law school!" her dad insisted. Then, a little more calmly, he added to Chris, "Megan here is the top of her class. Straight A's all through high school. Colleges already interested." He was actually beaming. Once more, Megan wanted to die. This attitude was beginning to be a habit, but her mother, shaking out a long cigarette, came to her rescue. "Jim, stop it." Then, as she found her lighter, Carol Simmons added, "Don't listen to your father's blustering, Meg. You know how he is—every once in a while he gets up on his soapbox and gives all of us the benefit of his years of wisdom. You go out for the team if you want to, but don't you feel that you're pushed into it! And, as for you"—she scowled in her husband's direction—"why don't you go put some more logs on the fire in the study? Or . . . something?" With that she slipped on a thick sweater and stepped onto the patio, where she lit up.

Later, after a few hours of television and leftovers, her parents finally went upstairs to bed.

When her parents had left the room, and their soft footsteps echoed from upstairs, Chris turned to her and winked. "Alone at last!"

For the first time that day, Megan was a little nervous. She had never been alone with him really, and that wasn't the only problem. Even at seventeen she'd rarely gone out on a date alone with a boy; she'd mainly hung out with a group of friends.

So now, on the couch, the television flickering and the fire dying, she felt a little awkward. When Chris leaned in to kiss her, she closed her eyes and felt his lips touch hers tentatively at first and then a little harder. A warmth spread through her blood, turning her bones liquid, and she wrapped her arms around his neck, kissing him back.

So this is how it feels, she thought as he held her close and she heard her own blood rushing in her ears. The world seemed to spin, to shine, and she wondered about letting go, touching him, feeling his body closer still.

A floorboard creaked overhead, and she nearly jumped out of her skin. She pushed him back and, breathing with a little difficulty, shook her head. "This . . . this isn't smart."

"Nothing happened," he said, but his eyes had darkened, and she knew he'd felt that same adrenaline rush as she had. His own breathing was ragged, his lips swollen, and she swallowed hard just thinking of the feel of his mouth upon hers.

"I know, I know, but . . . you know, Mom and Dad are just upstairs."

"We could go somewhere."

"No." She couldn't leave; her parents would have a fit. She wanted to kiss him again, to let him touch her, to let that wild child within her rise up and experience all there was to life, to step across those unwritten lines, to reach out, to live a little and . . . oh, God, no! She slammed that door shut, put that wayward imp back into a dark corner of her mind. This was happening much too fast. Thinking of doing more than just kissing Chris was a mistake. It was just way too soon.

"It's Adam, isn't it?" he said suddenly, and her head snapped up.

"Adam?" Her gaze found his, and she saw a bit of pain in the blue depths of his eyes. "I mean, why would you think that—".

"Because you're in love with him."

The accusation seemed to hang in the air between them, a dark, nasty idea, but the raw, unaltered truth.

"No." She shook her head, her tongue nearly tripping on the lie. "Adam? He's . . . he's Natalie's husband." Even now the word was hard to say and seemed to stick in her throat.

"Leslie said something to Ken."

Megan closed her eyes and wanted to strangle her friend. "About Adam and me?"

"About your fantasizing about him."

"I don't . . ." She started to argue, but let the words die away.

"About your thinking you're in love with him." Chris sighed. "And I saw it at the wedding. There you were, this beautiful girl with a fake smile and sad eyes. You couldn't give me, or anyone but Adam, the time of day. It pissed me off."

She felt suddenly miserable. How many people had noticed? Her mom, Natalie, maybe even Adam himself! Just the thought of it made her uncomfortable.

"So," he said, reaching for her hand and linking his fingers through hers, "I did something a little mean."

"What?" she asked, intrigued, and she saw a muscle work in his jaw.

"I decided to teach you a lesson."

"A lesson?" she repeated as she was beginning to understand. The kiss under the mistletoe. Oh, God, it had been some kind of backhanded joke?

"But, of course, it backfired. I kissed you and . . . Wow." He actually blushed. "It was crazy-good. And there we were in front of everyone. It was stupid."

She shook her head. "No, Chris. It was wonderful."

"Yeah, well, I thought so, too, and so instead of teaching you a lesson, it taught me one."

His self-deprecating smile was absolutely the sexiest thing she'd ever seen.

"So what about Adam?" he said.

"He's my brother-in-law. And yeah, I did have this whole fantasy thing going with him. An older guy, I guess."

"Is it over?"

Was it? She didn't really know, but she wasn't about to spoil this moment, so she lied, right then and there, staring into his worried eyes, touching his cheek with the tips of her fingers. "Of course it is, silly. Otherwise would I be here on this couch with you wondering how I could get you to kiss me again?"

"That's the easy part," he said, and kissed her just as she heard her father's heavy tread on the stairs. He lifted his head and swung to his feet. "I'll call you," he promised, and left as suddenly as he'd shown up on her doorstep.

From the window she watched him drive away, her gaze following the taillights of his car as it disappeared through a curtain of snow, the cat winding herself between Megan's ankles while Megan wondered if she could really ever give up dreaming of her sister's husband. God, she was a fool. And Chris? She sighed inwardly and wished she could kiss him one more time. Maybe then she wouldn't be lying when she said she wasn't in love with Adam.

Chapter 9

As it turned out she wasn't the only liar.

Chris didn't call.

Megan told herself she wasn't waiting for him though she jumped every time the phone rang. And things just got worse. She and Leslie braved the mall on the Monday after Christmas because Leslie wanted something new for her upcoming date with Ken. "I've got to get something cooler, you know, sexier," Leslie confided as they walked into the third boutique. "I know it sounds dumb, but Ken and I aren't going on this sledding thing alone. Guess who's coming along?"

Oh. God. Chris. And another girl. Megan's heart did a nosedive, and she realized how much the thought of Chris with someone else hurt.

"Claire and Brad," Leslie said, and Megan didn't know whether to be happy or disgusted. As Leslie picked up a sweater and set it back, she said, "I know, it's kind of weird. Brad's car is in the shop or something and he can't get his dad's, so anyway Ken's driving up to Mohawk Mountain for New Year's Eve."

Megan continued to browse through the sale racks, pushing the hangers a little too quickly as Leslie rattled on about the proposed trip. Somehow, she felt betrayed that Leslie was going to be on a double date with Claire Wakefield. It wasn't Leslie's fault—or Ken's for that matter—but still it was painful.

"Meg, have you been listening to what I've said?"

"Oh, yes, I'm just a little surprised, that's all."

"I thought that maybe you knew all about it," Leslie apologized. "Didn't Chris tell you?"

"I haven't seen Chris for a while," Megan admitted, and was surprised at how sad that made her. When had she become dependent on a boy to make her happy?

"Why not?"

"Well, thanks to you, Chris figured out that I thought I was in love with Adam."

"Ouch," Leslie said, then said, "'Thought' you were. As in no more? Come on!"

"I just don't know." That was the truth of it.

"Why didn't you just lie?"

"I didn't want to start out lying, you know. Seemed like a bad idea."

"A bad idea was admitting that you had a thing for Adam."

"Maybe."

"You need to fix that."

"I think it's okay."

"You'd better make sure. Or someone should." Leslie sent her a disbelieving glare, and Megan caught her drift. She skirted the sale rack and saw a sales person eyeing her, as if she expected her to shoplift. Pulling Leslie out of the store, Megan said, "Don't get any ideas. I'll handle this."

"Okay, okay," Leslie said, palms up, and they started shopping in earnest. By the time Megan got home, she was tired. The house was empty, her parents having gone out, no messages on the phone. "What did you expect?" she muttered, noticing that some of the Christmas decorations had begun to lose their luster; unlit red candles sat on the table with half-burned bits of blackened wick visible. Even the bright red holly berries on the mantel had started to wither and darken as if in anticipation of the season's end.

And how about you, Megan Simmons? she asked herself as she waited for Madonna to shoot into her room before shutting the door. *What will you do when vacation's over and the sparkle of Christmas is gone? Will Chris ever call you again, or was your relationship with him just a holiday fantasy?*

She flopped onto the bed and remembered when all of her unhappiness had begun, two years earlier when Adam had come into her life. No. That wasn't quite right, she reminded herself. He had come into Natalie's life.

Tired, Megan let her heavy lids drop over her eyes as she conjured up Adam's handsome face: olive skin with a nobility and a slight arrogance; his dark green eyes were nearly liquid. How could he unwittingly have caused her so many heartaches? Then Adam's image shifted, and she found herself looking into the blue eyes of Chris Johnson. He seemed amused, a dimple twitching in his cheek.

In her fantasy, they were beneath some sort of arbor, which was covered with mistletoe. Hundreds of people were watching them, and from the corner of her eye, she could see Natalie dancing with Adam. Natalie was wearing her wedding gown while Megan saw herself in faded jeans and an old sweatshirt with CENTRAL HIGH DEBATING TEAM on its front. Embarrassed and feeling out of place, she wanted to run and hide, or at least change into something more appropriate. She couldn't! Chris refused to let her go, his bright eyes twinkling with mischief.

From far away, she heard a ringing, and her eyes flew open. She ran to her parents' room and picked up the phone.

"Hey!" Chris said, and her knees actually buckled. She sat on the edge of her parents' bed. "How would you like to go sledding tomorrow?"

"I'd love it!" she said, and, at least for the moment, the spirit of Christmas began to glimmer again, if only in her heart.

Chapter 10

New Year's Eve dawned sunny but cold. Megan could see the icicles hanging from the eaves over her window. Although they reflected the sun's brilliant rays, they did not melt, but instead hung tenaciously to the sill. It would be an ideal day to go sledding on Mohawk Mountain.

As usual, Megan was ready long before Chris was due to arrive. Such was her nature. The myth that women were forever late bothered her, as she had just the opposite problem. If anything, she was always ready for a date far too early, much to Leslie's discomfort. Leslie was always late. "You're just too organized," she would shout at Megan, while rushing around and trying to get ready.

Now, Megan pulled on her new jeans and sweater and grabbed her ski jacket and some ski pants in case she needed them, both of which she crammed into a backpack. She also tucked in a swimming suit and towel, as Leslie had mentioned there was a pool at the resort. Slinging the pack over her shoulder, she was halfway down the stairs when the front door burst open.

"Surprise!" two familiar voices called out.

She hurried down the rest of the steps to find Natalie and Adam stomping the snow from their boots.

"We decided to stop by on our way home," Natalie explained, her arm entwined through Adam's. "It's great to see you!"

"But it's early."

"I know. We came home a day early, to get settled in," Natalie responded. "I've got to go to work the day after tomorrow. We took our chances and flew back here on standby tickets."

"I wish I'd known. I'm on my way out. Sledding," Megan said just as her mother, smelling of her last cigarette, hurried up and threw her arms around the newlyweds.

"Oh, my God! Natalie!" Carol was positively gushing as she threw her arms around her daughter and called over her shoulder, "Jim! It's Natalie and Adam!"

As her father came into the foyer, Megan caught a glimpse of Chris's car pulling into the snow-covered drive. She bit her lip and looked at Natalie. "Sorry. I've got to go."

"With Chris?" Natalie asked, obviously having seen them together at the wedding and guessing the rest. A dark eyebrow arched inquisitively before her father's arms swallowed her in a bear hug.

"Yeah."

"Interesting," Natalie said.

"Will you still be here tonight?" Megan asked her sister just as Adam gave her a big, brotherly hug that nearly squeezed the life from her. Another time she might have nearly swooned; now, spying Chris walking up the shoveled path, she couldn't escape fast enough. She opened the door.

"Sure, Meg, we'll be here," Adam answered, and bussed her lightly on the cheek. Spying Chris, he stuck out his hand, then dragged his cousin close. "Been busy, I see."

"A little."

"Good to see you!" Adam said, but Chris, his jaw rock hard, his eyes darker than usual, just nodded and grabbed Megan's arm.

"Ready?" he asked her.

She picked up her bag. "Yeah."

Adam called, "See you around, Chris!" as they headed outside.

"Later," Chris replied curtly, but never cast so much as a glance in Megan's direction as he opened the car door for her, then slammed it once she was inside.

They began the drive to the mountain in silence. She pretended interest in the snowfall, and he fiddled with the radio until, once they were out of town, he snapped it off and said, "So, Meg, are you in love with Adam?"

"No," she said, and for the first time in a long while, she knew she was telling the truth. Not that Chris really believed her. It didn't matter; the sky cleared as they reached the mountain and connected with the other kids from LaSalle. Leslie was stuck like glue to Ken and, of course, Claire Wakefield was with Brad, who, at least to begin with, seemed sober. They sledded on inner tubes and toboggans, and Megan felt the bracing cold of the mountain air, the bite of snow as she fell off, and the warmth of Chris, his body always close to hers. They laughed and threw snowballs and made snow angels and got to know each other. When they spied a sprig of mistletoe left over from Christmas, they kissed, then laughed, a special joke between them.

After a few more runs down the hill followed by a quick lunch, a group decided to hit the pool. Though outdoors, it was heated and sounded like heaven. "I'll meet you down there," Megan whispered to Chris as they began to head out the door to the pool. "I left my purse back at the table."

"I'll come with you."

"You don't need to. I need to change anyway."

Chris seemed dubious, but Megan hurried back to the

table, found her purse, and tucked it into her backpack before heading to the locker room, located down a short flight of stairs. Several girls from Upland-Gable were in the locker room, changing into swimwear. Ignoring them, Megan changed out of her sledding gear into her swimsuit, pulled out her lipstick, and found a mirror located behind a stack of blue lockers. The other girls were talking and laughing among themselves, but Megan didn't think that they had seen her.

She had just snapped her purse shut and was about to head back up the stairs when a loud voice attracted her attention. She would have recognized it anywhere as belonging to Claire Wakefield.

Megan froze. She didn't want to hear the conversation, but since Claire was on the other side of the bank of lockers, she had nowhere to go.

"Who's that girl that Chris is with?" an unfamiliar voice asked.

"Chris Johnson?" Claire asked innocently. "I think her name is Megan something-or-other." The contemptuous tone of Claire's voice indicated her opinion of Megan, which just about matched her own of Claire Wakefield. What a snob!

"I've never seen her before," was the other girl's comment.

"She's from *Central*."

"Oh." One word said it all.

"Isn't she the girl who was with him at the LaSalle sleigh ride?" another voice asked.

"I guess so," Claire commented dryly. "I really didn't notice."

"Come off it, Claire. You couldn't take your eyes off of Chris all night." Megan recognized the voice as belonging to Jeanette McDavis.

"I was with Brad, Jeanette, so I barely noticed Chris," Claire countered angrily.

Megan held her tongue.

"Yeah, but . . ." Jeanette's voice filled the locker room. "I know you were with Brad on the sleigh ride, Claire. I was there, remember? And, okay, so you're with Brad again today. But what's that all about? I thought you broke up with him."

"We got back together," Claire said.

Jeaneatte obviously wasn't buying it. "Because Chris wasn't interested."

"Give me a break." Claire sounded bored.

"Fine." Jeaneatte seemed tired of the argument. "Come on, let's go to the pool. The guys are probably already there."

"They can wait for a few minutes. I'm not ready."

"We'll meet you up at the pool then," Jeanette called.

Megan heard the sound of retreating footsteps. She and Claire were in the locker room, alone. She felt her mouth become dry and the sweat begin to bead on her forehead, then she told herself to get over it. She couldn't let one girl intimidate her. So Claire had been interested in Chris—so what?

Claire came around the corner of the stacked lockers and met Megan's gaze in the mirror. Her poise faltered for just a moment, but she recovered quickly. Adjusting the straps of the bikini visible through her cover-up, she stared pointedly at Megan.

"Well . . . this is embarrassing." Claire found a tube of lip gloss and touched up the shine on her lips.

"Yeah. Awkward."

"No doubt you overhead the conversation I had with my friends."

Megan nodded, wishing she could think of something clever to say. God, she'd be terrible on the debate team if she ever made it through tryouts. One look from this girl and she found her throat frozen. Claire tossed her blond locks behind her ears and pouted into the mirror as she surveyed herself. "How are you getting along with Chris?" she asked casually as she slipped the lip gloss into her purse.

"Fine," Megan answered noncommittally.

"He's a nice guy."

"Uh-huh."

"For the life of me, I can't *imagine* how the two of you ever got together."

"He's . . . a cousin of my brother-in-law." Why was she explaining herself to Claire?

"Oh, I see. You're related."

"No . . . he's related to my sister's husband."

"Cozy." Claire's eyes moved back to her own image. She smiled as she brushed her long, thick blond hair.

Though Megan wanted to say something more cutting to Claire, she only managed a quick, "It's just the right amount of cozy," then walked to the stairs to get out of Claire's dagger-like stare.

Megan followed signs to the pool area and found Chris and some other kids already in the aquamarine water. Steam rose from the pool, and the cold air was bracing.

"What took you so long?" he asked, taking her arm in his and pulling her closer to him after she got into the pool.

"I . . . I ran into a girl I know, down in the locker room," Megan replied, all too aware of his nearly naked body touching hers. Wet skin to wet skin. No way was she going to mention her conversation with Claire. Not today.

Chris smiled warmly and kissed her cheek. With a wink, he said, "Well, I'm glad you finally made it up here."

"Me too."

Claire had dived perfectly into the water, and come up near Brad. Leslie and Ken were making out in one corner, and the other kids were swimming and splashing. Several of the boys were loud, their voices echoing over the water, and Brad, again, was the ring leader.

Megan remembered the last time that she had seen them

act this way—on the night of the sleigh ride. She wondered if Brad and his friends had been drinking again. As the hours rolled past, Brad became more and more boisterous, pushing other kids into the pool, even a poor girl who was dressed in her ski clothes.

"It looks like Brad didn't learn his lesson," Chris said. "If Father Anthony catches him, he'll be thrown off the team and out of school." He shook his head. "And we'll all be in for it." Sighing, he added, "Maybe we'd better get going."

Other kids were already climbing out of the pool. Even Claire, dunked one too many times by Brad, had left him.

Megan glanced up at the sky, clouds now covering the moon, a few snowflakes beginning to fall from the dark heavens. She hated the thought of leaving, of ending the fun, but Chris was right, so they agreed to change in the locker rooms and meet in the parking lot at the car.

By the time Megan found Chris, he'd already started his car, the engine idling, the heater blasting. Snow was falling steadily again, and there was talk of the roads icing over. It was time to go. As Megan slid into the passenger seat she spied Brad, dressed in ski gear again, but walking cautiously as if staying upright was difficult. He nearly fell into the backseat of Ken's car and found the whole incident uproarious.

Chris's jaw clamped tight. "Ass," he said, then turned his attention to watch Claire, her hair pulled away from her face, her usually perfect makeup gone, cast a wistful glance toward Chris's car before sliding in with her date. What was going on here? Megan wondered.

As the other car pulled out of the lot, Megan got a glimpse of Brad kissing Claire; her eyes were open, staring over his shoulder, as if she really wasn't into making out, at least not with him.

Megan figured she knew why, and it had more to do with Chris than the boy Claire was with. As Chris drove down the winding mountain road, Megan said, "So I overheard Claire and some of her friends talking. They think she's got a thing for you."

"A thing?" he repeated, but he didn't smile.

"Whatever you want to call it."

"I don't want to call it anything."

"Something's going on. I saw how she looked at you, and, sometimes, it seemed like you were looking back."

"Jealous?" He slid her a glance.

"Should I be?"

"No." But then, to her surprise, he pulled off the road, stopping at a lower parking lot reserved for cross-country skiers. Chris's hands tightened around the steering wheel.

"What's wrong?" she asked.

"I haven't been completely honest with you," he admitted as the wipers slapped snowflakes off the windshield.

"About what?" Oh, God, was he going to tell her he was in love with some other girl, that they shouldn't date, that being together was all a mistake?

"Me. And . . . and the fact that I used to date Claire."

A part of Megan wasn't surprised. A part of her was. Another part was disappointed. As the windows started to fog over from their mingled breaths, she wished she could run away. If Chris still loved Claire, Megan didn't want to hear it.

"It's over," he assured her, but she wasn't convinced. "I met her late last summer when we moved here from Boston. She lives a few houses away from me and, well, she invited me over to her house for a swim one day."

"A swim?" Ironic, Megan thought as she remembered Claire in her little bikini casting flirty looks at Chris in the outdoor pool.

Chris shrugged. "It wasn't any big deal, at least not to me. She had another boyfriend. . . ."

"Brad?"

Chris nodded. "He was away for the summer, and so

Claire and I were together a lot. Until school started, I didn't know many of the kids at LaSalle, and then Claire and a couple of her friends at Upland-Gable. So we hung out." It explained a lot. "Anyway, Brad came back, and for a while we both dated her. I wasn't really all that interested in her, but she had been nice to me when I didn't know a soul."

Megan had trouble thinking that Claire could actually be nice to anybody, but she wondered if she had judged the Upland girl too harshly. It wasn't easy to lose someone you cared for, even if you did have a backup boyfriend in tow.

"Did you break it off with her?" she asked.

"I didn't have to."

"Because of Brad."

"Yeah, but I did call her, the day after Adam's wedding. The day after I met you," he said. "And I made sure she understood that I was interested in someone else and we could be 'friends.'"

"And how did she take it?"

"Like a dare, I guess." He looked over at Megan in the dark interior of the car. "It was like she didn't believe me, even though she was dating Brad. But seeing you, with me, I think she finally understood." He sighed. "It's funny."

"Funny?"

"Yeah, she didn't really want to be with me. I think she kind of used me to get back at Brad. But once she couldn't have me, she got a little more interested."

"And what about you? How do you feel?"

"It's over with her. You see, I've found someone else, a girl from Central. The trouble is, I'm not sure she likes me."

Megan felt herself smiling. "I think she probably does," she said, and he laughed, flicked on the ignition, and drove the rest of the way to her house. Once he'd parked, he carried Megan's backpack to the door. Natalie and Adam's car was gone. "I guess they got tired of waiting," Megan said, disappointed, though it was as much about missing her sister as it was about Adam, which was a surprise. She wondered if the change in her feelings was because he was married now, officially had become her sister's husband, or because of Chris.

It didn't take long for her to decide. She was falling in love with Chris. It was just that simple, and the thought of it brought a smile to her face. When he dropped her backpack onto the porch, she didn't wait for him, but put her arms around his neck and kissed him hard on the lips. He glanced overhead, as if searching for a sprig of mistletoe, but she giggled.

"It's not there," she assured him.

"No?"

"Uh-uh. No tricks this time. Just you and me and the fact that I want to kiss you very, very much." And so she did it again, and this time his arms surrounded her and he drew her close. She swayed against him, closing her eyes and thinking that she'd been foolish, mooning over Adam for far too long. Maybe it had been because Adam was off-limits and could always be a fantasy, but this boy with his sexy smile, devilish glint in his eyes, and way of looking at her as if he really cared, he was the here and now. Real.

And if she thought about it, she was pretty sure she could fall in love with him.

Maybe forever.

Chapter 11

"Megan?" Adam's voice caught her off guard, bringing her crashing back to the here-and-now of the waiting room at County General. With a start, she looked up to find him standing over her, his face a mask of concern. "How is he?"

"I don't know," she admitted, and turned her head to glance at the chart again. Nearly an hour had passed since she'd last read the information on his chart. Her heart sank. No change. "He's been in surgery for four hours." It seemed like a lifetime. "I talked to his admitting nurse, though." As Adam took the chair next to hers, she explained the situation as best she knew it and realized how little that was.

Once she was finished, he snorted, his jaw set. "And they're not telling you anything else? That's ridiculous." Jerking his head toward the woman manning the single desk, he said, "We need answers."

"I'm sure we'll get them as soon as there are any."

"I'm not so certain." His lips were compressed, and he was agitated. "I'll talk to them."

"It won't do any good," she said, and his eyes flared. There was nothing Adam Newell liked better than a challenge. "Look I've already tried." But her words were ignored as Adam was on his feet and making a beeline toward the unsuspecting woman who handed out the patient numbers. "Adam, please—"

Too late. He didn't push to the front of the line, but waited impatiently, hands in his pockets, as an older man who was in front of the desk and obviously hard of hearing was asking the information clerk to speak up for the sixth time.

A redhead seated across from Megan peered over the top of her beat-up fashion magazine, her eyebrows elevating a fraction as she watched Adam shift from one foot to the other.

Pushing forty-five Adam was still a handsome man, one who could turn heads. Though there was a bit of gray at his temples and he'd filled out a little over the years, and his face showed a few lines, he was good-looking and cut a striking figure in and out of the courtroom. He realized it and carried himself with the pride of a person who knew his place in the world, a place he'd worked hard to carve for himself.

This evening, though, his persistence and glib tongue didn't pay off. The woman behind the desk didn't and wouldn't tell him anything more despite the fact that he peppered her with questions.

"No luck?" Megan guessed as he returned to her side and dropped into the chair he'd recently vacated.

"Zero."

"I just don't think there is any more information to be had."

"Maybe." He said it as if she'd expected something more from him, as if he thought she believed he could move immovable mountains. Perhaps that had been the crux of her interest in him. Not only had she had girlish fantasies about him in her youth, but she'd seen a man who tried his best, though sometimes his methods weren't effective or the best choice. Years before, Megan had witnessed Adam try to save his marriage to a woman who had left him abruptly as she'd chased after her own dreams and a college professor who had convinced her to leave her "stick-in-the-mud" husband. Yep, that had been Natalie, ever flighty. Despite having thought she was marrying the love of her life not ten years earlier, she'd packed it in, left Adam a note saying it was over, and taken off for Paris, the city of light or love or whatever and where she now resided long after the college professor had turned his attention to another, younger student.

Adam, always stalwart, when he'd finally realized his marriage to Natalie was over, had remained single, throwing himself into what had become a successful career and dating a string of girlfriends, not one having lasted more than nine or ten months. And then he'd bought into the law firm where Megan worked just as her own marriage was crumbling. Even though she believed he was a confirmed bachelor, there had been the office flirtation with her, the rekindled fantasy when her own marriage had become rocky. Oh, geez, they were both idiots, she thought, leaning back in the stiff chair. They'd never dated, never kissed, never touched, but there had been an old spark that kept igniting, and, once her divorce was final, she'd thought she might just see what would happen between them. It would be messy, of course, probably too messy, with Adam still Chris's cousin and her kids remembering him as having been married to Natalie years before, but Megan would be lying if she said she hadn't considered what it would be like to be with him. To cut loose. To let the wild child within her free, if only for a few short nights.

Now, however, under the harsh glare of the waiting room lights, with Chris fighting for his life, she wondered what she'd been thinking. What kind of dangerous fantasies had she let grow in her imagination? All because she'd been unhappy. All because the romance had seemed to disappear from her relationship with her husband. All because she'd become lonely once the kids had moved out.

Foolish, foolish woman.

Did it really take a tragedy to wake her up?

How sad. How clichéd. How downright stupid.

"I don't suppose you called Natalie?" he asked. From the corner of her eye she saw the furrow of his brow.

"Texted," she said. "Time difference."

"Your dad?"

"Not yet, but I did send a quick note to Chris's parents." She glanced at Adam. "I'm surprised they haven't called. As for Dad"—she sighed, not looking forward to that conversation and all the questions—"I'll deal with him later, once I know more . . . oh!" She looked at the chart again and saw that Chris's status had changed from the blue square of surgery to the green of recovery. Her heart did a little leap. That had to be a good sign, right? Her husband was on the right track? "He's out of surgery."

"Thank God." Adam's phone beeped as he gazed at the chart. He yanked the phone from his jacket pocket, his eyebrows drawing together as he read the number on his phone's screen. "Looks like I'd better take this." As he pressed the phone to his ear, he answered. "Hey." Then he obviously saw the sign indicating that cell phones were banned in the room. With a nod to Megan he made his way to the hallway, his voice barely audible, the words indistinguishable.

Surprisingly, she was relieved that he was gone and she was alone again. She didn't need to deal with Adam Newell and how he'd woven his way in and out of the periphery of her life. Not now.

"Mrs. Johnson?"

Megan looked up to find a woman in scrubs in the doorway searching the faces in the room. On her feet in an instant, she said, "I'm Megan Johnson."

"Dr. Atwood." Probably in her late forties, she was a trim woman with serious blue eyes, sharp cheekbones, and a dimpled chin. Her hair was hidden as it was pinned beneath a surgical cap, and she didn't smile.

Megan's stomach knotted. "How is he?"

"It's serious, but he's stable," she said. "We can talk in one of the consultation rooms."

"He's going to make it?"

The doctor didn't immediately answer, but led her down the hallway and around a corner and through another waiting area to a small office not much larger than a closet. Dr. Atwood took one of the chairs by a slim table and Megan sat in the other, facing the woman as she pulled off the cap, letting it dangle at her neck, her ash-blond hair still restrained by bands.

"Your husband hasn't regained consciousness and might not for a while," she said, leaning her elbows on the table. "He suffered a head injury along with several broken bones in his pelvis. Both femurs were broken, his left more substantially, and he had some internal bleeding. . . ." She went on to describe Chris's injuries in medical terms and even showed Megan several X-rays, all of which caused Meg to cringe inside. Dear God, the extent of his injuries was phenomenal, but then, though the doctor didn't say it, Chris was lucky to be alive. ". . . To sum it up, he's in for a long haul." She left out the *if he does survive.* "Possibly another surgery to his pelvis, and with head injuries a lot is uncertain. When he is well enough to leave here, he'll probably need to spend some time in a rehab facility for intense physical therapy, then once he transfers back home, he'll need in-home care, if that's possible."

"Absolutely," Megan said without so much as a blink. "Whatever he needs."

"Good. Good. He'll be in ICU until he can be transferred to his own room, and I'm sorry, but I can't tell you exactly when that will be. If you have any questions, please, call the office." And then she was gone, leaving Megan alone in the small room. She closed the door behind the doctor and slid back into the chair. Alone for the first time since storming into the hospital, she dropped her head into her hands and let the tears flow, feeling the release and hoping beyond hope that Chris would survive. She'd been selfish, she thought, and possibly he had, too. Now, it was time to heal, not only his broken body but both their scarred hearts.

If it was possible.

Two hours later, in the intensive care unit, Megan stared down at the broken body of her husband and reached for his fingers. He was hooked up to tubes and wires, and an IV hung over his bed to drip fluids into his body, with computer monitors recording his heartbeats and other information she didn't pretend to understand. He wasn't alone, but cordoned off from the other patients by long curtains, the beds in the unit fanning out from a central nurses' station where each patient's vital signs and needs were accessed and controlled.

"Chris?" she said softy, all too aware of the lack of privacy. Five of the seven beds were occupied, a few other loved ones visiting for the allowed ten minutes per hour, nurses moving quietly from one patient to the next. "Honey, can you hear me?" She touched his fingers and expected some response, a change in the beeping of his heart rate, the miraculous fluttering of his eyes opening, the monitors strapped to him going as crazy as a million-dollar slot machine payout. But nothing happened, and the man on the bed, his head bandaged, his legs wrapped and elevated, didn't move. At all.

Nothing changed.

Invisible bands tightened over her chest.

"Chris, honey, it's Meg," she said, her throat thick and those damned tears she swore she was through shedding burn-

ing her eyes again. "I'm here, and I want you to know . . . I
want you to believe that . . . that I love you. I always have."
She blinked, trying not to dwell on the past two years, the
way they'd both faltered and fallen away from each other.
"I know that we lost our way, but that's over. Get well, darling, please," she said, and then, spying a nurse heading in
her direction, gave his fingers a squeeze. "I'll be back."

She left wishing that he'd heard her, hoping somehow her
words had pierced the unconsciousness, but of course, his
condition hadn't altered in the least. Her allotted minutes
had passed, and numbly she left his bedside.

When she reached the waiting area outside the intensive
care unit, Adam was leaning against a heat register near the
windows and looking outside to the view of the parking
area at night. Several other people were waiting as well, a
teenager slouched in a chair, his feet propped on a table as
he played some game on his iPhone, his mother nearby
reading a Bible. Another woman was knitting, and the har-
ried mother of a squirming two-year-old was pale and wan,
brightening when a man in his twenties hurried from the
area near the vending machines, a package of crackers in
his hand.

Adam turned, catching her reflection in the glass.

Before he could ask, she said, "He's still unconscious. No
change." Reading another question in his eyes, she added,
"No one's giving me any clues as to when he might wake up.
They just don't know."

He nodded slowly, processing, then looked at her intently again. "So how're you holding up?"

"Not very well," she admitted, her voice cracking a bit.
Too late she realized he intended to embrace her, but she
was too exhausted to care; she needed the support. Thankfully the hug was only brotherly, compassion for another
person who was suffering, two people holding each other
up as they worried about a loved one. "You should go
home, get some rest," he said, his breath moving her hair.

Vaguely she was aware of the woman who'd been knitting watching them. Who cared?

"Not yet." She shook her head. "The kids texted. They're on their way. And . . . and I can't. I just can't. They'll let me see him in another hour, and I want to stay."

"But you need to keep your strength up. When was the last time you ate?"

When had it been? "Lunch, I guess." She stepped away from him. "Don't worry. I'll be okay. I'm tougher than I look."

"If you say so." He hesitated, still close enough that she noticed the shadow of his beard darkening, then said, "Natalie's coming back."

"What?"

"She called earlier. From the airport. Flying standby."

Megan couldn't believe it, but felt a moment's ray of hope. God, she'd missed her sister.

"She'll be here in a few hours. I'm picking her up at the airport." He smiled then, a smile she hadn't seen in years, the one that had been reserved for his wife.

"Good." Megan gave him another hug, and he held her a second longer than necessary. Pulling away, she caught a glimpse of a man heading in their direction, a scraggly-looking dude just getting off the elevators and then, with a jolt, recognized Brody. He was striding purposefully, his gaze focused on his mother.

"Brody!" Her emotions collided in her chest at the sight of her firstborn. No longer clean-cut and military, he now sported long hair, an unkempt beard, and an army jacket that seemed to swallow him.

"Mom?" he asked, sending his ex-uncle a sidelong look as she quickly crossed the distance between them and threw her arms around her son. "What's going on?"

She'd cautioned both her children against coming, against risking the weather and traffic, but now she was grateful to hold him close. He smelled of cigarettes and something more, but she didn't analyze it, was just thankful to hug him. "Thank God you're here."

"Is Dad—?"

"Doing as well as can be expected, I think," she said, blinking quickly and clearing her throat, her thoughts turning to Chris, lying unmoving on the hospital bed still in critical condition, as she released her son.

"Can I see him?"

"Yes, yes, of course. Family is allowed, but only for a few minutes every hour and . . . brace yourself. He's still unconscious and has so many injuries and—"

"And I can handle it," Brody cut in, and held her gaze for a moment, his back stiffening; beneath the scruffy beard and long hair she glimpsed the army medic who had witnessed more death and injuries than anyone should.

"Oh, right. Sure." She managed a thin smile she hoped was encouraging.

At that moment, Adam stepped up, his hand extended. "Hi, Brody," he said, flashing a grin that didn't quite reach his eyes. He looked tired. Worried. Megan realized how much Chris's accident had taken its toll on Adam. "I'm glad you're here."

"Me too." Brody's voice didn't hold a lot of enthusiasm, but he shook his ex-uncle's hand, and if Adam noticed a coolness from the younger man, he didn't comment, just said to Megan, "I'll be back."

"Good."

As Adam made his way down the hall to the elevator, Brody's narrowed eyes followed him. "What the hell was that all about?"

"Your dad is Adam's cousin."

"I know, but . . ." Brody said, disbelieving, "he works with you, now. Right?"

"Uh-huh," she said, not wanting to go "there" with her son. "And he's off to the airport to meet Natalie."

"Aunt Natalie? Like, his ex? Haven't they been divorced for like ever?"

"Like, yeah."

"You were hugging him." It wasn't a question, and he was stone-cold serious, his tone almost militant as a soft chime indicated an elevator car had arrived.

"We're supporting each other." And that's all, she silently added, because it was the truth. No matter what she'd thought less than twenty-four hours earlier, she realized now how much she loved Chris and hoped with all of her heart that she would be able to tell him, to prove herself, to take another stab at their marriage.

Somewhere behind her the toddler laughed.

Since only one person was allowed to see Chris at a time and she'd recently been in the room with her husband, Megan walked Brody to the double doors of the intensive care unit and pressed a button. Seconds later the door swung open and, after a quick explanation to the nurse, Brody was escorted inside by one of the nurses.

Megan tried to catch a glimpse of Chris in the scant moments the door was open, but the drapes surrounding his bed blocked her view, of course. Not that she would see anything different than she had. If there was any change in his condition, the staff had promised to let her know. So all she could do was wait.

While Brody was with his father, Megan stretched her legs, walking to a vending area. Once there she saw the less-than-appetizing array of candy and crackers, then settled for a cup of coffee that she carried back to the area of couches, chairs, and tables that would probably become her home away from home for a while.

If Chris survived.

Don't think that way. He's going to make it. He has to.

In the few moments she'd been gone, the waiting area had cleared out. Now only one other person was there; the woman with her softly clicking knitting needles remained working tirelessly as she sat in a chair near a palm tree with skinny fronds.

Brody had to still be beyond the double doors.

Good.

Carrying her cup to the window Megan, as Adam had earlier, stared out at the night. The sky was black, the parking lot now only scattered with a few vehicles. Snow continuing to fall.

As she took her first sip of the awful brew she heard the elevator doors ding and footsteps moving rapidly from the hallway to the waiting area. "Mom?" Her daughter's voice announced Lindy's arrival. The knitting needles quit their quiet clacking as the woman looked up. "Mom!"

Megan turned, sloshing the coffee at the urgent tone of her daughter's voice.

Lindy's hair was caught in a stocking cap, her ski jacket zipped over a turtleneck and jeans, her face puffy as if from crying, anger and pain radiating from her.

"Lindy!" Megan's heart cracked. She stepped toward her daughter before she spied the fistful of papers clenched in her daughter's gloved hand.

"What the hell, Mom?" Lindy demanded, dropping her backpack to glare furiously at the woman who had borne her. Her lips barely moved as she said, "Are you really divorcing Dad? I mean, really?"

Chapter 12

"What?" Megan said, horrified, as her daughter wagged the crumpled papers in her face. "No!"

"Then what are these, huh?"

Megan's heart sank. She remembered rushing from the house, dropping the papers under the tree when she got the news of Chris's accident.

"I just go home to leave my bags, even have the cab wait for me, and when I go inside, the Christmas tree is all lit up and . . . and these damned pages are scattered under it." Lindy was crying now, tears running down her face.

"Oh, God, Lindy, I'm sorry." Never had Megan said those words with such meaning. She set her cup on the corner of a nearby table and straightened, staring her daughter in the eye. "I'm sorry for a lot of things. You weren't supposed to see those, and, in fact, I was going to burn them."

"Bull!"

"No, no, I was. But not earlier. Okay, I admit it," she said, feeling the weight of the knitter's gaze boring into her back. The needles were clicking again, but much more slowly. "I was considering it, but—"

"By 'it' you mean divorce."

"Yes," Megan admitted, sick inside. "But I've had a lot of time to think things over."

"Because Dad nearly died! That's it." Lindy was practically hysterical. "Not because you love him. You're unbelievable, Mom!" She was sobbing now, and though Megan tried to console her, to hold her, Lindy stepped away from her mother, her face contorting with an emotion akin to hatred. "Just leave me alone," she said, dashing her tears away with her free hand. "I just . . . I just want to see Dad."

"You can't right now."

"Why?" Lindy's eyes rounded in fear, and Megan mentally kicked herself.

"No, no, it's not that. He's okay, or as okay as he's been since he got here. But they only allow one visitor at a time in the ICU. Your brother's with him now."

"Brody's here?" Lindy's voice lifted a bit. She sniffed loudly. The needles clicked, and a disembodied voice asked a doctor to call.

"Yes. He got here a few minutes ago."

"Does he know about this?" Again the papers were shoved under Megan's nose, and this time she snatched them back, ripped them from her daughter's hand.

"No, but it doesn't matter," Megan said, refusing to become a victim or to be browbeaten any longer. She'd done enough of that herself; she didn't need Lindy to rub it in. "Look, as I said, I admit it; your father and I, you know, we've been having problems."

"You left him!"

Megan said, "It was mutual, and you know it. He moved out. It was a trial separation, and I thought, I really thought that divorce might be the only answer. But I was wrong. Okay. I think it's worth another chance, and, yes, of course, tonight had a lot to do with it. Almost losing your dad opened my eyes. I love him." She said it with all the passion that burned through her. "And I don't want to split up. No matter what. The doctor says his recovery, if he gets the chance to recover, will be long. Hard. On him. On me. On all of us. But we're going to see him through it. He's moving home as soon as he's able. When he's released."

Lindy was still suspicious, but there was a tiny gleam of hope in her eyes. "Does he know this?"

"Not yet."

"He may not be into it."

Megan nodded. That much was true. "Then we'll just have to find a way to convince him, won't we?"

"We?"

"Okay, me. I'll find a way," she said, and she meant every word. She only prayed that she'd get the chance. "I thought you might want to help, too."

Her daughter, still clearing her throat and blinking against tears, glared at her. Unwilling to trust. Unwilling to hope. When Brody came through the doors, she backed away from her mother as if Megan were a pariah and ran to her brother to embrace him the way Megan had longed to be held by her daughter. Clinging to her brother, Lindy sobbed brokenly, and Megan knew that Lindy's pain was partially her fault.

No one said being a mother would be easy, did they?

Oh, and no one said that marriages didn't have their weak points. It's up to the partners involved to keep a marriage strong, to make it interesting, to always find the love that came with that first blush, no matter what the trials, no matter how many years. Now, Meg, it's up to you!

She'd never backed down from a challenge, and certainly wasn't going to start now.

"Come on," she said to her daughter. "Let's see if they'll bend the rules a bit and let you in." With Lindy in tow, she headed to the locked doors again, and the nurse who answered took one look at Chris's daughter and said in a hushed voice, "Okay, but only for a few minutes. Just this once."

"Thank you," Megan said, and watched the door swing shut. To Brody, she asked, "How was he?"

"The same." Her son glanced down at her hands. "What's that?" he asked, pointing to the divorce documents.

"A mistake," she said softly, and then slowly, page by page, bit by bit, tore the document to shreds and dropped the fluttering pieces into a nearby trash receptacle. "A monumental mistake."

If Brody guessed the content of those pages, he didn't say, and when Lindy returned she, too, didn't mention the papers. As if by tacit agreement, the subject of divorce was dropped.

Megan hoped it was forever.

Megan and the rest of the family spent the next three days in and out of the hospital, alternately eating in the cafeteria or bringing in pizza, running back to the house for showers and to change their clothes, and camping out in the waiting area, sometimes napping on the uncomfortable couches, other times playing cards or games or texting on their phones.

For her part, Megan stayed close to the hospital. Adam and her assistant dealt with the issues at the office, clearing her schedule so that she could keep her vigil. It wasn't that big of a deal, she told herself, as she'd already slowed down a bit with her appointments for the holidays.

Natalie had arrived early the morning after the accident. Of course, she was as beautiful and regal-looking as ever. "Paris seems to agree with you," Megan had said, marveling that her sister, now in her forties, after a red-eye across the Atlantic was still as radiant as ever when she'd walked into the hospital as dawn was just about to break.

What was more astounding was that Natalie and Adam had seemed to reconnect.

"It's nothing," Natalie confided on the third day, though the light in her eyes betrayed her true emotions. "Adam and

I are over. Have been forever." She rolled her eyes. "Mom and Dad said we married too young, and they were right."

The same could have been said for Megan and Chris, but Megan held her tongue as her sister prattled on. "But you know, it's nice that we don't have to be so bitter." She looked longingly at her niece and nephew. "Maybe if we'd had kids things would have turned out differently."

"Maybe," Megan said.

Now, she was bone tired, far beyond weary. Chris's parents had arrived from Florida, and they, too, kept their vigil, splitting their time between the hospital and a nearby hotel. Megan's father and Lara had shown up, and they were camping out at the house, which was kind of weird, but not as weird as Natalie's staying with Adam, so all in all, Megan decided her nontraditional, splintered family was a family nonetheless.

So long as Chris survived.

On the fourth night Megan was in the hospital alone. It was Christmas Eve. Earlier the family had gathered for a grand Parisian dinner that Natalie had prepared. Megan had bowed out of the meal and the festivities, though the house, when she'd gone home to change, had smelled divine.

"It's all in the spices, you know," Natalie had confided as she bustled through the house, and Megan was reminded of Christmases past, when their mother had been manning the old stove that no longer resided in the kitchen and the kids hadn't yet been born. She thought again of her first Christmas with Chris and the sleigh ride that had been their first real date after Natalie's wedding. That entire Christmas season had been magical and emotional and the start of her adult life.

Her heart tore a little at the memories, and as she drove

to the hospital, listening to the same Christmas carols her radio station had been playing for weeks, she felt more than a little nostalgic, a trace of melancholy weaving into her heart.

At County General, she locked her car and wondered if Chris would ever wake up. The doctors were being cautiously optimistic, but she still had doubts.

And she missed him.

Oh, how she missed him.

When they'd been separated she'd felt that disconnect, the emptiness, but had told herself it was all in her mind. Now she was convinced she'd been wrong. The hospital parking lot was nearly empty and, as she walked through the snow that had been falling off and on for a week, she told herself to buck up, that no matter how long the wait, he was worth it.

She took the elevator up to the ICU and pressed the buttons to be let in. An unfamiliar nurse let her into the unit, and Megan noted that fewer of the beds were occupied than on the night when Chris had been life flighted to the hospital. Some of the patients had already been released to private rooms, but still he was here, connected to an array of medical equipment.

As she had every night, she walked to his bedside, sent up a silent prayer for his recovery, and took his fingers in hers. "Hey," she said softly, a lump in her throat. The heart monitor beeped steadily. "It's me, or I, if you want to be formal." No response. Of course. "So . . . how're you doing? You missed a helluva meal. A lot better than what you're ingesting," she added, eyeing the IV drip. "Who would have ever guessed that Natalie was cut out to be a French chef, huh?" She squeezed his fingers and tried not to cry. She was used to this, seeing him here in clean white dressings, a hospital gown, and strapped to all kinds of machines. This was their new way of life. "Natalie is still as slim as ever, and if I didn't love her so much, I could hate her." That was a lie, a pathetic joke; she hadn't been envious of Natalie for two decades. "So, how're ya doing, huh?" Her thoughts returned to Natalie's wedding and the night she'd first met Chris Johnson, the bold boy who had kissed her under the mistletoe.

Oh, how she wished and prayed that she could recapture some of what they'd once had. If only he would waken. She'd try. Oh, God, she'd try. If only he would stir. If only—

She felt a slight pressure on her hand.

What?

Looking down, she stared at him. "Chris?" she whispered, hope in her voice.

Nothing.

Had she imagined it? That was it. Her damned mind, always creating fantasies, overreacting. Still . . .

"Chris. It's me. Megan." She squeezed his fingers again. "I love you, honey." Her throat thickened to the point where she could barely speak. "Merry Christmas."

The silence was deafening, only the sound of medical equipment giving off the rhythmic beeps and—

Again the pressure. This time stronger. Her gaze flew to her husband's face. "Chris?" she whispered. Oh. Dear. God. Was it possible? Was he waking? "Chris?"

To her astonishment, his eyes blinked open for a second, focusing on her. His dry lips twisted a little in his unshaven face.

"Oh, God," she cried, tears raining from her eyes as in her peripheral vision she saw a nurse hurrying toward them.

Megan clung to Chris's hand, wouldn't let go. "I love you," she squeaked out. "I love you so much."

His eyes slowly closed. "I know," he rasped with difficulty, his voice so low as to be nearly inaudible. "I was . . . wondering . . . when you'd ever figure it out."

"You son of a gun," she said happily. "You damned son of a . . ."

"Mrs. Johnson, if you'll just step away," the nurse said.

Never, Megan thought, clinging to his fingers. *I'm never letting go. For as long as I live and breathe, I'm holding on to this man as if my life depends upon it.*

Because, she decided right then and there, it did.

The next morning, hours later, while Chris was sleeping, she went home to shower and change, then sneaked through the rooms quietly, hearing her father snoring in the guest room, seeing the bluish light from the television flickering beneath the doorway of Brody's room. Her hair still wet, her jeans and sweater clean, she donned her coat again and, as she did, she felt something in the pocket.

The ornament.

Retrieving it, she glanced down at the small picture frame once again and then, with infinite care, she kissed the old photograph and tied the fraying ribbon around one of the upper branches of the tree. Then she spied the sprig of mistletoe, hung over the door as it had been for each and every holiday season of her life. The tradition was that it went up the first of December and came down on New Year's Day.

"Not this year," she said, and, using one of the dining room chairs, she stood and pulled the sprig from its hook. Then, after returning the chair, she cinched the belt of her coat tight around her and made her way to her CR-V.

In half an hour she'd be back at the hospital, and she would wait until her husband wakened. He'd regained consciousness and by the end of the week, she'd been told, would be transferring to a private room. From there, he'd go to rehab and then return home. They'd already discussed it, and Brody, who had shaved and cut his hair, claimed he would move back and help his father. Lindy had insisted she was going to move home as well, come spring break, but Megan hoped she would stay in school and visit often.

Megan smiled to herself as she pulled into the hospital lot. Though she knew it was probably against all kinds of hospital rules, she decided to break them, to let the wild child within her free, and hold the damned bit of mistletoe over her husband's head and kiss him as he had kissed her all those years ago.

Today, she decided as she parked, was a new beginning. She clicked off the radio, cut the engine, and locked the car. Walking through the falling snow, she sighed happily. "Our first Christmas," she said as the hospital doors whispered open. "Again."